VIKING

THUNDER HORSE

by

Katie Aiken Ritter

Print copy ISBN 13: 978-0-9978765-9-8
Print copy ISBN 10: 099787659X

eBook ISBN 978-0-9978765-8-1

Nordic Horse artwork featured on cover
courtesy of Zaff Bobilin at Zaffworks.com

For my beloved oldest son Zach

You earned your horse, but I never paid up.
I still owe you, with twenty-plus years of interest.

This book doesn't erase that debt,
but maybe it will help me fulfill it.

Love you.

VIKING

THUNDER HORSE

In chronological order:

Book I: The Plains of Althing

Book II: Thunder Horse

Book III: The Green Land

Characters

Aldís	a free-ranging healer with some second-sight
Ankya	Naldrum's oldest daughter and favorite child
Eilíf	a widow, badly scarred in a farm fire
Fatimah	daughter of a modest freeholder family
Friedrich	bishop of a monastery in Germania
Haakon Sigurdsson	Jarl (earl) of Lade Garde, Trondheim, Norway
Josson	a ne'er-do-well cart-trader
Kandace	missing wife of Tor, abducted some years ago
Konradsson	young Germanic priest, once native to Iceland
Mani	Lawspeaker of all Iceland
Naldrum	headman of Bull Valley
Nenet and Nikea	Tor's children
Rota	agent for Haakon Sigurdsson, Jarl of Lade
Sauthi	a reclusive shepherd
Styr	friend of Tiller's, now a bondsman
Thorgest	a landowner friend of Tiller
Tiller	a *vikinger* (sailor) sent to steal The Nubian
Tor	an enslaved Moroccan man
Tora	common-law wife of Haakon Sigurdsson

Iceland, circa 979 A.D.
The north-way seas, just after the midsummer festival of Althing

Tiller Thorvaldsson had not sailed to Trondheim since his youth. How had he forgotten the wickedly-tight entry into this fjord?

His ship had cleared the marker island that morning, the one topped by a hulking stone that resembled a gigantic sea turtle. Once past it, they had dropped sail until the tide turned. When the waves lapped hard forward against their hull, Tiller called for the sail to be hefted again, made a hard-to-starboard pull, and their merchant *knarr* slid into the narrow mouth of Trondheim-fjord.

Imposing bare hills stood guard over both sides of the fjord entry. Atop them, armed men scrutinized every passing vessel. Crews on those ships also cast suspicious looks towards Tiller's unrecognized knarr.

The lookout called back from the fore. "Nearly every one of these ships and boats show the same flag! Do they *all* belong to Haakon Sigurdsson?"

"Don't worry about them," Tiller replied. His casual tone belied his thoughts. *Don't worry about them? Gods, how were they* ever *going to get out again past that nosy fleet?*

Another hard turn, this time to the ladder-board side. The wind freshened and filled their sail, pushing them fast fore-ward. By afternoon, the rooftops of Trondheim came into view.

Tiller's throat tightened as they came approached shore. He had remembered a tumbled cluster of huts, barns, trading tents, but nothing of any great note. Now, buildings of every description stretched as far as he could see, a great clutter of structures large and small. Around them, people swarmed like ants. The wind came alongside them now, and it carried the smell of habitation: smoke from innumerable cooking fires, fetid outhouses, and the good green-smell of crop fields.

How was he ever going to find one woman in all that mess? *I should never have listened to that cursed headman Naldrum or his promise of money for me to fetch her back. I'm a fool for taking this job, and I've brought this crew on a fool's errand.* But there was no going back now. The only way forward lay in figuring out how to find the woman, get her out of this place bristling with Sigurdsson's men, and make it back to the open seas alive. *Just that.*

It occurred to Tiller that of all the gods, only one might appreciate what he was about to do. A prayer to Loki, then: *if you ever loved this errant human, now would be a fine time to show it.*

Tiller swallowed hard, grasped the steering-board, and pointed the prow toward the teeming shoreline.

. . .

Chapter Two

Lade Garde: the seat of Haakon Sigurdsson, Jarl of Lade

The *knarr* slid perfectly onto the smooth beach of Trondheim harbor. Tiller turned the steering board just before the hull made contact to allow the ship to keel over onto the sand on its port side. As the crew lowered the sail and coiled ropes, Tiller dropped the ramp overboard and hopped onto the shore.

"I'm going out for a bit to see what opportunities might be here. I need you all to stay close to the ship for now." Tiller ignored the groans that ensued. Most of the crew would spend the day making salt, searching the shoreline for driftwood, hauling out small cauldrons for boiling. They could groan all they liked, but by evening, they would each be richer by a mark or two. Salt was always an easy sale and a highly profitable return for a day's work simmering seawater.

Tiller shouldered a pack of trade goods and headed towards the cluster of buildings. Lade Garde, Haakon's seat of power, stood somewhere ahead in that hive—and in Lade Garde, perhaps, was Haakon's slave woman, the one Tiller had sailed all this way to steal.

This entire town belonged to Haakon, Tiller reminded himself. None of the people he was passing were free in the way he always took for granted. The awareness that all these lives hung on one man's whims gave Tiller an uncomfortable sensation of being followed. *Nobody rules Icelanders like that,* he thought.

His father had had the same stubborn streak, but with a contentious nature. Always brawling. Always on the wrong side of a fight. Defiant to the end.

I won't share his fate. Won't fail as he did. Old bitterness clouded Tiller's thoughts.

Always the struggle. Always one man trying to steal what he envied from another. Only the names changed, generation to generation. Always men like himself at the bottom, scrapping to survive, while men like Fairhair and Bloodaxe and Haakon prospered and ruled. Why?

Tiller trudged along the path, past ship-building sheds and barns where barrels of trade goods were stored, straight towards the heart of Trondheim where the woman might be—and if so, where the greatest danger lay.

. . .

Mother of Odin, why does Haakon's place have to be so far from the shore? The further Tiller walked, the more somber his mood became. Trondheim had grown into an even larger settlement than it looked from the shore. Assuming he could wrest this woman from Haakon's home, how would he ever get her back to the ship? The quick sprint from house to ship that Tiller had envisioned would never work. *We'd need a hundred swords to fight our way out. I'll have to come up with another idea.*

And even then, once they reached the ship, he would still have to sail back through that confounded fjord with its long thin passage. It bent twice at hard angles, much like an arm at elbow and wrist. Not an easy waterway on which to gain speed and outrun pursuers.

We just have to stay ahead of the Haakon's men long enough to reach the open sea, Tiller reassured himself. Once he got back to Iceland, he'd unload the woman as fast as possible on Naldrum. Then she'd be the headman's problem, not his.

. . .

A bent beggar held out his palm and whined. Tiller dug in his pouch. "Which way to the home of the Jarl of Lade?" he asked

The beggar seemed to think the token Tiller offered deserved more than simple directions. He started limping along after Tiller, poking with his stick.

"Anything else you'd like to know about Lade Garde, seeing as how you're headed there?" the man asked. "I know the place well. I used to work there."

"Best way to get in without being accosted by a trove of guards?"

"You'll want the kitchen entrance," the man said. "Behind the main building. Merchants are always coming and going, so the guards there tend to be a little lax. I'll show you." He straightened and surprisingly spry, matched Tiller's gait.

"What's your business with the Jarl?" the beggar asked.

"Nothing I care to discuss," Tiller said.

"Oh, then," the man replied. "Not good business, I take it."

Tiller remained silent, which did not detract from his companion's wheedling. "Not as though many *have* good business with the Jarl, if I may say so."

"And why is that?"

"Haakon takes care of those who make him wealthy, but he steps all over those who don't. Cheats them, steals from them, appreciates nothing, does not know the meaning of the word 'truth'."

"You've no loyalty to him, it seems."

"I'm a beggar. What does my loyalty matter to anyone? But you're right. I'd cut his throat if I could get close enough," the man sneered. "I won't trouble you with the reasons why. Suffice to say that if you mean him any harm, I'm happy to help. For free." He fished the token back out of his own pouch and with a half-hearted gesture, offered it back to Tiller.

"Keep it. What do you know about the Jarl's household? About people who live in it? His wives…his slaves?"

"He has a wife, Tora. A sprawl of children, mostly not hers." The man looked about, although no one walked near them. "He takes the daughters of nearby farmers as a tax. Likes the untried younger ones best. He uses them for a bit and then throws them off. Any kids end up with him, by law. House is full of them, running like wild young dogs."

"And his slaves? Anything unusual there?" *Too dangerous to come right out and ask if Haakon had a dark-skinned captive.*

"Plenty of slaves. Most hate him, of course, but they fear him, too, so they'll rat out any threat to the house. He has a new slave now that's the talk of the town. A woman from far away. They say she has skin the color of a seal's fur, dark brown. Eyes, the same color. Said to be beautiful. His wife Tora hates her."

"Interesting," Tiller said. "What does she do there? Where does the Jarl keep her? I'd like to see such an unusual creature." *Excellent. The woman Naldrum wanted* was *here!*

The beggar shot a sharp look towards Tiller. "As would many. Word has it that Haakon keeps her under guard, deep in his household."

"'Deep in his house? Just how big is it?" Tiller asked. Turning a corner, his beggar companion pointed ahead.

"Lade Garde," he announced with some pride. "Home to Haakon Sigurdsson, the Jarl of Lade." A different voice at this, and he spat on the ground.

A building the size of ten longhouses loomed ahead, two stories tall, and the whole of it surrounded by a thick fence that stood just over Tiller's head. Without meaning to, he groaned.

. . .

The beggar grabbed Tiller's elbow, every movement eager. He pointed to a path that led through a small copse of trees. "We'll avoid the attention of the front-gate guard this way," he said. "Kitchen's this way. Look, here's a bit of luck." A cart filled with linen-wrapped meats passed where they stood. "We'll just walk along behind. Keep your head down. The gate guards will assume you're with the meat smoker's crew."

Tiller did as the beggar suggested. Soon they stood in the crowded alcove of a cooking room. The tantalizing aroma of pig being roasted over a spit came from an enormous fireplace.

After the cook finished haggling with the meat-smokers, the beggar sidled up to her. “Hey, Svienne. You remember me, don’t you? I’ve brought a fellow from a trade ship who might sweeten your palm,” the beggar announced. “New to these parts, and has some goods to sell.”

The cook ignored him. She directed the cinder-girl to turn the spit more slowly, then, wiping her hands on her apron, she lifted a cloth on a wooden tray of rising dough. The fragrance of yeast mingled with the roasting meat. Tiller’s mouth watered. *Wheat bread, aie.*

“What sort of goods?” the cook asked, never once glancing at Tiller.

“Amber beads, perfume, carved combs,” he began.

“Women’s stuff, then. Luxury.”

“You could say that, yes.”

“Ever traded with the Jarl before?” she asked.

“No.”

She held out her hand. Tiller placed a bit of hack-silver in it. She waited, her palm still extended, and he added more. Her eyes finally met his, but they held no welcome.

“I have some advice for you,” she said. “If you want to *sell* your wares—or at least take your unsold things back with you—show them to his new favorite, the one he calls the Nubian. If you want to “donate” your items,” she laughed without humor, “show them to his wife Tora. She’ll thank you for your loyalty to the Jarl, and that’ll be all the payment you’ll see.”

"Wise advice. I think I'll show my things to the Nubian. How does one arrange that?"

"You can't. I can't. Absolutely no one can visit the Jarl's new prize. But there's always a way to screw a man who screws others, isn't there? Cindergirl!" the cook barked. "Go tell Mistress Tora that a trader has arrived with fresh goods!" The cook laughed again, this time with real mirth. "That'll get you inside, at least. It's up to you to figure out how to make your way from one woman to the other."

. . .

It did not take long for a summons from 'Mistress Tora' to arrive. Tiller left the beggar in the kitchen whispering with the cook and followed the cinder-girl through one hallway after another until they reached an upper room. He could feel sweat rolling down his back between his shoulder blades. Getting inside Lade Garde had been unexpectedly easy. Getting back out would likely be the opposite.

"That door," the ash-girl whispered. She darted back towards the kitchen. Tiller knocked.

"Come in!"

Tiller bowed as he entered the room. A woman, attractive and middle-aged, lolled upon a chair covered in fur.

"I'm told you have fine goods of interest to women," she said.

"Yes, mistress. The Jarl told me to show them to a lady in his household. His favorite lady, he said. Thank you for receiving me."

Tora's smile warmed to flirtatiousness, increasing her beauty. "You flatter me. My husband has excellent taste. Spread your wares." She gestured to a table.

"Your husband?" Tiller feigned confusion. "You are the head lady here?"

"The Jarl's wife. Yes, of course."

"I think there has been some mistake." Tiller coughed. "These are…lesser goods."

"Then who *did* you come intending to sell to? The ash-girl said you asked for me!"

Tiller had opened his bundle of wares and had started putting items out on a small table. He hurriedly scooped everything back into his pack.

"I am thinking I misquoted him. Perhaps he meant one of his favorite lieutenants' wives? Or one of your personal favored slaves, who might have a bit of coin to spend? One who would see a bit of glitter and think it gold?"

The slight line between Tora's brows deepened. "But I thought—didn't I hear you say he specifically told you to show them to me?"

"My apologies, mistress. Your husband is a powerful man. I don't wish to offend in any way." Tiller backed towards the door.

My husband is a man besieged by his lusts. A hot flush began to spread up Tora's neck. "Tell me who exactly you thought you were meeting with!"

Tiller edged out the door, the latchstring in his fingers. "No one, madam. He did not give a name."

"Now I remember!" Her face grew angry. "You said 'his favorite lady', didn't you?" Tiller ducked as a wooden plate flew past and broke against the wall. "*Didn't* you!?"

"Perhaps he meant one of your daughters?" Another plate. "His mother?" A spoon clattered.

"I know exactly who he meant!" Tora's voice rose to a shriek. "You brought your trash to dangle in front of his horrid new amusement!"

She jumped from her chair and leaped for Tiller, her fists battering his head.

"Come with me!" Tora cried. "I'll take you to her, much good that it will do you or my husband!" She dragged Tiller along narrow corridors until they reached a door at the opposite end of the house.

A guard stood at the entrance. Tora shoved him aside and opened the door without knocking. She jerked her chin. "There she is! Show your cheap wares to his 'favorite lady'—and then get out of my house!"

Tora wiped angry tears from her cheeks and whirled out of the room. She slammed the door shut, then ran down the hall. Tiller could hear her bare feet thudding on the pine boards.

. . .

The woman Tiller sought stood alone in the center of an empty room. He had never seen such sadness in a face before, but that was not what captivated his attention. What made him stop in his tracks was her attire.

He had encountered women wearing clothing such as this when he had traded in other countries—always at a distance, always in a group. Never alone, and never close at hand.

An unadorned brown robe fell from her shoulders to the floor. Another cloth served as a simple headdress, white, and neatly folded over across her forehead. She wore no ornamentation, not in clothing or jewelry, save for a carved bit of wood hanging on a thin leather string around her neck.

"By Odin," Tiller breathed. "Naldrum never mentioned that his stolen property was a nun."

. . .

Chapter Three

"No…talk…no…" Long hesitations of uncertainty separated the nun's words.

In response, Tiller tried Gaelic, to no avail. He knew a smattering of *lingua franca,* picked up from Frankish slaves and trading runs. No response to that language either. Nuns, he knew, spoke something called Latin. No help there, because he did not.

Saxon, maybe? Tiller made an attempt, stumbling over the unfamiliar sounds.

'No anda, no dreogan andsaca! Winnan feond, gewinnan. Wiþ burh.' He gestured towards a small window. *'Faran sæ samod uhta?'*

No malice, no suffer! Fight enemy, win. Leave building—travel sea together, just before dawn? Not poetry, but it might serve to get across the idea: part question, part battle plan. Tiller held his breath.

She rushed towards him. Tiller felt reasonably certain that nuns did not normally fling their arms around strange men and embrace them. She kissed him repeatedly on both cheeks. As a torrent of Saxon poured from her, he stood stiff and unsure of what to do next.

. . .

Tiller held his finger to his lips. "Shhh," he said. He went to the door, opened it. The guard stood nearby, listening and watching.

The woman nodded. "Guard," she said in her strange accent.

"Doesn't look as if she's interested in any of my wares," Tiller remarked to him.

"She's not interested in anything," he grunted in response. "Barely eats. Cries a lot when she's alone. Silent as a stone when Haakon comes by. No fun at all, if that's what he was hoping for. I have to stand here bored day after damned day, 'protecting' her. From what? Seems a big nuisance, to my mind."

Tiller commiserated. "A big waste. Just like me coming here to sell her stuff." He glanced down the hall, trying to remember how it fit together.

Guards everywhere, long corridors, and a high wall. Ugh. Tiller thought rapidly. He needed to get out of this building before Tora betrayed him being there to anyone. He turned back to the woman.

"Big shouting, *uhta*, just before dawn," he said in Saxon. He pointed through a tiny window to where the fence was visible. "Go there."

She nodded.

Something about the woman's regal bearing made Tiller feel as if he should kneel. *Nonsense.* He was an Icelander. Icelanders knelt to no one.

Still, he found himself touching his forehead in a gesture of deference. "*Treow...ellen.*" *Trust. Strength.* Again, Tiller held his fingers to his lips. "Shhh."

She nodded.

Wonderful. Tiller now knew the woman was in fact here, and where she was housed. Now all he needed was the 'big noise' he had promised her—and he had absolutely no idea how that might come to be.

Tiller left the room and closed the door and let the guard direct him out of the house. To his relief, the beggar was nowhere to be seen, and the cook was preoccupied with putting her bread in the oven. Tiller left Lade Garde as fast as he could and began to explore the town.

. . .

Haakon Sigurdsson, the Jarl of Lade, had not regained the jarldom from his father's murderers because he was a stupid man. He was also a man with little patience for Tora's moods, so he ignored her as she sulked through the dinner.

Seeing that her approach was not working, Tora began to express her anger more directly. She slammed her wine goblet on the table after each sip.

"That's Flemish wine. You're spilling it, and it's damned expensive. Stop it." Haakon grunted.

It gave Tora the opening she needed. "Oh, so I cannot waste wine, but you can waste money on your dark treasure over there?" She glowered to where the nun sat, a guard on each side. "You can buy her trinkets she will refuse to wear, trying to gain her favor?"

"What nonsense is this? I didn't buy her any trinkets!" Haakon was starting to wish he'd never bought the slave called 'the Nubian'. Tora normally turned a blind eye to his lust-binges, but she'd been consumed with jealousy over this one.

Haakon chewed on a bone as he considered divorcing Tora. She'd been lusty in her youth, but after several children, she no longer wanted to share pleasure. When he wanted her, she feigned sleep. He could tell by her breathing.

I could give her a nice bit of farm, Haakon thought. *A few slaves to attend her.* But in truth, Tora—when she wasn't in a fit of jealousy—ran his household exceedingly well. Replacing her would not be easy. *She just needs her feathers smoothed,* Haakon decided.

"I'd never consider buying a slave gold or jewels. Not like the presents I give you. It would be a waste."

"Don't try to flatter me, Haakon! The trader you sent—"

He licked his lips and reached for another piece of meat. "Which trader?"

"That merchant! He said that you told him you wanted things for 'your favorite lady' and I was foolish enough to think he meant *me!* I was *mortified,* Haakon! And in front of a common trader!" Tears of hurt pride fell on her cheeks, this time genuine.

Haakon worked his teeth against the rib bone, gnawing and thinking. He worried it until not a shred of meat remained.

"My sweet Tora. No such thing happened. I invited no one here."

She wiped her eyes. "I talked to him myself. I don't believe you."

"Think about what you are saying, my wife. A stranger coming into our house asking to see the Nubian, and claiming I sent him, when I most certainly did not? What does that tell you?"

She frowned and looked at the untouched food congealing on her plate. Traced her finger against the wood grain of the table. Looked at Haakon, suddenly alert.

"A thief!" she exclaimed. "Planning to steal something?"

"Not just a common thief. Keep going, my love."

Tora sipped her wine, put the glass down carefully this time. Suddenly her eyes widened in shock. "He's a slaver! He plans to steal the Nubian!"

"Well done," said Haakon. He raised his voice. "Guards! A double complement on the wall from now on, day and night. I want men roving the streets as well. Someone is trying to take my most prized possession—" he pointed his eating knife at the dark-skinned nun— "and I will richly reward any who catches him at it!"

Haakon smiled, victorious, towards Tora, pleased with her cleverness. *No, I won't divorce her,* he said to himself. *She's far too intelligent. Quite useful.* He reached for another juicy rib, and did not see Tora's chin lift and her face turn away, with her eyes narrowed in bitterness.

His 'most prized possession'?

Haakon had used that exact term the last time he insisted on bedding her.

Tora drained her glass of wine in one gulp. She kissed her husband lightly on the cheek. "You like this dish? I am happy it pleases you. I had the cook prepare the pig a new way. Enjoy, my love." She tapped her finger on her chin. "You've fortified the walls and streets against this thief. I'll speak to the house servants and slaves. We will make sure this thief has no chance of success against Lade Garde!"

Haakon swallowed a mouthful of meat. He pulled Tora to him and planted a lusty kiss on her mouth. "Best first-wife ever," he said, and took a huge gulp of wine from his glass.

. . .

As the evening meal ended, Haakon went out to give his instructions to the wall guards. Tora summoned the household staff.

She drew them close, as if she had a secret. "We must all be vigilant," she half-whispered. "It seems a thief is trying to gain access to our home. If you see anything out of the ordinary for the next several days, come immediately to me. Me! No one else!"

As they bowed and returned to their duties, Tora touched the arm of a manservant.

"Beloved. A word alone, please?"

He dropped back into an alcove. She whispered briefly and he nodded.

Tora felt satisfied. By now the hall had been cleared of food and dishes, and people had begun to reassemble for the evening's amusements.

"Come, sire," she clapped her hands to Haakon as he returned into the hall. "Our new *skald* will sing tonight. Let us listen, shall we?" She gestured for the board and dice games to be put out. Soon a pleasant hum of conversation and music filled the room, and Tora filled Haakon's glass again and again.

. . .

"The tide will start going out late after middle-night. I want to ride it out of the fjord, so we need to leave sometime before dawn," Tiller announced to the *vikingers* around the ship. "Be on deck and ready to sail at an instant's notice."

"You're raiding, aren't you?" A voice from the back.

"No. It's just that the tides run early, so we might as well get a good start."

"What are you stealing?" Another voice.

"Who says I'm stealing anything?"

"We haven't seen any merchants down here buying wares from us. You've sold nothing. Your pack is just as full as when you left this morning. What's the hurry to leave, then?"

"I told you. I made a delivery to a private client."

"The only person in Trondheim who has enough gold to make a private delivery clear across the North-way sea worthwhile is Haakon Sigurdsson, the Jarl of Lade—and he's a notorious raider himself. He often doesn't buy from small traders, he *takes* from them. Are you stealing something from the Jarl? He'll kill us all if you do. Don't we have a right to know what you are getting us into?"

"Look, if you want to sign on with another ship, feel free."

"You know perfectly well no one will hire a bunch of strangers. If we want to get home, we're stuck with you. Besides, if we stay, Haakon will track us down to find out what we know about you." Grumbling sounds of agreement came from the rest of the crew.

Tiller remained firm. "Remember that we will be *very* well paid for this voyage, once we complete it."

"Who's your client? Who pays for a whole crew and a long trip, to sell nothing and buy nothing?"

"He said he wants to remain anonymous."

They looked at one another and shifted uneasily. "Something's up. This whole thing stinks."

"So, are we clear, then?" asked Tiller. "Be on the ship all night long, ready to go. Be ready to sail between middle-night and dawn, as soon as I get on board. Anyone not on deck will be left here, stranded. I mean that. As soon as I get back, we'll push off right away."

"You're raiding, and you're not taking us with you. That's just not right. Maybe we'll just follow you to get a bit of the action."

"Try that and I'll knife you myself. I cannot make it any clearer that I need you here on the ship ready to raise the sails. And let's have no more talk of raiding. We're honest traders, for Odin's sake, even if we are on a mission for *Gothi* Naldrum."

By Hel, he hadn't meant to let that slip out. Disconcerted surprise passed among the crew at the headman's name.

"Just get to work on something!" he snapped. Gods, he needed to think. Whatever plan he derived with was going to be half-baked, incomplete, and almost certain to get him killed—because he *was* raiding Haakon Sigurdsson, the brutal and feared Jarl of Lade, and he was doing it almost alone.

. . .

Tora plied the new skald-poet with promises of gifts, urging him to sing more and more outrageously about the merits of her husband. When Haakon began to nod, sleepy with the wine, she patted the cushions on which they reclined.

"Here, husband," she said. "Lie down here and rest. Everyone is still playing at the board games. No need to go to our bedchamber just yet. We have a house bursting with guests. Between that, and with so many guards posted, only a madman would try anything tonight."

"I shouldn't," Haakon mumbled as he sank onto the pillow, exhausted. He had ridden in that afternoon from farms far distant and exhausted, had not intended to drink so much. "Maybe just a short rest."

"I'll tell the skald to play gentle music. You are such a fine host. Everyone knows what excellent gatherings you hold. Just let the sounds of the party be a lullaby to soothe you. I'll wake you later and take you to bed."

She beckoned to a slave Haakon favored, a girl whose loyalty Tora had carefully cultivated.

"Lie here with the Jarl while he sleeps. Quiet him if he stirs. If he wakes, keep him in bed. He works so hard, and he deserves a good evening. I have my flow; I cannot."

She eyed the girl, who knew Tora had more to say.

"My Kalendar says that the gods will make this winter cold. You need a cloak. Do as I say, and you'll get my old one to keep you warm."

The girl nodded and slipped under the covers. She curled around Haakon. He threw an arm over her, found her breast with his hand, and snored deeply.

Tora watched to make certain that her husband would not wake for a long while.

"Your most prized possession," she snorted as she left the hall. "We'll see about that."

. . .

Tiller picked two of the *vikingers* to go with him to Lade Garde. "I need a little help tonight. You?" he pointed to one named Bót, who nodded. "And you."

The crew consisted of a motley jumble of men and women. The two Tiller selected were female.

Jeers followed his choice. "Are you taking them into Trondheim for a night at a brew-tent?"

Tiller shrugged off the remarks. "If so, it'll be a short night, I hope," he replied. The remark did not silence the crew so much as it elicited additional crude speculation regarding things 'short', specifically Tiller's anatomy and abilities.

He dug in the galley stores for the oldest cheese they had, and was gratified to find one blue with mold, slimy and rotting. Tiller tucked it into his pouch. On a wheelbarrow he loaded a bucket of ship's tar, a pine knot, a flint, a dirty blanket, a length of rope, and a large leather bag of the kind used to keep precious fabrics dry.

Only one more task remained, one that promised to be painful. Tiller selected two men this time. He sent the rest of the crew to wait at a distance and scooped an ember from the ship's galley fire.

"Say not a word to the others about this," he said. "The shock at seeing it needs to be genuine."

. . .

Chapter Four

The wheelbarrow creaked as Tiller pushed it along the roadway towards Haakon's house. His voice low, Tiller explained the plan, such as it was, to the two crew women who walked with him.

"Distract the guards. That'll be your job. Both of you, flirt with them. Engage as many as you can, by any means possible, and try to keep them occupied as long as you can." The women, both hardworking and no-nonsense, asked no questions. They simply nodded.

"I'll take the wheelbarrow. When chaos breaks out, head for the back of Lade Garde and find me there. There will be confusion. We'll need it to escape and make our way back to the ship."

His light tone belied Tiller's worries. This might be an easier feat on a dark night, but just past the midnight-sun of midsummer, there would still be plenty of light in the sky. He could only hope that the fog rolling in from the harbor might thicken a bit, to give him some cover.

Over and over, Tiller rehearsed what he needed to do.

Set the pine tar afire.

Run.

Run, to the part of the wall where he had told the Nubian to go. Run, and hope by some wild fortune that in the confusion and shouting about the fire, she would be able to escape from her room and get to the wall.

Throw the rope.

Hold it, blind to what might be happening on the other side of the wall. Feel the jerk of her clutching the knot. Pull, and hope to see a dark-robed nun coming over the wall.

Then run again.

He said nothing to the two women about what the large leather sack was for, nor did he tell them the second part, the escape plan. Only an idiot would try such a thing. But who knew? Maybe it would work.

. . .

The closer they came to the Jarl's house, the more Tiller fretted. *What an utterly shitty idea*, he chastised himself. Everything could and should go wrong. *No time to improve it now.* He considered Naldrum's reaction if he returned empty-handed. He had drawn them all straight into a mess, and it was most clearly all his fault for falling for Naldrum's promises. Even though it was the last thing in the world he wanted to admit, Tiller could not avoid seeing in himself the traits he had loathed in his father: too impetuous, too tempted by the promise of easy money, too hard-headed, cocksure, and swaggering.

He groaned again. No time to think of that now. But the ugliness of that comparison ate at him as he trundled the squeaking wheelbarrow towards Lade Garde.

. . .

Tiller directed the two women to the beaten pathway crossing the long front of Lade Garde. He left them there, pushing the wheelbarrow towards the back entrance.

"Distract the guards? What do we do?" one woman asked. She looked along the wall to where several men paced back and forth. "Should we—"

"We should start by ignoring Tiller," the one named Bót answered. "These are trained fighters. Not one of them would be distracted by a woman flirting with him, and especially not dressed in filthy crew clothing."

"So, what do we do?"

Bót laughed aloud. "Men of fighting love nothing more than a fight. Just follow my lead."

. . .

The guard squinted along the stretch of wall ahead. What was that? Two sailors wrestling?

"Ho, you two! Get away from there! Take your argument somewhere else!"

No response. He shouted again. "Hey!"

Damned vikingers. "I'll get rid of them," he said to his companion. He moved towards the twisting mess, hefting his weapon.

As the man reached the scuffling men, the pair suddenly parted and stood facing one another, bent over, hands on their knees, panting out of breath.

He noticed that one's shirt had torn. The rip exposed a creamy round breast. *A woman? No, two women!!*

"Trouble, girls?" he asked. The word was more leer than question.

"Stay out of it. This is a personal matter." Bót wiped her nose with the back of her hand, eyeing the other woman circling her.

The guard sized up the empty street. Nothing to worry about. *Bah.* Everybody who was anybody was inside at the feast with Haakon. By now they were probably watching bare-breasted slave women dance, except for unlucky him and the men posted out here missing everything.

He called to his companions. "You might want to see this!"

The other guards jogged over and had the same reaction. From force of habit, each glanced left and right. The roadway remained empty except for a hunched old man trundling a wheelbarrow slowly along the wall.

"I'll bet a flagon on the taller one," he grunted. Wagers were placed, and the men began to root for their choices. Other guards, peering around the corners of their side of the wall, came to see what was happening, curious.

The two women circled one another, taking their time, slow and wary. As they traded insults, the guards laughed more and more.

Bót knew what to do. Her insults to her companion became more and more lewd. The guards' laughter and shouting increased.

Finally, she pounced. The two women rolled together in the dirt, pulling hair and hitting at one another, and wagers flew.

. . .

Tiller heard the commotion, grateful for it, but did not pause to look at whatever was happening. He saw the side-wall guards leave and run around to see what was happening in the front of the property. *Good.* He pushed the wheelbarrow around the corner to the now-empty side and moved quickly down its length towards a stand of hemlocks that rose beside the high wall. He fumbled the bucket of pitch tar from under the blanket, climbed up on the wheelbarrow, berating himself *for Thor's sake, go faster!* and pounded the bucket upside down onto the pointed wooden pikes that topped the wall. Black treacle drooled down. Tiller added a bit of tinder, fumbled with the flint, his fingers shaking. A spark caught. A tendril of smoke curled, and an infant dragon of flame began to lick at the pitch.

It would be hidden for a little while, but soon would crackle, and reach towards the hemlock, hungry. Then the dragon would roar.

Becoming a hunched old trader again, Tiller turned the corner toward the back of the compound where the kitchen entrance lay. Two guards paced across it. Tiller wheeled his wheelbarrow near, tried to speak in a wheezing voice.

"Have any mead, boys? I'd love a swallow."

"Go away, old man."

"You should be grateful to me. I'm going to give you something, and all I want is a bit of mead."

A knife, waved in his direction. "You'll give it to me now, without any reward."

"Very well, then. There's something happening out front."

"What?" A look of lazy skepticism.

"Big fight." The old beggar pointed back the way he had come. "Front wall. They maybe could use your help."

Both guards reached for their swords. They raced around the corner of the wall towards the front of Lade Garde, running right under where the fledgling dragon licked, its brightness still hidden in the thick hemlock branches.

As soon as the guards left, Tiller dropped his bucket at the base of another hemlock trunk not far from the gate. This time his hands did not shake. Fire leapt from the dark stickiness in the bucket. Tiller watched just long enough to see it lapping against the resin-rich trunk of the tree. Soon it would jump to the timbers of the wall.

Time to hurry now. Tiller felt strangely calm, as if time had slowed to a crawl. He gave up the shambling walk and pushed the wheelbarrow through the kitchen entrance, open and unguarded.

. . .

Remnants of the hall feast had been carried back to the kitchen. A group of servants gleaned the bones for any bits of leftover meat under the watchful eye of the night cook.

"There's a fire on the side wall! And a fight on the front gate!" Tiller cried.

The gleaners shouted, catching the attention of the guard who stood at the house door. Food was dropped, brooms and blankets were grabbed, and servants spilled through the gate and around to the front of Lade Garde. Tiller stood back as the group thundered past to do battle with whatever they might find.

"Forget the rope and the wall!" Tiller exulted. "I'll just take her out the back gate here!" He moved the wheelbarrow against the kitchen shed and hoped that the dark-skinned nun would appear soon, wishing he had thought to ask her name.

. . .

Tora, lying her bedroom that overlooked the back yard, heard the sounds of yells and calls. She had stayed awake in hopes that tonight was in fact the night. Her lover slept beside her, his breath deep and slow.

"Time to wake," she nudged him. "My husband must have been right about someone trying to steal the Nubian. We need to get her away from whatever is happening. I'll wait for you and her at the back entrance."

He threw off the blankets and stood nude in front of the fire. Tora had only an instant to admire his legs before he pulled on a tunic, grabbed his sword belt, and ran down the hall.

. . .

Tora followed him at a more leisurely pace. She opened the door into the main hall and peeked through. There was the shape of her husband, a great mound under the blankets at his eating bench. She could see the pale arm of the slave girl draped across the covers. *Both of them sound asleep. Good.*

Most of the other guests and household staff slept as well. She had instructed the musicians to take turns playing all night, to drown out any sounds that might inconvenience her guests.

Tora closed the door again. She made her way out of the main building to the kitchen entrance. As she walked, she, too, drew a *saxe* and gripped it tightly in her hand.

. . .

The guard posted outside the Nubian's door had fallen asleep. Tora's lover kicked him. "Shift's over," he said.

The man came slowly awake, groaning and rubbing his eyes. "I wasn't sleeping," he said. "Just lying here resting with my eyes closed."

"And this big wet spot where you were drooling on the floor?"

The guard hung his head. "Nothing's happened all night."

"Something's happening now. Go to the front and help. I'll watch her."

The two men clasped hands and parted. The sleeping guard stumbled forward, yawning, and Tora's lover pulled at the door latch.

. . .

The Nubian stood in the center of the room, holding her breath—and holding a heavy candlestick, ready to hit whoever came in the door.

"Put it down, princess," he said gruffly, gesturing with his knife. She did not understand him, so he crossed the floor to her and took it from her hand. He gestured again. "Out."

They moved silently along the halls, his knife tip pressing the middle of her back. Just enough to feel it, no sudden moves.

The nun blinked at the sudden light of the pre-dawn sky as they emerged from the dimness inside. Tora met him at the back door, smiling.

"Here's your husband's prize, mistress. Safe and sound," he said.

"Excellent, my love," she purred. "We'll keep her out in the open here, where we can see. Is that smoke I smell? There must be fire somewhere! Haakon *was* right. Don't disturb our guests in the hall—they must know nothing of this! —but find the other guards and help. I'll stay here. She can't very well escape while I'm watching her, can she?" Tora wielded her knife, to make her meaning clear.

The man grinned and blew a kiss to Tora. He ran back into the building, closing the door behind him.

. . .

Tiller edged around the corner of the kitchen building, hoping to see the Nubian running towards him. She was there, all right.

But she stood perfectly still—and Tora held a knife at her throat.

. . .

Chapter Five

"You thought to steal my husband's treasure, eh?" Tora's voice came calm across the still air. Shouts of those fighting the fire were faint. Tiller clearly heard her laugh a little.

What was the correct response? He decided on the truth.

"Yes, Mistress Tora, I did. But not for myself. I was hired to take the Nubian by a man who claims Haakon stole her from *him.* I'm merely returning her to her rightful owner."

To Tiller's surprise, Tora threw her head back and laughed. Even the Nubian looked shocked at the sound. Her eyes rolled back towards Tora but she did not move her head; the knife still pressed.

"You might have saved yourself some trouble if you had told me your intent right away." Tora remarked, dryly. "I *loathe* this woman. Ten years with Haakon—the best of my youth! —but he saw her, and suddenly I was dispensable." The words tasted bitter on her tongue.

Tiller remained motionless. No telling how this might play out. Did Tora plan to kill the Nubian?

"So it would appear, my 'trader' friend, that you're doing me a favor. Stop gaping at me and hurry. I assume that the fire is a distraction you created? Well done! My personal guard is away to fight the flames, so he will see nothing. All of the kitchen staff and mongers have run off as well. Seems that no one is here to see you overwhelm me and steal this woman, is there?"

Tiller could not believe his luck. *I'll never doubt you again, Loki.*

"No, mistress. No one." He rummaged in the wheelbarrow, took out the large leather sack. "Here., We need to get her inside this."

Tora cut the woman's robe. She ripped two or three pieces of it and scattered them on the ground. "Deception relies on small details," was all she said.

. . .

The nun seemed to know not to argue. She wrapped her robes around her legs, put her feet into the sack, and wiggled inside. Tiller tied the canvas thongs tightly.

"Hurry," said Tora. "You need to be clear of Lade Garde as soon as possible. Go this way—" She gave him quick directions on some back alleys. "I'll point them away from you, as best I can. And know that if they catch you, you're on your own. I'll be among those calling for your death. This is the only help I can give you."

"Understood." Tiller turned the wheelbarrow to leave. But before he could take a step, a familiar voice came from the kitchen gate.

. . .

"So, you got her, did you?" the beggar sneered. "Snagged the Nubian! Well done, stranger!"

Tiller stopped. Behind him, he heard Tora suck in a breath.

"And here is the lady of the house, helping you to steal her husband's property. Haakon will be much surprised to hear this, mistress." He clapped his hands together, slowly, then executed a mock bow.

"I thought you said you hated Haakon," Tiller protested. "Yesterday—"

The beggar cut his words off. "Hate does not preclude convenience. I *do* hate Haakon, but I hate the cold of winter more. Haakon threw me out of his household. I'll never get work in this town again, but a small reward for loyal service will pay for a hovel and a blanket to keep me alive."

"I'll give you all the coin you need. Follow me to my ship."

"No, I think not," said the beggar. "You're too clever. That might not work for me as well as telling Haakon. I'll just go and speak with him now. Easy to get into the house with all this confusion you've created." He touched his cap, the same gesture of respect that Tiller had made to the Nubian, but this one heavy with sarcasm. The beggar pulled a knife from his belt and started to edge past them towards the house entrance.

"Here," said Tora. She lifted a heavy gold necklace over her head, held it out in her hand. "Haakon will never pay you this much. You could buy your own ship with this. Become a wealthy man."

The beggar's mouth dropped open. "By the gods," he breathed.

He stepped towards her, his fingers reaching, the knife still in his other hand. Tora flung the necklace onto the ground. The beggar lunged towards it and scrabbled in the dirt for the prize.

Tiller sprang. He plunged his knife, and the beggar lay lifeless on the ground.

. . .

"That could have been a mess for both of us," Tora breathed. Her words belied her still-calm composure. "Good thing you realized I was baiting him for you."

What a woman. Tiller hesitated. He needed to be gone, but still—

"Your husband is an utter fool, Mistress Tora," Tiller said. He strode across the small space between them. Pulled Tora against him, saw the amused invitation in her eyes, and kissed her. "What wouldn't I give to have a woman like you!"

"We people of adventure understand each other." She laughed, breathless. "My husband doesn't know who you are—*I* don't even know who you are! —but I'd certainly welcome a chance to learn. Come and see me if you're ever back in Trondheim. Now get away from here before anyone else sees you."

. . .

Tora watched Tiller until he was out of sight, then braced herself. The cut had to be deep enough to convince Haakon. He was a tremendously suspicious man.

She took the knife from where the beggar had dropped it. *What a foul, filthy edge this is.* She smeared his blade with his own blood, put the beggar's knife back in his hand. Ripped her sleeping gown at the shoulder. Took a deep breath, and positioned the sharp edge of her own *saxe* right along her hairline, where it would gush blood.

Another deep breath. Tora pulled her hair back, pulled the skin on her forehead tight, and sliced. She felt the blade grit against the bone—*too deep, by Hel*—and dropped, dizzy, onto the packed earth of the courtyard.

. . .

Out the kitchen gate, almost tipping over as he rounded the corner, running, pushing the wheelbarrow as fast as it would go. The two women from the ship, pointing. Sprinting towards him. The three of them careening down the narrow alley Tora indicated, their breath ragged wheezing, their hearts pounding.

Tiller had walked the town again and again the entire day. Six fields past Lade Garde, the road veered towards the beach. In his survey, Tiller had not seen the other path Tora described, another few fields down. It ran parallel to the main roadway, but offered a cover of thick brush and trees.

Go that way, Tora had said. *Nearly as fast, but less travelled.*

As soon as they reached the path, Tiller called a quick stop. Standing between the wheelbarrow and his two companions so they could not see what he did, Tiller untied the thongs of the sack in which the Nubian lay. Her eyes darted in fear.

"Safe. Stay silent," he muttered in Saxon, and tied the sack again.

"This isn't going to be pretty," he warned his shipmates. As he stripped off his tunic, they inhaled, appalled.

"Those marks on your body. What *is* that?" Bót asked, cringing.

"I have the white pox. We have to get out of town before anyone finds out."

Her forehead furrowed. "*White* pox? I've heard of the red pox, and the weeping pox, and the bleeding pox, and the black pox, but never the white pox." She made the sign of Thor and backed away. "It looks ghastly. How long have you had it?"

"It came on suddenly this morning," Tiller replied. "But what I had to do today couldn't wait, so..." He breathed heavily, coughed, spat on the ground. "I feel suddenly worse from all this excitement. I don't think I can walk. You'll have to get me to the ship. They'll kill us for bringing a plague into their city."

Tiller tossed his tunic over the leather sack in the wooden wheelbarrow and sprawled over it. A soft grunt came from the Nubian, and he felt her shift under him.

"Give me that blanket," he said. "Cover me up. I'm freezing with fever. And get us out of here."

. . .

They made it almost to the beach before someone accosted them. "You there! Halt!"

The women, each holding an arm of the wheelbarrow, froze in their tracks.

"What business do you have here?" A man with a drawn sword and a fierce expression.

Bót answered. "We're taking this man—he's a guest of Haakon, from the feast tonight—to our ship. He fell sick at the banquet. The jarl ordered us to take him to the harbor and get him away from Trondheim immediately."

A skeptical look. "Haakon Sigurdsson warned of a possible theft in the town tonight. He said to beware of all unusual circumstances.

Now you claim that the Jarl wants you to leave—and in a hurry? I highly doubt that. What's wrong with your man?"

Bót looked from side to side. "He has the white pox," she whispered, fearful.

"Never heard of such a thing. Let me see."

Tiller lay quaking with fever under the blanket. He heard the man's footsteps, hard with purpose. His head sticking out of the blanket, Tiller groaned and thrashed.

The harbor guard hesitated. The man did indeed look sick. Still, he had orders. "Take off that cover. Let me have a look at him."

Large white circles bubbled on Tiller's skin, oozing blood. They shone, a sickly putrid reflection of the night sun.

"By the gods, what *is* that?" the man asked. He leaned in for a closer look.

As the guard bent over him, Tiller retched. Foul whitish fluid spewed from his mouth onto the guard's tunic.

The man cursed and backed up, nearly tripping himself. "Ugh, that smells revolting. Which ship is yours?"

"Merchant *knarr*. Three vessels off Haakon's longship."

"I'll escort you there myself. And stay well behind me. I don't want any evil humors from that pox to reach me. We've got to get you out of here as fast as possible."

. . .

The *knarr* slipped over the choppy waves away from the harbor, heading for the infamous Trondheim pass. Tiller lay on board as if comatose, waiting for the next challenge.

A small longship cut through the waves and pulled parallel to their course. “Hold for boarding!” came the call.

This time, the crew had the name of the harbormaster and the code word he had given them. Tiller let the crew pull him to his feet, swaying with sickness and the smelly pale fluid drooling from his lips. Two other men—the ones he had chosen the night before—stood with him, their chests and thighs also covered with oozing, angry circles.

The sight of the bloody pustules and the harbormaster’s word, plus the repeated orders to ‘get that pox ship as far away as possible from Trondheim or I’ll hang the man who stops it’ resulted in a quick dismissal.

. . .

By the time the sun had reached her first-eighth, the *knarr* had maneuvered the sharp right- and left turns of the well-sheltered Trondheim fjord, and had left behind the stony hills guarding the inlet. Ahead lay only days of open sea, and the hefty reward promised by the chieftain Naldrum.

Tiller scooped the last bits of rotten cheese from his pocket and tossed them overboard. He threw back his head and laughed aloud.

“White pox! A bit of hot ember did the trick, didn’t it? Hurts, I know, but we’re clear of Trondheim and not a single sword drawn.” He tossed a container of beaver fat to one of the men. “Put this on your sores. It’ll sooth them.”

As they rubbed salve onto the burn marks, Tiller spoke again, his voice uncharacteristically husky. “We could all have ended up dead.

You two will each get a share from my wages for letting me burn you like that. Same with you." He nodded to the pair of women who had distracted the guards. "I won't forget what you did."

"So this whole trip was to snatch her?" Bót asked, pointing. She had helped trundle Tiller to the ship, completely unaware that someone lay hidden in the leather sack under him. They had been dumbfounded when, upon reaching the open seas with no one in pursuit, Tiller had untied the leather sack and a dark-skinned woman climbed from it. She now sat facing forward in the aft of their small ship. Her fingers moved tirelessly on a string of black beads, and her lips moved in silent words.

"Yes. Naldrum says she belongs to him. We just pulled off a rescue operation, for which he wanted total secrecy." No sense pretending now who the mission was for. He'd let it slip already.

Tiller watched the woman. *Poor thing. Whoever she was, she had to be terrified at being jerked around like this.* He climbed over thwarts and knelt beside her.

"Home soon," Tiller said in Saxon.

She cast a curious glance at him and shook her head. *How would this man know where my abbey is?* Tears came to her eyes. Hurriedly she touched the beads again, desperate, and fearful of what new danger might lie ahead.

"Hail Mary, full of grace," she whispered, but the ocean wind caught her words and blew them far away.

. . .

Chapter Six

Iceland, at the compound of the chieftain Naldrum

Naldrum's steward Kel glared at the headman. The stocky older chieftain kept slapping a riding crop against his leg. Naldrum's eyes had narrowed and his face flushed red at Kel's stubbornness.

The two men stood in a half-harvested field. Around them, a mix of workers—Saxon and Gaelic slaves, plus a few bondsmen—continued the rhythmic swing of grain-cutting, but they listened carefully.

"Put down those scythes and your wheelbarrows and come to the longhouse now!" Naldrum had shouted at the workers. "I want to break ground on the new storehouse today. All of the profit I have planned for this harvest depends on it!"

"They can't go!" Kel replied. "The grain fields need to be harvested. This clear weather could break into rain any day. What's the use of a storeroom that's empty of food? I need every single hand out here in the fields!"

Naldrum, incensed at his steward's refusal, shouted louder. "They're *my* workers so *I'll* decide what they do! I want that addition to the house done before autumn."

Kel stood firm. "If the harvest is spoiled by rain, you'll blame me—just like you did last year. The storeroom you already have holds enough to support your entire household through a bad year. We can wedge in extra crops and goods if you want. We can build a new one during winter, when there is so much less work to do. You always complain that the slaves and bond-workers are idle then."

"Did I ask you to make my plans for me? It's painfully obvious that you're not a man of business, Kel. Are you even aware that some farms are struggling up and down the valley? Think, Kel! Some of them will sell their harvests for cheap if I offer them a bit of silver now—and then pay me ten times over for the same grain when they are starving this winter! It's so easy! *That's* why I want the storeroom!"

Kel turned his face away, disgusted. He did not say what he thought. *Profiting on the pain of others. Vile.*

Naldrum took Kel's silence as resignation. "It's still light through most of the night. Make them finish here in the fields and then start on the building after the evening meal. I don't care how you motivate them. Threaten, starve, whip these lazy grifters. Make them work until they drop. From the profit I could make, I'll buy more slaves. Just get it done."

. . .

Now, two weeks later, several fields still needed reaping, and Naldrum's addition remained mired in chaos. Kel shouted, standing in the mud as exhausted workers careened around each other.

"Watch where you're going! Stop getting in each other's way! Someone is going to get hurt!"

The whole scene was a mess. There had been rock under the location Naldrum had selected, and the strongest workers had struggled to pry them from the ground and level it. Now, stone-layers wrestled foundation boulders into place where the walls would rise, side by side with men digging floor pits for sauerkraut barrels. It had rained last night, and bad weather threatened, again. It would start any instant. Kel had tried to call a work stop, but Naldrum had sent word that they must continue, no matter what the weather. Footing was already treacherous—a especially dangerous issue when working with heavy rock.

Kel's mood matched the threatening clouds. All he needed now was a dairymaid to show up, buckets sloshing with whey, and for the cooper to arrive with a jumble of staves and barrel-rings, and the field hands to dump a wagonful of just-cut cabbages. *Fukking chaos,* Kel fumed. The only thing that could make things worse would be Naldrum himself standing there.

As if some troll-spirit had divined his thoughts, Kel heard the headman's voice behind him—and Naldrum was clearly displeased.

"What is this mess, steward?"

Kel knew Naldrum did not want an explanation, only a response to rail against. Kel pretended to not hear as he squatted to help one of the slaves. He heard Naldrum grumbling as the headman picked his way through the mud to where Kel worked.

Kel stood, ready to pre-empt the verbal barrage he knew was coming.

"*Gothi,* you ordered this addition to your longhouse only half-a-moon ago. Did you really think we could get the site prepared, dig the foundation trenches, hire the stonemasons, get the stones carted here, lay the wall foundations and the floor stones, buy support pillars and roof trusses, do the turf-cutting for the walls, thatch the roof—*and* get the harvest in by now?"

Naldrum, faced with inarguable facts, puffed and bristled. "I still expect—"

"Excuse me, *gothi*," Kel bit out. "Every bit of time matters. I have to help get this cornerstone set straight." He turned on his heel.

Ever since Althing last summer, when he had tried to leave Naldrum's service and the chieftain had tricked him into staying, it had become harder to bear the sound of Naldrum's voice. But Kel knew the alternative: swallow his pride and stay, or Naldrum would hunt down Aldís, torture her until she begged for death, and then, mocking, refuse her. He had promised Kel as much at Althing.

I can't stand being around him. I can't leave. I just have to walk a fine line between open defiance and the bare minimum of obedience, and all to protect a woman who hates you, Kel mocked himself. Seeing Aldís at Althing after so many years apart had stunned him and delighted him—and then eviscerated him. She had shown up again, unexpectedly, to help with the slave boy Naldrum's son Drikke had injured. Painfully brief moments, but enough to confirm that his feelings for her still had not changed.

Kel's thoughts were interrupted by a cry of dismay. One of the slaves trying to heave a wheelbarrow full of stones lost her footing and slipped in the muck. The wheelbarrow tipped over and stones spilled everywhere.

Naldrum, wanting something on which to vent his frustration, rushed towards the woman and stuck her with his riding crop. She tried to get up, but Naldrum kicked her and she fell back down.

"You stupid, clumsy oaf!" he shouted. Red stripes already showed on her arms and face. "You nearly got mud all over me!"

Kel watched Naldrum thrash the woman. Slow realization swept over him. *It's me Naldrum wants to beat. As his steward, I carry more respect than nearly any freeman in our land, but Naldrum has no more regard for me than for this bedraggled Saxon slave-woman.*

She tried to protect her face from the whip. Naldrum screamed at her to move her hand.

No more respect than for a slave who dares not even defend her own life. No respect for anyone, or anything. Only for himself.

Suddenly, instead of the dirt-smeared woman cowering in fear under Naldrum's blow, Kel imagined Naldrum's crop slashing at Aldís' features. Without knowing he moved, Kel found himself between Naldrum and the slave. He grabbed Naldrum's forearm as it swung aloft for another blow, gripped, it, held it overhead. Lowered it, slow and deliberate, and let it go. Bent to pick up the riding switch that Naldrum had dropped in his surprise.

"You dropped your crop, *gothi.*" Kel's voice, deadly quiet. "We need this woman healthy if we are to finish your work on time."

The slaves had frozen in their work at Kel's defiance. He noted, not without humor, that Naldrum's face exactly matched theirs: shocked expression, mouth open.

"Thank you for your assistance in keeping your workers motivated, *gothi,*" Kel added. Only the faintest touch of sarcasm tinged his words. He might have been bowing to a man he truly respected. "I'll see that they increase their efforts on your behalf."

Naldrum, outmaneuvered, chose retreat. "See that they do," he grunted, as if he had been the one in control all along.

As the headman left, Kel turned back to the still-staring slaves. Now they crept backwards from him, not knowing whether to fear him too, or feel relief.

Kel said nothing, but only gave a slight shrug, as if to say *a man must do what a man must do.*

It was enough. As Kel made his way towards the sheep-fields, the workers watched him go, standing frozen with stones and tools still in their hands. Kel's protection of the woman had been such a small act, but one that mattered much to the defenseless. By dawn, every slave and servant in Naldrum's compound knew what had transpired in that muddy moment.

Kel, the unlikely hero of the *holmganger* duels at Althing.

Now Kel, the slave-saver.

Kel, defiant of Naldrum.

But the set of Kel's shoulders as he left told a different story. *Kel the discouraged. Kel the furious. Kel, not trapped as much as a slave—but trapped, nonetheless.*

. . .

Naldrum's oldest daughter Ankya stood in the doorway, watching Kel argue with her father. She felt excited at the manliness Kel had shown. She ran after Naldrum, who had strode off, cursing, to the stable. Rain caught her halfway there.

Naldrum stood under the dripping stable door, staring back at the storeroom construction. He pulled the thongs of his crop through his hand, his eyes narrowed.

"I know that look. You want to whip someone," Ankya said, pretending ignorance. "Who?"

Naldrum looked up sharply, noticed the unnatural gleam in her eyes. *Not again.* "How can you tell?"

"You were pulling your whip through your hand. You always do that when you want to hit someone. It's not magic." She laughed, pleased that she had impressed her father. "You know I love it when you punish those who misbehave. Tell me who!" She knew it was Kel, but wanted to force her father to say the words.

He whispered into her ear, as if was a secret between them. "My steward. Kel."

Ankya stiffened in his arms. Her eyes widened as if Naldrum had said something shocking. "Oh, no father! Not Kel!"

Naldrum pulled back in surprise. "Why not? It doesn't matter that he ranks high in our household. He deserves it."

Ankya shared more of her father's traits than a penchant for punishment. She had learned from him to be shrewd in hiding her motives.

"It's just that Kel has taken care of me more than once." She saw Naldrum's resistance, talked faster.

"Remember that time my horse threw me? And I broke my arm, and Kel tied it, and put me on his saddle in front of him, and brought me home? And the time he—"

Naldrum, put his finger against her lips. "Enough, daughter. If he has been kind to you, I'll let this matter go today. But if he misbehaves again—"

"Then you must let me strike him with the whip!" she cried, her voice oddly bright. *Perhaps I can make Kel obey me that way,* she thought.

"Ankya, please. It worries me to hear you say such things! I have ignored it, hoping it was a passing amusement, but I really must insist that you behave in a manner suitable for a jarl or a chieftain's wife! You're throwing away a fortune indulging in such nonsense!"

"Must you always measure me by what profit I might bright you?" Ankya cried. She dropped her submissive mask and glared at her father. "I don't care about some rich dowry a rich man might bring! I want to be Kel's wife."

"No! None of these rough locals for a treasure like you!" At her furious expression, Naldrum weakened. He tried a distraction. "We must talk of the harvest festival. I want all to admire my fine daughter." *The only daughter of the most important headman in the land.* "My lovely Ankya."

She let it go for the time being. They walked towards the longhouse, hand in hand. Ankya arranged her face carefully, and made happy chatter, but when Naldrum leaned over to kiss her lips, she gave him her cheek instead—and Naldrum, though he said nothing, noticed, and cringed inside. He would not lose Ankya. He could not.

. . .

Thoughts of his daughter troubled Naldrum during a sleepless night. *I love it when you punish those who misbehave,* Ankya had said. He had always felt justified in punishing others, of course. It was necessary to show he would not be disobeyed. In truth, Naldrum took some pleasure in asserting the power to do as he saw fit.

But his beloved daughter's pleasure came not from power, but something different, something deep and wrong. For the first time, Naldrum allowed himself to face the truth.

Something unnatural.

He expected better from his children. So far Ankya showed much more promise than the others—his son was an idiot, and the others too young and inconsequential to matter—but her strangeness had grown considerably in the passing year.

Troubled thoughts muddled and confused him. Why did hurting others cause such strange pleasure in Ankya? She would bring shame to the whole family if she didn't get it resolved.

What are you afraid of? A mocking, middle-of-the-night taunt from some wicked spirit.

The question made Naldrum flinch. *I'm not afraid of anything!* But he had seen the look in Ankya's eyes. She thought Kel had gotten the better of him today.

Fukking Kel. He should have let his steward go at Althing. The idea that she would prefer Kel to him made Naldrum's blood boil—as did the memory of how he felt when Kel handed back his riding whip. Yes, he had hated Kel today. Yes, he had wanted to punish him. Yes, it would have pleased Ankya to see her father punish a man. Yes, in truth, it would have made *him* happy, to beat Kel into the ground.

Naldrum's stomach churned. The night-sprite taunted. *You wanted so badly to strike your steward today, but you didn't. You're afraid of Kel. And worse, you're afraid of your daughter.*

"I'm not afraid! Not at all!" Naldrum rolled and tossed under his bedcovers. "Kel has a weak spirit. He always gives in to me. I could have whipped him, but what would the slaves think, seeing us brawling in the mud? As for Ankya? I must not encourage her strange interests."

Sleep refused to come. As servants groaned awake in the pre-dawn darkness and shuffled to their duties, Naldrum continued to lie, conflicted. Ankya's words sounded again and again in his mind. *You know I love it when you punish those who misbehave.*

That urging, so similar to what the woman Rota, Haakon Sigurdsson's messenger, had said at Althing two months ago. What had Rota said? *Show people that you will punish.* Something like that.

Rota had claimed that fear, hate and punishments would increase his power. Ankya took strange joy from it. *Power. Pleasure. Punishment.* The ideas circled deep within Naldrum's mind, but he could make no sense of what Rota meant, nor could he imagine a way to thwart Ankya's strange instincts.

In dawn dreams, Naldrum saw Rota and Ankya, snarling, circling, teeth bared, fighting for dominance. He stood aside, afraid but seduced by a new feeling that he did not understand. It throbbed, struggling to be born. In his dream, Naldrum saw himself strike Kel. He saw the look in Ankya's eyes.

Suddenly everything Rota had said made perfect sense. Hate, punishment, and power fell into perfect alignment. Naldrum nearly exploded in vengeful acceptance. The time had come to sow the seeds of hate and fear of which Rota had spoken—and to seize the power Haakon offered, and take it for his own.

. . .

When Naldrum's entourage had arrived home after the long trek from Althing, his enslaved blacksmith Tor had moved his anvil. In the new location, he could see the entire long roadway leading to Naldrum's property. He worked, and he watched.

Days passed. Another moon-day, another Tyr's-day, another Odin's-day, another Thor's-day, another Freya's-day, another bathing-day.

Then another set, and another. The days of the week became an endless, unbearable loop.

Tor swung his hammer. Sparks flew.

Three seasons ago—almost four now—he had set foot on this land. Not long after, he had left his children with a woman he had met only twice. He had not seen them since.

How many years had it been since he had seen his wife?

. . .

Tor had thought he would die of heartbreak when his wife Kandace had first been captured by slavers. But day by day, he had lived. Now years had passed. When he had left his children in hiding with the widow Eilíf, he thought he would die of sadness. But now nearly another year had passed, and still he lived.

When he had met the toothless sailor at Althing, all that pain had come back. Tor had learned so little, but so much of it dismaying. Someone had found Kandace, that Naldrum had hired someone to go get her, and that Naldrum already suspected that Kandace meant a great deal to Tor, but not that she was his wife. That much, only Tor knew—and that secret, he needed desperately to keep.

So he hammered. He pumped the blowing-bag to heat the forge fire. He counted the days of the week, and wondered if Naldrum's man had found her. He wondered about a ship, sailing across the treacherous waters of the north-way seas.

And he counted the days.

. . .

Such a sad thought, that he might actually prefer to see his beloved wife as Naldrum's slave, rather than floating wet and lifeless in the sea?

. . .

Chapter Seven
The Passing

The healer Aldís lifted a horn brimming with funeral ale to the sky. Foam sloshed over the rim and ran down her wrist. She ignored it.

Such an unfortunate time for a man to die, these weeks after Althing when harvesting was in full swing. Those who would normally honor and mourn old Vitha's passing might feel the need to work instead. But there was always work, all year long, and people died, all year long. Mourners always found a way to come.

Summer-spirits which roved the land in the sunny months harmed no one. They eased the passing of the dead; everyone said so. But as the year swung from summer towards autumn, one worried how the *dökk-álfar*, the dark elves of the cold months, might respond as they grew impatient for their turn to roam the earth. Who knew what they might do?

Aldís no longer dreaded the dark elves from underground as she once had. She had told no one about the prior autumn when she had inadvertently spent the entire dreaded night of *álfablót* out of doors. They had been so close to her that she had smelled them and felt their breath. But they had not hurt her.

Still, their mysterious powers must be respected. Dark-elves marked humans who might not last the year. They could be grudging as well as giving. One trod lightly over their barrows and burrows, especially now, when their time approached and the barrier between life and death drew thinner. Too easy for the *álfar,* impatient with their dank loneliness, to reach for living beings.

Thinking of Vitha going to the afterlife, Aldís fretted. She hoped the *dökk-álfar* had not marked her, and would not grow hungry for her spirit. She made a quick prayer to the goddess who ruled the underworld and commanded them dark-elves.

I'm not ready to come to you, Hel. I have unfinished work to do here, even though I'm not sure what it is. I'll be yours one day, but not yet. Please.

But today was not her funeral, and this was not autumn, not yet at least. This day, the words of honor must be spoken on behalf of old Vitha, who had lost his battle with disease and age.

Aldís sipped the ale. The cool bitter taste filled her mouth. She swallowed, lifted the flagon again, and passed it along the line of mourners.

Each offered blessings, adapting the ancient words. "May Vitha ride the wind to the afterlife. May he cross the edge of the world to Hel's dominion, where he feels no more pain, knows no more worry." No more wasting of his bent old body, his aged wife watching as he seemed to melt away from the inside. No more groans, as he tried to hide the anguish from her.

"Ah, Vitha, you were once a wild young vikinger. May you taste youth again." Even when he had grown sick and old, one could still sense the energy of the young man who had once walked in those bones, felt the ready energy of his laughter.

"May the gifts we offer sustain Vitha in the afterlife." Precious animals had been killed to accompany Vitha's spirit to Hel. His elderly wife was determined he would not go hungry there, even if it meant she might this winter.

"May we never forget you. May we raise your memory with love and with honor, and with laughter." Vitha with the bright blue eyes, always ready for mischief—and who had struggled with inner darkness of which few knew. Aldís had known.

"May your example inspire us to live larger lives, braver ones, better ones." She spoke the final blessing, naming the gods he had loved the most. Beside her, observers murmured to their own gods of hearth and harvest, asking them to watch over Vitha.

Aldís fought back tears. Such deep sadness at losing her friend. "Spirits who walk among us unseen…beings who move with tree and stone and river…companions in our daily passage from dawn to dusk to dawn, invisible, present, and aware, Vitha belongs to you now. We release his spirit to you, and we pray that you hold him with as much love and friendship as we have."

A good tribute meant the release of shared pain. At the celebration feast afterwards, friends would release pain in laughter, telling stories about Vitha's outrageous pranks and daring deeds, which needed no exaggeration to make them astonishing. But now came the time for his final journey.

Aldís gave the signal. Men and women on the sides of the funeral pallet knelt down, lifted, and raised him as one, the bier resting heavy on their shoulders. Behind them came the torch-bearers.

They carried Vitha to the middle of a scythed meadow where the wood stood ready. The slow music of the crossing-chant started.

Soon, Vitha's thin old body was wrapped in young flames that would carry him away. The crackling of the good-fire roared. The crossing-over smoke rose to the sky, and the invisible world claimed Vitha as one of their own.

. . .

The faces of the watchers burned, too, from the heat of the funeral pyre. They stood in silence for a long while, from time to time wiping tears, watching the smoke rise and knowing it betokened a good crossing-over.

When the embers fell to a flickering dance, a light rain started, so gentle it was little more than mist. A fine signal to leave the fire, to go back inside. Amid backslapping, hugs, and gentle arms proffered to the widow, the group made its way back to her longhouse. They would eat, and then, because harvest demanded, hasten back to their own farms to return to work.

Aldís stayed at the burning. Her friend the widow Eilíf had wanted to come, but Eilíf still not been able to bring herself to show her scarred face in public. She had made excuses—*Tor's children, I cannot leave them*—but Aldís knew.

She breathed in the cold fresh air, drawing the funeral smoke deep into her lungs. Vitha was now one of the *álfa*. Aldís spoke with him at length, asked for his help with Eilíf. He had been Eilíf's beloved uncle. Perhaps he might look kindly on his niece. Perhaps he could speak with the *dökk-álfar,* and ask their underground brotherhood to send some of their earth-strength to her, support her.

The light had nearly faded from the sky when Aldís finished. She looked around, half-expecting to see a shadowy form flitting at the edge of the meadow. *Goodbye, Vitha*, she said, and raised her hand to the wind.

. . .

Tiller considered having the crew bring down the sail. They had been tacking against a strong wind, and he was worried the huge sheet might tear. But they needed to make progress as fast as possible.

Tiller swung around, looked over his shoulder at the rising moon. He could see its light through the rainclouds, but not the moon itself. No matter; he had seen it last night.

He counted. Althing had started on the full moon closest to Longest-Day. Tiller had left the festival after Naldrum's request soon after, working his way down the river from Thing-valley and along the southern coast. One stop, and an unexpected delay. By the time they had reached the open sea, the moon had dwindled to half.

Would he have time to make it to Thorgest's before the deadline? Certainly his old friend had been joking, Tiller reassured himself.

They had made remarkable time to Norway, reaching Trondheim in only a few weeks. Now, the moon was nearly full again.

But rain fell, darkening the skies, and the seas ran high. Did they dear go back to a harbor along the North-way coast for shelter? But it was too dangerous. Surely the Jarl of Lade had sent out ships to search for them along the coastline. They would have to rough it on the open sea.

Tiller made his way along the small walkway to where the Nubian huddled under a woolen blanket. At his insistence, she had changed from her nun's habit into clothing more suitable aboard ship.

He squatted down in front of her. Her fingers still traced along the string of small beads and her lips moved, as they had done without ceasing since land disappeared behind them.

"You've a good stomach for strong waves," Tiller greeted her.

She did not understand, of course, and he did not feel up to the arduous task of trying to translate. Instead, he pointed to himself. "Tiller."

Her lips paused. Her eyes rested on his face.

"Tiller." He pointed to some of the other crew, called their names. Each responded, just a nod or hey.

"Tiller," she said.

A quick smile.

"Kandace," she said. He noticed that her voice held a tone of pride.

Tiller held up his ten fingers, closed his hands, then ten fingers again, spoke in Saxon. "*Dægrím hámfæreld.*" Twenty days to the 'home-fields', more or less.

Again, that puzzled expression on her face. *Why does this man—Tiller—keep saying home?*

Tiller gave Kandace a quick pat on her shoulder. "Soon you'll sleep in your own longhouse," he said. Privately, he wondered what kind of relationship existed between this nun and Naldrum.

It's none of your affair, Tiller told himself. *Get her there, get your silver, get to Thorgest's longhouse, collect your pillars from him, and get to your own land. Spend the winter building your longhouse. That's all that matters.*

. . .

Kandace had watched the fore of the knarr intently, searching each day for a coastline, hoping to see the familiar fields of Saxony. From Tiller's clumsy words, she dared to hope that he was taking her back to Wilton Abbey, her home.

Beautiful Wilton. A merchant woman in the nearby port town had seen Kandace in the street and had covered her bare body with a cloak. She had taken Kandace to the stone archway of Wilton and asked for the Abbess in charge. The abbess had called for a blacksmith to remove the rough iron bands that had cut into Kandace's wrists, and gave her clothing to wear and a place to sleep, and food to ease the gnawing hunger. The sisters had treated the infections. Their Saxon words, so strange at first, had become her language.

If only their ministrations could replace her memory. Before Wilton, nothing existed in Kandace's mind. Only swirling emptiness, only bits of something she could not fathom. She had given up wondering, but at night, dreams still came. A child whose face she could not see, screaming, running after her, crying *mama.* Terror, but of what, she knew not. A man. Kandace could not see his face, but in the dreams, she desired him.

But the dream man, whoever he was, was not real. Kandace knew this, because she lived in purity, sworn to Jesus. When she woke to dreams of the child, she woke sobbing. When she woke from dreams of desire, she flinched, dismayed. For both, she reached for her beads to bring peace.

Hail Mary full of grace. Kandace's fingers moved along the strand, and her lips moved in unison with them. Eventually, the feeling of not being able to get in air would leave. Calm would come, and she would breathe easily again.

. . .

They were not heading to where Tiller had promised, Kandace realized. The air through which Wilton Abbey's bells echoed had seemed warmer, tamer. But the winds and current against which their ship pushed seemed fierce. And colder.

'Home' was not where Tiller was taking her.

. . .

Chapter Eight

Tor, hammering a broken handle on the cook's favorite cauldron, glanced up to see travelers coming along the curve of the Bull River valley. His heartbeat quickened. He strained to see.

Three figures, no, four, all on horseback. All of him demanded to *run, run, call to her, see if it is Kandace.*

"I can't go. They cannot know I know her." Tor sat down heavily on a nearby stone, his fists clenched along his thighs. "But please let it be Kandace."

The approach to the compound from the river road took a long time. Watching seemed an eternity. Hope alternated with pain, as Tor forced himself to stand and walk to the pit where the fire glowed, as he forced himself to add more charcoal to the glowing embers, forced himself to take the rod of iron, to heat it, to strike the hammer against it, to watch the gray-blue ashes flake away from the glowing bar, to slowly curve the repair work into a proper handle for the cook's cauldron.

Tor did not let himself stare towards where the sun glinted on the shallow waters of the Bull River as it ran over its gravel bed. But he might as well have stared. Every other heartbeat he looked up, anxiously watching the slow progress of the distant horses. To pass the time interminable time, Tor swung his hammer, heated the iron, and breathed again.

. . .

The four travelers brought only disappointment to Tor. They turned out to be a group of men only. Two wore tunics that draped all the way to their ankles, and had oddly-shaven heads, plus their guide and a servant.

Shortly after they arrived, Tor heard calls come from the longhouse for chickens to be plucked. A cinder-girl stacked wood in the outside pit, which meant a piglet would be roasted. Obviously, Naldrum wanted to impress whoever had arrived.

When Tor finished his stack of repairs, he scattered the coals of his forge and untied the leather blacksmith apron and headed to storeroom construction to help with the heaviest stones. When that was finished, he would fall exhausted onto one of the crowded benches in the longhouse, and hope to sleep without dreams.

. . .

Two monks knocked at Naldrum's door. He had met them both at Althing that summer, and they had taken the long coastal road around, meeting the people of Bull Valley on their way to accept his invitation to visit.

The younger monk paced and muttered as Naldrum kept them waiting.

"Be patient, young Konradsson," the older monk said. "You know what we discussed about this man. This is just his way of trying to show that he is more important than we are. A petty, childish act.

Do not be pulled into his silliness. We are men of God." Friedrich, the older monk, sat on a bench along the sunny side of the longhouse, glad to be out of the saddle. "And for heaven's sake, stop pacing."

Konradsson tried to sit calmly, but in no time at all was once again striding back and forth along the building, oblivious to the flock of geese that ran first one way and then another, as he crisscrossed where their grain had been scattered.

Ankya drifted towards them. She sized up the older man on the bench and the nervous young one walking the grounds. "You're the one people call a 'bishop'," she said, directing her comments to Friedrich. She plopped onto the bench beside him. "You met with my father at Althing, didn't you?"

Konradsson stopped in alarm and stared at Ankya as if she might bite him, but Friedrich answered in a gentle voice.

"I did." Something told him to pause, and immediately, he was glad for it.

"I'm glad you have come to visit us. I have been thinking and wanting to talk to you, because we are alike, you and us," Ankya said. Her eyes became shrewd, calculating. "Or at least our gods are. Don't you agree?"

Friedrich concealed his surprise. Konradsson did not fare as well. He edged closer and glared in disgust at the girl. "Your pagan gods are nothing like my Lord! Whatever do you mean?"

Ankya stroked her fingers through her hair, unruffled by his outburst. "I heard you talking to people. I heard you talking to your gods and praying. You spoke of sacrifice, and of drinking blood from a cup in honor of your deities. Likewise, we sacrifice animals and drink from a blood-cup at the *blót* feasts."

Konradsson started to protest. "But our blood comes from—"

Ankya interrupted him, excited. "I know—from *a man!* That is the best part. *Our* sacrifice-meat and blood come from animals, but yours comes from *humans!* I heard you say it at Althing, how one of them sacrificed his body and then told others to *eat* it in memory of him, and to drink his blood! He *told* them to do it!" She gazed in happy awe at them. "How brave that is!" She imagined Kel saying the same brave words.

Aghast, Friedrich found himself at a loss for words.

Ankya pulled her knees to her chest and clasped her arms around them. "Since your sacrifices are human instead of animals, and since that one even volunteered to be the *blót*-offering, doesn't that mean your gods are more powerful than ours? Which makes me wonder if our gods are maybe even afraid of your gods?"

Friedrich choked. How could he possibly to answer this strange young woman whose pale eyes darted about, settling on nothing?

He made an attempt.

"I think that *people* who worship in one way may feel fear about another faith. Perhaps the people who believe in your…" again, he choked over the words, "…*gods*…might fear the people who worship Our Lord. They might therefore fear me and my fellow priest, young Konradsson. But let me assure you that we mean harm to no one. The God I serve welcomes all and forgives all. It is not His way to fight, but to offer love."

Ankya challenged Friedrich. "My father said that Harald Bluetooth kills those who keep to the Old Ways instead of praying to your gods. It's one of the reasons so many Icelanders left the Nor'way lands. Killing people seems like fighting to me. How do you explain that?"

Shocked again, Friedrich pressed on. "Even kings do things—in the name of God—which grieves God's heart. Such actions do not please the Lord, I think."

Ankya drilled him with her shrewd eyes. "Shouldn't your god punish the king, then, for disobeying the rules?" Friedrich noticed a tiny tremor of excitement in her voice at the word *punish.* The sound of it deepened his discomfiture. He decided to change the subject.

"I saw many young women your age at the bride-fair at Althing. Have you a betrothed?"

She snorted. "Not yet. My father says he is saving me for someone special. But," her voice lowered, as one conspirator to another, "I have chosen my mate. The man just doesn't know it yet."

Friedrich noticed that Konradsson had backed away from Ankya and watched from a distance, gnawing at his knuckle.

"Well, miss, when it is time for marriage, perhaps you will have learned of my faith, and perhaps even come to believe in it. If so, perhaps let me perform your marriage ceremony, if your father permits."

Ankya snorted. "I don't need my father's permission. Yes, you can marry me to my intended!" Her eyes sparkled with happiness. "I would love that! Because then *I* would get to taste the human blood as you white-christ folk do—and eat human flesh instead of our blot-sacrifice animals!" She clapped her hands. "Body and blood! That's what you say isn't it? Body and blood?" Ankya skipped towards the longhouse door. "Body and blood! Drink the blood and eat the meat, all as part of my wedding feast!"

The two monks stared after her, horrified. The door of the longhouse opened and Naldrum greeted his visitors.

"Ah, my sweet Ankya!" he said, putting an affectionate arm around his daughter. "I see you have met our guests. What do you gentlemen think of my favorite child?"

Naldrum did not see Ankya put her fingers to her lips, as if she and the monks shared a secret that her father must not learn. He also did not see the smile Ankya flashed to Friedrich, a smile which chilled the bishop to the bone.

Friedrich forgot the greeting he had planned for Naldrum. He pulled off his cap and stammered a hello, never taking his eyes from Ankya.

. . .

Chapter Nine

Bót sailed with Tiller from time to time. This trip, due to the hefty reward promised, had tempted her away from farm work. She had promised her headman a share of the reward.

"Kind of odd, isn't it?" she asked Tiller.

"You mean her being a slave *and* one of those 'nun' women?"

"Well, yes to that. But I meant I'd never seen someone with that kind of dark skin, not my whole life, until that huge slave man we met at Althing. And now this woman—and she belongs to Naldrum also? Two amazing beings, likely the only of their kind in all of Iceland, and both from the same farm?"

"Well, not many who can afford such expense. I heard Naldrum paid an ungodly amount."

"True. Still, something seems odd about it, don't you think?"

Tiller shrugged. "I don't know, and I don't care. I'm in it for the bounty." He adjusted the steering board. They had left the Orkney Islands, and now the North-way current pushed hard against the port side of their hull, trying to shove the ship back towards the Nor'way lands. Tiller would be fighting the current the entire rest of the trip.

Tiller saw Bót picking at a sliver of wood on the ship's rail and laughed inwardly. Bót never let an idea go once it started to interest her.

Sure enough. "I wonder if maybe they knew each other before Naldrum bought them," she said. "Same slave market, or something, I guess."

The question jogged a memory for Tiller. "You know, I spoke with that big slave of Naldrum's over a brew one night, just before we left, talking of all the places we'd traded."

"Did he say anything about Kandace? Do they know how the Jarl got her away from Naldrum?"

"Honestly, we never spoke of her." Tiller, watching the sail, was aware of Bót's head turning sharply towards him, the sound of surprise. "I know," he laughed. One would think the topic might have come up, but my mind was full of thoughts about getting down the river in time for the tides, about how much we were going to earn, how many crew I'd need. And the slave man seemed preoccupied himself. I didn't want to pry."

"Rumor at Althing was that Naldrum bought the man from a cart-trader named Josson, last year, late autumn. The prior year at Althing, did you hear anyone talking about slaves with dark skins from far away? No! Just that fellow this year. That means if nobody heard anything about them at *last* summer's Althing, only *this* year's, Naldrum had to have gotten both of them after last summer, in the autumn sometime. Yet somehow, she ends up in Trondheim in the spring? When nobody sails during the winter?"

Again, both men rode the waves in silence, turning the two bits of information over in their thoughts.

"Damn it, Bót! Why do you put such nonsense in my head? I was just happy we managed to get her out of Trondheim, and now you've got me wondering if Naldrum's got some trickery planned!" An uneasy feeling filled Tiller's chest. Naldrum, he knew, could not be trusted. Why had he not questioned the chieftain more before accepting this undertaking?

"Well, you have to admit that *something* doesn't fit," Bót continued. "I'm wagering that they do know each other. Might be a coincidence, but they both arrived at his compound right around the same time last year? I find such a 'coincidence' interesting."

"I know that tone of voice," Tiller said to his friend. "You're sorting something out. Let me know when you arrive at your far-fetched conclusion." He sniffed the air. "Rain is going to be on us soon. We should get the sail ready for a blow."

. . .

Chapter Ten

Ankya, supervising the women weaving linen, leaned back against the wall in the shadows and pursed her lips, considering. Ever since she had spoken to the white-christ men about their blood-sacrifices, thoughts of it intrigued her more than ever. To her delight, the older white-christ had peeked into the weaving alcove. He had looked around, almost furtively, and seeing only the weaving women, he had stepped inside the space where they worked. Their faces had brightened, Ankya noticed. He reached his hand to them and place it on their heads, one by one, saying a few words.

Ankya stayed where Friedrich could not see her until he had touched each weaver's head, and then hopped off the bench to resume her questions of earlier.

The bishop's face changed from kindly to alarmed at seeing Ankya. He backed slightly away.

"We cook our sacrifice animals once they are killed, so that we can eat their meat in our blood-feasts, what we call a *blót*-feast," said Ankya. "Do you do that too? Roast your human meat? Or do you eat it raw? And where does it come from? Do you keep a slave, to cut off a bit when you need it?"

Friedrich, continually horrified by Naldrum's daughter, prayed that he would be able to bring some light to this unfortunate pagan.

"We do not kill. Neither animals nor humans. Once, long ago, a single man offered himself as sacrifice—with the idea that after him, no other sacrifices would be needed." No sense explaining the Son of God to her at this point. One small concept at a time.

But Ankya was ready for him. "That's the man you call Jesus."

"Yes."

"But they *did* eat him at the blood-feast, yes? He told them to?"

"Not quite. They ate a lamb."

"But I heard you say differently! *'This is my flesh which is given for you, eat this in remembrance of me'* and *'this is my blood, drink it in memory of me'* is what you said! I wondered at first if you had cut a little piece of your *own* flesh off. I'm confused! Is it a lie about the flesh and blood, or is it true?"

Friedrich despaired at the strange young woman. His earnest intentions of converting pagan minds of Iceland had seemed well-founded in the peaceful monastery in Germania. Now, one odd young woman was illustrating the challenge such work entailed.

Daily, Friedrich willed himself to keep trying, but despite his prayers, godly self-assurance dwindled and impossibility grew.

. . .

Ankya considered the shape of Friedrich's back as he hurried away to visit the slaves in the fields. He looked hunched.

Perhaps he needs to make a proper *blót sacrifice. His god must be hungry and weak, if he's just been doing pretend ones.*

Ankya stroked the hair of one of the weavers, a girl of ten or twelve with sad eyes. The girl flinched a little at the touch, but an older weaver gave her a wordless gesture to stay quiet.

"What a pretty face you have," Ankya told the girl, who gave a shy smile. "I think I will wash your hair myself, the next bathing-day. Look at these tangles in it. Has it ever been combed, even?"

The weaver-girl passed the shuttle through the fibers on the loom. She shook her head. *Not since your father bought me from the farm where I was born.*

"I have an ivory comb. You'll have fleas, but I'll comb it to get rid of them. You'll be as pretty as a little goddess then."

"Thank you, miss," the child said. Her expression brightened.

"After that, maybe I'll present you to my father or my brother for a *frill.* They like favors. A young bed-girl is a pretty present to make!"

The child looked in alarm as she heard the other weavers gasp. Their shocked expressions told her enough of what Ankya meant.

"I'm just a little girl, Miss," she whispered.

Ankya smiled sweetly. She took the girl's chin in her hand and turned her face side to side, squeezing more and more tightly.

"Silly thing. You're just a slave. Why trouble yourself about things you can't change?" She laughed and let go.

The marks of Ankya's fingers showed as angry red blotches against the girl's jawbone. Ankya settled herself on the bench back on the bench again, pleased with herself for an excellent idea.

"Weave faster," she commanded. "I have an idea for a new dress I want."

. . .

Friedrich tried to avoid Ankya as he returned from the fields, but she had walked out to meet him, full of excitement.

"I had the best idea today!" Ankya exclaimed. She did not refer to the bed-girl for her father, no. That was a splendid idea, but she had thought of something even better. "You seem so worn out by care. I think your Jesus-god feels hungry. I know just the thing for him!"

Friedrich crossed himself. Ankya, wanting to gain his favor, mimicked him. She adored this gesture that she had learned from watching him and that fool Konradsson. Such an earthy, seductive motion: touch the forehead, tap herself *there*, then touch each of her breasts. She took care to pat each of her nipples with her fingertips, exactly as she had just seen Friedrich do. Perhaps she would add this gesture to the goddess-ceremony of the Egg, when spring came. It seemed fitting.

Again, Friedrich blanched.

"It is this," said Ankya. "I know of someone. A *bad* woman. I think she—"

"Ah, you are concerned that she will be going to Hell when she dies," Friedrich replied, thankful for once to be on solid ecclesiastical ground with Ankya. He prepared to explain 'sin'. Perhaps now he could get her to understand.

"But of course that will happen! Hel welcomes everyone who dies. It's her whole purpose for being." Ankya felt confused. "Unless they are warriors, of course, and then—"

Friedrich, not understanding, cut off Ankya's words before she said Valhalla.

"No, child. Hell is where sinners go to be cleansed of their misdeeds. Not good people. Hell is not a woman. It is a place."

Ankya considered that for a man who looked so learned, Friedrich could be terribly stupid. Ankya tried to help.

"Of *course* Hel is not a woman. Everyone knows that! She is a *goddess,* who takes the dead to live at her home which is also called Hel, which is why you are probably confused. Now, as I was saying—"

"No, Hell is the underworld, where the wicked go."

"No, you've really got it wrong. The underworld is where the dark-elves live, the *dokk-álfa*. But they're not really wicked. Just different." Ankya beamed at the priest. "Like I am."

Friedrich gave up. "What is your question about this woman you say is bad. Does she need my help?"

"Help?" Ankya snorted in derision. "No! She can *give* you help! That's my idea."

As they walked back from the fields together, Ankya described Aldís, carefully omitting the part about Kel's connection with the healer. When they neared the longhouse, Ankya finished her plan.

"I thought about this for a long time today. If that bad woman were to be a sacrifice—the way the Jesus-man was—how happy would your god be? Then he would have a man-sacrifice *and* a woman one, a matched set! If it has been a long, long time since the man died, your god must be so hungry. Famished! We can accomplish two good things together. We can get this bad woman out of these parts, where she causes nothing but trouble, and we can feed your god. How wonderful is that?"

Friedrich clutched his throat, gurgled something and rushed off. Ankya followed more slowly, musing her plan.

Her father clearly did not like that woman Aldís. The horrid creature had surprised and embarrassed Kel when they rode back from Althing. Ankya decided that after she presented the weaver-girl to her father, all clean and pretty for him, she would suggest her idea. Her father would be so pleased at her cleverness in finding a way to get rid of that annoying woman, and to simultaneously honor his guest the Bishop Friedrich.

Profit without cost. Pure profit, as Naldrum liked to say.

Ankya crossed herself again—forehead, pubis, nipple tap, nipple tap. She skipped back to the longhouse, smiling and thinking of Kel. She composed a little song to hum about blót-hunger, Jesus, Hel, and hungry gods.

Something about Aldís wove itself into the song. Something familiar, something about the healer Ankya could not quite remember, no matter how hard she tried.

But Ankya had a strong feeling that whatever it was, it mattered, deeply.

. . .

Far distant, Aldís stood and stretched from the middle-day break and prepared to go back to work. She detested threshing, but the chore had to be done every year, regardless. At most farms, every able-bodied person over the age of four had been working dawn to dusk to thresh the just-harvested grain crops.

Stand on the sack and twist your feet. Swing the sack in your hands, and pound it against the ground. Twist the sack in heavily-gloved fingers. Like the others, Aldís steadily changed her motions as one set of muscles tired.

She and the other workers—farm owners, their children, their bond workers, any slaves, and even passing travelers pressed into service—filled their rough sacks again and again, stuffing handfuls of scythed crops from brimming wheelbarrows steadily trundled in from the fields. As each wheelbarrow was emptied, another would take its place.

But the work, though hard, was not all bad. With everyone out of doors working together, a relaxed atmosphere took over. The threshers chatted together, and sometimes sang as they worked to separate each head of grain from its stalk. Aldís had noticed that as they worked day after day to break the grain shafts, strict boundaries between slave and master, bond worker and farm owner also tended to break down, as the group strove against rain and time to process the harvest. After that came the far easier task of winnowing the grain, separating the seed heads from the chaff. Mysteriously, she had noticed, the separations between those with less and those with more returned each year.

Such thoughts filled Aldís's mind as she worked, chatting idly with the people around her. The endless line of wheelbarrows seemed to be nearly finished. It betokened a good meal and the camaraderie of work done well together, a good evening and a good rest, and usually, a day in which everyone except those who milked the herds could sleep late.

The sun went behind a cloud, but the sudden chill that made Aldís pull her shoulders forward did not come from that. The cold came from fear that had paralyzed her limbs at what she had just glimpsed.

Weeks had come and gone since Vitha's funeral. Aldís had told herself that it had been her imagination, that she had not seen a face that she dreaded above all others lurking behind the mourners. But just now, as she had glanced up at the sound of a horse riding by, the same fear swept over her.

Had she just seen the man with the small cruel mouth and evil eyes riding past the farm, leering towards where she worked with the others?

That man had held her, tied and gagged, in front of the headman Naldrum at the Althing this past summer. Aldís had boarded the first ship leaving Althing to run away in terror, not from what had happened that day, but because that was not the first time she had seen his horrid face.

Fifteen years ago, a man with a cruel mouth and evil eyes had tied her and cut her. The scars still marked her arms. His companion had snatched her small daughter, and had ridden away with the child and killed her.

Aldís, dizzy, dropped her sack of grain. She fell on the ground and for a brief while, knew nothing.

. . .

Chapter Eleven

Aldís walked without stopping for days in the opposite direction from where the rider had been heading, fleeing again from the specter of that man.

Perhaps it was not him at Vitha's, she tried to reason with herself. The longhouse had been crowded with people. She had drunk ale on an empty stomach—how long had it been since she had eaten that day? —and the drink had gone straight to her head. *Perhaps I just imagined seeing him.*

But logic did nothing to allay the terror his face inspired in Aldís. She ran, her traveling pack across her back, without knowing where she was going, or why.

. . .

Aldís panted up the steep hill of the mountain path. With no direction in mind, simply running from fear, she had ended up at the exact same hillside where she had spent *álfablót* last year.

In that night of dread in which nothing should be unprotected, and out of doors, she had found a kind of angry strength. But it had been an accident last year. To find herself here again, of all the places she could have gone, seemed to be no accident.

Something had called her to this place again. But what, or who?

For the thousandth time, Aldís cursed the uneven nature of her *seeing*. Why must it always be so mysterious, making her guess what it was about?

She spread a sheepskin on the ground and knelt, her face to the valley. Her hands lay in her lap, open, palms up, and she listened.

And waited, afraid to hope, but hoping, nonetheless.

There it was. The same sense of someone, or something, calling, just as Aldís had felt the prior year on this same hill. *Are you there?* This time, Aldís heard it more clearly, but she still had no idea who or what was trying to summon her.

What she longed for could never be. *But what mother wouldn't hope? I'm only human,* Aldís told herself. She had been on this hill the night that the dead and undead spirits walked the land. Was it possible that this mountain held special powers, allowing the voices of the dead to reach more easily from the afterlife to this lonely hillside? Was that what she was hearing?

Aldís had thrown a leather bag of water and a bit of dried beef in her traveling knapsack. Blueberries, round and ripe, surrounded her, filling bushes on the hillside. They glowed, plump and deep in color, promising sweetness.

She would not go hungry. She was safe up here. No one knew where she was. Tonight would be a time to listen and wonder—and be safe, far away from the man with the small cruel mouth and the evil eyes.

. . .

Chapter Twelve

Kandace now felt certain the ship was not heading anywhere towards Wilton Abbey. But Tiller's inability to speak Saxon properly meant she could not ask.

She glanced at Bót and Tiller, talking in the aft of the ship. *They are looking at me and talking about me.* Panic about what lay ahead set in. Kandace prayed through her beads with furious intensity.

But the faces of those men did not look unkind, as had the men who had come up the river in their dragon-prow vessel and hustled her away.

We should never have left the walls of the abbey at Wiltshire. The nuns' little outing, so innocently planned, had proved disastrous. Three of the other women who had been snatched and loaded onto the ship had been taken all the way up a long coastline with Kandace to Lade Garde, but she had not seen any of them since their first night there.

Of the others who had been taken—Kandace named them silently in her prayers—they had disappeared almost right away, at the first harbor they had come to. A man on the ship had held out his hand, money had been dropped into his palm, and one by one, the shaken sisters had their wrist-rope handed to a stranger, who led them away. Kandace had no idea at all where they were, or what horrors they experienced daily, now.

The words of her bridegroom Jesus came to mind. *My god, my god, why have you forsaken me?*

The small ship pitched on the waves. Dusk faded into the short night of summer. The sail was taken down, and Kandace lay down and covered herself with a blanket. In the sky, an endless number of stars began to fill the sky over her, as tears fell slowly along her temples and into her ears.

. . .

Tiller pulled on the steering board as the knarr neared the mouth of the Bull River. Kandace stood near him, bracing herself for landing. She had heard the call of "Land ahead!" and had watched the shoreline rise up from the sea in front of them. She searched anxiously for something, anything familiar.

To her utter dismay, the landscape looked nothing like the slow river near Hamwick where her abbey was located. No gentle salt marshes, no flocks of songbirds chirping and darting over the swaying grasses. No clusters of stone houses along the riverside, and no steeple of a church rising among them. *What is this desolate treeless place?* Kandace's heart sank. *I have utterly no idea where I am.*

When Tiller ran the ship aground, Kandace opened the crate where he had stored her nun's habit and pulled it out.

"No," Tiller signed. "We'll be on horseback." He pantomimed riding, mimicked the skirts getting in her way.

Kandace pointed, insisting. "Wherever you are taking me, I do not plan to arrive looking all woebegone and helpless," she said in her proud, strong voice. "I will arrive there as you found me in Trondheim, calm and trusting in the Lord to protect me, as He has always done." *Nearly always,* the small voice inside her reminded, but she brushed it away.

"Whatever you say, mistress," Tiller replied to the torrent of foreign words. When she began to disrobe, her face set and stubborn, he took her nun's habit from her and put it back in the crate.

"Many days, horses, ride," he said in Saxon. "Ride, ride, ride, ride, ride."

Kandace stood on the lonely riverbank in defeat. She started to reach for her beads for solace, but instead sank down on her haunches on the gravel shore. Too sad to weep, to overwhelmed to pray, too confused to take any action, she heard Tiller blow the arrival-horn, and waited, empty. By the time the *vikingers* had furled the sail, someone from a shoreline farm had arrived with horses for hire, and they prepared to ride.

. . .

Kandace straightened in her saddle. *By the Mother, did this man intend to ride all night?* Any land, even a strange land, seemed an improvement over the cramped, damp ship. The entire voyage she had longed for dry clothing and a dry bed. Now she longed for any bed at all, dry or damp.

And yet still they rode, pressing hard. The knarr had been left far behind, beached on the gravel bank of wide river that had opened to the sea. Now that river had diminished to a smaller flow, but the gravel bed had widened. A wide riverbed with a small flow in the middle generally betokened floods. Kandace tried to imagine what kind of spring flooding would create such a landscape, but failed. *They must be violent and massive*, she thought.

Kandace kept a steady pace on her horse, just behind the man called Tiller and the one called Bót. She saw clusters of farm buildings from time to time, but the men gave no signs of stopping.

If they can ride, I can ride. No help for it now. They passed waterfall after waterfall where torrents poured straight down dizzying mountain precipices, and in between the steep hills lay wide valleys, each with its own wide gravel streambed joining the river they followed. All Kandace could think to do was to try and remember the way, should she ever need to retrace this route to the sea.

. . .

They kept the spurs to their horses' flanks for days. Finally, near nothing at all, Tiller called for a stop. Dismounting, he rummaged in the panniers for Kandace's habit.

"If you want to dress for your owner, now's your chance." He handed it to Kandace, and with Bót, turned his back as Kandace pulled off the rough ship's kyrtill and pants. They made no attempt to look or leer. *Definitely not the same as the men who had stolen her from the abbey.*

As she smoothed her habit and pulled the crucifix over her head, an odd feeling drifted through Kandace, something almost motherly. Tiller and Bót looked to be close to her in age, but it was clear that life had not come easy to either of them. Still, they had offered small kindnesses which mattered to Kandace. Surely such men would not take her to a place of danger. It certainly must be somewhere good, even if strange to her eyes. She breathed deeply. *I will trust them.*

. . .

Chapter Thirteen

Haakon Sigurdsson, the Jarl of Lade, furious at the loss of his prize possession, had flung ships into the North-way seas, hard on the trail of Tiller's knarr, carrying descriptions of Kandace. No description of Tiller was available. Tora claimed she could not recall the details of his face, nor could the harbor master who had recoiled in disgust when Tiller spat up on him.

One of the ships was directed to locate Haakon's agent in Iceland, the mysterious woman named Rota. Standing before Rota now, the messenger fought to not show his triumph.

He had bet a substantial wager with his travel companions that the news he carried would shock 'Madam Ice-for-Blood' Rota, who prided herself on never losing her composure. Meat shares and silver had been gambled.

I shall dine well tonight. The messenger smiled to himself, for as soon as he had delivered the message, Rota had pressed her hand against her mouth, aghast.

"Say it again. The entire thing."

"The Jarl of Lade sends word that a prize bit of property called 'the Nubian' has been stolen from him. Taken straight out of Lade Garde itself, on a night with double guards on all sections of the wall. A man was killed on the scene, but others were involved. There was a fire on the walls—" He corrected himself. "Two fires, I mean. With all the attention given to the fire, the loss of the Nubian was not discovered until much later. One ship is known to have left the port that night, and traders came and went by ship the next day as well. It is unknown at this time if the woman was smuggled out by ship or over land. The Jarl asks—"

The messenger paused. Hopefully, Rota would not have him whipped for the next part, because he was duty bound to say it. "The Jarl wishes to ask what knowledge, if any, you may have of the matter."

"The Jarl doubts me? Doubts *me?*" Rota all but shrieked. "How *dare—*" She caught herself just in time. Every syllable she uttered would be repeated back to Haakon Sigurdsson. "How dare anyone insinuate that I might be disloyal to the Jarl"

"Is that your return message to him?" The man's voice held a sly edge, but not enough that she could openly accuse him.

"Of course that's not my answer! I'll decide what it is, and I'll keep it short so that you get it right."

He caught the slur, ignored it.

"Did someone in the household betray him?" Rota asked. "Does he have any suspects at all?"

"The Jarl did not say."

Rota's brow furrowed and her mouth set in a thin line. Who would be stupid enough to risk Haakon's murderous temper?

"Was anything else taken? Valuables? Other slaves stolen? Anyone else hurt?"

"No, madam. Just the one woman was kidnapped. The only two people hurt in the incident were the man I mentioned earlier, a beggar who once worked for Haakon and who appears to have been part of the gang of thieves, and the Jarl's wife Tora. It appears that she fought with him. She was the one who killed the beggar, but he cut her in the process, and pretty badly."

Tora, injured? No! "Will she live?" Rota could barely ask the question.

The messenger's tone softened. "She is improving."

Rota felt shaken to her core. "Should I return home?"

The messenger could hardly believe his ears. Was Rota actually asking his advice? He started to reply but realized his error from her scathing glance.

"I will dictate my message to the Jarl now. Then I want you to return quickly to your ship and sail immediately."

She spoke the words that needed to reach Haakon. The messenger repeated them, three times. He bowed and left.

Rota pushed fear about Tora from her mind. Nothing she could do here, and the man had said Tora was recovering. Rota would go back to Trondheim after the summer, as they had planned.

But for how, she had other matters to attend to. This same day, she had also received a message from Naldrum.

She had kingmaking to plan.

. . .

Naldrum found himself in an exceptionally awkward position. He had been summoned out to the stones in front of his house at news that an important delivery had arrived, and half the household had followed to see what it was. Beside Naldrum stood his guest, the esteemed *bishop-of-who-cares-where-in-Germania*, practically a king among white-christ believers. With Friedrich, his constant companion, the younger priest Konradsson, wearing his stupid expression that wavered constantly between nervousness and disgust, and on his body, the same odd long tunic that Friedrich wore.

In front of them, wearing the same rough ship's clothing as the *vikingers* who had brought Friedrich and Konradsson to Iceland, stood a man who said his name was Tiller, claiming to be a ship-steerer Naldrum had hired at Althing, announcing delivery of a female passenger he had smuggled out of Lade Garde in Trondheim and demanding payment from Naldrum for delivering her to him.

And here stood that female passenger, the woman with skin the rich brown color of seal's fur who Naldrum had once surmised was Tor's wife—and she, too, wore the odd long tunic of the white-christ faith.

Kandace, Tiller had said her name was.

Kandace kept looking at the bishop and Konradsson, and they at her. They had said briefly spoken words to one another that Naldrum could not understand. After the words, silence, and they kept staring at one another.

Naldrum felt confused. Did she actually belong to them instead of Haakon? Naldrum could not ask the bishop, nor dared he ask Tiller. By Loki, what a confused mess.

"You *kidnapped* a sister who serves God?" First the bishop, his booming voice an indictment of Tiller.

"I did not use that word. I simply retrieved from Lade Garde, at *gothi* Naldrum's request and with great trouble and personal danger, this woman who belongs to him."

"Belongs to him? As a slave? That's preposterous! She's a nun!" Again, the bishop.

The woman spoke rapidly in Saxon. No one paid attention to her.

"You hired this fellow Tiller to wrest this woman from her home in Trondheim?" The bishop directed the question to Naldrum, but Tiller answered.

"It wasn't her home. She was in captivity in the house of Haakon Sigurdsson, Jarl of that area. Haakon had stolen her from *gothi* Naldrum, which is why Naldrum hired me to fetch her here."

Would Tiller not shut up? Naldrum tried a distraction. "Yes, Haakon's captive. I heard of it and sought to obtain her freedom, as I'm sure you would approve."

"For what purpose? This man said you claim to 'own' her, like a common slave. Such a thing is not possible!"

"Oh no, of course I don't own her. I knew you were coming and hoped to surprise you with her presence. Surely you are delighted! A white-christ woman, captured by pagans in Norway and now set free, so that she may be returned to—where does she live?" Naldrum fumed. What a mess.

"You plan to send her home to wherever her abbey is?" The bishop, slightly mollified.

What in Thor's name was an abbey? "Of course! What else would I want with her?"

Tiller spoke, frowning. "I'm confused. You most definitely said at Althing that she's your property, and you wanted her back here. If she's not, and she's to go somewhere else, why did you have me bring her all the way up Bull Valley? Who's taking her to this place called Abbey? Where is that, even? And most of all, I don't care about any of that. I just need to get paid and get back to my ship. I have other pressing matters to attend to."

"We'll talk in private later about your payment."

Tiller knew enough about Naldrum that he would be fooled into such a ploy. "We'll talk about it now, and in front of others! I just raced to Trondheim and back, risking my life and several of my crew to get her for you. You promised me a fortune to get her for you. Don't think you can get refuse to pay now!"

"I said we'd talk privately later!" Naldrum, red-faced, shouted at Tiller.

The bishop could no longer tolerate the ridiculous conversation taking place in front of him. He put his palms up to silence the others.

"I am the most senior representative here present of our Lord and Savior Jesus Christ. As such, I will accept custody of this woman. Whatever sums were promised, *vikinger*, you must discuss with headman Naldrum. Regardless of that outcome, she must be returned as soon as possible to the closest the abbey to here, and they will get her back to the one from where she was no doubt taken by this Haakon you speak of."

As Tiller and Naldrum began to shout in disagreement, Friedrich boomed, "My decision is final! We will give Sister Kandace a few days to rest and recover from what was undoubtedly a terrifying voyage, then we will ride down Bull Valley and seek a ship—perhaps yours, Tiller, if you are inclined to wait. Kandace will accompany us. Now, our first need: does anyone here speak her language, who will be able to help us learn where she came from?"

Naldrum stared, furious. *How dare the bishop claim rights to this woman?*

Tiller stared, furious also. *Now, for certain, Naldrum would refuse to pay. All these weeks, wasted.* He felt sick, and disgusted with himself as much as with Naldrum.

. . .

Kel had come around the corner from the storeroom construction and observed all of this. He immediately knew that Naldrum was trying to cheat the *vikinger* Tiller. Oh, to be able to confront Naldrum with the truth somehow!

An idea occurred to Kel. He spoke directly to the bishop.

"We have a slave who has dark-toned skin, just like this woman. I don't know if he comes from the same land that she does, or knows here language, but it's worth a try, perhaps."

Naldrum suddenly looked even more apoplectic, if such a thing was possible. The bishop, however, nodded his head vigorously.

"Of course! Of course! We should try every means at our disposal. Bring this fellow to the hall right now and let's have him try!"

. . .

Tor had been summoned to a far field, his great strength requested to assist in pulling a sledge filled with stones. Head down, straining with the horses hitched to the sledge, he did not see Kel until someone called to the steward.

Tor lifted his head and saw Kel sprinting across the fields.

Kel never runs was all Tor had time to think before the steward, out of breath, arrived.

Kel panting, beckoned to Tor "Come with me. I'll tell you as we go." Tor dropped the traces and left the sledge. As they jogged back to the longhouse, Kel explained.

"A *vikinger,* a man named Tiller, arrived today with a woman he brought from Trondheim. He claims that our headman hired him 'to fetch back a slave stolen from Naldrum.' Naldrum is denying it, but I'm pretty sure this fellow is telling the truth."

Tor's hand went to his chest. He fought to breathe.

Kel continued. "Naldrum doesn't deny he sent Tiller, but he claims it was to rescue this woman out of the kindness of his heart. I can tell you for a fact Naldrum's never laid eyes on her before, whoever she is. As far as rescuing her? Naldrum doesn't care about helping anyone but himself, not ever—so why would he go the expense and danger of rescuing a total stranger from Trondheim? From Haakon Sigurdsson, for the gods' sake?"

Tor could barely hear Kel for the blood rushing in his ears. He tried to keep his voice noncommittal. "What does the woman say?"

"That's the problem. None of us can understand a word she speaks. This Tiller fellow seems to know a smattering of her language, but not enough to sort things out. You've traveled more than any of us. Maybe you can make out how to talk to her. They're all waiting back at the longhouse. Do you think you can help?"

Tor imagined kneeling, touching his forehead to the ground. *Allah, thank you, thank you thank you,* but he had to keep pace with Kel.

"I can try. Whoever she is, if Naldrum's involved in any way, I'm sure he's up to no good. I'd help her for that reason alone."

"Good to know," Kel said. "Same here."

They hurried across the rough-cut stubble of the harvested fields. Tor longed to sprint, knowing he could easily outrun Kel, but forced himself to stay with the steward. As Kel pushed open the big carved door of the longhouse, Tor drew a deep breath to steady himself. He was certain he knew who the woman was—but a small part of him feared that if he saw another woman instead of Kandace, the disappointment might crush him.

. . .

Chapter Fourteen

But it was Kandace.

In what seemed almost a dream, she stood halfway down the longhouse room, proud and composed, the light of the longfire glowing amber against her skin.

It is really her. So many years. Tor wanted to run to her, pull her close, reassure himself that this was not just another hopeful dream. He gripped the doorframe, weak at the sight of her. *Oh, Kandace. Oh, my love.*

Kel looked back to see what was keeping him. Tor could not walk. He feigned a stumble.

"Tripped," Tor said. He knelt, pretended to be re-tying his boot. Caught his breath, tried to think.

"Ah, here is my slave man." Naldrum puffed and rubbed his hands. Ever since meeting the toothless sailor at Althing, Naldrum had imagined this instant. Tor would be shocked and dismayed. The woman would fall to her knees in tears at seeing Tor humiliated. Now, at last, Naldrum would have long-awaited victory over his belligerent giant of a slave.

He had often wondered about the woman. Was she Tor's daughter? His sister? His wife? Naldrum had pictured Tor, ashen-faced as Naldrum took the Nubian to bed, pulling the curtains of his private sleeping area closed. Tor's misery at seeing Naldrum dress the woman in fine silks one day and making her dig in the fields the next. A new idea came to him: he could beat the woman, and make Tor watch. On second thought, he realized that would stir up Ankya's oddness. Naldrum shook off the thought, repulsed.

"My *slave man,"* Naldrum repeated, his words louder as if the woman could understand what he was saying.

To his dismay, the Nubian regarded Tor with no sign of recognition. Nothing at all, when there should have been so much. Naldrum frowned.

Had he been able to hear Tor's thoughts, however, the headman would have been ecstatic with triumph. Tor had tied his very existence to the hope of one day finding Kandace. Seeing her alive and healthy made Tor vulnerable—and realizing Kandace was utterly indifferent to him did in an instant what years of fearful worry could not. He began to crumble inside.

Naldrum had no way of seeing this, however. His delighted anticipation of humiliating Tor switched to abrupt anger.

"You know this woman, don't you?" Naldrum shrieked. "You know her! Tell me that you know her!"

His tantrum, that of petulant child, steadied Tor as nothing else might have. He forced himself to match Kandace's expression, the polite but disinterested look in her eyes.

"Sorry to disappoint you, *gothi*," Tor said to Naldrum. "I've never seen this woman before in my life."

. . .

Friedrich, oblivious to what had just happened, spoke to Tor. "Steward Kel suggested that you might be able to understand my sister in Christ," he said. "Because you have traveled so widely. Perhaps she is even of your land, wherever that is."

Tor nodded. He stepped closer to Kandace. *How does she not know me?*

"They call me Tor here," he said gently in the language of their home. He had a fleeting hope that the sound of the words or his voice might change her expression, spark recognition, but nothing happened.

"Can you understand me? Do you understand what I am saying?" Tor kept his words low, quiet, kind. *Has she even forgotten our language?* Another sad thought occurred to him. Had she forgotten their two children as well?

Kandace seemed confused. She looked closely at Tor, but did not answer.

"I am a friend," Tor said. "You are in danger. Do not speak."

She did not move, but her eyes darted to Naldrum. *Danger,* this tall man had said. From whom? Kandace already felt she could trust Tiller. Two other men in the room had kind faces, and they were clearly monks. Another man, tall and strong, his face more closed than unkind, stood at some distance, and seemed no threat.

Danger from the man who had just screamed? As soon as she had arrived at this place with Tiller, Kandace had not liked the look of that man. He carried himself the same way Haakon had: pompous, entitled, selfish. If the person speaking to her said 'danger', he probably meant from that one.

Tor saw the flick of glance at Naldrum. She had understood something of his words, he felt certain.

"Yes. Danger, from him. Do not say anything to me. Know this: I am a friend. You can trust me. If you understand, blink your eyes twice."

Two rapid blinks, while she still scanned the room. *Good.*

"Do you recognize me? Blink twice again if you do."

She looked at him, quickly looked away. An almost-imperceptible shake of her head *no.*

Tor swallowed hard. *What happened to you, my love?*

"I need you to say something to me. Anything. Tell me how you fared on the voyage. Just speak and say something."

Kandace stumbled to use the same words as Tor had, the sounds so long-unused strange on her tongue. Slowly at first, and then with increasing speed, she spoke, making a reply of a few short sentences.

Tor turned to Naldrum. "This woman must have experienced some trauma. She seems to speak a similar language as mine, but many of her words are garbled and do not make sense."

But Kandace's words had made perfect sense. She explained that she had been captured and taken across the sea to a town where she was mostly kept in a small room, alone. That Tiller had come there one day and had smuggled her out. That he had told her he was taking her home, but he had brought her here instead. That she did not know where this place was, or why he brought her here, or who any of these people were.

. . .

Naldrum could hardly contain himself. "Are you *certain* you do not know each other?" he shrilled.

"I regret not. This seems to disappoint you, gothi. How very unfortunate." Tor's voice, dry with sarcasm. Inwardly, he prayed *Allah, forgive me, for this lie, and for the many more lies I intend to tell.*

Now Naldrum felt even more frustration. He had promised Tiller a fortune in silver so that he could torment his insolent slave, but apparently for nothing, seeing that neither Tor nor the woman had shown the slightest sign of recognition.

I could strip her of those robes fast enough and sell her to another chieftain, of course. But she belonged to the Jarl of Lade—Loki, what if the Jarl found out that Naldrum was involved with taking her? And now this fool Friedrich had claimed her. Did he own all the white-christs? Were they all his slaves? Was *that* why they had been bowing to him at Althing, and ever here?

Naldrum's head spun. What to do? Someone had made a mess of things. His expression grew more sullen. *By Hel! What do I do now?* Kel needed to fix this mess for him. But Kel had been so disrespectful lately, he'd probably humiliate Naldrum in front of the bishop.

Tor saw the temper tantrum approaching. For the first time ever, his tone to Naldrum bordered on being respectful.

"I think, *gothi,* that she does not fully understand what I am trying to say to her. Her words are similar to my native language, but different. She might be confused and overwhelmed with fatigue. Kel said this sailor Tiller took her in violence from somewhere far away, and brought her here?"

Naldrum appeared slightly calmer. Tor pressed on. "Whoever she is, this woman has only just arrived here after an arduous journey. Perhaps you might let her rest for a few days. I can try again each day to see if I can learn more. What do you wish me to ask of her?"

Naldrum had no option but to continue the lie he had told to the bishop. "You must find where she comes from. A place called 'Abbey,' the bishop says."

"I will do my best, headman." *He would ask Kandace whatever he wanted, not what Naldrum desired.*

Naldrum looked around the table. The bishop's face, frowning in concern. Konradsson, looking anxious as usual. The brown-skinned woman, glancing in confusion from Tor to the others, saying nothing now. Tiller, ready to fight for payment.

Only Ankya seemed nonplussed. She had moved close to the woman and now picked at her robes. Finally, the nun looked at Naldrum's daughter and cocked her head, as if to ask *what do you want?*

Ankya understood the gesture. "Does she drink the blood too?" she asked the bishop, never taking her eyes from the nun's face. "Eat the flesh and drink the blood? I want to ask her!"

The bishop groaned and crossed himself. This woman-child's inner evil frightened him. He suddenly longed to be far away from Naldrum's compound.

But Konradsson answered Ankya's question, his voice hard.

"She does. But it is a Flesh you do not understand, and Blood you do not deserve to taste. If you wish to learn, you must put aside your pagan ways and humble yourself. You must earn the right."

"You will teach me?" Ankya reached for his hand, eager.

Konradsson shook off her hand as if it were poison. "I will teach you to pray to our Lord. The rest is between Him and you."

Ankya clapped and laughed, the sound full of unnatural joy.

"Enough of this!" Naldrum cried. "Ankya, please, for once just *stop!*" His thoughts raced in confusion. With his goal of tormenting Tor disappearing, with this bishop-man here claiming the woman, Naldrum simply wanted the whole mess to have never happened. He rubbed his fists on his temples. Whose fault was all this?

Tiller brought her here. The thought brought instant relief. Such a simple matter, he realized. Tiller had brought the wrong woman.

Ankya, however, stared at her father in shock. He had never spoken sharply to her, not ever, but just now he had yelled at her as if she was a common slave, in front of her new favorite people.

Ankya's eyes reddened with sudden tears. "I'll do as I choose, you mean old troll," she whispered to herself. She traced her finger along the nun's shoulder, across the woman's chest and down her arm, and lingered her fingertips on the back of the woman's hand, drawing rune-magic on that fascinating skin, just like Tor's.

"We'll be like sisters," Ankya sighed. She pushed her father's mean words aside where she could fester on it later. "Sister Kandace, they called you, right? I'll be sister Ankya." She smiled, and Friedrich groaned again.

. . .

The two men's faces nearly touched, both nearly spitting in fury.

"How dare you refuse to pay me!" Tiller cried. "I did exactly as you asked. I went into Trondheim, as you directed, into the Jarl of

Lade's home, *as you directed,* and found a dark-skinned woman, the *only* one who matched that description, and got her out of there to bring to you. I'm not responsible if your information was wrong! You owe me and my crew the amount you promised!"

"I pay when and who I choose, and I owe you *nothing!* You can pout here all winter, and it won't change my mind!"

. . .

In the end, Naldrum won. Loyal landowners nearby received hurried summons to appear at his compound, armed, and soon arrived. Before long an ugly mob swarmed, demanding that Naldrum send out the 'traitorous cheat'.

Naldrum walked among them, the very model of peaceable forgiveness, begging them to show understanding to the very man he had fetched them to disparage. "I wouldn't want any of you to run him through," he said, winking. "I wouldn't want any of you to cut his throat!" More winking.

They knew just what he meant. The mob called out offers to defend Naldrum, but he laughed.

"We wouldn't want any harm to come to this sorry fellow, would we?" Naldrum asked. The crowd cheered *yes,* and he shook his head as if they were suggesting a game rather than mortal harm. "No, no, nothing like that." More laughter.

Finally, Tiller gave up. He mounted his horse and rode through the jeering crowd, fuming with bitter fury.

Naldrum watched him ride away. "What a terrible deal he turned out to be. We should do something," he said to Kel. "I can't have that man going around telling lies about me."

Kel had just seen what amounted to a robbery. *Tiller's an honest man. He doesn't deserve this.*

"I bet your friend Aldís would know what to do about this Kandace woman. She probably has a potion for addled brains."

Why must Naldrum always bring up Aldís?

To threaten without appearing to do so, Kel knew. Not as blatant as the threats Naldrum had made to Aldís at Althing, but they were threats nonetheless. *Stay here and serve me, or she gets hurt* was Naldrum's consistent message.

Aldís was out there, somewhere. For some reason, Naldrum hated Aldís *because* of Kel, though the gods only knew why. She didn't deserve to be crippled because of Naldrum's temper tantrums. Kel would say what he needed to keep her safe, even if it made him sick to do it.

He choked out some placating response. "Every man makes mistakes. Tiller may make a bigger one, sooner or later. If he's foolish enough to get himself outlawed on some matter or another, no one will pay attention to anything he says, you won't have to worry about him anymore."

"You're a loyal steward, Kel," Naldrum glowed. "I think he *will* be outlawed on some matter or other."

Kel felt no relief at turning Naldrum's thoughts from Aldís, but only despair. *I can't keep doing this for him,* he thought. Once it had felt fun, almost daring, to pull off such tricks for Naldrum.

Kel watched Tiller ride away and regretted the words that had come from his mouth. *Be careful, man,* he thought towards Tiller. *Watch every step. You've made a powerful enemy through no fault of your own.*

. . .

Tiller knew his crew waited on the knarr at the mouth of Bull River. With Kandace delivered safely, they would be celebrating, he was certain, expecting to hear that they would be wealthy this winter, able to buy meat and mead no matter now dear the price. What was he going to tell them now?

The temptation of so much silver took my good sense away. I should have known not to trust this headman. He cheats everyone. Why did I think I'd be different?

He realized now that Naldrum had manipulated him with all that promised of wealth, almost daring him to run a raid on the feared Jarl. *What an idiot I am,* he thought. *Naldrum played me for a fool.*

The grain-field harvest was in full swing all along the Bull River valley. Tiller rode past farm after farm where families and servants worked with scythes in the tall grass fields, the peaceful scenes totally at odds with his emotions. *A stupid, stupid fool.*

. . .

Chapter Fifteen

Friedrich had not believed Naldrum's flimsy protests about getting Kandace home. He wanted to take the nun with him and Konradsson when they left, but without Tor to translate for her, he realized what a burden he would impose on her. But he could not, as a man of faith, buy a slave from Naldrum, not even for a good cause, not even if Naldrum would consider selling Tor.

In the end, the bishop realized he had little choice, for the nun—according to Tor—said that she wanted to stay at Naldrum's compound.

"She wishes to pray for Ankya," Tor told the bishop. "The headman's daughter seems to be quite taken with Kandace. Your white-christ sister believes she can help Ankya." *By heaven, the lies he told every day now.* Tor pushed the thought far from his mind. *Surely Allah would forgive him, since he lied for a greater good?* "I will strive to learn more about her, to find out where she came from."

In truth, Friedrich felt relieved. Perhaps Kandace *could* help Naldrum's perplexing, unsavory daughter find salvation. For himself, Friedrich wished to be thoroughly away from Ankya.

Tor saw the bishop wavering. What was the man saying?

"And Kandace *still* has no memory of the abbey she lived in?"

Tor's answer to this was at least partially true. "I have asked her several times where she comes from. She simply becomes distressed," he said.

"Keep trying, good fellow," the bishop directed. He looked left and right, bent closer. "I do not wish to speak evil of any man, but I fear that this headman you serve is not—" he hesitated, "entirely trustworthy."

Tor nodded. "I give you my word that I will do my best to protect her in every possible way," he promised. "Even against Naldrum, if it comes to that."

"Thank you, Tor. I am in your debt for taking care of my sister in the Lord."

. . .

As Friedrich and Konradsson rode away, the young monk waited until they were out of earshot before he burst out. "You treat that man as if he were an equal to you—even though that slave is every bit as wicked a heathen as these pagans here!"

"Is it that he is a slave that offends you, or his beliefs in the prophet Allah?" Friedrich asked. "If because he is a slave, you know that means nothing in the eyes of the Lord! How many of our brothers and sisters have you seen enslaved here, without any hope of return? Have they stirred no pity in your heart? These poor people did not choose to be taken from their homes and families and sold here!"

Konradsson was shocked to realize that his view of slaves as inconsequential beasts came from his old days, long before the monastery in Germania, before he had ever left Iceland.

Contrite, he replied, "That was wrong of me. It is not that Tor is a slave. It is that he worships—"

"Differently that you and I?"

"Yes! How can you be so accepting of that? It is wrong!"

"Listen again to the words of our Savior, young Konradsson, who said 'treat others the way you wish to be treated.' Tor has been the very embodiment of those words. Should I think less of a man who acts as our Lord instructed?"

Konradsson felt confused. Was the bishop suggesting that Tor's beliefs were not wicked?

Friedrich could not say to the younger monk that he felt equally confused by the whole situation. Instead of admitting his predicament, he deepened it.

"We are guests in this land. We do not worship the idols they hold to be sacred. But we wish these people to be respectful to us. To be welcoming and friendly, and to listen to our preaching, yes?"

"Yes, of course," Konradsson said. His head drooped a little.

"Then that is how we must first act to them! Be welcoming, friendly and listen to them and their concerns," Friedrich replied. Happy light filled his face. "Now, where shall we go next? We could well travel from one valley to another and explore the entire land across a year. Let us stop at each farm and speak a few words of comfort to these people. I understand from our host Naldrum that harvests were poor last year and may be again this year. Since we will spend at least one winter here, it behooves us to help these unfortunates in wherever we can."

Germania felt very, *very* far away. Certainty about his mission wobbled. But for some reason, Friedrich felt a peace he could not explain, and longed for more of it. The sound of their horses' hooves on the track leading away from Naldrum's compound comforted him. Soon he was lost in thought and prayer.

. . .

Chapter Sixteen

"Why do you seem intent on keeping me here?" Kandace asked, her manner serene and proud as always, but determined. "And what are you working on today?"

Tor bent to inspect the glowing metal on the forge. "Shoes for the horses," he answered. "Do you remember ever hearing horseshoes clang on the stones along the harbor streets?" Tor slipped in small memories of their home city whenever possible. "These are not quite the same as the ones from our land. For instance, see this one has an iron spike, to help the horse hold its footing on winter ice. There is no ice, of course, where we once lived."

Kandace watched as Tor hammered the piece of metal, held it in the fire with tongs, heated it, hammered. Being around him felt comforting to her.

Tor hoped that Kandace had forgotten her first question, but she returned to it.

"I asked you something. Not about the horse-shoes, fascinating though they are." Her voice was dryly humorous. He knew her well enough that she would not be distracted again.

As he considered his response, Tor again wondered what had happened to her. He had tiptoed around the subject several times, but a curtain shielded Kandace from her past. She had told him she could remember being taken in by a group of women, who bathed her and fed her and treated her wounds. She could remember learning the women's language, could remember choosing to live with them, taking vows to do so.

Before that, nothing. No hint of what had happened to her, save that she had been injured. No idea of who had mistreated her, or of where she had been, or how she had gotten there. Nothing. Just an emptiness, a void. Not even any fear. Whatever had happened was gone, and along with it, all the years with Tor before the slavers had taken her from him, and gone from her memory the children they had had together, and life in their happy home.

Every day Tor had prayed for patience, and for Kandace to heal. But as the weeks passed, he had begun to see that wish as selfish. Now, with her calm determined expression and her question hanging in the air between them, he felt at an impasse. What would remembering do, but cause Kandace more pain? He could not go to the children, and neither could she. If she remembered that she was married to Tor, how long would she be able to conceal that from Naldrum—or even bear staying in his compound?

For now, Naldrum had left her alone, oddly intimidated by her relationship to Friedrich—but Tor knew it would not last forever.

He delayed his answer a trifle longer, and thought about escape. The river road to the sea was bordered by farms, at least half of which felt strong loyalty to Naldrum. Passage on a ship cost precious silver that Tor did not have. Getting their children from Eilíf and to a ship that could carry them all to a place of safety—a ship whose crew would never speak of the striking foreign passengers to Naldrum's allies—was such a feat even possible? What if Kandace recovered their children only to see them found, snatched away, and sold?

Daily, the journey away from the present to any kind of future seemed more and more impossible.

But she was here, and for now, safe. Their children were safe. Tor resolved to be satisfied with the smallest of things each day, and to have the least possible expectations or hope. At least he could manage to survive that way.

He told the truth to Kandace, but not all of it. "I want you to stay here because you are safer here than elsewhere in this land."

She was not to be easily deterred. "Why do you say that? And why do you care about my safety?"

A heartbeat, during which naked emotion shone in his eyes. Again, he chose a partial truth. "I feel connected to you. I cannot explain to you exactly why or how, but I do." *Cannot because I choose not to.*

She bit her lip, looked away. "I understand, I guess. I feel connected to you to. But you realize that real connection with a man, any man, goes against the vows I took with the Sisters?"

"Are those vows permanent? What if you wanted to change them?" He held his breath, waited.

Kandace looked surprised, as if such a thought had never occurred to her. "Why ever would I?"

An easy smile that told nothing of the painful longing in his heart. "If you ever do, I'd like to be the first to know."

She laughed, her eyes cast down at the compliment. "I promise."

The moment all but passed, but Tor needed to say one more truth.

"Kandace, when I say I can't explain how I feel connected to you, I need you to understand something. It is not that I cannot explain. It is that I feel it best not to say those words to you."

Her expression froze between the laugh and alarm. “And why is that?”

“Because you are not ready to hear it, beautiful kind Kandace. But I swear by all that I hold holy, I will tell you when you *are* ready.”

She had asked a question, and he had answered. Few words, but ones which carried profound weight. Tor had taken the first step on the road—no matter the consequences.

. . .

Tor had been called into the longhouse to work on an interior door. He used the chance to speak to Kel, after having made certain that Naldrum was in earshot.

“The woman Kandace,” Tor said, in a false loud whisper.

“What about her?”

“I think she wields strange magic,” said Tor.

“Such as?”

“She says words I do not recognize. Words that have no meaning. I heard her do it recently, when that silver trader came through. s here. She said strange words, and he gave her a ring. She wears it now.”

“Any man might give an attractive woman a ring.”

“But he had said just said that the ring was for display of his handiwork, and was not for sale at any price. Then she spoke the words, and he just handed it to her—and at no cost.” In truth, Tor had scraped together enough to buy the ring for Kandace at Althing, a hopeful gift.

“Really?!” Kel exclaimed. “That’s a power I’d like to have!”

"But it wasn't just that." Tor saw that Naldrum was actually leaning towards him from the high-seat, trying to hear better. "I've seen other things. She whispers things to the animals. And one of the slaves came to her crying, pregnant by Naldrum's son Drikke, the slave said. Kandace said words, and touched the woman's belly—and now her stomach has shrunk to nothing."

"Why are you telling me this? If she has powers, I'm not likely to confront her. She might curse me."

"I know. But you're the steward here, and I just think someone in charge should be aware of it. That kind of magic exists in my land. There are powerful sorceresses who practice it, and they are widely feared. The gods only know what terrors she might unleash on any of us who offend her."

Kel mused, imagining terrors he might like unleashed on Naldrum.

"Likewise," Tor continued, "There is benefit to be had. If she is pleased, she could bring great boons to this household." He noted with satisfaction that Naldrum now had openly put his hand to his ear to hear better.

"I leave it to your judgement if you want to tell the *gothi.* I am only a slave, and it is not my place. But you are his steward, so it would be wrong of me not to speak of it to you. I may have my differences with your headman, but I don't want to hold back such an important truth."

"I'll discuss it with him when he's in a mood to listen." Kel, needing to get to harvest counting, waved Tor back to work.

As the enslaved man hammered on the door hinge, apologizing to his Maker for yet another lie, Tor heard Naldrum call Kel over to his chair, speaking in an eager voice.

"What's that I just heard about magic?"

. . .

Chapter Seventeen

Tiller rode towards his friend Thorgest's longhouse through an unseasonably early snowstorm. Large soft flakes drifted down without wind. Soon serene whiteness blanketed everything in sight, and the only sound was the soft crunch of his horse's hooves in the snow.

Tiller welcomed the peace. Soon he would reach Thorgest's, where the well-stocked woodpile always stood dry and covered, where the longfire always crackled and where one could always smell the fragrance of something good, just about ready to eat. He hoped for dumplings cooked in rich chicken broth and spurred his horse, longing to be there already.

The image of Thorgest's cozy longhouse blurred into thoughts of the dwelling Tiller planned to build. That stupid trip for Naldrum had cost him precious time as well as money. *I might have had it under roof already, and even the turf walls well under way. If this winter is as cold as this early snow indicates, I may have to wait until spring to get started, and that will mess with sailing.*

Nothing he could do about, though. For now, it would just be good to have his pillars back in his own possession. He would work every day from now until the seas were navigable again in the spring, preparing the building. *Progress will be made, even if slow.* The thoughts cheered Tiller, and after the debacle with Naldrum, he badly needed cheering.

Matters with his crew had been ugly. Tiller had used nearly every bit of his saved silver to pay the wages the Naldrum had reneged on, and had promised additional payments he could not afford. Still, a way would be found. Naldrum's cheating was no fault of the crew, and Tiller would not see them suffer.

The pillars. Tiller lapsed into a pleasant reverie, imagining the carved high-seat stocks in a broad new longhouse, perhaps with a proper glass window like Naldrum had. *That pompous ass. He thinks his longhouse so fine. Compared to most here, it was, but how long since the headman had travelled outside his own island? Had he seen the great stone buildings of other lands that scraped the clouds? The size of Haakon Sigurdsson's huge dwelling, or the sprawling town of Trondheim? No. Naldrum was a petty, puny little lord of nothing, great only in his own mind, a swaggering land-lord respected only by those who had no idea of the glories in other parts of the world.*

Tiller brushed off the irritation, resolving to not think of Naldrum again for the winter. A new longhouse, a proper window, a doorway carved with dragons. Space for visitors to sleep, and for children.

Children! Where had that thought come from? He had never cared about children. Tiller realized that the thought was not really about them, but the woman who might bear them. But even for her, Tiller had no image, no face of love long lost. Life these past years had been all about struggling out of the mire, about changing his past, about fighting for his name to be respectable again. No time for women. But now, thinking of a home of his own, for the first time Tiller pictured a woman in his longhouse, hair loose from her braids, gleaming in the firelight. He remembered the kiss with Tora. Yes, a woman like that.

He kicked his horse. Thorgest, a warm welcome, a future longhouse and a lusty wife beckoned.

. . .

Thorgest, however, met Tiller outside in the cold.

"I heard you stabling your horse," he explained. "Weather's ungodly today."

"No, I enjoyed the ride through your valley. I see you have increased your herd of goats. Lots of good ewes, it looks like."

"Aye, we did. Sheep are doing well, too."

An awkward pause ensued. This was when Thorgest was supposed to slap Tiller on the back, make a joke about it being so long since Althing, ask what had taken him so long, why those damned pillars were still cluttering up his cowshed. Instead, Thorgest coughed nervously.

The silence lengthened. Finally, Tiller made small courtesies. "How are your wives and those boisterous sons?"

"Boys are fine. The two young ones are working over in Hawk Valley, building a stone lining for a hot-pot there. Havlide and our oldest both worked on a merchant knarr across the summer. Thought they'd be back to help with the sheep round-up. I expect we'll see them ride in any day to eat us out of house and home for the winter, bragging about how they're real *vikingers* now." Thorgest could not hide the pride in his voice.

Another long pause, the only sound the hissing of the snow through the still air.

"I expect you've come about your pillars," Thorgest began. Again, Tiller noticed the nervous tone. This was not the man he knew his friend to be.

"I have, Thorgest. I'm truly sorry it took me so long. Went on a wasted errand for damned *gothi* Naldrum."

But Thorgest cut him off. "Doesn't matter what the reason. It's been fourteen moons."

"Has it?" Tiller counted on his fingers. "You're right, it has."

Thorgest shifted, blew on his cold fingers. "Fourteen moons," he repeated. He looked everywhere but at Tiller.

"What are you saying?" An uncomfortable feeling in Tiller's gut.

"I'm saying that it's been fourteen months, and the law is twelve months plus one. I warned you, at Althing."

"You *warned* me? You just said it—we were joking—I told you I'd be right back after the job for Naldrum."

"One of us was joking."

The dismay spread from Tiller's belly to his chest. "You can't be serious."

"I am."

Now, finally, with the thing said, Thorgest met Tiller's eyes. The older man squinted in defensiveness, fearful that Tiller would push him too hard and he might give in to his young friend, give the pillars back. The knowledge that his second wife was watching through a slit in their longhouse door made Thorgest stiffen his back.

"My new wife wants them," Thorgest blurted in a rush. "Harvest bad last year, so we couldn't afford a proper wedding ceremony. She was already pregnant, too. She's making my first wife miserable, wanting everything to be even. I'm at my wit's end, Tiller. She wants the pillars for our longhouse."

"She's *not my problem!"* Tiller shouted. "Those pillars are mine. You *know* what they mean to me!"

Had Tiller pleaded, Thorgest, knew, he would have relented. The young man standing in front of him had befriended Thorgest's sons, had taught them how to sail. He had worked on Thorgest's farm, had supped at his table. Tiller, who had lost his own father too young, had for years been like another son to Thorgest.

Tiller apparently was thinking the same thing, but he did not plead. He had turned pale with fury.

"You've been like a father to me! You could have *been* my father! You know how mine let me down, and how I learned to trust you, came to think of you as more than a foster-father. How could you betray me like that? *Those...pillars...belong...to...me!"*

Thorgest closed his eyes, knowing that he was closing the door forever on a relationship that mattered to both of them.

"I'm sorry, Tiller. Nothing I can do about it. I have to live under my roof, and I need peace. I've had none since this marriage. I'll make it up to you in the spring, help you find new ones. But the law is the law—and nobody in this valley would side against me about it. Twelve months and another moon you left them here—and another moon after that even, with no compensation. They belong to me now."

"You want compensation? Have my silver! Here it is!" Tiller pulled a pouch of silvers from his belt, all that he had left after paying his crew. "Have the last of it! Those pillars are all that matter to me in my life now. Can you replace the carvings on them, the runes and images carved by my grandparents and uncles and aunts, and great grandparents? Can you give my family back? You can't replace that! Silver is nothing to me next to them!"

"No, I can't replace the carvings." Thorgest felt a deep sadness. "But that's what she likes about them." White breath billowed from his mouth as he breathed heavy and deep. "So that's it. I'm going inside now." His blue eyes dropped the shielded look, and for once he spoke to Tiller as a friend. "I would like nothing more than to invite you inside. But I can't imagine how that would work, given the circumstances. Do you need food to take with you?"

"I need nothing from you. Not now, and not ever again." Tiller aimed his voice at the door, still barely open. "Congratulations, you greedy wretch! With a heart like that, you'll never find happiness, no matter how many gifts Thorgest gives you."

He slammed his palm against the stable wall, and for an instant, bent his head against the freezing stones of the door frame.

"Tiller," Thorgest started, but Tiller shot him a look of pure hatred, and Thorgest closed his mouth.

. . .

The snow fell faster as Tiller rode away from Thorgest's settlement. The old farmer watched until he could no longer distinguish Tiller and his horse from the whitening air.

"Farewell, son," Thorgest whispered to the valley. He turned to go inside. His new young wife would crow and brag on about her victory and her new possessions. Despite her round breasts and bottom, Thorgest longed to ride away, to be on horseback beside Tiller, riding, with no angry words between them, with *nothing* between them but the jingle of horse bells and the pleasant falling snow.

. . .

Chapter Eighteen

Tiller slept that night at another farm, as far up the valley from Thorgest as he could ride. He did not know the farmer, but the law of hospitality demanded that visitors be given shelter and a meal. The farmer's daughter, a young woman with a remarkably pretty face, had welcomed him as she opened the door. "The pottage is still warm. Bring in a load of dry wood when you come back from the stable."

To Tiller's surprise, he saw a man he knew working in the barn, mucking the horse pens.

"What are you doing here?" each man said in surprised unison. They both laughed.

"You first," Styr said to Tiller.

"I'm on my way back from being betrayed by Thorgest. You?"

"I live here now."

"But I just saw you at Althing! What happened?"

"Same problem as everybody. Too much rain, too many hayfields got muddy and trodden-down and hay couldn't be made. We were going to have to slaughter over half our animals because not enough feed to make it through the winter. Fewer animals meant not enough milk, not enough *skyr,* not enough whey to sour the cabbages, not enough cheeses, not enough butter to sustain us through the winter. My father is getting too old to work at heavy chores. While we were at Althing, we made the decision. Sell the land, hire me out as a bondsman. The fellow who bought our place is a decent man. His family had outgrown his farm. He gave ours to his daughter and son-in-law and their four children. In exchange for our land and our stock, my parents can stay, doing whatever work they can. He'll keep them safe and warm and fed in their old years. And I work here now. Thought I'd be a prosperous farmer there myself one day, with a strong wife of my own and our gaggle of kids to help, but not anymore."

For the second time that day, a friend did not meet Tiller's eyes, but this time out of pure sadness. "But the folks here are nice," Styr forced a smile. "And that pretty daughter brightens the days. One day I'll get a fresh start."

. . .

They supped together after Tiller had helped Styr finish the stable and feed the animals.

"Meet Fatimah," Styr said, as the attractive young woman refilled their *sup* bowls. "Fatimah the lovely."

The young woman blushed, then glanced at her mother, her face tense. *No, she hadn't heard. Thank goodness. They wouldn't have to hear her usual rant over Fatimah's name.*

A slight shake of her head at Styr, a secretive smile. Tiller grinned to himself as well. That girl was clearly sweet on his friend. Not a bad situation, if you had to be a bondsman.

Fatimah's father glanced over from where he stitched a pair of boots. "Fatimah," he said. "Attend to your work." The little smile on Fatimah's face vanished, and she scurried away.

. . .

Fatimah. 'The beautiful one', it meant, a ridiculous name her father had chosen over her mother's shouted objections. Fatimah paid for his stubbornness each time her mother introduced her, saying *and here is our oldest daughter, Fatimah* but her mother would not stop there, no. The old bitterness forced her to add, her voice dripping sarcasm, *my husband chose that absurd name, probably a remembrance of some whore in Persia or Kiev from his viking days. And you see Fatimah has a clubbed foot, poor thing, but her father named her 'the beautiful one' anyway. How silly of him.*

Why did her mother need to say that every time? As if people couldn't already see the way she walked.

Styr did not seem to care about her foot, but only her face. He had shaken Fatimah's father's hand at Althing, trying not to look too proud for his new circumstances, trying not to look defeated. He had started work for her father right away at Althing, with the bearing of someone who had known prosperity and now wore servitude like a tunic that was cut awkwardly. But as soon as he saw Fatimah milking her family's goats, he had smiled and shrugged off the awkwardness. Her younger sisters had giggled and whispered *our handsome new bondsman fancies you, Fatimah!* She had felt ashamed of her daydreaming about the strong-shouldered and hard-working man. When they had returned from Althing, one day she could stand it no longer and had hobbled all the way across a field he was plowing, *let him see, damn it, I won't even try to hide it,* and straight out asked Styr if he was blind, had he not noticed that she had a club foot, was he just making fun of her? He had laughed and said *that little thing? It's nothing! But that face of yours—Fatimah, you truly are so beautiful. Why would I care about a silly limp?*

She had looked at Styr, furious, not daring to believe. Had her mother put Styr up to mocking her? But he was sincere. Styr had gone on talking, not noticing her astonishment, relieved to be saying the words to her at last, now that she had given him an opening.

"My mother had a silvered looking-glass. We sold it when we lost our farm. I wish I had it now. You should get to see your own face, Fatimah. The next time a rich-ware trader comes past, I am going to offer him something, I don't know what. I don't have the means to buy you a silvered-glass, too expensive. But maybe I could buy you a look, a peep, just for little while. You deserve to see what your name means. You *are* lovely, and clever, too, and sweet. Everybody has a flaw. At least you know where yours is. They're harder to see when the bad is on the inside."

The feelings had flooded Styr the instant he saw Fatimah, and the words poured out of him.

Fatimah had goggled at Styr like an idiot, feeling stupid. No one ever spoke to her that way, with such an astonishingly earnest tone and his eyes shining and those ridiculously flattering words coming out of his mouth. She had put her hand over her own mouth, shy, but Styr took it away and at last, she knew what a kiss felt like.

Styr with the strong hands that looked elegant even when dirty. Styr with the dry wit who could make her serious father laugh until tears rolled down his cheeks. Styr, who could do anything, fix anything, figure out any problem. Fatimah thrilled at what passed between them when her eyes met his, at the sweet melting inside when they held hands beneath the table at meals.

Fatimah, knowing she was falling in love, had even gone to the sooth-sayer at Althing, wondering what might be possible. The woman had said the strangest thing.

Silver will ring, silver will sing, silver will offer a way before Spring.

But the woman had cautioned her as well. Something was connected with the silver, something the sooth-sayer could not see. Something deadly, she said.

. . .

The snow that day had turned to ice overnight. When Fatimah's father asked for help clearing a path to their sheep-pens, Tiller eagerly agreed. He needed heavy work to clear the fury filling him.

A day turned into another, and another. With nowhere to go and no longhouse to build, Tiller stayed on, first to finish a wall for Fatimah's father, and then to help thatch the roof with fresh hay. Fatimah's father accepted the help gladly. *He's a good worker,* he said to his wife, who snorted.

Time each day working with Styr helped. People stopping at the farm, coming and going, helped. Seeing the new sheep-pen wall rise little by little, strong and sturdy, helped. The hurt Thorgest had caused eased, but only a bit.

. . .

Dusk approached. Tiller came into the stable, and Fatimah noticed that his normally-taciturn face shone with almost boyish excitement.

Styr and her father worked together, rubbing fat into the strap-leathers for the plow. Styr tossed one to Tiller.

"Here, give us a hand. It's almost time for supper and we want to finish." The three men chatted through the task. Fatimah felt happy, listening. *Styr must have been like this before he became a bondsman, just easy-going and relaxed. How had he never married?* His kind face daily grew more attractive to her. As Fatimah scattered grain for the hens and geese, the sound of their voices rising and falling made a pleasant music.

She had just turned to milking the cows when someone called her father back to the longhouse. Fatimah set the bucket below the cow and sat on the milking stool and reached for the cow's pink udders.

As her father's footsteps faded, Tiller pulled Styr into the cow byre, and Fatimah had heard sudden urgency in his voice. Unseen, she kept her head down and listened intently, hardly daring to breathe.

The words came in fragments. "Thorgest will be away for a midwinter festival…a wedding, I think…we'll have a *Jul* adventure…raid his longhouse…after all, the pillars belong to me…and then there's *this*…"

The sound of *this* came clearly, something metal dropping from Tiller's palm onto the low stone wall of the cow byre. Fatimah knew the clear chime of coins striking against one another.

They bounced as they fell, chinkling against one another, spinning, twirling, an eternity of possibility sounding between stone and silver. A final whirring and the gleaming circles settled flat against the lichen-covered rock. Then silence, as Styr stared at the coins and Tiller spoke.

"Four of them for you, if you come and help."

Fatimah stayed motionless. *Tiller was offering to pay Styr four silvers? For what?*

In that moment, she heard the sounds as sudden loveliness, the sweet promise of freedom. Fatimah held her breath. *What was Tiller proposing for such a staggering sum?*

Styr whistled long and low. "Four silvers? Four *apiece?* For each of us that goes with you?" He looked at the coins, hungry for them to be his. Each one of them meant a quartet of sheep. Four silvers. Son of Odin, three of them would buy eleven ewes and a ram. With luck, that would mean twenty-two sheep in his flock by spring, with wool to spin and sell and wear. And the fourth coin, a cow, for milk and skyr and cheese, or a goat? He hesitated, spending them in his mind, testing the idea before he agreed to the work.

Fatimah's hands froze absolutely still on the cow's teats. She tried to hold her breath, but small warm clouds floated from her mouth in the cold air. She listened, leaning forward, her whole being reaching towards Styr's *hmmm...hmmm...hmmm* as he thought.

Her parent's farm, even with good land and good herds, had had to cut back after the poor harvest last autumn. She could almost hear Styr thinking a path forward, not just for himself, but their whole farmstead. The spring had been badly wet again, and another lean harvest might tumble them from a prosperous freehold to the edge of hunger. Her father's shoulders hunched every day at the wet weather. Her mother said nothing, but the lines around her mouth deepened.

“You’re absolutely certain Thorgest will be away? His entire household?”

“Maybe a few shepherds would be about, keeping an eye on Thorgest’s animals, but they would offer no challenge,” Tiller said, and added, “This may be my only chance.”

Hmmm…hmmm…hmmm…

Tiller added, “It’s not as if we’d be doing something wrong. They’re *my* pillars. I’m just taking them back. I could be an ass and leave a gap in his longhouse, but that’s not my way. I’m not looking for revenge, just to get back what’s rightfully mine. We’ll bring a pair of pillars to replace the ones we take from him. If he files a protest at the regional spring Thing, as long as I’ve replaced them, I doubt he’d get a unanimous verdict against me. Everyone’s heard about his new wife and how she’s running the whole house. She’s not making any friends in the valley. His first wife has family here. As long as I do right by Thorgest, they should see it as a case of restoring her honor without hurting Thorgest. The whole nonsense will be dismissed.”

Tiller did not let his friend see the fierce desire he felt, how much he needed Styr to say yes. As he waited, letting Styr mull over the decision, Tiller heard once again the true regret in Thorgest’s words. *I think even Thorgest would be secretly laughing at his wife. I’m doing this as much for him as anybody.*

Even so, anger burned deep within Tiller, feeding on shame, feeding on betrayal. No need to speak of that to Styr.

. . .

“Four silvers. Who else are you asking to go?” Styr asked.

Fatimah inhaled quickly. Styr was going to say yes. If he was not inclined, he would have offered objections for Tiller to overcome. *Look how well I know him already. I am meant to be with this man.*

The cow lowed impatiently and kicked at the bucket, wanting the milking to start. Fatimah hesitated a few more moments, listening again to the magic sound of the silvers as Styr played them through his fingers, hesitating just a bit longer before he gave Tiller an answer. She yearned to touch the coins, to see the small, gleaming vision of hope cradled in Styr's palm. Those bits of metal might mean the only thing that mattered to both of them: the chance of a future together.

Four silvers. Oh, goddess Freya, four! But would Styr be safe?

Styr had picked up one of the coins and put it to his teeth. "You've bitten it, to verify?"

Tiller looked at him without answering, but his expression said *how long have you known me? You think me a novice?*

Styr had laughed easily. "Just checking. You know me. Always careful."

Fatimah's breath had caught at the deep throaty sound. She loved Styr so much. She touched her fingertips to her lips, and trembled, remembering the kiss, and blushed, and the cow complained again.

And then she remembered. *Silver will ring. Silver will sing. Silver will offer a way before Spring.*

Fatimah had assumed the *saith* had meant a wedding-ring of some kind, not coins. The danger the sooth-sayer had spoken of…. oh, Freya, what exactly was Tiller planning?

. . .

Chapter Nineteen

Kel surveyed the obscenity of Naldrum's newly-finished storehouse. Casks sunken into the ground brimmed with soured cabbages. Above them rose shelf after shelf of aging *gammelost* cheeses. The roof hung with all manner of smoked meats: sausages, hocks, flanks of pig, lamb, beef, horseflesh and fish. Baskets along the wall brimmed with root crops of carrots, turnips, and parsnips, and rough nettle-cloth sacks of grains lay slumped in stacked piles against another wall.

What Kel considered the worst of all was the butter. *Barrels of it.*

How many daily milkings had contributed to this vast store of Naldrum's? Year after year, season after season, day after day, morning and evening milk had streamed into wooden pails, and set to wait until rich cream rose to the top, to be spooned off and churned. How many thrusts of a milk-maid's arm with the churn until the mystery happened, when creamy white abruptly turned to golden butter, to acquire such a hoard of the magical stuff?

Butter. Third only to gold and silver as trade value in this land, it sustained humans through the dark cold of winter. Not just a food, but a balm. The taste of it somehow imparted a sense of well-being, of goodness.

Every farm made butter, every day, and used it every day. When they could, they put a tiny leftover portion each day into the farm's butter-tub, especially in spring when the milk came richest with cream. In good years, by harvest time, the tub brimmed with enough to last through the lean-cream months until spring. In very good years, they had a little extra to trade, or to splurge for holiday meals.

But Naldrum did not have one butter-tub. He had dozens of them, more than his entire household could eat in years. Who needed that much wealth?

. . .

Ankya lurked behind Kel. Her boot gritted a small stone against the new storeroom floor, and he turned.

"Look what superb work you did, creating this!" she applauded Kel. "My father must be so pleased with you."

Normally, Kel would have given some noncommittal response. Today, though, disgusted between a combination of Naldrum's greediness and miserly cheating *—he could have paid that vikinger Tiller ten times what he was owed!* —Kel spoke scathing words.

"Your father has bought up all he can of other farmer's wares. He intends to profit from them this winter, when food is scarce and they will sell their children because they're too poor to feed them. Look at all this! Look at this mountain of butter! It's revolting!"

Ankya, startled, pulled her hand from caressing Kel's shoulder. "You do not think my father is a good businessman?" she asked.

"I think your father is a cheat and a crook. He would willingly watch people starve—people who *trust* him, Ankya! —just so he could make a bigger profit. I can't understand how someone can live that way."

Ankya had never heard anyone disparage her father in such a way. She knew that Kel had spoken dangerous words, traitorous words. She quivered, knowing the power that gave her over him.

But Kel had trusted her, too. Kel, this man her father said was so unworthy.

Inspiration struck. She would learn what would make Kel happy.

"What would you have my father do with all this extra food?" Ankya asked, her voice innocent.

"He could show that he wants to help the valley farmers instead of profiting off them. Really help them. He could start by giving each of them some of this butter and cheese to help those who have had to kill their cattle this year and who will have too little milk and cream over the winter. Show them that he understands their plight, and will help them until spring comes and their herds build again. They will be more than willing to pay him back when they are able!"

. . .

Ankya waited until Naldrum had eaten his fill. She saw him stretch in satisfied contentment and lean back in his high-seat.

She stood behind her father and stroked his shoulders in a way he liked. "Your new storehouse is a thing of beauty," Ankya said.

"Mmmm," Naldrum grunted.

"So much food. So *much.*"

"Mmmm."

"I heard that *gothi* in other valleys who have much food are doing something new this year." Ankya timed her words to the motion of her fingers. "Something unusual."

"Mmmm. What is that, my pet?"

She had rehearsed her words carefully. "They give something to get something."

"Mmmm. I like the sound of that."

"Many people say you should do it as well. That if you are the first to implement this, they will see you as even a greater leader. The greatest leader!" She waited for her father to take the bait.

Naldrum, relieved that for once Ankya was talking of business and not her fascination with blood, encouraged her. "Tell me more, daughter."

"To help people with food in this winter. Perhaps the farmers were lazy, yes, or didn't work their slaves hard enough, but still, they will suffer with hunger. Other chieftains spoke of how distressing that would be for their people."

Naldrum stiffened. Before he could protest, she added, "And if you help them, they should have to swear complete loyalty to you."

Ankya knew that Naldrum never, ever gave something without getting far more in return. She had weighed Kel's angry suggestion at length, knowing that her father would never accept it unless it profited him somehow.

Kel would still be happy. She would have done him a favor, so he would also be in her debt—and her father would be pleased with the deal as well.

She knew that Naldrum would make a decision quickly, and once made, she would have no chance of changing his mind.

"I was thinking, perhaps we, too, could give people a bit of extra butter this year," Ankya offered. "Since other chieftains are considering it for their clans. And do it first, so that you will be seen as the leader and not the follower."

Naldrum considered. "How much do I have?"

"Kel says there is more than we all could eat in years. You are so rich, father!" She kneaded his neck.

"I am rich." He smiled with his eyes closed. "But what do the problems of these farmers who have planned badly matter to me?"

"Because hunger and fear will make them stretch out their hand to you in fealty—even the ones who are always causing you trouble. You cannot lose!"

Naldrum sat up and opened his eyes. He twisted around to face Ankya.

"My daughter, you are a true child of mine. I'll speak to Kel tomorrow. We'll ride to the valley farms and make a little show for them of how they can count on me. I'll go myself, to make sure they swear."

Ankya had more plans to go along with this, but she had accomplished the most important part. Across the next couple of days, she intended for her father to three more things.

Kel would go with him.

Kandace would go with him, because Kandace was body-and-blood, and she wanted Naldrum to show off her favorite new amusement.

And Ankya herself would go with them. Not to gloat over having Kandace. Not to ogle Kel, although she certainly would. No, Ankya had a bigger goal altogether.

Someone in the valley farms would know where that woman Aldís was working—and Ankya intended to find out.

. . .

Butter beckoned. Word spread quickly through the river valley that Naldrum intended to open his vast store of it to anyone who pledged fealty to him. About a third of the farms in his quarter had done so at Althing, but many had instead pledged to other headmen in the area. But at the promise of such largess, and in the face of a winter of hunger, they reconsidered. All along Bull Valley and the trackways that branched from it, freeholders considered the growing power Naldrum wielded and pondered the best course of action, whether to reject Naldrum on principle, or join with him whether they despised him personally or not.

But kissing Naldrum's sword carried fearful implications. Those who longed for security at any cost eagerly planned their trip, but those who valued freedom struggled. They feared Naldrum's growing power, and tried to explain their concerns to old friends.

But the words fell on ears unwilling to listen. Farmers who had for years shared butchering days and had traded tools began to see their friends as 'the other', and frost began to grow.

. . .

Chapter Twenty

"I want to know, and I want to know today,", Kandace announced, her hands on her hips. "When will I be sent back to my abbey? Your Naldrum has kept me here for weeks now. While I appreciate learning much about your country, it is long overdue time to go home. I long to see the Sisters again, to be back at holy orders."

Tor felt defeated. Kandace had prodded him nearly every week, but until now he had avoided answering. Although his wife's memory seemed to be gone, her personality had not changed. Tor recognized the tone of voice that meant she absolutely would not be denied this time. As if to emphasize that, Kandace blocked his way.

But what could he say? Anything to keep her here, to buy another day, another week. Who knew when the wall of memory might suddenly dissolve, when she would recognize him, ask about their children? He could not afford to let her go even if she wanted to, but he was running out of excuses.

Naldrum, too, had begun pressuring Tor about Kandace's recovery. Tor saw though the chieftain's intentions. Naldrum intended to sell Kandace to a slaver as soon as Tor said she was fully healthy in her mind again, if not before that.

"You have seen that we have fewer and fewer visitors, Kandace. Everyone in the land—*everyone*, I promise you—is preoccupied with the harvest. No ships leave at this time of year. I know, because I arrived here this time last year, on perhaps the last ship of the season."

A cloud passed across Kandace' elegant features. "You came here only last year?"

Tor held his breath. "Yes."

The smallest line between her brows, as she stared at him. "I am sorry. I stupidly assumed that you have been here for your whole life, like so many of the other enslaved people. I've been so concerned with myself that I have not thought of others. You are a stranger to this land as well? Where did you live before this?"

Be careful, be careful, Tor cautioned himself. "A place far, far away. A land where the sun always shone, bright and warm, where it never became pale and weak and moved south as it is doing here. A place where the breezes cooled hot days, and nights smelled sweet with flowers."

She smiled, momentarily distracted. "It sounds lovely. Even at the abbey, I shiver most of the year. Tell me more about your home. I'd love to live in such a place."

You once did, my love. Tor fought to keep his voice steady. As he talked, Kandace leaned forward eagerly at his descriptions. But when he mentioned orange trees, her face suddenly went blank, and her eyes wandered.

Abruptly, Kandace stood, smoothing her robes. "Forgive me. I am interrupting you. I came here to be measured for a saddle. You remember that you translated your chieftain's invitation yesterday to accompany him on a short trip, yes?" Again, the small line between her brows. "For some reason I cannot remember what we were talking about. Perhaps we can continue the conversation later."

"As you wish," Tor replied. "There are saddles I can easily adjust to fit you. Wait here. I'll fetch one of the quieter horses, and we can see how long your stirrups need to hang."

He headed out over the pasture. She had never asked anything about him before. Something about the oranges had disturbed her. But she liked the idea of life in a warm land.

Patience, Tor reminded himself yet again. Breaking down the wall in her mind might open Kandace to all sorts of pain. He had to be careful.

Tor did not admit to himself that he had just omitted telling his wife an important truth. Soon the last ships would sail away from Iceland or settle for the winter here, and stay put against winter gales, until equal-night-and-day in spring signaled safer seas.

Naldrum won't let her go anyway, Tor consoled himself. But he had once again all but lied to Kandace.

Such a confusing puzzle, doing wrong things while trying to do good. Where lay the compass, to keep him from succumbing one day to true evil?

The good I seek to do must never enrich me in any way. But even that thought felt suspect. Wasn't protecting Kandace also for his own benefit? More and more, he felt himself adrift and questioning, a man who desperately needed safe mooring when none could be found.

. . .

Chapter Twenty-One

Lingering over supper, Naldrum watched his daughter Ankya working embroidery. The firelight cast a soft glow on her smooth straight braids. *Lovely.*

He tipped his *sup* bowl, ran his finger through the last of the broth, and shouted to Kel, who sat as far as possible at the other end of the long table.

"Kel, I plan to leave tomorrow morning for a short tour of the valley. Just a friendly visit to some of the farms. You'll come with me."

Kel stopped mid-chew. "Me? You usually take your son Drikke for visits. Don't you want me here to oversee the last of the harvest?"

Naldrum's eyes narrowed. "Why must you always feel the right to question me, Steward? Drikke will be going with me. So will you."

Kel took the wiser course and did not answer. "I'll have the horses ready. Will the any of your wives be going with you?"

"No. I plan to take the Nubian. People in the valley are curious, so I will show her off to them. They'll enjoy it."

They'll enjoy it, or you'll enjoy flaunting her? Kel just nodded his head.

Naldrum continued, counting off on his fingers each instruction for Kel. "Tor must come also, to translate, plus I'll want a couple of slaves, a couple of guards. Have two packhorses loaded with large butter casks. We'll be offered guest lodging each night, so no tents needed. Have everything ready after the morning meal."

Ankya paused her stitching, her fingertips white where she gripped her needle. "And me? Did you forget?" She had suggested the idea to her father. He damned certain had better not intend to leave her behind!

Naldrum smiled as if he were indulging Ankya, but did not answer. What good would it do to have her there? None. And what damage, if she started prattling on about sacrifices or blood or any of the nonsense she spouted? Possibly quite a bit. He did not want to be embarrassed by his daughter looking a fool.

Naldrum's false smile did not deceive his observant daughter. Ankya removed the needle from her embroidery and placed the tip against her wrist. Slowly, slowly, with Naldrum watching, she drew the sharp iron tip across her vein. Drops of blood showed from the scratch.

Naldrum's face whitened. "What are you doing, Ankya?"

"Proving my willingness to be your protégé, Father," she said, her voice clear and strong. "I am as wise in business as any man. If you are to be our land's Lawspeaker, you will need trusted advisors around you. This offers an opportunity for you to introduce me as such to your loyal clans. Instead, leaving me home, feeling distraught, unwanted and unappreciated? How unfortunate that might be."

Shaken, Naldrum had no answer. Ankya *had* suggested the clever idea of giving butter in exchange for allegiance, that much was true. But was his daughter *threatening* him? Naldrum could not believe such a thing possible, but he dared not test her. Ever since Friedrich and Konradsson had come, she had behaved more and more erratically. *Those revolting white-christs*, Naldrum thought. *Her stupid fascination with their faith has made my daughter stranger than ever. All of this is their fault.*

"Certainly you will come!" he forced a hearty tone for Ankya. "Everyone must see that you, of all my children, sit at my right hand!"

Ankya fluttered her eyelashes at her father. "I'm thrilled to accompany you and learn from you." She walked to his high-seat, leaned over, and placed a demure kiss on his cheek. As she returned to her seat, sucking the drops of blood from her wrist, Ankya picked up her embroidery again and flashed a look of triumph towards Kel.

Kel pretended not to see. He dipped his spoon into his *sup* bowl again and stirred it without eating. Naldrum loathed staying in the homes of others. A tour of the valleys with a quantity of butter? And Kandace on display? Naldrum's plans almost certainly had nothing to do with goodwill.

Naldrum still held all the power. But little by little, Kel's intention of destroying his chieftain had hardened. One day he would find a way.

. . .

"Make certain the Nubian wears that thing she calls a cross around her neck for this journey," Naldrum instructed Tor. "I want it visible at all times."

Tor wondered at the reason, but Naldrum offered no explanation.

. . .

Chapter Twenty-Two

The farmer and his wife argued behind their longhouse in irritated whispers.

"Must I prepare the smoked loins for Naldrum?" she hissed in an irritated whisper. "Because he always expects the finest! I told you not to pledge to him at Althing. He's just a greedy man, all promises and no real action. But you listened to your brother. Now our harvest dinner will be ruined because his group will gobble all the best meats I was saving!"

"Does he know we even have those loins tucked away for the harvest meal? No! Stop fretting. Make what you would for any traveler who stopped in for shelter, on any ordinary night." Already the man rued listening to his brother's advice. Naldrum rich and powerful in the heady atmosphere of the Althing was one thing. Naldrum up close, shamelessly eyeing every woman in the house was quite another.

His wife fretted still. "I'll not do less than we are able. The honor of this house!"

He grabbed her apron, pulled her close, kissed her ear and whispered. "Stop worrying. The *gothi* said he's traveling the entire valley. By the time he gets home, he won't remember a bit about which house served which meal. You love planning your harvest table. I won't let Naldrum ruin your pleasure just because he barged in here today."

She leaned her head against his chest. For a brief pause they held one another.

"Wipe your eyes, and go on in," her husband said. "Flatter him and make a fuss over him. He likes that. Insist that he sleeps in our bed-space. Do all the showy things that mean nothing, and feed him goat or chicken meat." He ran his hand along her thigh. "The loins here are too good for him anyway."

She laughed and slapped his hand away. "I love you," she said, and reached for the knife. Chicken for supper it would be.

. . .

"Tor, go to our horses and bring in the cask for me. Kel, go and help him."

As the two men left the hall, Naldrum leaned forward to the others around the table, conspiratorial. He gestured to Kandace, who sat next to him. He tapped her carved wooden cross with his fingertips, lifted it so that it caught the light of the longfire.

"This, my friends," Naldrum paused for emphasis, "This is the sign of a powerful god of the Saxon lands. You may have seen others in our own land wearing them." He sighed, heavily, as if in distress. "More every year, it seems. Did you know that those who wear them secretly preach that our gods are not good enough for them? That they mock our beliefs, saying that their god is the only god? Have you ever heard such disrespect?" He laughed, derisive.

An uneasy laugh echoed around the table. While the rules of hospitality decreed that they must extend a gracious welcome to Naldrum's dark-skinned guest in her odd garments, they also needed to honor *gothi* Naldrum's farfetched claim.

Now even derisive humor left his face. "I welcomed this woman, fleeing danger, into my household as I would any guest. Others like her travel among us, also welcomed as any strangers would be, unchallenged and accepted—but what has happened since they started intruding in our land?" Naldrum pitched his voice even lower. "What has happened to our weather? To our crops?"

He waited for the thoughts to connect. He had revised this little speech at each farmstead, perfecting it so that those around each successive night would reach the desired conclusion. Most remained silent, unsure of what Naldrum intended, and afraid of disappointing him with the wrong answer.

Naldrum led them. "Has it seemed to you that each year your crops have worsened? That the forests which once covered our entire mountains dwindle, smaller and smaller? Not only do they not flourish and regrow, things are worse. Landslips happen regularly now. Where will our firewood and charcoal come from, if they disappear? Where will we get wood to raise and repair our buildings?"

He paused to allow this new concern to sink in, then continued. "Every year, belts tighten, Every year, worse and worse."

Look at those sheep. So eager to follow, right to the slaughter.

The occasional dissenter infuriated Naldrum. "But *gothi,* should we blame those who wear the cross instead of the hammer of Thor?

What if they are right? What if our gods have become weak, and adding theirs may help us?"

Naldrum fought the urge to have such speakers taken outside and thrashed. He made his voice soft, patronizing. "Our gods have protected us for fifty years. Now, suddenly, they fail? I think not."

Most subsided with that, but a clever few would still disagree. "But many of the old ones, the first settlers of our land, believed the white-christ faith. After all, their god guided Aud the Deepminded!"

Aud the Deepminded! Must they always bring up that hardheaded woman? Aud and her ship of loyal men. Aud, who freed her slaves and gave them land. *Aud, Aud, Aud!* Naldrum loathed that name, nearly revered as a goddess herself by now.

He learned to deflect the issue of Aud. "Yet many of the children of Aud, and grandchildren and great-grandchildren worship Odin and Thor as we do. So, which is greater?"

There could be no answer to such a question. The 'renegade sheep' would subside bleating, frustrated, and Naldrum could continue.

He smiled warmly. "My personal theory—don't tell anyone, it's just between me and you—is that Loki has sent these white-christs, either to test us, to see if we're loyal, or to trick us, as Loki is so fond of doing. We must not fall for his nonsense. Of course, the laws of hospitality demand that we be courteous to all people. But bear it in mind, the day may come in which you must choose between the Old Ways and these dangerous new ideas. It bodes well to consider in advance what your decision will be. I know what mine is. Dark days may come, my friends. Dark days, when we must name those who bring hardship upon us, and punish them!"

He reached for the cross on Kandace's bosom again. Held it up, twisted it so all could see it clearly. Kept on his face an expression that indicated his intention not only to prevail, but to do so in the most vindictive way possible.

His guests had never heard someone speak so openly and so hatefully. It went against every tradition in their land of hospitality, fairness, generosity, obedience to law. Despite that, they nodded, and pulled their beards, and agreed.

Sheep, Naldrum laughed to himself again. But little by little, even he began to believe the lies and venom that came from his mouth.

. . .

Rota's recommendation—to name a fear, and to promise punishment—had worked astonishingly well in these little speeches. Naldrum could not resist one last dig at Tor before the enslaved man and Kel returned with the cask.

"Perhaps this year, I'll take that cross-wearing Loki-test as a *frill.* I'm not saying I will, but I think I will. Once I finish with her, we'll send this white-christ witch back where she came from—to Loki and the immortals!" Naldrum laughed uproariously. His guests, nervously at first, followed suit.

He smoothed his features into a generous smile as Kel opened the longhouse door for Tor and they came back into the hall. "Ah, here are my steward and my slave again, returned with a gift for you. When you decide who to stand with in the coming days, a wise choice might be to side with those who butter your bread."

With this, Naldrum signaled, and Tor opened the cask to show it brimming with butter. A cry of delight sounded around the table. Ankya, pleased to be the center of attention, ladled a huge scoop of the rich stuff into a bowl and offered it to their hosts.

"Plenty more where this came from, my loyal friends!" Naldrum exclaimed. "I promise that those who pledge loyalty to me have nothing to fear this winter, no matter what the weather brings!"

. . .

Kandace, unable to understand Naldrum's words without Tor to translate for her, had followed the expressions around table, mirroring their smiles and looking serious when they did as well. She wanted to be a good guest, hoping if she pleased Naldrum that he would in turn release her to finally voyage back to the abbey.

But as they supped at one farm after another, the listeners increasingly stared at Kandace with narrowed eyes. They drew away from sitting close to her, and glanced sideways at her, suspicious, as Naldrum began to buy their freedoms for a golden bit of butter.

. . .

Finally, Kandace found a snatch of time to talk to Tor alone. "When he sends you and Kel out of the room to get the butter casks, he says something about me, the same thing every time. He points to me, points to the cross I wear, talks a while, makes a joke. But it doesn't seem to be a funny joke."

"I'll find a way to learn what he is saying," Tor promised.

At the next farm, he listened against the almost-closed door listening while Naldrum spoke, disgusted to hear the headman accuse Kandace of being complicit in causing crops to fail. He did not know what Naldrum meant by a frill, or what 'send Kandace back where she came from' implied. Return her to Trondheim, perhaps? Tor only knew that whatever Naldrum was planning would be terrible for Kandace—and for him.

. . .

The next morning, Tor lifted the butter cask to strap it back in the pannier straddling the packhorses. As he tightened the buckle, he heard a voice nearby.

"You love her, don't you?" Ankya's lispy voice, calculated to be soft and sweet.

Tor could not ignore the headman's daughter. "I'm sorry. What are you speaking of?"

"That woman they call a 'nun'. The one with skin like yours. You've fallen in love with her."

"Why ever would you say that?"

"I saw how you looked at her when you came into the hall tonight with the butter-cask. So worried. It's how I felt when my favorite dog started hunting sheep, and Father said they would have to kill it."

Tor kept his gaze on the panniers. "I'm sorry, miss."

"Don't be sorry. I understand love. Especially when you can't have what you want." Ankya watched as Kel readied the saddles for the departing riders. "It's so much harder then."

She lost interest in Tor, but the wanting for Kel lingered. To distract herself, Ankya said, "I can't wait until the *álfablót,* right after the harvest-supper. I think Father might burn the nun as an offering, the way they say that the old ones did, long ago. Or perhaps hang her from a tree, like the legends of Uppsala. Can you imagine? So exciting! I've never seen someone be hung to death! And surely, the crops will improve in our valley if we give the gods such a special, important gift, yes?"

Tor became stone.

Ankya patted him on the arm. "I'm just guessing, and Father would hate if I spoiled his secret, so please don't tell anyone, will you? But I guess if you *do* love this woman Kandace, you might feel sad when they burn her. You'll probably feel the way I did when they killed my dog, the one that hunted sheep. I was so angry with Father when they cut its throat." She paused, remembering. "Of course, it was exciting, but still, I loved my dog. I always laughed when it would come home with its mouth all bloody from tearing a sheep apart, and sleep all day, relaxed and fed." Ankya had confused herself in what she wanted to say. Happily, she remembered.

"Anyway, Tor, take heart! You'll be fine. I have a new dog now, and I love it just as much as the old one!" She thought of her chubby puppy and giggled. "I'll look for a puppy for your own! There won't be any until spring, but I'll keep an eye out."

She drifted off, as always her eyes on Kel, hoping for a word. Tor, sick to his bones, stood shaking, grateful for the horse to lean against so that he did not fall to the ground in despair.

. . . .

Tor whispered to Kandace. "At the next dinner, offer to say a prayer over the meal. Right when I bring the butter-cask in."

Her expression lit up. "Really?"

"Yes. Say it in those words you use with your bishop Friedrich, what you call Latin. I'll nod at you when it's the right time."

"Happily, but why?"

"Naldrum is talking about the challenges these farmers face, with crops and weather and sickness in their animals. He will appreciate you helping him deliver his message. And Kandace," Tor fastened his eyes on hers, "I want you to say a long prayer, and make your voice fierce, too, to drive evil spirits from the room. Say his name, *Naldrum*. Point to his food when you bless it, and point to him, and point to his daughter Ankya who he loves so much. Say her name, too, slowly and loudly—so he can clearly hear it.

She frowned, doubting. "Are you sure?"

"I promise you, it is for the best," Tor said.

Allah, forgive me.

. . .

Kandace did as Tor suggested. Her expression severe, she stood and pointed, said Naldrum's name and Ankya's, and blessed the food, pouring out a long stream of words.

Naldrum had started eating, his mouth full of mutton. "Tor! What's all that she's saying?"

Tor came from the far end of the table. "Your lordship, I cannot," he said, feigning distress.

"You cannot what?" demanded Naldrum.

"I cannot say those words to you. You would have me flayed. They are too dangerous!"

"What is it? I demand to know!"

Tor drew a deep breath. He spoke in a low, loud voice, clear enough for all to hear.

"She has cursed you, *gothi.* She says that if you raise a hand to hurt her, the magic of her cross will cause you to suffer endless torments, and that—no, I cannot say more!"

"Tell me!" Naldrum demanded

"Sir," Tor whispered. "She said that if you harm her, your daughter Ankya will sicken. That her intestines and lungs will fill with pus, and she will die."

Naldrum paled. The meat dropped unnoticed from his mouth.

"She would not. Tell her I order her not to do that."

Tor ignored Naldrum and continued. "But that is not all, *gothi.* She has placed a terrible curse on you as well. Any woman who lies with you with will find something growing deep inside her. A child, but not a child. Something horrible, half-human, half-troll. It will never be born. It will live in the belly of the woman, gnawing at her innards, until the pox-infant eats the woman from the inside out—and when it has eaten its way out of her, it will writhe along the roadway, crawling to you, mocking you and calling your name, *father Naldrum! Kiss me, father Naldrum!* as it seeks to come home to you."

Girls of the household who had preened the rich chieftain in hopes of a gift or a bracelet stepped away and put their hands in their apron pockets.

Naldrum, cruel to others, expected cruelty from others. He therefore believed every word Tor spoke. He blanched, then colored, then blanched again, and scrabbled on his plate for his spoon and pretended to inspect it.

Kandace could see that her blessing had somehow upset Naldrum. *Perhaps Tor did not translate it properly?* Little she could do. Kandace smiled broadly at her horrified hosts, nodded to one or two, and helped herself to a bit of bread.

. . .

Tor had bought Kandace a little time, but how much? More than ever, he needed to get her away from Naldrum. The only one place he could think of was the widow Eilíf's farm, where his children were hidden. But how to get her there?

Perhaps Loki heard Naldrum mention his name. Perhaps Loki did not appreciate being used in such a manner by a human, or perhaps he found Tor's deadly-serious prank wildly humorous. In any case, on the very next day, the trickster-god played a prank on Naldrum.

. . .

Chapter Twenty-Three

Naldrum's custom when traveling was to send his messenger ahead of him each morning to announce his arrival to the next farm. But as the group rode towards it, Naldrum grew alarmed at seeing his messenger galloping back towards them. He rode forward so that he could hear the messenger's words in private. The man skidded to a stop.

"*Gothi,* the stables are already crowded with horses," the man panted. "Another party is there. A rival *gothi.*"

Naldrum laughed, but the sound rang false. "What does that matter to me? It is still early. They are probably departing soon. We'll wait here and jeer at them as they ride past."

"No, *gothi*. They are staying again tonight. And another group of travelers also arrived this morning, a little before I did. A goat has already been slaughtered for the evening meal, since so many must be fed."

"Who is in the second group?"

"The house servants told me it's a woman travelling under the flag of a ruler in Norway." The messenger hesitated. *What did they say her name was?* "Ro-something."

"Rota?" This time Naldrum could not keep the panic from in his voice.

"Yes, *Gothi.*"

What was Rota doing in his valley? How dare she travel here without alerting him! A ghastly idea occurred to Naldrum. Perhaps Rota was courting the rival headman also? His thoughts veered towards what her motive might be. Did Haakon plan to provoke a long hostility into open fighting, then swoop in and take over both their lands after?

Beyond those concerns, Naldrum knew that Rota must not, under any circumstances, see Kandace with him. His theft of Haakon's property would be immediately discovered.

Naldrum's head swam. He rode back to his group and seized on the first excuse he could think of. "I will not be second-guest! We must change our plans." Naldrum's ego would not suffer the possibility of giving up the seat of honor for dinner, or the use of the freeholder's own bed-space, and the best bedding. He kicked his horse cruelly and jerked its reins, furious. Even those who knew to keep their faces impassive leaned back in surprise at Naldrum's outburst. "We'll just bypass this farm and ride to the next one. It's not that far."

"It is *quite* far, *gothi*," Kel said. He did not care how long they were in saddle. Kel could ride all night if needed. He was just enjoying seeing Naldrum discomfiture at the messenger's words.

The headman considered another distasteful fact. Even though the farm compound was well off the road, Rota may have posted a guard where the fork rand from the main track. Any guard would surely report to Rota on groups that passed. What if even that man saw Kandace?

If he did, Rota would surely send a messenger to Haakon Sigurdsson that Naldrum had just ridden past with a dark-skinned woman who fit Kandace's description. His dreams of becoming Lawspeaker would be over.

An idea formed in Naldrum's mind. A stupidly dangerous, but the only option he could think of.

"Drikke!" Naldrum shouted to his son. "Tor! Kel! The three of you, come here!"

. . .

The small group around Naldrum frowned as he announced his plan.

"As you all know, Kandace cursed me in front of my guests last night. As punishment, I intend to send her home straight away. I am in such an angry mood about it that I no longer want to stop at this farm. We'll skip this farm and ride to the next one."

"If they see us pass, they'll insist we stop," Kel said, hiding a laugh. *Was Naldrum too thin-skinned to share a table when he wasn't the guest of honor? No, there was something else at stake. Naldrum looked* afraid.

"That is why I plan to take a different route." Naldrum pointed to the mountain that ran along the east side of the valley. "There's an old track along the base of Hekla. When we reach it, we'll separate into two groups. Tor, you'll take Kandace up and over the mountain. My son Drikke will go with you to prevent any ideas of running away. Kel, you and the rest of our group will ride with me. We'll follow the track at the mountain base until we are well past this large farm, and then we'll return to the main road."

Drikke protested. "Ride over Hekla? Whatever for? Even in midsummer, snow can come with no warning. We are closer to the *Equal-Night* than to *Midnight-Sun.* Do you want to send me to my death?"

Kel agreed. "Drikke's right, *gothi.* It's dangerous. If you're determined to pass up perfectly good hospitality here, why not just refuse it, but keep all of us will stay together? If you want to get Kandace back, that's the fastest way."

The protests only fanned Naldrum's fury. He looked on his son with spite. "How dare you both argue with me? Drikke, stop acting like such a coward? Look how bright it is today! And early! You'll be off the mountain by afternoon."

He mounted his horse again. "If the woman Rota ever comes to our compound, hide Kandace immediately. The Nubian is too valuable! We must always guard against someone stealing her. Rota must never see her. Now ride!" He turned and gestured wildly toward his standard-bearer. "And take down our flag before anyone sees it and announces us!"

"Rota? Why are you talking about her?" asked Naldrum's son Drikke.

Kel looked at Naldrum's messenger, shaking his head in agreement, and realized what had made Naldrum afraid. Rota was at the farm ahead.

He decided that secret should not be kept.

"Haakon's agent Rota is the guest," he shouted to their group. "Our headman needs to protect Kandace. His valuable property must not be stolen by Rota and Haakon. Forget the warm bed and good food of the farm ahead, and ride toward Hekla! Do as our *gothi* instructs. Hail Naldrum!"

Naldrum purpled. Kel spurred his horse towards the mountain, not bothering to hide his smirk.

. . .

The servants and slaves who followed Naldrum exchanged telling glances, careful to not be seen. No one wanted to be the target of Naldrum's notorious wrath.

But what fools did their headman take them for? Ever since the *vikinger* Tiller had stood on Naldrum's flag-stones, shouting to be paid for stealing Kandace from Haakon, everyone at Naldrum's compound had gossiped about what a stupid thing their headman had done. Now, to hide his secret, Naldrum was sending his own son, his most valuable slave, and the Nubian over Hekla?

Each gave thanks that they, too, had not been chosen to travel to over that mountain—and each whispered prayers that Tor and Kandace would emerge safe from deadly Hekla, the dreaded Gateway to Hell.

. . .

Kandace called ahead to where Tor rode. "Should we worry about the weather?" She pointed. The sun, so bright when they had left Naldrum's group, had become hazy as they rode further up the mountain track.

“We absolutely should.” He glowered back at Naldrum’s son, who sauntered along behind them. Drikke kept his hand on his sword hilt, as if that little show of force would keep them compliant.

As they rode higher on the shoulder of the mountain, the horses’ hooves began to crunch on patches left over from an earlier snow.

He called back to their guard. “Drikke, bad weather could come on us with these clouds closing in. We should ride faster.”

Drikke dropped his chin and lifted his eyebrows in a mocking expression. “Should we, slave?” he drawled. “Or should we trust in my father’s judgement?”

. . .

They paused for a quick break. Cold gusts of wind had increased to a steady blow.

Drikke gnawed at his knuckle. He tried to hide his nervousness from Tor.

“Do you think the weather will hold?”

“How should I know? You have lived in this country your entire life, and I have been here less than a year, and never in the highlands. You should be answering that question for *us*!”

“What did you call this place?” Kandace asked. She had pulled gloves from her pack and held out her wrist for Tor to tie the fastenings.

Drikke laughed weakly. “We call it Hekla—cloak—because the summit is so often hidden in mist.” He looked about as though he were nervous of being overheard, even in such a remote location. “My father says we will be fine, but he would never ride up here himself No one ever does except for outlaws hoping to escape notice."

"And why is that?"

"You'll see when we get higher. I've never been here. It's supposed to be a fearful place. Smoke comes out of the bare ground. Not like a hot-spring, just smoke oozing up everywhere from the ground." Drikke looked around again, nervous, as if something evil could hear. "Back in the Settlement days, some long-ago white-christs gave it another name. They called it the 'gateway to hell'. Not our Hel, home to many in the afterlife, but a place of fire and demons where they said evil ones are tormented forever."

Kandace shuddered, but not from the cold.

"We need to keep riding. It could begin to snow any time now. We can't afford to be caught up here." Tor's voice sounded grim. There was no need to pretend.

. . .

True to Drikke's description, they soon passed jagged crevices where steam rose. Drikke continued his steady stream of complaints, lagging farther and farther behind despite his earlier exhortations to ride quickly. As the first white flakes fell, Tor lashed out, impatiently waiting once again for Naldrum's son to catch up.

"If we're going to get over this beast of a mountain and back to the valley, why are you dithering so?"

"Don't tell me what to do, slave!" Drikke lashed at Tor with his reins, but the tall blacksmith easily avoided them.

Red-faced, Drikke tried again, standing in his stirrups. He reached towards Tor with his whip. Drikke's horse, overbalanced, lost its footing on icy stones. It scrabbled with its hooves trying to regain balance, but failed. As it fell, an earsplitting scream echoed across the snow.

. . .

The three stood over the horse as it tried to stand, crying in pain.

"You damned fool," said Tor. "Your mare's leg has broken. Look there, where it's lodged between those two stones."

Half-sobbing, Drikke yanked at his horse, but it continued its screaming. "It's not my fault!" He covered his ears, half sobbing.

"Give me your knife."

"What are you going to do? Are you going to kill me?" Drikke backed away. Tor reached for Drikke's belt and pulled the knife from it. He walked to the horse and knelt. His lips moved in a silent prayer, and the pitiful crying stopped. The mare's blood turned the snow-white ground a harsh pink.

"You've killed my horse! Now what will we do?" Drikke whined. "This is all your fault!"

"If I had a bit of silver for every time I've heard your father say the same thing, I'd be a free man," Tor said.

"How dare you!" Drikke stopped sniveling, shocked that Tor would speak to him in such a way.

"We're down a horse. The snow's coming harder. We have no shelter. We might die on this damned mountain today, so I'll say whatever I want. Do you really want to blame everyone the same way that your father does? I've seen your face when he does it. You hate it."

A flicker crossed Drikke's face. In an instant, it disappeared. "My father is a great man!"

"The great man you were cursing a little while ago? I believe you called him a *fukking* fool for sending us across this cursed mountain."

"He must have had good reason! First this stupid weather and now your insolence! It is too much!" Drikke darted about in confusion. "What will we do now? Give me back my *saxe!* Am I the next target for the knife? Please don't kill me up here on this horrid mountain!"

Tor rolled his eyes. "I don't kill men."

"I bet you do! I bet that was your plan all along!" His voice raised to a shriek.

Tor shook his head. *Just like his father.* How could a boy grow into a strong man, raised without love in that shadow?

"Here," said Tor. "Take my horse. I'll walk, and hold Kandace's halter." Anything to get Drikke from wasting more time.

Drikke put his foot in Tor's stirrup. His words belied the shame on his face. "I'm in charge, do you understand? Whatever I say, you have to do."

"No one questions that. Can we just please get moving again?"

"I'm going to give you an order, and you're going to follow it," said Drikke. "Do you understand?" He mounted Tor's horse.

"Whatever you say! Just hurry!"

"Ride along this ridge. It's the only way to keep going forward. When you get to the end, keep following it. It'll descend the mountain. As soon as you get lower, the snow and mists will clear and you'll see the path to follow. Once you get all the way down, keep going straight forward and keep Hekla to your back. You'll come to a track. Turn left on it. Stay on it and it'll take you directly back to the road we were on. Turn right on that road. Follow it until you come to another trackway, then turn left. You'll come to a small river. Ford it, and soon you'll recognize my father's valley."

"Why are you telling me all this?"

Drikke's voice was evasive. "What if we get separated? You should know how to get home."

"Fair enough."

"Remember what I said. Follow the ridge, left on the track at the bottom of the mountain, then right on the main road, and follow it around—"

"Left on the next track, cross the river. I remember."

Tor helped Kandace mount her horse again. He took the lead line, and they started off.

After a few paces Tor glanced back, and knew then why Drikke had directed him. Naldrum's son was heading back in the direction from which they had come, riding so fast that his horse's hooves spurted up little dustings of snow.

"If you follow me, I'll turn and cut you down with my sword!" he cried over his shoulder. "My father will believe me when I say you attacked me!"

Tor rolled his eyes. *Cowardly fool.*

"Going after Drikke seems as bad as continuing ahead," he said to Kandace. "Don't worry. We'll go fast. We'll be off this mountain and in the sun again soon."

"I'm not afraid," Kandace replied. She kicked her horse gently and they started forward again.

. . .

The snow thickened.

. . .

Chapter Twenty-Four

Tor bent against the howling wind. He could no longer see ahead of them, or behind them. *If I had known it would be this bad, I'd have taken our chances following Drikke.* Tor had had no knowledge of the Icelandic highlands, and how treacherous the weather could be on the white-capped mountains.

Kandace bent over the pommel of the saddle with her head against the horse's neck. She had pulled her cloak over her face to protect from the animal's mane, whipping in the gale.

Suddenly the horse stopped dead in its tracks and refused to move. Tor jerked on the lead. Even with his great strength, he could not budge the horse. It dug in and pulled backwards.

"Hia!" he yelled. "Come *on!*"

Just that quickly the wind rose to a scream. Tor's boots, thick with snow, slipped as he pulled the horse. They could not go forward. Nor could they go back. The way Drikke had taken had disappeared.

. . .

Kandace, in a fog of cold and hunger, became aware that the horse had stopped moving. She pulled a small opening in her cloak and peeked through it. "What has happened?"

"I can't get him to move. I'm going to try and turn him around. We passed a crevice in the rocks just a little bit back. We might be able to shelter in it until the snow stops."

"Here." Kandace jumped down from the saddle. "Maybe it'll be easier without me on him."

"Can you walk? It's only a very short way."

"Of course I can. You've been walking all this time. Let's go."

Tor had almost no thought save the need for safety in this storm, but at the farthest edge of his mind, he felt admiration for Kandace. *How did I never know my wife was so strong?*

. . .

They leaned against the stones of the crevice Tor had found.

"It's not much better than being out there." He shivered.

"It's much better! We're in the lea of the wind, at least. Let's see what we have here."

Kandace dug in the horse's panniers. "Oh, blessings!" she cried, and pulled out a large tent-wool. "Kel must have packed this even though Naldrum said we didn't need any!"

. . .

Setting up a tent in the stones and wind proved impossible. Tor stamped his feet. *So cold.* They pulled the horse closer, leaned against it, discouraged again.

Kandace spun around and eyed the stone wall behind them. "Here." She held the tent-wool blanket against a small ledge, pointed with her chin to a loose stone. "Put that on top to hold it in place."

Tor grasped her intent. As she held the wool, section by section, he piled stones on top of it along the ledge, until one whole side hung secure, draped down the stone wall.

Tor bowed to Kandace in open astonishment. "You're brilliant!" he said.

"And freezing," she laughed. "But thank you. It'll give us a little bit of shelter, if we stand under it."

"We can do better than that," said Tor. He lifted the loose bottom of the wool. "Hold it up as high as you can."

Tor guided the horse, spoke to it gently. "Now lift it over him."

Between the two of them, they got the exhausted animal to stand under the tent-wool, then had it to lie down, trapping the loose edge of the tent blanket under its substantial body. It sank in exhaustion against the blanket, lowered its head, and drew its legs close. Billows of moist warmth came from its nostrils. It groaned in relief, and barely noticed when the two humans crawled under the tent-wool and pressed next to its great body.

. . .

Kandace and Tor sat side by side under their improvised tent, their backs to the horse, grateful for its thick winter coat and the warmth that came from its belly. Outside, the storm screamed and beat against their tiny shelter. From time to time, Tor or Kandace would lift an arm and push against the tent-wool to dislodge snow from piling up and collapsing their precarious shelter.

"The storm can't last long. We'll be clear of it soon," they reassured each other. But those words came less and less often, and the periods of not talking grew. Soon the only sounds were the hissing of the snow and the howling of the wind across the ragged rock landscape of Hekla.

. . .

By sunset, the storm still howled. The dim light in the tiny tent faded, and the cold became bitter. Even with the horse next to him, Tor began to shiver uncontrollably. He could no longer feel anything in his feet.

Time became fluid, and memory wavered. Tor leaned closer to Kandace, eager to breathe in the scent of oranges. His tunic brushed her drowsy face.

"Tor, your clothes are soaking wet!" she cried. "Drikke should have given you a cloak, at least!" Kandace ran her hand along his waist and down his leg to his boots. They, too, were sopping wet from walking in the snow.

"By the blessed Virgin, you are going to die of cold if you don't get these off," Kandace said.

Had he heard her correctly? Tor could not remember.

"What?" he asked.

Had Kandace said something? How long ago? He lay back, drifting.

Kandace could no longer hear Tor breathing. She could not see him in the snow-covered darkness of their improvised tent.

"Tor!" she screamed. "Tor! Don't leave me alone here! *Tor!"*

What was that sound, that howling? *So tired.*

. . .

Kandace slapped at Tor's face and chest. "Wake up! Please!"

"What did you say?" His voice, no more than a throaty whisper.

"Do you still have Drikke's knife? Give it to me."

Tor tried to remember what a knife was. He fumbled under his cloak, his fingers stiff. Kandace untied his boots, took them off. She unwrapped his leg windings. In the cramped space, she managed to get his tunic off. The pants were harder. Tor could barely move.

Kandace stripped herself of everything except her nun's habit. With the knife, she cut the neckline, opening it wider.

"Here," she said. She lifted the hem. "You must wriggle inside this with me. It'll be another little tent inside our blanket tent."

Tor struggled to do as Kandace directed. One instant he could feel her knees and hips next to his, and the next he felt as if he was floating, free as a snowflake, uncaring of his next breath.

Kandace tucked the bottom of her robe over their entwined feet. She wriggled tighter against the horse's flank, her warmer skin curled against Tor's chilled body inside the voluminous fabric.

She breathed into the robe, and hoped.

. . .

In the sunny valley below, Rota inclined her head to a servant who whispered in her ear.

"Oh, really?" she murmured, drawing out the word and holding back laughter. "How wonderfully amusing! Send my flagbearer with a fine gift to offer him." She turned to her host, a freeholder whose property lay along a fertile curve of the Bull River. "I'm so sorry to interrupt. I just learned that your chieftain Naldrum rides across your land."

"Naldrum?" the man spat on the ground. "He's not my chieftain. I've never pledged to him, and I don't intend to now. That pompous pigshit." He did not explain his reasons to Rota, nor did she inquire.

"In any case, I'm actually riding towards his compound to pay him a call. It would be good to meet him now, perhaps." Again, Rota shook with barely-concealed mirth.

She had posted a guard posted some distance up the roadway. Naldrum's group, crashing down a steep hill through a thicket of brush, had nearly collided with him. Her man had drawn his sword and caught the bridle of a young woman who rode with them.

"My guard seems to have convinced Naldrum that he should come here to your longhouse. I must confess, I'm intrigued as to why they were trying to skirt your lands. Perhaps we might ask him together."

The man snorted. "They saw your flag, maybe? You clearly know the man. Has he reason to avoid you?"

Rota tapped her finger against her teeth as she considered the question. "None at all that I know of. In fact, he should be *wanting* to meet with me again—which makes his behavior even more interesting. Hearing his reasoning is something I shall much anticipate. I'm sorry to ask you to endure it on my behalf."

"It's nothing. It'll make him squirm. Anything that causes that horse's ass distress is welcome entertainment to me."

. . .

"I know you, don't I?" Naldrum pointed at Rota as he entered the hall, pretending to not recognize her.

She stood silent, a slight smile on her lips.

"But where have I seen your face? Don't tell me! Ah—was it at Althing? I meet so many people there. No wonder I could not place you at first." Naldrum did his best to beam at Rota.

She stood stone-faced and did not answer him.

Naldrum sweated a bit. "Althing, I'm sure. I've been so busy since then, building my new storehouse, you know. I've barely travelled. It must have been Althing."

Still, she stared at him.

Now Naldrum grew impatient. "Speak, woman! Why do you stand there so rudely ignoring me?"

She gave a small smile, sardonic, unhurried. "You know perfectly well who I am."

Naldrum glanced around wildly, as if someone might give him an answer to make him seem less stupid. But his own entourage found the floor of utmost interest, while the freeholder's household members hid smiles behind their hands.

"What an unmannerly greeting," he finally replied, all pretense gone from his voice. "I thought your Jarl wanted me as his ally. Your mockery seems a strange way of encouraging a friendship."

"And your avoidance of me seems a strange way of doing the same." Rota sat at the longhouse table. She smoothed her dress, adjusted the circlet of gold on her forehead, and prepared for an interesting conversation.

. . .

Chapter Twenty-Five

Kandace dreamed.

She lay, stretched and comfortable, in a warm place. The sun-shutters had been thrown open to welcome the cool breeze after the heat of the day. Late-afternoon sun glowed across the floor. Motes of dust danced in the beams of light.

Kandace stretched and yawned. The sheets, silk as light as air, slid across her bare skin. Her husband lay sleeping beside her, his strong tall body completely relaxed. She sat up in bed and watched his belly move up in and down, his breathing slow and peaceful. Kandace bent and kissed his navel. She thought about another, lower kiss.

No. He needs rest. She got out of bed, opened the door to the children's room. The girl watching them waved a palmetto fan over the small sleeping bodies.

Kandace closed the door, went to the window, leaned on the sill. The orange tree in their courtyard hung heavy with fruit. Kandace smiled. No kiss now, but later tonight, she would peel one of the fruits, and twist the skin, press it against her throat. *He will kiss my neck. He will know.*

She lay down next to him again, content for the time being to simply touch his skin. Her husband moved, and she adjusted her body against his. “Shhhh, my beloved. Sleep.” She kissed the dusky skin of his beautiful throat, whispered his name.

. . .

Only Tor’s eyes moved. They opened wide in the dark of their makeshift tent. He had not heard that name for years. Should he wake his wife? Was this the change for which he had been hoping so long?

The soft sound of her breathing told Tor that Kandace had fallen back asleep. He tightened his arms around her and lay in the dark without moving.

Breathing, and hoping.

. . .

Kandace nestled against Tor, secure in the feel of his body curved with hers as it had every morning since their marriage. She drifted back to sleep again.

After a while, she began to wake a little. Even though Tor’s skin was warm, she felt chilled. Kandace reached for her sheets, but her fingers touched only some kind of wool wrapping. She opened her eyes, expecting to see moonlight in the large windows of their home, but she saw nothing. All was darkness. The wind howled outside the room, but inside, all was silent.

Where was she? Too tired to care, Kandace reached for Tor’s hand, wrapped her fingers around it, and fell asleep again.

. . .

She came suddenly awake. *Where was she?* She lay in pitch dark, rigid with confusion. A dream of sleeping next to a man flitted at the edge of her thoughts. Tor murmured in his sleep and Kandace realized that her dream was no dream. A man lay somehow entangled in her clothing, his naked skin touching hers.

She screamed.

. . .

Tor came thrashing awake at the sound. For a short while they struggled together inside Kandace's nun's robes, her clawing to get away from Tor, and him grasping Kandace to hold her and calm her down.

"Kandace! Kandace, stop! Be still!"

Her breathing, panicked. Her body, iron in fear and shock.

"I'm not going to hurt you," he said. "Shhh. I'm not going to hurt you! Do you remember the storm? Riding? Drikke leaving? How cold we were? How you told me to sleep together with you, to stay warm? To survive? Remember, please!"

Still rigid, but she managed a nod. "What was I thinking? I took holy orders. I cannot lie with a man!"

"You were thinking with true kindness. You almost certainly saved my life. Beyond that, nothing happened. Nothing at all."

Her breathing came in small warm puffs near his face. "I believe you." She tried to not move, to avoid touching Tor.

"I think you were dreaming earlier." He had heard her say his name in sleep, his real name. Tor held his breath.

A long silence. Fragments of the dream filled Kandace's thoughts. That place, so familiar. Those rooms. Her children—

Her children?

Her children.

The wall of dis-remembering began to fall, sand under a sea wave.

"Oh my God. Oh my God. Oh my God—" Kandace collapsed against Tor. Nothing came from her lips save a moan of agony. "Oh God Oh God Oh God—"

"Kandace," he tried. "Are you remembering?"

"OhmyGodohmyGodohmyGodohmyGodohmyGod," she wept. "Where are the children? Are they safe? Where are *we?*"

And then, in a tone of horror. "How long has it been?"

. . .

Chapter Twenty-Six

At the top of Hekla, the Gateway to Hell, a kind of miracle had occurred. The pain at the opening of her memory came sharp and swift, a long clean slice, razor sharp. Had she been anywhere else, she might have just started running wildly in any direction—but she lay wrapped in a cocoon of robe with Tor, trapped in a tiny tent on top of a mountain in a blizzard in the middle of the night. There was nothing she could do, and nowhere she could go.

"I'll tell you everything I can," Tor said. "Either one or both of us could still die on this mountain. You must learn all that has happened—and if you are the only one to survive this night, you need to know the secret of where our children are. I will go through it all quickly, because there is much to tell. But Kandace, the hearing of much of this will be terribly hard for you. I promise to take care of your pain later, but first, you need truth."

Tor did not say that he needed to tell Kandace everything for another reason. He, too, needed something: an end to the long, solitary journey of sadness and searching, however brief their time of togetherness might be.

. . .

There were parts Tor did not know, and parts that Kandace could not bring herself to tell him.

About the betrayal that had led to her capture.

About the day the slavers took her away from the city where the orange trees grew.

About what had happened in the weeks after that, before the nuns found her without a stitch of clothing, bruised all over, and her memory gone.

One day, she would tell her husband, but for now, all that could wait.

But Tor kept his word, speeding through everything he knew. As the blizzard continued to rage around them, and faced with likely death, they knew at last the bliss of being together again.

. . .

"We have nothing left at all? You sold everything? The house? My gold necklaces and earrings? Everything?"

"Yes. I had looked everywhere in our city, and only found the slimmest of clues. But based on them, I knew you had likely been taken to one of the lands that lay to the north. I sold our horses, the house, and everything in our storehouses. Sold everything we once owned except the clothing on our backs and our soul-stones. I took the children, and we boarded a ship and started traveling toward the routes that the slave traders take."

"Oh, beloved." It would do not good to tell him of the slavers breath in her face, of their fingers probing her crutch. The memory made her ashamed, even though she had fought with all her strength against their coarse taking of her body.

"It was such a slim chance that we might find you. So many rivers, so many lands. But you had to be somewhere. I asked everyone I met, in every port, if they had seen a woman of your description. From time to time, there would be a bit of a trail, but it never led anywhere. A different woman in her own trail of misfortune. Such anguish, Kandace, to see others of our land, captured and enslaved just as you had been, who I could not help—or who I *chose* not to help, so that I could keep looking for you."

Tor could not speak for a short while. "I could have bought any each of them with the silver in my money box. But if I had, there might not have been enough to pay for you, once I found you. They begged me, knowing I had to means to free them, but I walked away, Kandace. Walked away from women just like you."

He wept. Kandace held him close, murmured words of comfort.

"We were in some Frankish town the day my funds dwindled to a single piece of silver. I walked along the port until I saw a merchant who looked honest—and Kandace, I sold myself to her."

She did not understand. "What do you mean, sold yourself?"

"As a slave, Kandace. As a *vikinger* man who would work for only food and for the right to sail with her, to keep looking for you."

Kandace wept at the enormity of what he had done for her.

"And the children?" Her voice shook, needing to know, but terrified of what Tor might say.

Instead, he laughed. "You would be astonished to learn what fine sailors your son and daughter became! All the years we traveled as passengers and the years I worked as a slave, they lived on the ships with me. In the summers we went north, and in the winters, south. Life on board became normal to them. Our children, who might have grown up spoiled and coddled and throwing tantrums over a pet monkey, can sew whippings and mend sails and paint tar with the best of *vikingers!* Nenet and Nikea can climb a ship's rigging as fast and high as any sailors born to the work. They are strong, Kandace. I am so proud of them. *You* will be so proud of them!"

The next question, also hard. "Tell me where they are, please."

. . .

Tor described the harrowing events of the previous autumn and how the trader Josson had bought him from the ship merchant Indaell, the man's clear intention to sell the children away from Tor, and how Tor had come to the sad conclusion that their best chance for safety lay away from him.

"We stopped one day at the farm of a woman named Eilíf who lived alone after she'd endured a terrible accident. A widow, grieving and damaged, but a woman with a good heart who longed for a family. It was the safest place I could find."

"They are still there now?"

"I heard this past summer that they are, so I am guessing yes. No one but me, the woman Eilíf, and one other person knows that the children are on that remote farm. I do not go to see them, not ever. I cannot take the chance of someone following me there."

Kandace's throat choked. "How far away? I need—" She could not finish the sentence.

He told her how many days she would have to walk or ride to reach Eilíf's valley

"So close! We must—" but Tor cut her off.

"No. I know it will break your heart to hear that, but we must keep their secret safe until we can find a way to escape Naldrum. Otherwise it will mean disaster to all of us."

Kandace stifled a sob, her fist against her mouth "Naldrum! That horrid man! I cannot bear that you are enslaved to him!"

"Try think of it another way. It is he who brought you here, Kandace. Without him, I might never have seen you. The Great One works in mysterious ways, my beautiful wife. Yes, he is a horrid man, no doubt about that. But even a man such as he might serve God's purpose."

"You are far kinder than I am. You always were."

Tor kissed her, kept his lips against her temple. "I am so glad to have you back I can think of nothing else for now. Naldrum, pah! He is far from us, here and now."

"So, what's the plan?" Kandace's crisp, practical side.

"The plan? To get safely down from this mountain."

"And after that?"

Tor felt a moment of confusion. Deep in his being, a great laugh began to build. It grew and grew, and finally burst from him, a rolling wave of relief and joy.

"The plan for the last several years has been to find you. That was the *only* plan. Then you arrived at Naldrum's, but you did not remember anything, and the plan became helping you to find your right mind again. Now that has happened—so for the first time in years, I have no plan!"

Tor roared with laughter again, a sound so infectious that Kandace found herself laughing along with him without quite knowing why.

The long, crazy laugh turned to tears of sadness and grief, and then to relief as they clung tightly to each other. When the storm had subsided, they wiped their eyes.

"Listen. The wind has stopped." Tor peeked outside. The snow had stopped falling as well. Sun glittered over soft white mounds that hid the treacherous stony pathway.

"It has," Kandace agreed. "We will sort out how to get down this mountain and back to the valley. And as we do, we will come up with some kind of plan to get you, me, and the children off this island as soon as possible."

Easier said than done, Tor thought. But he did not share his concerns with his wife. She, too, had grown stronger in unexpected ways. The young wife of a decade ago would have faced the snowstorm aghast and trembling. The Kandace of today had courage and resourcefulness.

But he knew this land better than she did. Four people of foreign coloring could not help being noticed and reported up and down the valleys, both by people eager to curry favor with Naldrum and those who had no idea from whence the dusky travelers came.

Any plan, whatever it might be, would have to be a remarkable one, with nothing left to chance. How could that possibly be?

. . .

"Tell me about this mystery woman," Kandace resumed as they picked their way through the snowy path. "The one who knows about the widow Eilíf's farm."

"Her name is Aldís. She's some kind of healer. I honestly don't know much at all about her. I've only met her twice, and both for only a short period of time."

"And yet you seem to trust her implicitly. I can hear it in your voice."

"I do. I can't explain. It's just something about her."

Kandace thought. "Where does she live?"

"I don't know."

"Does anyone know? Could you ask someone?"

"I guess I could. I never did because I didn't want to call any attention to the fact that I knew her."

"Let *me* ask. I can just say I've heard of her and want to learn more. Remember, nobody knows the connection between you and me, do they?"

"No. I've taken care to never indicate I know you in any way. In fact, your first day here, I told Naldrum I'd never seen you before. He believed me."

Kandace gave Tor a quick grin. *That beautiful, mischievous smile.* His heart beat faster.

"We'll have to keep him thinking that. All of them. For starters, I'll keep calling you Tor."

He groaned. "It's going to be so much harder to hide it all now."

Silent agreement on her part. They walked for a while, each mulling over the difficulty of living a lie now that the truth had been revealed.

"We keep talking about going back to Naldrum's," Kandace began.

"Yes. I don't want to, but strangely enough, it seems safest for now.

"Drikke abandoned us," Kandace said in a tone that told Tiller she was thinking of an idea. "We might be dead up there, for all they know. Nobody has any idea that we're even alive. Why do we have to go back?"

"You have another idea?" Tor asked.

"Maybe." Again, that smile that melted his heart and heated his thighs. "Maybe not."

. . .

Once Kandace's question had been spoken aloud, it flew about in their thoughts, a strange kind of bird that sparkled with dangerous excitement. They talked about where they might go, and how to remain unseen. How to get to the widow's, where to go after they took the children.

Little by little the bird of hope began to die, as the myriad ways they might be found and captured became painfully obvious. They had almost reached the road, resigned to returning to Naldrum's, when Kandace drew a quick breath and grabbed Tor by the arm.

"I have it," she said.

Hope sprang again. "Tell me right away."

"You're not going to like it. It's so dangerous—and it might not work."

"Tell me!"

"We just came through what they call the Gateway to Hell. And look, here we are, fine. Better than before, in fact. I think it is a sign from Heaven."

"What does that mean?"

"I propose," Kandace said, rushing her words, "that we walk straight forward—towards, and into, Hell itself!"

She told him what she meant. Tor listened, sickened, and flinched. But if Kandace was strong enough to do this, he could too.

. . .

Tor had learned in his own journey what it meant to risk all, but Kandace astonished him with the courage her idea required. At first, Tor protested, but she insisted he hear the whole thing through. When she finished explaining, Tor pulled her close. They leaned together, gathering strength from one another.

"To hell it is, then," he agreed. He pulled at the horse's reins, and they resumed walking.

. . .

Chapter Twenty-Seven

Aldís bent over a young woman who groaned on the longhouse bench, rolled into a ball and wearing only a shift.

"The pain started at the quarter-moon," someone said. "Sudden. Right above her stomach."

"Lie on your back so I can feel your stomach."

The girl rolled over and tried to lie flat, the effort clearly causing her agony. Aldís touched where the woman's abdomen felt too warm and the woman groaned. She put her ear against the girl's stomach and listened with her ears and her inner senses.

Listened longer. Imagined inside the young woman, picturing bone and bowel. Drew upon everything she had ever seen in slaughtering season, the mysterious shapes of organs. With no idea what was wrong, tried to sense the right thing to do.

"What makes it worse?" Aldís asked, grasping for some idea, any idea. "She ate cheese this morning. That made it awful."

"She should stop eating cheese. Milk, butter, anything from the dairy. Nothing but clear soup."

Aldís stood and shook her head. "I'm sorry. I don't know what it is. But it feels like something that will go away. Just let her rest."

She took a deep breath and closed down the inner-listening part of herself. As she did, an uneasy feeling surged. It had flowed through her, day after day, and it had increased. *That calling.*

A little girl tugged at Aldís's apron. "I saw you fight," she lisped.

"What?" Aldís, distracted.

"At Al-fing," the child said.

The girl's mother picked her up and gave her a kiss. "She saw you in the holmgang duels at Althing when you fought with Kel Coesson. She's talked about you ever since. One of the farms you and Kel saved belonged to my brother. You're quite the hero to her."

Aldís smiled. "Glad we helped." She did not want to talk about Kel.

But the mother did. "He's a good man. You seemed to be friends. You're unmarried, aren't you?"

The old familiar longing for what Aldís had once shared with Kel bloomed inside her, and then the familiar bitterness. She pictured Kel paying the family to pay for Drikke's hurt slave, and the sharpness eased a bit.

"But there's something else about him," the woman continued. "He was involved in some matter with a neighbor and his grandchild. I only know because I recognized him riding to them one day. My neighbor would never speak of the matter."

Once again, the cold hatred swept over Aldís. "Good luck with this sickness. I have to be going. I'll stop on my way back to check on her again."

. . .

Chapter Twenty-Eight

Rota crossed her legs and leaned back in her seat. Across the last few days, she had made her leisurely way along the valley to Naldrum's compound, just as he had dreaded. When she presented herself at his longhouse door, Naldrum, frantic, asked Kel for the hundredth time about Tor and Kandace. It would not do to have them show up now, at the most inopportune time.

Rota could hear only bits of the whispered conversation "I gather that you have lost a slave?" she asked.

"A small matter, certain to be resolved soon." Naldrum's words belied the panic she had distinctly heard in his voice. Fortunately, Rota had learned that simply staring at Naldrum would cause him to blurt on.

"Apparently, the fool ventured up on Hekla. There was an early snowstorm, and heavy. He must have gotten lost up there, or injured."

"Just the one man?" Her tone was solicitous. "Surely that is not a large matter, the loss of a single slave."

"He cost quite a bit," Naldrum rambled. "Perhaps you saw him at the Althing. A very tall man. Dark-skinned, from a distant land. And—" Naldrum stumbled, started again. "He may have had a companion with him on Hekla. So I might have lost two slaves." A brief hesitation. "But of course, that is nothing to a man of my means. Please don't be concerned on my behalf. What news of the Jarl?"

"Ah yes," Rota mused. "I recall the slave of whom you speak. Fine looking fellow, and an excellent blacksmith, as I recall. Shame to lose him." She cocked her head at Naldrum, as if considering something. "Regarding the Jarl, I can tell you that we have exchanged messages since I saw you at Althing. He was quite pleased to hear of your interest in working together."

"Very good, very good." Naldrum could barely focus, fretting that Tor and Kandace might burst in any instant and ruin his negotiations.

Rota seemed not to notice Naldrum's agitation. "The Jarl, of course, is still interested in the other half of our proposal, regarding how you will be of value to him."

Naldrum grimaced. "*Me* be of value to *him?* I am not a craftsman, applying for a serving position. We are men of business. I await our first official trade."

"Oh, but my understanding is that there has been a trade already! And I believe Jarl Haakon feels some equaling-up needs to be done, so he will want something quite significant from you, given the nature of the existing *exchange*."

Always this woman had to speak in confusing vagueness! "What do you mean, a trade already? Who does the Jarl think he is to demand anything?"

"Perhaps you have something that the Jarl values highly?"

Naldrum thought wildly, casting about for what she could possibly mean. Then he brightened. Of course!

"My daughter Ankya! Yes! I have great interest in arranging a royal marriage for my beloved child. She is worth the hand of any prince, or a king even, as first-wife!"

"No. Not your daughter."

"Exclusivity in my trade routes and wares?"

"No."

"By Loki, woman! Stop playing games with me! I have *many* things that the Jarl would want! Which of them is it?"

Rota sighed. "Perhaps you could notice that my glass of mead is empty and offer to refresh it."

"Perhaps you could act like a decent negotiator instead of a stupid *fitta!* Get to your point!"

"You bore me," Rota laughed. "You have utterly no skill in negotiations, and no intelligence at all. You're a stupid brute who has only gotten ahead because you're rich. You dangle your wealth to make greedy people want to be like you, and to make good people afraid of you. But I'm not greedy, and I'm not afraid of you, *gothi* Naldrum."

Naldrum nearly exploded in anger. Rota sighed again. She tilted her head at her servant, who left without a word.

"Stop being a troll and sit down," Rota said. "My trade terms will be clear to you very soon." She laughed inwardly again, thinking about Naldrum's missing slaves, and how much fun she intended to have at this arrogant, boorish man's expense.

. . .

When Kandace and Tor had left Hekla behind, they had headed directly back to the farm where Rota was visiting. Tor had explained that Naldrum was avoiding the farm for some reason. He told her of their journey across Hekla, and how Drikke had abandoned them with only one horse in the storm.

Rota listened, but with growing rage. Haakon's messenger had dared to question her about the Jarl's missing slave called the Nubian. She was all but certain that the woman in front of her was that exact creature.

Kandace, silent as Tor's voice rose and fell in unfamiliar words, frowned at Rota. Had she seen this woman's face at Lade Garde? Something about it seemed familiar, but still different.

"Your companion," Rota asked, nodding at Kandace. "You say she lives in Naldrum's compound. For how long now?"

"A *vikinger* brought her, after this summer's Althing and before the autumn harvest festival. My understanding is that Naldrum hired the man while at Althing to go and steal her from Haakon." Tor did not add the part about the toothless sailor at Althing.

"Interesting," Rota kept her face calm, her rage in check. How could Naldrum possibly be enough of an idiot to steal from the Jarl? How dare that stupid, stupid man put all of her hard work in danger!

"You say Kandace had been captured from the Saxon lands and sold to Haakon. She may not be much better off with Naldrum, but she is free of the Jarl. Yet you two have come directly here to me, Haakon's agent. Why? What could you possibly hope for?"

"Nothing," Tor admitted. "We know full well that you might confront Naldrum and return Kandace to Haakon for the reward he has offered. It would serve your master and your career well."

"It's a substantial reward. Haakon would be pleased with me."

"Or you might say nothing to Haakon, and simply show up at Naldrum's compound to return his two missing slaves. Either way, you would gain additional favor and power with one or the other man."

"Or?" Rota said, knowing that something better and far more intriguing was about to be offered. She enjoyed the challenge Tor and Kandace presented. Most people were far too easy.

"Or you could do what you came here to do," said Tor. "I saw you at Althing. I heard the rumors about all the silver you spent at the trade booths in Haakon's name, and the gifts you gave to various headmen. Haakon didn't send you all this way and give you that much silver just to enhance trade relations. No, it's clear that you're working on something big. Something important. Naldrum is part of your plan, whatever it is. Your knowing that Kandace is here puts Naldrum in a terrible, precarious position—which gives you an enormous amount of leverage over him. Because of his foolishness, him knowing you know it, you can control him. You can bend him to your wishes."

Rota almost laughed. "And you want in return?" she said.

"What are we to you? Slaves. Nothing. In truth, we matter little to the Jarl or to Haakon. We're amusements, or workers, easy to replace. But you have it in your power now to set us free from both of them. That is worth whatever you might ask in return."

Oh, delicious. Rota could have taken their faces in her hands and kissed them. Instead, she stood and offered space at the table where she sat. "Eat, my friends," was all she said.

. . .

As they arrived at the border of Naldrum's land, Rota gave Tor and Kandace explicit directions.

"As you know, the road now takes us directly through Naldrum's compound. It'll be dangerous for you. My wagon is the only thing big enough to conceal you both while I figure out what I'm going to do."

They had lain side by side amid the poles under the tent-wool of Rota's traveling-booth, holding hands and wincing at each rough bump along the rutted roadway. When Rota arrived at Naldrum's compound, they heard voices shouting. Now the wagon had stopped.

They recognized familiar sounds of the cook calling for eggs, the sounds of a barrel being rolled up the flagstones to the longhouse door. The sounds of Rota's horses being unharnessed, and her belongings taken into the longhouse. What was happening?

They huddled, trying not to move, to not be seen, and prayed that Rota would keep her word.

. . .

Bishop Friedrich had started his exploration of Iceland via the summer Althing festival. Since then, he had made up his mind to travel to every part of the land, looking for opportunities to make converts from the pagan folk of the land. What he had not expected was how at every turn, people would approach him, almost fearful, and ask to talk.

Icelanders typically began the conversation with the Great Settlement of Iceland several generations ago, and how their forebears had been Christian.

"My great-grandmother came here as one of the first ships from Norway. Like Aud the Deepminded, she was Christian, but her children married those who followed the old gods of Norway. I have often wondered…" After that, an invitation would be issued, to please visit this valley or that relative, to stay for a week or so at various farms and chieftains' homesteads and engage in conversation.

To preach, and Friedrich hoped, to convert.

He noted, however, that a troubling addendum usually followed those invitations. "What with the crop failures, and the troubles in our land, perhaps our old gods are not as helpful as they once were. Perhaps we should give yours a try again."

How did he explain to a worried people that worship was not the same as trading a lame horse for a different one? That professing the faith in the One True God was not a whim because of a bad harvest, to be dropped again when times were better? How could he tell them that their gods—in whom the peoples of Norway and Sweden and the old tribes of Germania had put their faith for so many millennia, *did not even exist?*

Such a statement would not endear him to his listeners. Little by little, Friedrich had come to realize that they saw the Lord Jesus simply as a convenient addition to their family shrines. What an abysmal failure of his great plans to follow the example of Saint Patrick, who had gone to the Eire lands and found triumph there!

But Friedrich had also grown to admire how these stubborn Icelanders celebrated the wisdom of the being they called Odin. They admired the strength and honor of Thor, put their hope in Freya for children, prayed for justice from the one they called Forseti. To say to them that those creatures of virtue had never existed, and that their wisdom, honor, compassion, justice came from imagined idols—and then to mentally slay those beings? Such an undertaking was a far more delicate matter than Friedrich had reckoned on.

Yes, he had come to Iceland with good intentions. Certainly, converting pagan followers to his faith was the joyous center of that plan. But Friedrich could barely admit the truth to himself. Was it fair to take away their many hopes for help, in favor of a single God who promised eternal salvation after death—but who held only mysterious, undecipherable parables? What help were parables to those whose children cried for food and who, looking in the larder, saw dwindling sacks of grain and only a few withered carrots on the shelves?

Given that, Friedrich even understood, reluctantly, why the people of this beautiful but harsh land had turned from Christian beliefs back to old pagan ways. A hard winter, a harvest of hunger, and they would grasp in desperation for any help—just as they grasped now at his words for hope. His most enthusiastic prospective convert to date had been Ankya, but Friedrich had put as much ground as possible between himself and that disturbed young woman.

The comfortable monastery in Germania suddenly seemed so far away. In his memory, Friedrich walked through the quiet of well-tended gardens inside the high old walls that kept out the noise of the city. He imagined the steady drone of honeybees—how he missed that sound! —drifting among apple trees and squash blossoms. The sweet smell of fresh-cut wood in the cooper's shop where brothers fitted together oak staves, making barrels to hold their renowned beer. The peaceful rhythm of the day that started with prayers at *matins* and ending with *compline.* The quiet chants of evensong. The smell of beeswax candles burning in his chambers. The taste of the

Memories tightened his throat. Friedrich swallowed hard.

His lips moved in quiet prayer. "Lord, let me not fail by doubting Your will. Whatever work you sent me here to do, please help me to do it." The vision that had come to him telling him to go to Iceland still raised goose bumps on his arms.

Friedrich called to the man who guided them along the valley pass. "How much longer until we arrive at our destination?"

"Another day or so to the settlement at Akureyri," he ventured.

"Come, Konradsson," Friedrich called. "We must ride faster. It would be good to eat fresh fish instead of another meal of boiled eggs." He straightened his shoulders and sat taller in his saddle. The Lord had sent him on this mission. Who was he to question God?

But despite his resolution, Friedrich could not rid himself of the shadow which had come over his spirit. Their horses' hooves thudded soft on the heavy grassland trails, a calming rhythm that also brought back memories of his own country. Instead of looking forward to the place where they rode, Friedrich's thoughts drifted again and again towards home.

. . .

Rota's assistant lifted the canvas tent fabric and beckoned to Kandace and Tor. They stretched sore muscles and clambered from the pile of booth-poles, fearing the worst.

"Come here," she said. "My mistress needs you."

. . .

Unhappy, feeling betrayed, Kandace and Tor stood facing Naldrum, the two of them almost as shocked as he was. Naldrum had gone from purple to almost gray. He struggled to stand, and even to breathe.

"What is this trickery?" he gurgled. "Why are these two here?"

"I was hoping you might tell me that," Rota said, her voice as smooth as cream.

. . .

Chapter Twenty-Nine

Naldrum's mouth hung open. He could not think of a lie fast enough, or an excuse.

"You are surprised to see them?" Rota asked. "I thought you might be pleased to learn that your slave man is not lost in the snows of Hekla, but is here, hale and hearty."

"Of course." Naldrum could get out nothing more.

"And this woman was with him. I thought you say that he had a companion—another damned nuisance slave, I believe were your words—with him?"

"I have many slaves. I don't keep track of them all."

Rota feigned surprise. "You didn't notice a woman whose skin is as impressively black as lava sands? Sitting right here at your table, night after night? Dressed as a nun? You didn't notice *that?*"

Naldrum, sulking, stared at the opposite wall. "What of it? I suppose she may have been visiting my household for a short while. Is there some crime in that?"

"Of course not, my dear *gothi* Naldrum. But Jarl Haakon has been deeply concerned about her safety. He would undoubtedly be glad to know she is found, and safe. A man of his wealth might offer a substantial reward for such news."

"Well, you can just run along and tell him that," Naldrum replied. "I don't *expect* any sort of reward, but of course, gifts are always appreciated."

"*Substantial* ones," Rota tempted him. "He has been *quite* worried about her!"

"If he so wishes." Naldrum considered the jeweled rings on his fingers.

"No doubt. Just the one small matter, though. Perhaps you could help me."

Naldrum pursed his lips. *Ah now we negotiate.* He felt pleased to be on familiar territory at which he excelled. He looked down his nose at Rota, puffing with his own prestige. "Anything you wish, lovely woman."

"Perhaps you can help me explain to the Jarl exactly *how* Kandace came to be living in your dwelling, so far from his home?"

Naldrum waved the question away as if it was of little consequence. "By ship, I'm sure. Unless nuns can fly?" He laughed, pleased with his joke.

A cold silence from Rota. "Perhaps we should start before that. At her sudden departure from Norway, perhaps? A man called Tiller apparently took her from the safety of the Jarl's home. I understand that he brought her here, directly to you, at your request. And just this morning, you described Haakon's valued property as *your* slave? So very perplexing."

Naldrum had no training in self-control. "That is a rude, rude question! You're twisting my words!" He swept his arm, sending dishes and mead horns flying from the table. His youngest wife covered her ears at his shouting.

Rota remained lounging on a cushion, smiling happily. Tor and Kandace stood like stone, staring with disgust at Naldrum in full tantrum.

Rota stretched and got up. She strolled to the hospitality table and considered the spread, her mouth downturned. "Yes, I'd love something to eat, thank you, but something better than this mess," she said. "Bring me a flask of your best imported wine, and have your cook roast for me the heart of a lamb. In the meantime, we will speak about you returning what you stole from Haakon."

. . .

Rota put her heels to her horse's flanks as she rode from Naldrum's compound. Tor followed her, along with Kandace. Rota had enjoyed seeing Naldrum's expression when she called for Naldrum's prize mare to be saddled as Tor's mount, and for Kandace to ride Ankya's new gelding.

"It's nothing personal. Just collateral of a sort," Rota said to Naldrum. "It's good for your slave man to be considering the cost of your favorite horses if he does not return promptly. He'll ride faster that way, I think."

Tor's heart sank. Rota was as wicked as Naldrum. She had betrayed them both.

. . .

Ankya had been delighted to see Kandace again. Now it was all so much worse, seeing Kandace about to ride away again. Ankya squeezed her fat puppy. It yelped as her fingers around its ribs pressed too hard.

Angry, Ankya pictured the road along which Kandace would ride. Her puppy yelped again.

"I got my father to go to the valley farms," she told it. "I got him to say I could go too. I asked people about that healer Aldís. I would have found her."

The puppy squirmed, protesting.

Ankya's eyes filled with tears.

"No one loves me." Ankya buried her face in the puppy's warmth. "My father sees me as a prize, to earn him some kind of profit. Kel thinks I am a child, and now Kandace is leaving me too."

She made the sign of the cross as Kandace rode away. *Heart, pubis, nipple, nipple,* and wondered if one could die of heartbreak.

. . .

Rota waited until her flag-bearer had cleared the last markers of Naldrum's lands. She waved her servants away so that she could speak to Tor and Kandace in private.

"Well done, both of you," she said, as Tor translated for Kandace. "I think your headman may need a bit of time to recover from his excess of temper." She permitted herself a small laugh, then grew serious. "Tor, you heard what I said about you returning to Naldrum. You're his property. Much as I might want, I can't just take you."

He had no answer. Cruel though it was, the law sided with Rota.

"I did, however, make it clear to Naldrum that I intend to check on you regularly, to ensure that you suffer no ill consequences from him. I told him that he cannot even so much as raise his voice to you. That's all the protection I can give you, but he will abide by it, I am certain, for he will suffer much if he betrays this command."

"It is not my safety that matters, Rota," Tor said.

Kandace looked from one to the other. "What is she saying? What happens to us now?"

"I don't know," he said.

Kandace began to cry. Realizing Naldrum's desire to avoid the woman at the valley farm, it had been Kandace who on Hekla had proposed seeking shelter with the very woman the headman clearly feared. *To go into Hell itself*, she had said to Tor. In the snow and desperate, the idea had somehow made sense. Now, seeing Tor's sad face and Rota's implacable expression made Kandace fear the worst had happened.

"She's going to send me back to the Jarl, and send you back to Naldrum, isn't she?" Kandace guessed. "I'll kill myself if she does that. I'll throw myself overboard as soon as we get to sea. Her precious Jarl will never see me alive again. Tell her that."

Tor closed his eyes. There were limits to what one man could translate.

. . .

With no hope or ideas, Tor could not ride on and on, dreading what lay ahead. What could he do if Rota confirmed that they were heading towards a ship? Tor imagined himself leaping towards Rota's horse, taking the reins, pulling her horse towards his. Her knife hung at her side. He could have it at her throat in an instant, and fend off her guards. With a weapon, he could destroy all of them, Tor knew in his heart.

What is about this savage land and its people that has me thinking like a madman? Yet he knew he would do anything to keep Kandace from being taken away again, including murder. He tried to not think of Rota being dead by his hand.

He reined in his horse. “Stop! I need to know!”

Rota had been waiting for the question. She recognized in herself a kind of meanness, knowing the fear the nun and Tor must be feeling. Still, she could not help pretending to be confused at what Tor was asking. Rota made him squirm for it until at last shame overcame her.

“Your headman believes I’ll have Kandace on a fast ship to Lade Garde. I intend for him to think that, and to let him fester, worrying about what Haakon will do to him.”

Tor hesitated at the glimmer of hope. “You said ‘he believes.’ Am I hearing that you may *not* return her?”

“I’m equally sure that this woman Kandace dreads going back to Haakon. I don’t blame her. He’s a rutting boar, and it’s only a matter of time until he savages her.”

Fear beat alongside the tiny flicker of hope in Tor’s heart.

“What really happens now?” he asked.

“I have no intention of returning Kandace to the Jarl, for personal reasons that I won’t discuss with you,” Rota replied. “But I need Naldrum to *believe* I’ve sent her back. How will he know? He’ll never dare raise the subject with Haakon!” She laughed. “Since you seem to care so much about Kandace’s wellbeing, I would advise you to get her as far from Naldrum as possible. Find her somewhere safe to stay, then return to your master Naldrum, and inform him that I put her on a ship to the Jarl and continued on my way. Naldrum has no way of knowing otherwise. Do you know anywhere she might go?"

. . .

Rota had not seen a kiss like that for a long time. She put her hand up to halt their entourage. The riders waited, silent, watching as Tor and Kandace held one another, sobbing with relief.

Rota watched too. Her face had returned to its usual cold mask. A sarcastic thought flitted. *It seems I was correct that he cares for her wellbeing.* No one could see the longing that lay beneath her practiced expression.

What does it feel like, to be loved like that? Rota wondered.

. . .

Rota told her guards to wait for her at a fork in the road. Only three of them—Tor, Kandace and Rota—followed the almost-invisible track that led to the widow's home.

They came to within shouting distance of the longhouse.

"We'll separate from you here," Tor said. "This way leads to another valley, and another, secluded." It did not. The track led only to the widow's house, but better to be cautious. "As soon as I find a place to settle Kandace, I'll take the horses back to Naldrum." He held Rota's bridle, looked up at her with gratitude, and started to say his thanks.

"The less I know, the better," she cut off his words. "One cannot be too careful dealing with snakes like Haakon and Naldrum."

As Kandace and Tor rode out of sight, Rota drew a deep breath and relaxed in the fresh autumn air, enjoying a short time of being alone.

That vile Haakon. How had her twin sister Tora ever fallen in love with such a man? Haakon's messenger about the Nubian had told her more, over beer and wine that night, of how Tora hated the Nubian, and how jealous she had been of Haakon's favorite new prize.

Happy birthday, my sweet sister, Rota thought. *Your cheating husband will never lay eyes on this dusky treasure ever again.*

Rota laughed to herself. Best of all, the sheepish Naldrum would now follow her every command, terrified about what message she might send Haakon.

Rota pulled a bloody rag from her pouch and wrapped it around her hand. What did Tora always say? *Deception relies on small details*. She waved gaily to the valley were Tor and Kandace were mere dots on the horizon, then turned her horse and rode back to her entourage, unhurried.

. . .

"What happened, mistress?" her guard asked. "Where are they? Where are the horses?"

Rota tossed her head and laughed. "The horses have run off. But they have Naldrum's brand. Someone will return them to him."

"You're hurt!" he cried, seeing the blood on the rag. "You should have let me come with you!"

Don't worry, I'm fine. He was big, and the attack came fast, but he's not much of a fighter. And the woman, *ffffft*." Rota blew through her teeth.

"Really? They are dead?" He stuttered a little, as he often did when nervous. His mistress Rota had a lethal side. "I should have done it for you."

"Oh, it's good for me to keep in practice. It's just a scratch." Rota tied the rag more tightly around her hand. "Look, already the blood has stopped."

When her guard turned and rode forward again, Rota touched a finger to a tear that ran down her cheek, thinking of Tor's expression as he had turned to ride away. Tor loved Kandace, but in that instant, he had loved Rota, too. His eyes had filled with adoring gratitude. *To be loved by someone like that.*

Rota pushed the hood from her head and let her hair blow in the breeze. She did not deceive herself with hopes of such romance. *I'd ruin a man like Tor. Better for those of his ilk to love good women. Not vipers like me.*

. . .

Chapter Thirty

Bishop Friedrich sagged in his saddle as he and the young priest Konradsson left the family with whom they had spent the last two days. As they rode, Friedrich began to murmur to himself. At first, Konradsson ignored it, assuming that the older bishop was saying prayers. As the mutters grew louder, Konradsson thought that the bishop might be distressed.

"What is it, Father?" Konradsson asked, but the bishop seemed deep in thought, and made no reply.

They continued, winding along the broad valley under clear blue skies. Konradsson tried not to watch but was unable to stop himself.

They crossed a burbling stream. The bishop said nothing about the power of water to heal, as he inevitably did. Konradsson dropped back a little, so that he could keep an eye on the bishop unobserved. Soon, Friedrich began to sway back and forth on his horse.

The younger monk tried to make conversation, hoping to distract Friedrich from whatever troubled him.

"That fine farmer last night. She had so little to cook with, but it tasted good." The woman who worked the farm had given them measures of beer she had brewed, and warm flat loaves of oat bannock.

"The wine and the wafer," Friedrich muttered.

"She had only a few eggs, but she boiled them all for us." Was the bishop even listening? Konradsson raised his voice. "She offered some of her chickens for us to take with us, but I told her to please keep them, because she had too few in the flock to share."

"If the mother is sitting on the eggs, you shall not take the mother with the young—" A snatch of biblical verse Konradsson recognized.

"Father, please look at me. Are you all right? You seem not yourself."

Friedrich stared at Konradsson as if he did not recognize the young man. "No. I am not all right." His eyes wandered, full of distress and confusion. "She had the dragons carved on her door—like all the others! She had the graven images in her house—like all the others!" He pulled on his horse's reins and the animal reared a little, stopped short. "But she gave us the wine and the wafer. All she had—"

He swung off the horse, dropped to stand in the roadway. "We carry gold in our bags, *gold,* in the hopes of buying land to build a first church here. We give nothing to the people who have sheltered us, save our thanks and prayers. But they have given to us of *all they have!*"

The blood beat in his temples and Friedrich found it hard to breathe. *More blessed to give than to receive.*

He haphazardly threw his horse's reins towards Konradsson and crossed himself. He began to say the words of confession. Sweat broke out on his brow, and Friedrich wiped it with a shaking hand, and confessed, and confessed again. He half-fell from his horse and stood on the roadway.

I thought I came to prove my faith. My belief that as one of those loyal to God, I should command the dark forces of this place to yield to Him.

I was wrong.

The reason he had come had had nothing to do with God. It has to do with his own pride. *I was so wrong. I came here to judge a people I did not know. I came here believing myself superior to them.*

All at once he gave a great cry and sank to his knees, right in the middle of the road. He stayed there, praying, as the sun moved across the sky.

Konradsson dismounted as well. He held the reins to both horses, fretting about what to do. Finally, he hobbled the horses and knelt beside the bishop, and his lips moved along with the torrent of words pouring from Friedrich.

. . .

Friedrich had prayed all day but it had brought no relief. His young companion still knelt beside the bishop, fatigued and aching. Several times, Friedrich had urged the younger monk to leave him, to go on to the next home, but Konradsson had demurred.

"No, Father Friedrich. Whatever trials you are suffering, let me suffer them with you." He could not bring himself to ask his mentor what could have caused such anguish—and Friedrich was too ashamed of himself to offer an explanation.

The bishop began again. "Oh Lord Jesus, Redeemer and Savior, forgive my sins—"

Konradsson shivered in the brisk wind and pulled his sleeves over his chilly hands. His lips moved silently along with the bishop, and he wondered, but did not dare to ask.

. . .

Sunset streaked the sky, and still Friedrich begged for atonement. To Konradsson's relief, a family came along the edge of their fields, carrying a pitcher of beer, looking about wide-eyed.

The great dark bulk of the bishop kneeling, swaying and moaning in the road caused them to clutch at their throats in horror and shrink back.

"What is that thing with you?" the farmer asked, her voice fearful.

"My employer," Konradsson replied.

"Oh, just a man!" she cried, relieved. "We need to get you both inside!"

Konradsson whispered to them that the bishop steadfastly refused to move. At last the farmer had planted her feet and refused to budge unless they came to her home.

"It's *álfablót* tonight, stranger. We're not leaving the two of you out here." Outnumbered, the bishop let them drag him to his feet He trudged along, his lips still moving.

At the longhouse door, he waved away the family's urging to come inside and choose a place on the sleeping benches in the warm home. "No, kind sir. You have done more than you should. I will stay in the stable. It was good enough for our Lord."

"Father, I will stay with you." Konradsson offered, hoping the bishop would refuse. Of course, he no longer believed in the álfablót—but still, that meant that All Hallows Eve had come. Even if he did not believe that trolls and dark-elves walked about, still, the souls of the undead were said to stream across the land tonight. He crossed himself.

Friedrich regarded Konradsson as if the young priest was someone Friedrich knew but could not place. “No. No, you stay here where it is warm.”

The freeholder’s husband and Konradsson watched as Friedrich staggered across the field towards the goat shed.

“No one sleeps outside the longhouse tonight,” the man observed. “I do not think your friend is at all well.”

“I do not think so either.”

“Perhaps we should send a slave woman to him?”

“For whatever purpose? He refuses to eat.”

“To lie with him. To keep him warm.” The man elbowed Konradsson. “Cheer your friend up a bit.”

Konradsson registered shock at the suggestion. “Oh no!” he cried. “He would not want that at all, I am certain!”

A quick side glance at Konradsson. “Ah. I thought perhaps.”

“You don’t understand,” Konradsson cried. “He is a man of God—and has made a vow not to lie with women!”

“Suit yourself,” the man said. “If he wants to freeze in his unholy hell, let him. Just as well. I’m loathe to leave a valuable slave outside during álfablót anyway! Now come inside, young man. You don’t look so well yourself. It’s simple in here, but we’re happy to share.” He stepped back and held the longhouse door open. Konradsson, with a glance at the dragons and serpents carved into the wooden frame, went through to fire and warmth and something that smelled quite heavenly.

. . .

Friedrich threw himself on the freezing stone floor of the goat shed, but did not feel the cold. His head swam. The bishop frowned in the darkness, trying to make sense of his confusion.

He and Konradsson had travelled along river valleys and fjord margins, moving from farm to farm every day or so. They had followed the same pattern, day after day: bid farewell to the family who had given them shelter, ask directions to the next homestead, and set off for there.

Upon arrival, Friedrich would ask Konradsson to introduce them—the young monk's native Icelandic far exceeded the small vocabulary the bishop had garnered since their journey had started—and to ask for lodging for a night or two.

The farmers invariably complied. At first Friedrich had not understood the law of hospitality, unspoken but of critical importance, that each homestead must offer food and shelter for any travelers who asked. But even after Konradsson had explained it to him, the bishop still found himself regularly astonished at the warmth of the welcome they received.

We explained that we worship our Lord, the one true God, and they did not argue. We explained to them that they, too, must convert to our faith, for it was critical to their souls.

He had expected protests. He had braced himself for arguments, for forcible ejections into the night.

He had not expected the heads nodding, the willingness to kneel, to say the unfamiliar prayers. He had nearly wept with joy to see them fashion small crosses from bits of twig and thread, or from straw. The first time such acceptance had happened, and the next and the next, Friedrich had been ecstatic with joy—until the time for the evening meal, when the family idols were still offered bits of meat and mead, and songs were sung to them, and thanks were given, and requests made.

Instead of getting rid of their idolatrous tokens, each family had added the small crosses to the small shelf that held a collection of icons for their own gods, and prayed to all of them together.

Friedrich mumbled to himself, recalling his first struggles. "I felt anger at them. They did such insults to our Lord." But he had watched their faces in the firelight, earnest with need, tentative in hope, full of love for the unseen beings that they believed cared about them.

"They are just human beings," he said, half in prayer, half in argument, with whom he knew not.

He had seen other expressions.

The woman at the farm they had just left, the one who Konradsson had spoken of. She had opened her storeroom to make the evening meal and *tssked* a quiet dismay at the contents—or lack thereof. Yet she had fed them of what she had. The mother who had cradled a sick daughter, holding in her hand a ragged bundle of bone and hair and herb, weeping to Freya to help the child live. The man who held his elderly father's hand, who tenderly fed the weak old man with a spoon.

He mused in confusion. "We are told that only those who believe in Jesus will go to heaven. But these people, Lord, they have fed us, when they have so little themselves. Is that not what your Son taught? They have sheltered us, when they have had sick and old ones to attend to. They have done everything—*everything*—that Jesus taught. Are they to be denied entrance to your Kingdom simply because they never heard the Word? How is that fair, Father? Konradsson and I are the first to preach to them. How cruel it seems to deny these good people, when so many of your own defy what you teach, yet you profess that they are already forgiven, be they murderers, even!" Friedrich thought of burghers in faraway Germania who cheated the church-tithe, and of kings who professed the faith but warred ruthlessly. Of even those in monasteries who took money from the poor-box and spent it on fine things for themselves and their whores. He seethed, asking again, "How is that right, when *so many* of your own do far less good, and far more harm?"

The bishop had not noticed that his voice had risen nearly the level of an angry roar. Taken aback, he spoke in a whisper. "And I, who thought to come here judging them—*yes, despite your commandment*—I *did* judge them, thinking them to be lacking in humanity."

Where had it all started, this passion to reform?

"I heard young Konradsson's confession when he came to our monastery! He did not know it was I who sat in the confessional. He spoke with great pain. I know what some of these people—these men—did to him. And I felt something akin to hatred towards them for it. And when I prayed on the matter, I resolved to bring Konradsson here to face his past and finally overcome the terrors it holds for him. I thought he and I would 'forgive' these people for the heathens that they are." His voice rose again in frustration. "But I know now that I did not really *want* to forgive them! I had judged them, and found them wanting as human beings. And now? I have seen such goodness in them instead of the evil I expected! Of course, some are evil—there are evil men and women everywhere—but most are decent, hardworking, kind people. I have seen so much kindness and generosity—and—and—and—" he broke down and covered his face in his hands, filled with doubt.

What Friedrich had told himself would be evil in nature had turned out to be good. What he had believed was true about those who would be given or denied the path to heaven, he now questioned. Every bit of faith on which he had built his life had begun to crumble about him. In that cold stable, the renowned bishop Friedrich scrabbled in despair, far from all he held dear.

"I am lost, Lord," he cried. For the first time in a long, long time, Friedrich felt his own soul in deep need of forgiveness—but forgiveness for what, and to whom he prayed, he barely knew.

. . .

Chapter Thirty-One

Naldrum still felt angry, just as he had since Rota rode away with Kandace and Tor. He paced the longhouse, staring out the door and fuming, cursing Tor, cursing Kandace, cursing Rota, cursing Haakon, cursing Tiller. He knew his own actions had been reasonable and well-considered, but schemers and saps around him had all but ruined his plans.

"Every single one of them has tried to shame me! I will exact revenge on any who even dare to *think* of defying me!"

Drikke had said that Tor had attacked him and run away on Hekla. Unforgiveable. He would beat Tor within an inch of his life when he came back. Tiller had taken the wrong woman from Haakon. Look what trouble that had caused with Rota—and now both Rota and the woman he could have sold for a fortune were gone because of Tor. Kel had grown more and more disrespectful. Naldrum resolved to find a way to hurt his steward in a way that would also shame him. And even Ankya had shown signs of disobedience. Blame for that probably lay with Kel as well. Naldrum counted all the wrongs done to him, grinding his teeth.

"And that damned bishop with h is stupid white-christ beliefs! He got here just in time to interfere with Kandace arriving! His kind have been here since the first of our people came to our land, but did they last? No! Because our gods are *better!* We are pagan!"

Naldrum did not admit to himself that he hated paying homage to any deity. Invoking the gods was more a matter of business. Say the words others wished to hear, and reap the profit from pretended devotion. For the first time, he considered using the gods differently, as a means of punishing those who had acted against him.

"I have killed enough sacrifice animals on their behalf. They owe me," Naldrum said to his ale-horn. "As for bad harvests and famine, they come and go. Some, surely, will starve. Perhaps many. Is that any fault of mine? Of course not! And is it such a tragedy? People die every year anyway, don't they?"

What mattered was how to *use* famine. "If there is any constant in the world, it is that in every circumstance there is opportunity for wise men to glean profit." He considered his words. Brilliant, except for one change. *Glean* implied poor folk going over a field, searching for stray grains. "There is opportunity for great profit for men of vision," he amended. *Perfect.*

He and his family would have plenty of the best foods to eat. His slaves would have enough to keep them working. Any extra beyond that, he might sell, if he could get the right price for it.

"Food will be at a premium this winter," Naldrum reminded himself, pleased with his great storeroom. "And those I help—and I will help only those who have the ability to help me in return, those who are already wealthy—they will know their debt to me." An excellent prospect all around!

But for once, even thoughts of wealth to be earned did not console Naldrum. He wanted more. Naldrum thought again of the bishop.

"I can tell you this!" he shouted. "Whatever that man has, I want! People reverence him! He wears no gold. He carries no sword. He wields no lash, yet they kneel as if they are his slaves— and *willing* slaves, at that!"

The chieftain drank deep of the bitter nectar of jealousy. He pondered the means to power and profit. As the season of growing yielded to the cold months of autumn and winter, Naldrum thought, obsessively, of those he admired and desired to emulate. Men like Haakon, with regard for none but themselves. *Wise men.*

. . .

Without Kandace to flaunt in front of the valley famers now, and with rumors of the curse sweeping from farm to farm, Naldrum sulked through the harvest supper celebration. He paid lip service to the álfablót ceremony, even giving the ceremonial knife to Ankya, who barely concealed her joy at being the one to cut the throat of the kid goat and collect its blót for the ritual.

He barely paid attention to the annual sheep roundup. Because he never rode out to the far fields, because he did not go into the *rett,* the sheep-separating pens, Naldrum never noticed the furtive shepherd named Sauthi, who kept his hood low and his face averted.

Kel, overseeing the rounding up and separating of sheep, saw his reclusive friend Sauthi. As he had every year, Kel wondered why Sauthi kept so far from all the festivities that accompanied the boisterous days. But swamped by work, he brushed the question aside as he had every other year.

. . .

On the last night of the *réttir,* when all the sheep had been sorted by their earmarks, the farmers of the valley crowded into Naldrum's longhouse for the closing party. Naldrum went through the motions of lifting the beer to accept toasts in his name. Afterwards, he sat brooding on his high-seat.

"This valley bores me. Leaders of other lands have far more," he confided to his youngest wife, the one with thieves' eyes.

"You have the winter and the spring until Althing," she said. "You say you want to be Lawspeaker. What have you done to make it happen? Your failed butter tour?"

Naldrum flinched. He had not told his wife the reason his tour had been cut short, but she had learned the reason from household gossip.

"Why don't you use this time to plan instead of sulking all day? Haakon wants an ally. Rota says it's you. Act like it. Otherwise I want to hear no more about your grand aspirations."

She was the youngest of his wives. The others Naldrum mostly ignored. This one he respected and feared, because in his heart, Naldrum knew she was tougher than he—and that made him love her, as might a child who craves love from a cruel parent.

"All right," he replied. "I will erupt from this valley, come spring. I will smother others, spreading influence like lava from the forge-fires below the earth. I will acquire more power than anyone in this backwards land has ever dreamed possible. And I will let nothing stop me."

. . .

Chapter Thirty-Two

Kel made excuses every day to ride away from the longhouse. A fence in a far field needed inspecting. A delivery wagon had broken down and needed his supervision. A lease-holder needed assistance with a rotted roof. He wondered why he had never before taken advantage of the quieter work of winter to get away from Naldrum for days at a time.

. . .

"Didn't we stop here for something a while back?" Kel asked his horse Thor-Thunder. He did not think it was a child-claim farm. Each of those unfortunate locations of the last many years were burned in his memory, and he avoided them at all costs. This farm had a pleasant feel to is, as if something good had happened here.

He and Thunder had trotted some distance past the farm when Kel remembered. He reined in Thunder.

"Of course! We always take this road home from Althing. Remember, Thunder? Stupid Drikke managed to get his stable-boy's leg broken right. These rocks here, are where the boy fell."

Now Kel remembered why the place had a happy feeling. He had seen Aldís there. She had galloped up on a borrowed horse, answering one of those strange calls in her head that help was needed.

"We could go back for a bit," he said to Thunder. *She's not there, you fool,* Kel reminded himself. *And she doesn't want to see you.*

"I'm just going to check in and see how the boy is doing." His chin set, stubborn. "It's the least I can do."

. . .

People stood around the stone yard of the longhouse, tossing wheat into the air from wide shallow baskets. Kel realized they must have finished their threshing. Time to winnow the grain from the chaff.

A few faces looked up, acknowledged a visitor, and returned to work. One dropped his basket and ran to Kel. It was the boy who had had the broken leg. He practically knelt in front of Kel.

"I don't know how to thank you," he said over and over. "I've wanted to thank you so long."

"Get up, son," said Kel. "No need to thank me. I just did what I thought was right. How's the leg coming?"

"I can't even tell which one was broken and which wasn't," the boy said. "Can jump and run as well on both. Your healer friend Aldís saved me."

"And the dog bite? That healed as well?"

"Just a bit of mark left is all." The boy lifted his tunic, showed the line of small pale scars where the dog's teeth had closed on his hip. "Aldís stayed with me the whole time. She rubbed oils into it, and hot water. It never got infected. Healed up as nice as can be."

Kel smiled at hearing Aldís's name. "She's good at what she does, eh?"

"Better than good. I want to learn to do what she does." His eyes grew moist. "Thanks to you and her, I have a chance. If you hadn't freed me from Drikke—"

"It's behind you. How's this family to live with?"

"They're kind. Only thing they hate in the world is Naldrum and his family. They've welcomed me as if I was one of their own. I'm so grateful."

As they spoke, the boy's foster father joined them. "Good to see you, Steward Kel." He held out his hand, and they shook.

"What's that look for?" Kel asked.

"Just that you may not realize that you're getting quite a reputation among some of the valley folk. Word came a while back that it's not only our boy here you've stood up for. That you also intervened in Naldrum beating one of his slaves."

"I did. Not a big deal."

"It's a bigger deal than you realize, Kel. I'm going to give you a bit of advice, and I want you to seriously consider it."

"And that is?"

"Only a landowner can be elected as a headman. You've been to Althing often enough that you're familiar with the *gothar* who represent the many valleys and settlements in our land. Some are like Naldrum, greedy and thinking only of themselves, even if they hide it. Some are fine leaders. We need more of the latter sort. You'd be a welcome addition to their number. Is there any way you could gain ownership of a farm? An elderly father, or an uncle or aunt, perhaps?"

Kel stepped back, more than a little surprised at the idea. "I've never considered such a thing. Me, a *gothi?* For a long time, I figured

I'd grow old as Naldrum's steward, but that's not going to happen. I never really thought about what came next."

"We all have to earn our way. Farming is hard, but it's an honest living, at least. Not as hard as serving a man you despise."

"There is that. But no, I'm not in line to inherit acreage from anyone. Getting land presents a big obstacle."

"I don't pretend to know how it might come about," said the farmer.

"But think about it. Lots of us long for an alternative to Naldrum, but too few of us are leaders—and even fewer have the potential to challenge Naldrum and defeat him. You might be just the fellow. Keep it in mind, will you?"

Kel remembered a long-ago conversation with Tor. *Set your intentions. Don't worry about how a thing might come to be. Just decide what you hope to do, and you will be guided.* Something like that.

"I will." He clasped the farmer's hand again, gave it a firm shake. "I will."

"Good. Now turn that beautiful horse of yours loose in the meadow and plan to stay with us for supper. I won't take no for an answer."

. . .

He had not expected to see Aldís at the table.

"I… I…" Kel stuttered. "I'm not stalking you. I didn't know you'd be here."

"I'm not upset. You have as much right to visit this family as I do. They hold you in pretty high regard."

"I'm grateful. Not much of that in my life, I can tell you." An impulsive idea came to him as he thought of the good feeling he had had passing the farm, the desire to revisit it. "Aldís, I was riding past here, and I felt almost a compulsion to stop. A good feeling."

"Is that a question?"

"I guess it is. Is that what it's like for you? That feeling of needing to help with a sickness or an injury? As if something is pulling you?"

"Something of the sort. It's a mystery to me, but yes. I just feel a feeling, and I follow it. I always feel a little stupid until it proves itself to be true." She blushed a little. *Why am I blushing at Kel Coesson? Stop that!*

The farmer and his wrinkled old mother exchanged glances. Her eyes twinkled.

Aldís turned to the elderly woman. "How did the winnowing go today?"

"We should be finished by *lauger*-day. I hope! My hair feels as if it's full of chaff. I can't wait to wash it." She turned her smiling old face back to Kel. "Did my son tell you that news of your recent exploits preceded you?"

Now it was Kel's turn to redden. "No need to talk about it."

The old woman leaned in to Aldís conspiratorially. "He's a bit of a hero. First a friend to the downtrodden at the holmgang duels at Althing, and now a man who stands up for those who have no power."

"Please," Kel said. "Aldís fought in those duels as well. She deserves as much credit as I do." He stood and cleared his *sup* bowl from the table. "I need to go check on Thunder."

As Kel left the longhouse and walked through the cool evening air to where his horse knickered, the old woman kept her grip on Aldís's arm. She fully intended to make sure this most excellent woman knew exactly what a good man Kel was.

Aldís listened, unwilling but surprised. When the time came for all to find places on the sleeping benches, she took her traveling bag and slipped out the longhouse door before anyone noticed.

It was one thing sharing a meal with the new favorite of the valleys. But spending the night with him sleeping a short distance away was not something she felt ready for—or wanted.

Which way to go? She chose east, and struck out on the quiet track. Enough moon to light the quiet track, she knew. It would rise shortly, and was waxing gibbous, so nearly full.

But in addition to the moon and the quiet for thinking, Aldís received another reward for her lonely travel. In the northern sky to her right, the dancing lights that sometimes came with the cold months began to stream upwards into the sky.

But not just the usual glow of one or two colors blending together. A dizzying array of colors drenched the dark skies with ribbons, swirls, shafts, rivers, fingers, flows of glorious wonder. Aldís stopped walking and stood awestruck in the center of the track, face lifted to the sky.

She found herself wanting to go back to the farm, to call all outside to see the glory in the night sky.

To tell Kel.

Just keep walking, Aldís told herself. No need to act like a lovestruck girl. But as she walked, she thought of how it had made her feel when Kel fought the *holmgangers,* and how he had paid for this farm family to take in Drikke's injured slave boy. Something about the majesty of the northern lights stirred an old feeling in Aldís's heart.

I loved Kel because of what Althing means, she knew. Maybe the Kel she had once loved was shaking off the loathsome crust of Naldrum.

Maybe not. Maybe there was too much she could never forgive him for—but she felt, for the first time in years, that she could manage civility.

. . .

Kel brushed off invitations to stay longer at the farm. "If I do, you'll put me to work winnowing. I much prefer heavy work," he protested, knowing that they had more than enough hands to finish the task.

The former slave boy walked with Kel to the meadow to get Thunder. "I'm never going to forget you, you know," he said. "I don't mean to impose, but it would mean a great deal to me if you'd stop in every so often. These folks think highly of you as well. Please let us host you when you travel through here."

The request brought an unfamiliar hoarseness to Kel's chest. "I'd like that," he said. On impulse, he stopped and turned to the boy.

"I've no children. No family of my own. Maybe I could be a kind of uncle to you."

An eager smile lit the young man's features. "Even though these folks have taken me in, I've no family of my own anymore either. I'd like that very much."

They exchanged an awkward hug that did not match the glowing warmth that swelled in each one's chest afterwards.

"I'll give you my first bit of uncle advice, son," said Kel. "Adults look as if we have our lives sorted out. But we mostly haven't. Most adults are just like people your age in older skins. We are uncertain, making it up as we go along, fearful of looking stupid to others. Never be fooled by someone's age into thinking they are a good person. Never assume that years give wisdom. You think I'm a good enough fellow, but my own life is a bit of a mess right now. I don't know what my future holds, but I'm pretty sure it's going to involve a lot more chaos and unhappiness than peace and pleasantries."

The features of a young man in his teens showed exactly the kind of confusion Kel expected at such words. "Why are you telling me this?" he asked.

"Because I want you to look to your own self for wisdom and guidance first. Then look to people you *know* to be good, and learn from them, knowing that even they are imperfect people with hidden flaws. Don't assume, *ever,* that you have less value than someone else because he or she has wealth, land, prestige, or age. You matter. I matter. Aldís matters. We all matter. Even Drikke, boor that he is, matters. Find your strength and trust your gut. And always work to learn the truth instead of being deceived by assumptions."

"That's a lot to learn," the boy said, and Kel laughed.

"The fact that you realize it tells me you'll figure it all out one day. Now let's get my horse saddled and I'll give you a riding lesson before I leave."

. . .

He caught up with Aldís by the time the sun reached middle-day. *Gods, had she walked all night?*

Aldís heard the horse's hooves cantering along the track a distance away. Might be Kel. Might not. She considered stepping off into the tangle of tall blueberry bushes that lined the roadway. Kel would never see her in the thick brush.

Or I could be decent. Aldís put down her sack, shaded her eyes and waited.

. . .

Chapter Thirty-Three

Kel saw a figure standing on the roadway ahead. Even from there he could see the stubborn, half-defiant set of her body. Why was she always so defensive when he was around? She had nothing to fear from him.

Kel realized with no small amount of surprise, that although he was pleased to see Aldís so soon again, the old worry that she would run away was gone. If she stayed and talked, good. If she left, good. Something had changed.

. . .

A careful conversation, in which they spoke of small nothings. They might have been two strangers who had just met over supper last night, not two people who had lain together in love, and who had fought bitterly and said words difficult to forgive. Not two people who had wielded sword and saxe and shield together in the holmgang duels that summer.

. . .

The morning was cold but crisp, with no wind to chill the bones. They walked together in the bright sunlight, Kel leading Thunder with Aldís's pack tossed on his saddle. Their breath came from their mouths as little clouds while they talked.

. . .

A stream to cross. The curve of a hill. A wide valley. Still they walked and talked.

A horse passed them coming from the other direction, almost hidden beneath a towering load of flax bundles.

"Good day to you," said the woman leading the horse "Taking this flax to our neighbors. They have a better field for *retting* than I do."

Another person approached, his horse pulling a small cart loaded with bones. "I'm taking these to the carver for processing," he said. "Had to kill one of our horses so we'd have enough meat this winter. Might as well get every bit I can from the poor thing."

"Hard times," agreed Aldís. She asked the name of the carver, and then added, "They do good work. Tell them to make a comb for you, or a set of dice, so you have something to remember your horse by."

As they passed, Kel glanced at her. "Does everyone tell you who they are and why they're on the road?"

For the first time in ages, he saw Aldís smile at something he said. "Yes."

"I guess they know you're a good person and they can trust you." The compliment, he knew, came close to dangerous territory. She might turn on him in anger. But still, she deserved it.

"Everyone has a little bit of the sixth sense that I do," Aldís replied. "When people along the road feel the instinct to talk to me, I'm glad."

"You know, I've ridden this road several times since boy was hurt. Never had the desire to stop in before."

"That was your bit of sixth-sense talking to you. Maybe it was just the good deed of looking in on your young friend, or maybe it was something more."

Kel plunged ahead. "Don't you find it a pretty astonishing coincidence for us to run into each other several times in the space of a season?"

Aldís had been wondering the same thing. Sudden awkwardness overcame her. "One just accepts it as best one can."

Kel went at his question a different way. "But have you been at that farm for long?"

"No. Only since last Thor's day. They had started flax-cutting and appreciated the help, but no one was there who needed care with sickness or injury. Maybe we *were* supposed to meet and talk like this. That's what's so strange about these sixth-sense, second-sight communications. They're never clear. But there they are, nonetheless, calling us or warning us."

"You don't talk about it much, do you?"

"I don't. I'm never sure if they are real or not, so I feel a bit foolish sometimes saying them aloud." Aldís did not mention the call that she had felt off and on ever since last autumn, the one too faint and too different to follow.

Kel changed the subject. "The boy healed so well," he said. "I'm sort of grateful to have seen how badly he was injured before, and how sound he is now. I've heard bits of talk from time to time about the work you do. Never really had direct experience with it before. You have a gift."

She took the praise, but her lips thinned and her face grew tense. "I never meant to be a healer. Just kind of happened, after—" Aldís stopped. They had talked, those long years past, of her youthful dream of being the first woman to serve as Lawspeaker and how those hopes had been suddenly dashed. Too much had changed since then.

Kel missed her expression and change in mood. "I have to turn off on this track now," he said. "I have to say, it's been wonderful, this bit of walking and talking. Thank you, Aldís."

"I've enjoyed it too, Kel Coesson," she replied. A measured response, in which he heard no feeling, but not hatred either. It was the best Kel had had from her in ages.

He grinned, mounted Thunder, and saluted Aldís. As he rode away, his chest filled with happiness. He resisted the urge to turn around and wave, but he did lift his hand once more in a wave, fingers spread wide. *Fare well, friend.*

Aldís shouldered her bag again. No particular destination called. With nowhere she needed to go and nothing she needed to do, Aldís walked until she saw a bit of flat grass a little way off the track She spread her blanket and stretched out, her face to the mild sun and her hands open to the sky, and gave herself time to sort out what had just happened.

The events that had destroyed the love and trust between her and Kel could never be changed, but Aldís reminded herself that grass eventually grew over fields completely destroyed by fire. She thought of the people she knew, the friendships she had. Plenty of acquaintances who were glad of seeing her, with whom conversation flowed easily, who welcomed her to stay as long as she liked, knowing how hard she worked. But how many did she count as true friends?

She had once loved Kel because he had been the first person who seemed to truly understand her. That feeling had flickered inside her again today. Aldís realized that something in her thirsted for the sort of connection she once had with Kel. How many friends did she have with whom could she talk of deep ideas and wide thoughts, explore the past and consider the future? Kel had shared her love of the law, for example. It was something one could not touch, but which shaped nearly everything about how people lived. He had understood that, had liked how her mind worked. Back in those lost days, Kel had listened, shaking his head in fascination at how her mind worked.

"I loved being understood. That is what drew me to Kel." Aldís said it aloud in a kind of defiance, but of what? She had avoided thinking about Kel for so long that even the simple spoken admission gave relief.

"It's not just that," Aldís said to the air drifting over her. "People want to share things from day to day. They *need* to. Small successes, like the boy's leg and the wound from the dog bite healing, or having a neighbor to help with *retting* your flax. Or someone with whom you can unburden your spirit, knowing they will share your sadness about having to butcher one of your horses. Someone with whom to share hope when things are hard. To share fear that you dare not admit to anyone else. Someone to encourage hope despite that fear. Little things, but they are the stuff with which people build a life."

She lay quiet, slowly falling half asleep, peaceful and drowsing. In that quiet, Aldís understood a truth. Yes, she had served the community as best she could since that long-ago Althing with Kel. Yes, she had done good, and was appreciated, but she had not built a life. She had drifted, tethered to the pain of her past, too afraid to trust or try again.

"I don't even know how, after all this time," Aldís said, sitting up. Still, it felt as if she had arrived, somehow, at a place inside herself to which she could go again, and rest, and think. A place of peace, and near it, thoughts of Kel that were no longer quite so angry, quite so dangerous.

Aldís folded her blanket, picked up her satchel, and walked back to the road from the small meadow. The sun would be behind her the rest of the day. Somewhere ahead, her life waited.

. . .

Chapter Thirty-Four

No need for a Kalendar to call *day-eighths* as autumn dwindled quickly towards full midwinter. The *equal-day-and-night* that signaled *álfablót* also meant the beginning of the darkening-days, the first half of winter. People rushed their outside chores to completion, as daylight in which to work grew shorter and shorter. First the grain harvest got underway, then plowing before the soil became too cold, and planting of barley and wheat and oats for next year. After that, flax was cut, and last of all butchering started. Much to accomplish in three short moons.

Across those weeks, children checked the sun-mark sticks each morning and evening. They watched with excited anticipation as the sticks neared the mark where Sól had sunk lowest the prior year, chattering about it as they helped in their own small ways with tasks.

"Tell me again why the Sun goes away?" they begged.

"You know that when *álfablót* begins, the dark elves take over the earth. They set traps for bright Sól, trying to capture her so that they can take her down to their world under the earth, so that it will be bright like ours is. She fights back, but she becomes so tired she can barely rise! Say your prayers to her so she will escape them. Be good, so that she will remember to come back to our land. We need her. We are not dark-elves. Without the sun, we would die."

Despite the prayers of many, the sun-goddess continued to sink lower and lower and to shine shorter and weaker. Eventually, in the coldest darkest days, Sól barely had the strength to drag herself above the horizon before she disappeared below it in exhaustion again. She shone terribly weak, and her light gave no warmth.

By Longest-Night, those who lived in the western fjords reported that she did not rise at all. One question dominated every valley: would Sól actually come back this year?

. . .

But midwinter brought Jul, the merry celebration of harvest-done days when work ceased and visiting started, with ready barrels of ale and music to be enjoyed, and clapping of hands, and dancing and singing. Who did not look forward to the short dark days when they brought bonfires, friends, family, feasting?

This year, the worry came hard on the heels of equally troublesome matters. Too many families knew that even if she returned as she always had before, they could not manage feasts and festivities to mark her return. This year, not only the sunlight had waned. As Longest-Night had approached, housewives had halved and halved again the amount of food to prepare each day. The daily terrible re-deciding about whether to butcher another animal for food or to hold on, half starving, knowing that each of the herd or flock that survived meant milk and eggs through the winter, and each laying chicken or ewe in foal meant increase for the next year. Each night, an anguished discussion, weighing the remaining geese and hens against how much grain they would eat all winter against how many eggs they might produce: one or two night's *sup* in the pot would fill bellies, but dozens of eggs would not be laid…but eating a hen meant more seeds available to plant in the spring.

Farm women and men began to lock their larder-boxes to prevent theft of even the smallest bit of food. Cheekbones, collarbones, and hip bones showed sharp through skin.

. . .

Naldrum had promised butter and food, but when poorer farmers petitioned him for help, the chieftain let his face fall in false regret. He had once grown tired of his amusement of mocking the white-christs, but now they gave him a convenient excuse for his broken promise.

"It's terrible. All of the supplies I set aside for safety against starvation have been claimed. And the worst of it? By those who pray to the white-christ."

But to landowners with large farms and influence, he gave or sold, according to their wealth. Those who had the most to offer him got the best of his supplies.

Naldrum cautioned each of them. "You're the only one I'm doing this for. Tell no one, or I'll cut you off."

All too easily, men and women rich in silver but poor in spirit accepted his prices and terms. Loyalty bought favor and protection. They eagerly accepted whatever scraps Naldrum chose to spare.

But well off or poor, all whispered to each other about the greed of neighbors they thought might be white-christ worshippers.

All along the valley farms, anger smoldered, rumors flew, and fear grew as the days deepened in dark and cold. Misgivings and misfortune rasped against the dry flint of worry. Sparks of envy and disquiet fed on tinder of distrust and dismay. A fire of fear flamed, feeding on Naldrum's words. From them, a weapon began to take shape, a wicked little blade of hunger and hate.

The small knife scraped suspicions between master and worker, neighbor and neighbor, family and friend. The wounds, though tiny, were many, and multiplied faster than they could heal.

. . .

Rumors spread of a gyrfalcon hunting Bull Valley. The sale of a gyrfalcon would bring enough to buy food for a multitude.

But even this most elusive of falcons became a divisive issue. Perhaps it, like the ravens of Odin, carried news to the gods about the world of humans. Maybe it was a *fylgja*, a good spirit bringing promise of better times to come, and capturing it would bring more hardship instead.

Or it might be a *gandreith*, a wild-hunt wind-rider, harbinger of doom. Better to stop it before the spirits of the dead brought storms and fierce weather.

Traps were set, but the falcon somehow remained free. No one saw who untied the bait-birds, or how some were eaten although the trap was never sprung. And even that fed the burning, bitter flame of anger.

. . .

Chapter Thirty-Five

Rota, after divesting Naldrum of his prized Kandace, had ridden far from Naldrum's compound to once again explore more of the remarkable country in which she had landed. She returned to Naldrum again in late autumn to speak with him about the means of gaining power.

"Your first step must be the law councils," Rota explained. "Control those who vote on laws and legal cases, and you control the whole land."

Impatient, Naldrum waved her comments away. "What do I care about disputes of whose sheep is whose, and who insulted someone else?" Both at the local spring quarter-*thing* and the formal court of Althing, Naldrum felt bored by legal proceedings. "I prefer to leave such matters to my law-arguer. Laws. Blah, blah, blah."

"How can you be such a powerful *gothi* and still be so profoundly, utterly stupid?" Rota shouted at him. 'The *thing* courts of your land have a weakness you can exploit! Now listen to me, you nitwit. The courts are supposed to base decisions on the law of people rather than the law of a king, yes?"

Naldrum yawned. "We hear it every year at Althing. Ridiculous how many put their own profits aside for a failed old code of honor."

"You must be different from those people," Rota replied. "You must corrupt the courts in your favor."

"How? No one dares go against the law." He made a mocking face.

Rota put her palm to her forehead. If a man of any intelligence was as corruptible as Naldrum, she might actually enjoy the task to which Haakon had assigned her. Instead, she had to flatter and lead this idiot as if he were a spoiled troll-child, greedy for some prize.

"It's so easy!" Rota forced her voice to be comforting and exciting. "Does someone owe you a favor? Nominate them for the local *thing* council. Someone needs to borrow your slaves or bond workers for a task? Usually it is a thing done in friendship, for the common good, but you can make it a transaction. Lend your slaves only in return for a favor on the courts. Do not say it directly, because people will take affront. Say it as a suggestion. A wish. Offer your expectations simply as something that would make you happy. Nominate that person, and let others know how pleased their votes for this person will make you. Follow your words up with a small gift or favor."

"Why should I do that? I can get whatever I want with my own silver!"

Rota gritted her teeth. *Such an arrogant imbecile. He thinks he knows everything, yet he knows nothing.* "Because those who defy you will soon see others gaining in favor, thanks to you. Then the dissenters, just like sheep, will fall in line and follow you too."

. . .

Naldrum stewed for weeks on Rota's insulting but intriguing words. He would never admit that he was wrong, no. Finally his youngest wife, the one people whispered had thief-eyes, could not stand his slow stupidity any longer. She had grasped Rota's plan immediately. It galled her to see Naldrum ponderously mulling it over, trying to understand.

"Tell me again what Haakon's agent Rota told you," she suggested.

"She said that once I control the courts, whatever I want can happen," he replied.

"Perhaps it's true." She saw Naldrum bristle at a possible insult and rushed her words. "If the law and the courts cannot stop you, you can do *anything!* Maybe it would be well heed what she says."

Naldrum, a little afraid of this wife, agreed. "Perhaps." She saw in his reluctance agreement the fact that he had no intention of actually agreeing with her, and pushed harder.

"You could test it out during the spring *thing*."

The idea of having a bit of fun and mocking the solemnity of the local court pleased Naldrum. "I guess I could!" He laughed, thinking of the fools the farmers of his valley were.

"If it works, perhaps by the time of Althing next summer you'll have enough influence that you *will* win as Lawspeaker over Mani's son Bright?"

Again, he glowered. "You doubt I will win? Of *course* I will!"

"And the Althing after that, *you'll* be the Lawspeaker." She smiled, sly. "At which time, it then will be up to you to decide which cases get heard, and which do not. Those who support you will get legal satisfaction. Those who do not will go home as losers."

"Ha!" Naldrum chortled. "The yokels of this land think the law is strong enough to contain men like me? They are fools! And once I am Lawspeaker, I'll change the laws to give myself greater wealth and power than they could ever dream of!"

"How clever you are for this idea!" his wife said.

Naldrum looked at her sharply. Was she mocking him? He knew, but would never admit to anyone, that she was far more intelligent than he was. But she seemed to be sincere.

With the decision made, he felt excited about starting the process and rubbed his hands in glee. "I *am* clever. I understand such matters as these very well." Naldrum pictured himself standing on the Law Rock in Mani's place, with the crowd below cheering up at him in adoration. A thought came to him. "Mani took such care to welcome those among us who worship other gods. But look how easy it has been for me to turn people against each other in this valley. I've made a laughingstock of our Lawspeaker. I'll do a much better job than he does."

As Naldrum mused pleasantly on Mani's foolishness and his own prodigious talents, his wife interrupted.

"You know, after that man Bishop-friedrich left, I heard talk of that new god everywhere. Perhaps his people really are the reason for so much distress among the farms." She laid her snare patiently, knowing that Naldrum would need time to grasp her meaning. Her recalcitrant husband could not accept advice easily, even from her. But she had noticed that Naldrum had begun to believe the rumors he himself had started. She had found it was always easier to convince him about something he already wanted to believe.

Naldrum squirmed, thinking of Ankya's eerie fascination with Friedrich and her insistence on saying 'body and blood' nearly every damned day. Desire to protect his innocent young daughter filled

Naldrum. Besides, he felt more and more embarrassed by Ankya. He settled for a half-admission to his daughter's step-mother.

"I used to amuse myself poking fun at the white-christs. But lately I have begun to believe that their true intent is to prey on impressionable minds like my darling Ankya."

His darling Ankya! Naldrum's young wife nearly gagged, but took the opening he had given her.

"Perhaps it would be best to root those people out, while there are still few of them? After all, the old gods protected our forefathers in the days of Settlement. Of course they will protect us—you, I mean—now."

Naldrum had only no actual liking for the old gods beyond a vague desire to keep Ankya innocent and dependent on him. His wife continued to fit his thoughts together for him, bit by bit.

"What matters really is not the old gods, but you. People *believe* in whatever you tell them. Who cares if the Old Ways and old gods are even real? You can still ride people's faith in them as a ship might ride the waves!"

He smiled, and she knew she had him. "People are afraid! They fear hunger. They fear loss. They *loathe* those things which *cause* hunger and loss." *By Frigg, could she lay it out any more clearly for him?*

At long last, with his wife guiding him, Naldrum finally came to understand what Rota had meant about using what people feared.

"They loathe whatever causes them hunger and loss," he repeated slowly. "So we must seek out and punish those who do."

"You must offer people a place of safety, whether imagined or real."

Naldrum crowed in triumph. "Of course, I saw this coming all along! Did you know I disparaged the white-christ worshippers at my butter visits? How wise I am!"

"For certain, my husband. Now, perhaps the time has come to make your efforts larger."

Naldrum, with a turnip in his fist halfway to his open mouth, scowled, not understanding.

"Perhaps you intend to do more than just speak of the worshippers and their nasty practices. Perhaps you mean to go to the gut of the matter, and spread fear of their god itself. After all, your dear daughter…" She paused to let Naldrum pull the trap closed on himself.

Naldrum chewed his turnip, anger filling him. "That revolting bishop thinks he can steal Ankya from me? I will excite men and women once again to power of the Old Ways. Soon that bishop fellow will find himself on a ship back home!"

"Husband, your genius knows no bounds." His thief-eyed wife rose. She knew what the smug excitement in Naldrum's face indicated. "You must excuse me, my love. Regrettable, but I have to go with some of the bondwomen to check on *álfablót* preparations. Enjoy the rest of your supper." She headed for the longhouse door, smiling to herself.

The sheer brilliance of Naldrum's plan made him almost giddy with self-congratulatory pride. He did not mind that his wife had left the room. She had made it clear to him long ago that their marriage was a convenience only, his to boast of such a beautiful young companion, and hers to enjoy the position and wealth she had always craved. Naldrum peered through the longhouse to see which of the slave women were nearby working.

"Drikke!" he shouted to his son. "That big-breasted Gaelic you've been at night and day. Where is she?"

Naldrum's wife, leaving the room, kept her gaze down, as if she could not hear or see her husband's betrayal. She had heard of Kandace's curse and was curious. Far better for the Gaelic to bear the risk than one of her own favorite slaves.

Drikke pointed. The woman, huddled in a corner at the furthest point in the room, sagged in dismay. Was it not enough for Naldrum's son to constantly force her? She, too, had heard rumors of how Kandace had cursed Naldrum. *I don't want a troll eating my insides out!* The slave woman hunched down between two others, clutched her sewing, and tried to be invisible.

"Don't you dare refuse me! I'll have your every tooth pulled if you do!" Naldrum sat erect and impatient on his high-seat.

The Gaelic woman groaned and closed her eyes. Monks of her youth in faraway Ireland had taught it was a sin to take one's own life. Was this entire life not a worse kind of sin?

Slowly, making herself numb, she rose. As she trudged towards Naldrum's private sleeping area, she thought of the priest's lurid, terrifying descriptions of hell, and wondered if God would send her there for eternity if she was able to get a blade close enough to Naldrum's gizzard to slit his throat.

. . .

Chapter Thirty-Six

First, the rumors: our misfortune is because our gads are angry. Second, the solution: find those to blame and punish them.

. . .

"Naldrum says our neighbor's Frankish wife doesn't observe the blood-festivals properly. We share a sheep-field with them. Maybe it's her fault so few of our ewes are quickening."

"That whore! How dare she endanger your livelihood with her false beliefs!"

"Naldrum's servants heard that a place near the coast had chickens lay eggs with no yolks on the god-days last month."

"No yolks! Do you think it's a warning?"

"Without doubt it is! They'll have no chicks come spring. If they go hungry, it's their own fault!"

"Did you hear that a raven went mad and flew into Naldrum's longhouse window and shattered it to a thousand pieces?"

"I did—and I also heard that Bishop-friedrich said the window was nothing compared to cathedral stained glass. What is stained glass?''

"I don't know. But who is Bishop-friedrich to insult our headman?" The glass window and the reasons for the raven's madness had been discussed so far and wide that the damage felt personal. In very little time, speculations arose that perhaps Sól would not return this year because of the dangerous practice of wearing crosses. Perhaps, they wondered, the mad raven was a sign that on this Longest-Night the white-christs would unleash upon the land the Days of Prophecy, the legend that spoke of *Ragnarök* when all life would end, all gods die, and the whole world would be covered with floodwaters.

And as the days until Longest-Night passed, the weather worsened. Instead of soft white winter snowstorms followed by blue skies, rain came, relentless, raw, windy, cold, and gray.

"Again, rain! So much rain this summer, and last month, and now all this week again. All these angry torrents, as if Frey was trying to tell us of his displeasure." Unspoken were the words that Frey, the god of rain and the brother of Freya, might abate the floods if only those who did not love the old gods would leave Iceland and never return.

Others whispered about the wickedness of men and women purchased at the slave-market at Althing, and the children of slaves from earlier generations.

"Our new man-slave made a symbol. Two sticks crossed like this. They call it a cross." Fingers formed a 't' shape. "I found him wearing it under his tunic. I took it away and I've given him no food to eat for three days. Let's see how long it takes him to bow to Odin."

"My slave as well. He says it's nothing, so why does he hide it from me?"

"We hired a girl, the daughter of a Saxon, to spin and weave. She has one. She kisses it daily when she thinks I do not see."

"Naldrum says they are putting evil spells on us. You should whip that wench."

Freeholder after freeholder began to search out those who wore the small crosses, and to beat those who carried them, as an example to other servants. Yet still the rains fell, and still the sun sank into the southern horizon, and still the sheep did not quicken.

. . .

Naldrum encouraged his staff to repeat to him such conversations, and rewarded farmers who had said them with small gifts of meat and ale. One came from a neighbor who rode over to borrow leather to repair a torn saddle. Another from someone who asked for mighty Tor to repair a broken wagon-wheel. The cheese-slave heard from a nearby midwife that her cross had been taken and she had escaped a whipping only because she had helped with a difficult delivery. The cheese-slave repeated it to the ash-girl in Naldrum's hearing.

He listened to each one with growing pleasure, and the Gaelic woman heard her name called again day after day.

. . .

Chapter Thirty-Seven

Give them hope.

. . .

As midwinter drew imminent, not a scrap of salvageable harvest remained in the fields. Every fistful of grain had been carefully dried, and threshed, and stored. The flax had been cut, its husks had been rotted and stripped off by wickedly-sharp hatchels, and the freed inner core, soft as maiden hair, had been stuffed into loose sacks for winter weaving.

As the weather grew colder, herds were culled. First, fattened pigs, for they did not give milk or work on the farm. After the pigs, horses. Then, if the rafters in the longhouses hung crowded with joints from the horses and pigs, the cows, goats and sheep would be spared for their milk and cheese. But if the pigs and horsemeat would not be enough, some of those, too, were slaughtered

The next animals harvested were geese, their feathers plucked and their soft down sewn into quilted fabric. They had pride of place, for crisp brown goose was always the dish at the center of the Jul feast.

The cook summoned her ash-girl and a handful of teenage servants to work outside the longhouse plucking and gutting geese.

They sang mid-winter songs and debated exactly when the Jul festivities would start—for the instant a flame had been coaxed from the Jul-log, no work could be demanded of any slave or free servant until the last ember gave up its glow. Their pleasant conversation took a different course when a heated disagreement about this year's log broke out—and they inadvertently handed Naldrum another weapon in his quest for power.

. . .

Every year in rare moments of leisure, bond workers and thralls roved nearby hills in search of the biggest pine tree they could find. By autumn, they had made their choice, and felled it, leaving it hidden in the forest to dry. Come midwinter, they carried it in triumph into the longhouse where it would be set ablaze to mark the start of Jul celebration, Stories were told of *Jul* logs in the old country that had burned for as long as a week.

Today, the tree-hunters had carried their prize log from the woods. They placed it in close against the longhouse foundation, well back under where the thatch roof overhung, where it would stay dry even if rain came.

Other workers in the compound saw it immediately, of course. An argument began to sound.

"This scrawny thing is the best tree you could find? With all summer to search?" The cook stood with a cleaver in hand and goose entrails all over the outdoor table. "I'll barely get a nap before that thing is burned to bits!"

Those who had selected the log reacted with defensive anger. "Have *you* gone into the forest recently? Any woodcutter can tell you we must choose from smaller and smaller trees every year—and even these 'scrawny things' are hard to find. We searched every hill. This was the biggest one anywhere!"

"It's our one respite of the year. I feel cheated!" To the disappointment of all, this log would give less than a day's freedom from work, if that.

Tempers flared. The fracas increased.

"You don't believe us? Ask the charcoal burners! They know the forests better than anyone!"

"You idiot. You think the charcoal burners will tell you where the largest trees are to be found? No! They want those for themselves! It's they who are at fault, for taking too many trees!

"I think *Iceland's* at fault! Too many people, too few forests—you figure it out. It's not just more trees we need. We need more *everything*. More forests, more fields. We need a new land!"

Naldrum had at first only felt annoyance at the bickering. "Quiet those louts down!" he had shouted at Kel.

But later, when the log had been set afire and the holiday began, the house poet told the story of the first arrivals to Iceland, and the rich fields and forests they had found. Again and again, the skald sang of *hope* and *joy* and *new land.* At last the words attracted Naldrum's attention. He leaned forward in his high seat, his fingers interlaced, thinking.

Rota had told him to look for things people feared, and something to give them hope. His skald had just laid it all out for him.

Ankya," he asked. "What do you think would happen if our people could enjoy new land as they had in the days of settlement?"

She considered the idea. "They would flock to it like sheep to a fresh field of grass. Whoever gave them rights to use it would receive grateful and generous tithes. He will be seen as a great benefactor."

Naldrum kissed his daughter's hand. "When people first came to Iceland, so far away from other land, they discussed an idea: perhaps even *another* island existed beyond ours. Some searched, but nothing was ever found. It may be time to resume looking again."

"It would give people hope, that is for certain."

"Hope is all I need. Only the hope matters, not any results," Naldrum mused. "An actual discovery is not only unlikely, but completely unnecessary to my purposes. If nothing is ever found, people will still see me as the one who gave them hope. They'll consider me their great benefactor—and all it will cost me is one measly ship."

What a beautiful scheme! Naldrum rubbed his hands in glee as idea after idea unfolded.

"I'll promise other headmen that if they support this venture, I'll give them first choice of any lands found. I'll end up paying nothing—*nothing!* —yet I'll get all the credit."

He called for his skald to stop singing. "I want you to compose a new poem about me," Naldrum demanded. "At the festival of spring, I want you to perform it in my honor." He listed the elements he wanted in the story. The skald grimaced, but his livelihood depended on Naldrum's favor.

"It will be the finest tribute ever sung," the poet promised.

Naldrum smiled at the pitiful Jul log. A good thing that his servants would have a short holiday. He wanted a glorious new cloak for Althing next summer, and perhaps a larger wagon. Better that the servants stop slacking about and get to back to work.

Naldrum summoned his messenger. "I need you to ride tomorrow to Bjarni the shipbuilder." Old Bjarni could work without pay at first. By the time he wanted silver, Naldrum would have secured more than enough from those who begged for a share of the glory.

. . .

Chapter Thirty-Eight

Styr's dog ran ahead as if to say *here this way here is the path follow me, I'll find a way for us,* wagging its tail happily despite the fearful rasping of the man who panted along behind. Styr's fingers clawed at crevices in stone and dirt and moss as he struggled upwards, following his dog. They scrambled over rocks, higher and higher into the unfamiliar terrain. Styr flung himself exhausted onto the ground. *Here, fellow,* he called the dog, gulping for breath *Here, fellow. Come.*

Styr patted his dog, reassuring it. He felt anxiously in his pocket for the silver coins. Still there. Immediately he was ashamed that they had been his first thought, but no, *she* had been his first thought, and what those coins meant to her.

Get out of here, Tiller had said. *Thorgest probably sent his sons after us and he's right behind them with his sledge, thinking he'll force me into giving the pillars back. I'll stay here and face them all. He'll be furious, but I'll make him listen to reason.*

Styr had wanted to stay, but when the howling began, they knew Thorgest had brought his hunting dogs. Tiller had insisted then, saying *Einarr will stay here with me. Thorgest knows him. The rest of you, go now, before they see you. No need for them to know any of you were here.* Styr and the others had run, scattering in different directions as they each headed for home.

Styr's own dog for once bounded in front of him, instinctively knowing what was needed: a place to hide above the road crossing where far below, Einarr stood with Tiller, Einarr's knife out just in case, even though Tiller had sharply told him to put it away.

Styr's breath slowed a little. He was drenched with sweat and fear. He wiped his face, rolled over and sat up, slumping and stunned, shaking his head. *Sweet gods, what had happened? Thorgest wasn't supposed to be home for days!*

Still, he laughed a little at the absurdity of it all. Tiller, with those massive pillars blatantly visible. They had been trundling along the roadway, the sledge creaking under the load. What could Tiller say, caught red-handed like that? *Well met, Thorgest. Something missing at home?*

But the coins were safe. Fatimah's silver. *Hope.*

. . .

Styr shimmied to the steep edge of the hill, trying to get a view of where Tiller and Einarr waited. Would Thorgest listen to them, or react in fury at the sight of the heavy carved pillars?

Early that morning the small group with Tiller had laughed and joked about the prize-taking to come. They had mimicked Thorgest's face as he walked into his longhouse and saw that the high-seat pillars had been swapped with plain ones. '*What? Where are my pillars! Damn you Tiller! I know it was you!*'

Hefting the heavy pillars out of place and wedging in the replacement one, the men had still laughed as they grunted. It had all been such a joke. Boys playing a prank.

Not so funny now.

Styr thought about climbing back down the hill. Thorgest in a good mood was an amiable man, but Thorgest angry was an altogether different thing. *Why did I forget that?* It had been the soft gleam of the silvers, the imagined sounds of eleven ewes and their new lambs bleating—more, if he was lucky and some had twins. It had been the hopeful light in Fatimah's eyes as they talked about renting the small field on the edge of the farm from her father Rolf—who had practically invited Styr to try for it, saying, *That field there has too many stones to farm and I can't afford any more stock, but a young man with a few goats or sheep could use that field, use it to earn money to afford a wife.* Fatimah's father never used her name to Styr out of respect, but they both knew what he meant. Love of Fatimah formed a secret bond between the two men.

Will Rolf send me away from the farm if he hears I was involved in this mess? Styr wondered. That would be unthinkable. Since last year, men and even some women and children without farms already roamed the countryside, all of them looking for work, any kind of work where food served as payment. Without Rolf, Styr might well starve to death. At the very least, he would have to say goodbye to Fatimah forever.

Surely Tiller would not say to Thorgest the names of the men who had helped him pull the ancient carved pillars out and push the plain new ones into place, no, surely not. But when the news of it swept the valley—as it certainly would—how then could Styr explain suddenly having four silvers, enough to buy a herd of sheep and a ram and four goats? How?

Thorgest knows Tiller. Didn't Tiller teach Thorgest's sons how to sail? This will blow over, Styr told himself. The two men had done business together for years. Surely Thorgest would be reasonable. *Maybe they'll argue, and maybe knock each other about a bit, and then laugh and it'll be over, and Thorgest would say you damned hardheaded vikinger, and Tiller would answer back you wish* you *were a vikinger because then I wouldn't have had to teach your sons how to vik, which I did it for free as a favor to you and then you went and stole my pillars and Thorgest would hang his head and apologize and Tiller would clap him on the back and say it's nothing, it's over.*

But Styr did not know that Thorgest had been backed into a corner. He did not know the anger of betrayal that burned in Tiller's heart. Styr did not know how deep a rift had opened between the two men over these beautiful, treasured pillars, a rift as abrupt as the cliffs at Althing, as hard and stubborn and real.

From far below came faint sounds lifted on the wind. Shouting? Styr chewed on his knuckle. What to do? Should he go back, or head to Fatimah's farm and hope for the best?

. . .

Styr waited. No sounds had come from the valley below for a long while. He cautiously descended. There was no one in sight on the roadway, but Styr's dog growled, low and dangerous.

"What is it, boy?" he asked. The dog stayed right at Styr's side, the deep sound reverberating in its chest.

Styr walked to where the road intersected with the track to Thorgest's farm, where Tiller had waited with the sledge. The dirt looked wet, and his dog sniffed it, his hackles high. Styr knelt by the dark stains.

Oh, good gods, no. That could not be blood on the road.

But it was. Styr stumbled getting to his feet, horror growing in him. What had happened? Had Thorgest killed Tiller? Or had Tiller…?

Instinct drove Styr's feet. He raced away from this waking nightmare back towards Rolf's farm.

. . .

Styr had almost reached the post that marked Rolf's holdings. For a while now, the noises of a cart-train had been increasing behind him. As they drew near, Styr stepped aside to let the people and animals pass.

A string of thin horses came first, probably to be sold for meat, then a wagon of household goods. Pig iron, baskets of seeds, and a loom precariously balanced on top. Behind the wagon, a man led a ram on a leather leash.

Skyr gestured in greeting, and then jammed his both hands into his kyrtill pockets. No one needed to see the bruises and scrapes from wrenching out Thorgest's pillars. He made his face relax. The silvers were safe. Styr had wrapped tightly in cloth and jammed them into his shoes to keep them quiet, two silvers to each foot.

"Well met," Styr greeted the horse-handler. He got a grunt in reply. Nothing coming from that one, Styr guessed. But the man leading the ram knew that conversation oiled the wheels of barter.

Besides, he was a talkative man and enjoyed conversation, sale or no sale.

"Odd stuff happening on the road today. Know anything about it?"

"No," Styr answered. "I just came over the hill from the opposite direction. What do you mean?"

"A fellow driving like a madman passed us back a way. Had two high-seat pillars on his sledge. All carved up. Never saw their equal. Remarkable things. Beside them on the sledge, something else. Something covered up. Not as long. About the length of a man."

Styr could not speak.

"We tried to stop the fellow, to make a trade maybe, but he never even slowed down, just drove the horses. Nearly ran us off the road, and then veered down a narrow track I'd never taken before."

Styr cold not respond. What was on the sledge? Where was Einarr?

"And further back, near the cross of the roads, it looked as if there had been a terrible fight."

"What kind of fight?" His heart in his throat.

"I don't know. Blood everywhere. Something or somebody got cut, that's for certain. And far back, earlier, before we even reached the road crossing, we saw another man with his horse pulling a sledge. Something covered up on it too, also the length of a man, but wider. Have to ask oneself what it means to see three mysterious shapes and blood on the ground? Something happened. Something bad."

. . .

By nightfall, Fatimah's worry turned to panic.

Her father grumbled. "What is keeping Styr? He said he'd be back from his day-trip by now. By Hel, where did he need to go so badly?"

Despite Rolf's angry words, Fatimah could hear the worry under his annoyance. Her mother made it worse with irritable comments.

"Maybe it's time to get rid of him. I've seen how he looks at Fatimah! That's trouble if you ask me."

Fatimah dared not go all the way out to the gate where she would get a better view of the road, not with her mother's hawk-eyes watching and her sharp voice nagging, "Fatimah, you don't need to go looking for him. Stay away from that man. What does he have to offer you? Nothing! Don't be an idiot."

"Styr, where are you?" The stars offered no reply.

As Fatimah worried, she began to hate the memory of little soft chimes of the silvers jingling in Styr's hand that night, the two of them laughing, giddy with happiness as they leaned against the fence after Tiller had left and she had turned the cow out to graze. *Look at them, Fatimah! Four silvers! These mean something I had never dreamed possible.* He had jingled them once more, softly, not wanting anyone to hear and ask where he had gotten them, and he had had just enough time to whisper *I love you, Fatimah* when her mother had stomped around the byre and glared at them.

Styr, please be safe. Fatimah lingered near the longhouse door, open to catch the air, the light from the longfire within spilling out across the yard. She took the supper scraps out for the pigs, returned inside, forced herself to work, staying near the opening and glancing as often as she dared into the night beyond.

The sound of her name drifted on the wind, a breath just outside the door, still propped open to bring air into the stuffy longhouse on this mild winter night.

"Fatimah."

Yes, she definitely had heard that. Fatimah made an excuse and before her mother could argue, hobbled down along the turf sides of the longhouse back beyond the chicken coop and they held each other in the dark and her head was against his chest and he was kissing her hair and Styr sounded as if he was crying, his voice all raspy and he said *Fatimah, it all went wrong, so wrong.* He could not bring himself to say anything to Fatimah about the bodies—were they bodies? And if so, whose? —not yet, not until he knew more, but he whispered *I am so worried about Tiller, I don't know what happened.*

She whispered back. "Styr. Stop. I don't care about anything as long as you are safe."

He held Fatimah and told himself that Tiller was strong and resourceful. It sounded worse than bad, it sounded devastating, but this might be the only chance he would get to take care of Fatimah. *We can finally be together. We have a chance.* He held the woman in his arms, her gentle shoulders, the softness of her breasts against his chest, those sweet round cheeks those luminous eyes raised to his.

"Fatimah, no matter what happens now, I have the silvers. We are going to buy a herd and I am going to rent the field from your father and work extra hours to pay it off. My beloved, one day I am going to be your husband." He said it as if he believed it.

Once again, she could breathe. The memory of the silvers tinkling together softened to a chime, almost sweet again, and Fatimah felt almost safe again.

Almost.

But in her arms, Styr still shook. *What had happened?* Fatimah held him tightly to steady him. Whatever it was, whatever danger Styr had risked, came from his love for her. With four silvers, he could have left, could have headed for a ship, could have bought passage to another country where the crops were better than here, were people were not always in threat of hunger, where his strong arms and quick brain could find work that paid well – but he had come back to here, to find her, to be with her. For the first time in her life Fatimah knew what it was to be fiercely strong. Power surged from somewhere deep within her.

"Shhhh," she whispered. "Shhhh, Styr. Everything will be all right."

. . .

It did not take long for the terrible news to sweep through the valley.

Thorgest's two sons had been killed, he said, in a fight with Tiller and Einarr. Einarr was dead as well. With no witnesses alive to refute his words, Thorgest accused Tiller of the murder of all three men. The trial would be held at the *thing* to be held at Thornes, come spring, three months away. Until then, Thorgest warned, he intended to kill Tiller on sight—if he found him and had the opportunity.

. . .

Chapter Thirty-Nine

Dísablót, the opposite of *álfablót.* One in autumn, one in spring. One a private, fearful negotiation between individual families and the dark forces of under-earth, and the other a sprawling celebration of female fertility bursting forth, when each valley held a *thing* to celebrate the *dísir*, the collected body of female spirits, from deity to waterfall sprites to white-elves.

Soon the *dísir* would take charge of the world from its male winter-keepers, the dark elves. Stepping forth with the returning sun, every *dis* blessed and brightened her own small realm. Water *nixies* rolled and laughed, bubbling in springs, streams, waterfalls and rivers. Dryads stood tall and strong in the shapes of greening birch trees. Ancient hearth spirits that had drowsed through the long winter nights woke again to keep watch over food and fire. Nymphs peeked from groves at their sisters, the fertile and ever-youthful goddesses of field and furrow, who blew warm breath over young crops to protect them from frost. In any barnyard, an elusive horn-spirit might run a hand over the back of a pregnant mare in labor to ease her pain. *Dís* drifted everywhere, where women could reach out to them for help at any instant. Such a relief to have them back.

. . .

Naldrum's Kalendar had counted the days and weeks from Longest-Night at midwinter. She knew the valley families each would be doing counting of their own, setting their sun-sticks to keep track of the approach of Equal-Day-And-Night, when the dísablót was always celebrated.

But each elected *gothi,* who bore responsibility for hosting the spring *thing* for their own valley, held final authority on which day was Equal-Day-And-Night, because they needed time to prepare for the many tasks of the *thing* and its associated dísablót: food and firewood for guests, seating for the law councils who heard regional cases, and the longhouse readied for important visitors.

Naldrum's Kalendar started her count at Longest-Night, making little marks on her kalendar-staff. When six and a half weeks had passed, she informed Naldrum that the goddess Brigid had arrived in the land, bringing the first lambs—and starting the time for preparations for the spring *thing* and the *dísablót*. Naldrum had let it be known that all residents of Bull Valley would enjoy a sumptuous feast.

After Brigid's day, the count seemed to go faster and faster, as if the *dísir* themselves felt eager for the end of winter. Every day burst with new birth. The joy of spring overflowed.

But Kel loathed spring, for it meant that the killing season had come.

. . .

Each year, always the same. Nine months after the summer gathering, a certain kind of knock sounded at the heavy door of

Naldrum's longhouse. The door-boy would summon Kel and whisper that the visitor insisted on speaking to the chieftain Naldrum—and Naldrum only—regarding a personal matter.

After years as Naldrum's steward, Kel knew what to expect on the other side of the door. No trader's cart, no bleating lambs for sale, just a single person with hat in hand, embarrassed. Usually a man, father to a youngish woman, usually one of the poorer sort.

Some held their heads high, proud and angry. Others gasped, seeing at last the richness of Naldrum's famed longhouse.

Perhaps Naldrum would offer silver, they hoped. *Silver would buy food.* After the brutal winter, hope flickered. But anything would help.

Whatever their differences, they all had the same reason for coming: a child, just born, and fathered, they claimed, by Naldrum. If so, they had legal rights. Naldrum owed the child's birthright of support.

Go away, Kel longed to say to them. *Your situation seems difficult now? I promise you, it will only get worse by your coming here. Go away.*

Every year, the knocks. Each year, the secretive meetings, and Naldrum ranting afterwards that these women had made false claims.

"Do they fool themselves that because I am a rich man, I can be tricked into parting easily with my wealth?"

Every time, the petulant denials that only Kel heard. *You let yourself believe him. You should have known better. You should have questioned him.*

You should have refused.

Now, each knock might feed a needle-thin hope, that one would be a family member of the girl he had heard in Naldrum's tent the summer before. Then everything might change. That girl held the key to a legal charge against Naldrum: *rape.*

If no one came from her family, Kel had only one other option, which was to put a knife into Naldrum's back. But he knew too well that it would not stop the sickness already growing along river valleys. Other chieftains and headmen had already begun to mimic Naldrum's ways of holding long-standing decency in contempt.

Until either of those things happened—a witness who might hold the key to destroying Naldrum, or Kel murdering and running—he had one single, disgusting duty: to keep up the foul charade of serving Naldrum.

The headman must not suspect anything, even if it meant that Kel must stomach doing the unthinkable one last time this year.

. . .

Eight and a half moons had grown and gone since Althing, yet still no knock had yet summoned Kel to the door. He chafed, dreading but anxious for them. He muttered to himself. *What was taking so long?*

Sounds of morning farm work yielded to afternoon, and no knock came. Kel found himself snapping at anyone who crossed his path. He gnawed his fingernails to nothing, he picked at his cuticles. The cook sounded the dinner meal, and the longhouse filled with servants talking about the upcoming festival and the work to be done.

Kel sat alone, brooding. "No," he said to the ash-girl. "Not hungry." He pushed away the bowl she proffered.

Soon the fires were banked for night. Kel lay rigid on the dark sleeping bench, wrapped in woolen blankets, unable to relax, his neck tight with apprehension. When the cocks crowed the dawn, he stared bleary-eyed. *Surely, today. The sooner started, the sooner the whole mess will be finished.* As much as he loathed the ritual, he yearned for it to begin, because once begun, it would sooner or later end. He just had to get through it.

But no knock came that day either. By nightfall, Kel's temples beat with pain. Once again, he tossed and turned through the night.

The next day passed.

Another.

Another.

At last, when he felt he could bear it no longer, a knock.

. . .

Chapter Forty

The man reeked of tallow. *A soap-maker, likely. A poor man who had probably borrowed a horse to get here.*

The man spoke, but Kel did not listen to the words. He did not need to. Instead, he watched the man's face, and wondered. How many times had he done this ghoulish duty? Naldrum's reputation for cheating and dishonesty was well known. Why did they come anyway, hopeful year after year, expecting in the headman to be decent?

Desperation, Kel wanted to tell himself. But his conscience stabbed. *They keep coming because of* you. *You've helped Naldrum keep his dark secrets.*

"You've come for child-rights," Kel interrupted the man. "Go away. I promise you, I will personally send whatever payment you want."

The man stiffened. "Don't dishonor me. The father must answer to me. I have the right."

Kel leaned close, grabbed the man's tunic. "This won't end well. Trust me. I speak truth. Get away now while you still can!"

The man stepped back, furious. "Naldrum!" he bellowed at the top of his lungs. "I demand to speak to *gothi* Naldrum!"

Naldrum's shouted back from deep within the longhouse. "Who calls me?"

Kel pushed his fists against his temples. "Follow me."

Their footsteps echoed through the longhouse to the small chamber where Naldrum gave private audiences. The room held a single carved chair and a table. Candlelight, an elegant display of wealth instead of an oil sconce, gleamed across the polished wood. Kel tapped on the doorframe.

"A visitor with a private matter." The code words he had used the year before, and the year before that. *So many years.*

Naldrum looked up in puzzled surprise, as if such a thing had never happened before. "Let him in, please," he said. He gestured to the man to sit. The man looked around for another chair. There was none, by design. Naldrum motioned for Kel to wait outside the door to prevent interruptions, and began to question the visitor. Kel listened, sick, as the familiar litany began.

"The Festivities of Spring begin in just a few days. I have much to plan for the many guests we are expecting. Since my steward has allowed you to disturb my work, this must be important. Tell me what brings you here today."

Kel knew the sound of Naldrum faking reassurance, his murmur of concern at the story of a daughter, barely of age, or an especially attractive young woman already with a husband. Always the speakers mentioned that the girl tended to be shy, that she had kept the pregnancy hidden until she could no longer. Who, when the child was born, had finally made a reluctant confession and named Naldrum as father.

Since they were coming for a settlement, the visitors did not add what else the young women had said, the other details had been eked out in shame and sobs.

Naldrum always listened fully. A long silence, in which he appraised the speaker as if weighing the man's honesty. A flat reply. *I certainly don't recall this happening.* Naldrum would let the silence stretch out, let the man grow more and more uncomfortable. Still even more silence.

Finally, Naldrum would sigh in exasperation and proclaim that although he, Naldrum, doubted the woman's claim, he understood the difficulty of an unexpected child.

"I am a generous man. But certainly, you must understand the problem this presents. People constantly try to take advantage of my wealth and good nature. But I hate to see a poor family suffer." Another long silence. "I suppose, as a leader, I might help you."

Naldrum's voice sank almost to a whisper. "I require only one thing in exchange for the silver I will give you. You must say nothing about this child being mine. Nothing, to anyone! For its own safety, you understand? Those who dislike me would use your precious newborn to hurt me. So, to keep the child safe, you must not say a word to anyone about this. Do any others in your valley know you came here? No? Just your wife, and the infant's mother? Excellent. Pledge them to secrecy. You seem like a good man. Perhaps, in due time, I might bring the child to my home. Teach it a trade, give it opportunity. Rest your mind on this matter. All will be well."

Kel fumed in bitterness, knowing what came next. A threat clouded Naldrum's voice.

"Do I make myself clear? Do not even *think* of telling others about this conversation. It is critical if you expect my help with this bastard child. Now, my steward will show you on your way. Go home. He will come to your farm shortly with a payment."

. . .

The man tried to engage Kel in conversation as they walked back towards the door.

"*Gothi* Naldrum seems quite a good fellow," he said. "I have to admit I was a little nervous coming here, such a great headman, so wealthy. Didn't know if he'd even see me, or if he would believe me. But our daughter is so young, and we have not the means." The man choked. "For her sake, I had to try. Do you have a daughter of your own? If so, you'll understand."

Kel did not answer. He could say nothing to the soap-maker about what was to come. The poor fellow would know soon enough. At least let him ride home in peace.

As the massive longhouse door creaked open, Kel lifted his chin towards the roadway. "Weather's clear. Get back to your family in time for the festival. The days are still short, so make good riding time." As he watched the man ride away on his borrowed horse, Kel plowed the dark furrows of the human mind, and feared what he was about to do. *Begun.*

. . .

When Kel returned to Naldrum, the headman's knuckles showed white where he gripped the arms of the chair. The pleasant mask had disappeared.

"Again, this year?" Naldrum actied as if his steward had somehow personally caused the man to appear. "Every rotten spring,

Steward! What a nuisance these silly girls and their deceived parents are with their trumped-up claims of fatherhood."

Kel's face betrayed no reaction. "Sir."

"The infant must bear some sort of flaw. Why else would they come to me instead of going to the real father? False claims! I cannot allow my name to be tainted in this way. A flawed child, with my name? No! I cannot bear the thought. The infant cannot live. It must be exposed."

Naldrum began to spell out the unpleasant task he expected Kel to perform, as if he had never before said the words. Kel kept his face frozen. *Oh, to be free of this man!*

At last, the command. "Go now. You know what to do."

Bu this year, Naldrum said more.

"Kel, I have begun to question your loyalty to me. You shook my hand at Althing and contracted to fulfill my orders. So that you do not think of shirking your duty, my son will ride with you and will report back to me. If you have any thoughts of disloyalty, remember your friend Aldís. Let's hope she never experiences any sort of pain again."

. . .

Kel left the room. The painful knot inside tightened. He strode to the stables without speaking to anyone.

Naldrum's eyes narrowed. His fingers drummed on the table as he watched Kel leave. Had it been his imagination or was his steward sweating? He could not afford the man to break, not now. Still, anyone could be replaced. *I need to test his loyalty before we get much farther.* Naldrum pushed back the sleeves of his tunic. His rings glowed in the candlelight as he made marks on fine sheepskin, counting and planning.

"Drikke," he called his son. "Go saddle your horse. You must accompany Kel on a journey. Grab a sleeping sack and leave, right now."

. . .

Chapter Forty-One

The tallow-renderer guided his horse along the road towards the small settlement where he worked, looking for a waiting figure. A maroon shawl, yes, there was his wife. He waved, eager to share the amazing news. This year they would celebrate the spring *dísablót* festivities as never before.

At his wave, he saw her entire body change from stiff worry to relief. She lifted her skirts and ran towards him, mindless of the deep mud on the trackway.

He leapt from the horse. Her arms went around him as his feet touched the ground. “It went well!” she cried. “I can see it in your eyes! Tell me everything!”

He buried his face against his wife’s shoulder. The long ride home had filled him with hope. So much could happen now.

. . .

“Just think! Our grandchild in Naldrum’s own household! Living on that grand farm, in that house!” He looped the horse’s reins around his arm. Hand in hand, he and his wife walked back to their modest dwelling.

“Is it true that Naldrum has a glass window in his longhouse?”

"It is. I saw one as we walked through. I wanted to go over and touch it, but no one is allowed."

"But you saw it!"

"I did. The sun shone through it onto the longhouse floor!"

She marveled. So many years of struggle, of worry, now perhaps at an end. She asked him over and over to repeat Naldrum's words, and he said them, laughing. *'All will be well!'*

She felt like a girl. "I can't wait to tell our daughter! Walk faster!"

"Wife, I've ridden so long," he protested, but she would have none of it, and laughing, dragged him into a run. He dropped the horse's reins to let it graze, and together they tumbled through the longhouse door, calling to the fretting young woman who held a tiny bundle in her arms.

. . .

Kel had followed, keeping his horse Thor-Thunder at a distance as he always did. Rounding the same curve in the road, he watched as they went inside. He yearned to turn around, to leave them to their happiness. The ache in his chest flamed.

I can't do this again. But Drikke rode behind him, sulking.

Kel gritted his teeth. *Just this year. If that one girl comes, if she gives me proof, I'll go back to Mani and file a claim. Either way, after this spring, I'll find a way to be free of Naldrum. I'll find Aldís, bodily put her on a ship to another land, and put the knife in Naldrum where he cannot recover.*

He groaned. What would Aldís think of what he was about to do? What he had done so many times? She would detest him even more.

But she would be safe from Naldrum's threats as long as Kel carried out his headman's grisly orders.

At least he, unlike Drikke, could show the family some respect and kindness in this dreadful deed.

. . .

Kel willed himself to become iron. He dismounted his horse and forced himself to walk towards the small dwelling. His boots crushed the tender spring grass underneath into slippery wet muck.

. . .

As always, the family goggled at his words. Their mouths sagged open, their eyes unbelieving.

"What do you mean, no support? But Naldrum promised—"

"I cannot explain his change of mind," said Kel. Would it help to tell them how devious and dishonest Naldrum was? *No.*

"I can only tell you that he gave me these instructions right after you left." Kel rubbed his chest with his fist again, the pain worsening. *Look at that young woman. So innocent.*

"Tell me exactly what the *gothi* said." The father needed to know the worst.

Kel repeated the instructions word for word. "Naldrum decrees that your daughter must be punished, because she is telling false stories about him. Her claim is a lie. He told me to whip her as punishment, and to make you whip her as well. He wants her pain to be a reminder to you to never again speak his name in such reckless, unfounded accusations."

"We will do no such thing! Our daughter is telling the truth! And we've never whipped her!"

Kel gave them Naldrum's final instruction. "He instructs that if any of you breathes a single word of this—and these are his words, not mine—*'your lying slut of a daughter will die in bloody anguish.'*"

"What are we to do?" the girl cried to Kel. "I only told my parents because we need his help! Food costs more than we have! We have no *skyr* left, no cheese, no smoked meats. We eat only the thinnest of pottage these days, and my parents cannot feed another mouth. I never asked for this child. I never wanted Naldrum's attention! But it is just an infant, innocent and helpless! Who can look at that tiny face and deliberately do it harm? Naldrum wronged me then, and he wrongs us now!"

Kel could see the bones of her hand through the skin. She trembled so hard the baby shook. He felt as if he could not breathe. *Just finish it.*

"The headman Naldrum instructs that I—" He had gotten the words out so many times before. Why would they not come now?

He tried again. "Headman Naldrum instructs that the child be—"

"No!" She had guessed already. "No!"

Kel felt almost relief that he did not have to say the actual words. His voice sank. "There is nothing you can do. Naldrum will not tolerate otherwise."

She thrust the bundle holding the newborn towards her mother. In one swift movement, she knelt before Kel, her young face upturned, pleading. She gripped the leather of his breeches.

"There *must* be another way. I can see in your eyes that you do not want to do this. Please!"

Kel sensed himself slipping, felt his hard resolve melting into a muddy mess.

"No! I *don't* want to do it!" he cried. "You're just a girl! You did not ask for this! But believe me when I say *you have no choice.* Naldrum may have lied to you, but he will not let you defy him. What I offer is painful, but at least you will survive."

The mother, father, and girl stared at him aghast. Kel sagged, his head in his hands. Only the crackle of their tiny fire broke the silence.

The child wailed. Out of instinct, the young mother took it and opened her tunic. She held the small mouth to her breast, cupping its head with her thin hand. Tendrils of blonde hair escaped from its ragged cap.

Kel stared at the floor, listening to the sound of the hungry little mouth. The sickness that roiled inside him bubbled up into his throat. He tasted foulness. "Survive," Kel muttered to himself. "Just survive." He could not move.

"You claim that *gothi* Naldrum lies," the tallow-maker said. "Why do you not lie to him in return? Tell him that you took the child as he directed. Say that I whipped my daughter. Tell him that we, frightened out of our wits, vowed never to speak his name again in this matter. How would he ever know you defied him? We are nothing to him!"

"Because his own son waits outside, to see it is done."

The father walked to the doorway and looked outside. Drikke sat slumped on his horse, annoyed impatience in every line of his body.

Again, the sad silence. Each one weighed the options, rejected them. Hoped, but found only failure.

"I cannot help you, much as I might want to," Kel finally muttered. "I understand how terrible this will be for you. Let me spare you the worst of what Naldrum would inflict. I will be quick. Your child will not suffer, I promise you."

Their faces turned to stone. Hating himself, hating Naldrum, Kel took the infant from the girl's breast and carried it outside. She clutched Kel, begging, but her parents held her as he walked away.

. . .

Chapter Forty-Two

Kel made it back to Naldrum's holdings as a blinding red sunrise stained the sky. All of the routine motions soothed Kel and stole precious time from Naldrum. The horse was unsaddled, the leather saddle and bridle hung and the stable boy reminded to rub oil into them, and oats poured into the bucket for Thor-Thunder. Normally he brushed his beloved horse himself, but fatigue pulled at every bone.

Kel's footsteps grew slower and slower as he walked to the longhouse. Chickens scratched in the dirt, and a woman bent over a mound of carded sheep's wool, ready to spin it. Another hurried to join her. The two women would work in companionable conversation.

"Health to you, Steward Kel" they called. "Not long until the *dísablót!*"

He nodded and wiped his mouth. Gods, for something to eat, for a drink.

A gaggle of young boys burst out of the longhouse accompanied by a couple of dogs. "Good morning, sir!" They bowed, barely stopping. Kel wanted to kick the dogs out of his way, to cuff the boys' heads, to hurt someone, anyone. To tear the damned longhouse down pillar by pillar, to set the whole damned thing on fire and to drag Naldrum into the flames and watch him scream in agony. *For* Aldís. *For all the young women you've hurt.*

He went in, knocked on the door to Naldrum's private room.

"Who is it?"

Kel opened the door. Naldrum's face disgusted him. Kel said nothing, just lifted his chin to indicate *it is done.*

Without waiting for Naldrum to respond, he slammed the door shut, strode away, and returned to the stable. He threw himself onto the stone floor beside his horse and fell into a tortured sleep.

. . .

The following week, another knock. Another attempt, pleading with the man to go away, but another 'private interview' with Naldrum. Another dreaded ride, trailing a poor but joyous man, and being trailed in turn by Drikke.

This time, drenching rain suited Kel's bitterness.

. . .

The child lay squirming on the rain-wet stone, crying. A perfect little boy. Kel gripped the stone, trying to force himself do what he had done before, but his fingers would not let go of the edge of the rock.

Oh, Aldís. Her name came from his lips, more invocation for help than prayer for her safety.

"You want your mother," he said to the infant. "I wish I could give you back to her."

He lifted the baby in his arms, held it close to his chest. His lips brushed the soft fuzz of hair that tufted the small round head. Why did the gods not stop him in this evil act? Why did they not stop Naldrum? How immoral could one man be before Frigg, mother of all women, finally took notice and intervened?

The girl and her family watched at a distance. He knew it was cruel to keep them waiting.

Kel wrapped his hand around the infant's nose and mouth, gripped tightly. "Shhh," he said. "Sleep, wee one."

It struggled. Kel held the baby closer, his mouth against its tiny head, whispering comfort. When the small body went limp, Kel wept, ashamed of what he had done.

He lay the child back on the stones and knelt before it in sadness, unable to move. *Those people. This grief belongs to them.* Kel cleared his throat, stood, and carefully arranged the tiny limbs as if the child slept. Gently tucked it up in its swaddling clothes. When he had finished, he faced the family, but kept his distance. Words of sorrow would ring hollow and only add to their pain. He palmed the center of his chest and bowed, the sign of respect and submission. Then Kel wheeled, mounted his horse, and kicked it to a gallop, passing Drikke without speaking.

He drove Thor-Thunder cruelly. Every lash of the reins heightened his loathing of Naldrum, of himself for serving the man, and the aching, desperate grief for this family, this child, and for a woman he loved and would never see again.

The rain fell harder. Kel threw back his hood, wanting to feel the sharp cold of it cut against the face of a man who had no kindness and no heart.

. . .

Chapter Forty-Three

To the relief of all at Naldrum's, the weather had cleared a few days before the *thing* was due to happen. The entire compound had labored to prepare for masses of expected dísablót guests, and the thought of visitors tenting in fields full of mud and the longhouse overflowing with cranky, rain-ridden guests had threatened to spoil a great deal of hard work. Naldrum had had tantrums. The sun gave his staff some relief.

Kel rode back towards the compound through the sprawling lands owned by his headman. Already the trail was choked with those who intended to arrive early and get the best sites to set up their booths.

. . .

They had survived—barely, for some—two years of bad harvests and a grueling winter. The fresh spring air lifted spirits, and for the time being, the tensions of the valley neighbors eased. Ceaseless greetings went back and forth as cousins, in-laws, and old acquaintances mingled along the roadway.

"Spring greetings!" "May this *dísablót* burst with meat and ale and cheese!" "Happy *equal-night-and-day* to you and yours!" "May the goddess bless our farms with plentiful lambs!" Their celebration had already started. After a winter of such strain, this lighthearted mood promised to become more and more raucous in the last days until the festival, where the celebration of womanhood would spill over into other matters of wooing, coupling, lust, and love.

. . .

Even more visitors had turned out than usual. *No surprise there,* thought Kel as Thor-Thunder picked his way among them. Many of these early ones had more on their mind besides a good tent-site. Before the festival got underway, they would line up to ask Naldrum to forgive their debts for one more season, or for the loan of extra seed.

Kel replied to their greetings in a monotone without thought. He could almost smell the worry lurking beneath their gaiety. Fear stalked them along the roadway, the dreaded possibility that even now, their precious seeds lay black and beginning to rot on too-wet ground. If that if that happened, some might not manage another winter.

The crowd swelled, almost tumescent with the need for optimism that something would signal a change in luck. They streamed forward, a herd that looked happy on the surface but walked fraught with inner fears, trampling lean and empty toward Naldrum's richness, longing for hope and certainty.

Naldrum's beautiful daughter Ankya will perform the Ceremony of the Egg. The seeds will take root and thrive. The torrential rains will stop.

We will survive. And if we survive, surely, things will get better one day.

. . .

Kel could not put his finger on it, but a nagging thought troubled him about their too-hopeful words. At last he gave up thinking about it, and instead considered his own state of being.

The thought of death preoccupied him daily. *To be free of Naldrum, even if it meant death.* He did not much care how it happened, or if it would hurt. In fact, the more he suffered, the better, to atone for the hurt he had caused in others.

Perhaps one day the Dísir will tear me limb from limb. Kel shuddered. Maybe they had not yet because they understood that Kel would sell his soul to Loki if it meant he could escape Naldrum. Or perhaps not. He greatly doubted that the *dísir,* with all that lay under their auspices, cared much about his motivations.

In the midst of the bursting of spring, of new life, the darkness in Kel deepened daily. More and more, he longed for the release of death.

. . .

But only after one more thing, he promised himself. If another knock came, he desperately hoped it would be that girl from Althing.

Yet almost as fervently, he wished for the opposite. Perhaps the unwanted spring visitors had finished for this year, and there would be no more children to kill.

. . .

Such was not to be. Late in the night, Kel stirred from sleep, hearing the dreaded sound echo through the longhouse. Kel groaned and rolled over, stuffing the coverings around his ears.

. . .

The knocking sounded again. Kel cursed. Why did the door-boy not answer? He waited, hoping he had imagined it, but yet another one came, quiet and hesitant. Kel tossed in his blankets. *Not my job to answer the door in the dead of night.*

Louder this time, but still tentative; a half-knock, almost, and then a little louder again, as if someone had built up their courage.

Go away, he fumed.

The rapping against the door continued, growing louder, faster, and more demanding. *Damn them all, how could everyone sleep through this?* Cursing, Kel threw off the blankets and stumbled through the main room, furious at the sleeping figures under other blankets. To Hel with them. He couldn't go back to sleep now if he tried.

The door lamp had gone out. Kel felt around the threshold for the small stone bowl filled with tallow and a twist of cotton-grass. His fingers found it, and he held the wick to an ember in the fire pit. When the lamp sputtered alight, he reached for the door-string, and held the lamp high so he could see whoever stood on the other side of the door.

No one was there.

Odd. Maybe it had been revelers from the camping field, drunk and playing pranks. Kel slammed the door closed and put the lamp on the floor. He kicked the sleeping door-boy and turned to go back to bed.

The knock came again, this time a sharp rapping, insistent.

Fuming, Kel reached for the lamp again He pushed the door open. Once again, he saw only darkness.

"What are you playing at?" he shouted into the night. "If I catch whoever is trying to make trouble for this house, I'll horsewhip you!"

He waited, glaring. Nothing moved.

Kel strode outside and stood barefoot on the flag stones ringing the longhouse entrance. He saw nothing but Naldrum's flagstaff, its banner hanging limp. A light mist flowed along the ground. The flag-stones gleamed, damp, reflecting the small light of the lamp.

Kel looked more closely at the stones. Their smooth surface showed only smooth and even wetness. No footprints or any marks of shoes coming and going. What in Hel?

If anybody knocks again, they can be damned. Let them wait until morning.

Kel stepped back inside the longhouse door, his feet cold from the wet stones. Just as he pulled the door closed once more, the same knock pounded against the wood.

"I have you now!" Kel cried, and crashed the door open.

A woman's pale skin reflected the dim light of the lamp. A cloak covered most of her face. Kel could see only her eyes, impossibly large, impossibly dark, and a bit of her hair, sodden in the night mist.

Kel stared. Too young to be Aldís, but in the weak light, someone who might be Aldís stared back at him.

He reached towards her. His arm felt difficult to move, as if it was partially frozen. Kel touched the woman's jaw, clumsy and awkward. She stood without speaking as he groped at her mouth.

"I cannot see clearly. Is that you, Aldís??"

The hood fell back from her head. Angry red welts covered her face. Kel stepped back in shock, then grabbed at her, but she drifted away, just out of reach.

"Naldrum promised me he would leave you alone. *He promised!"* Kel's voice rose in fury. "All that I have done for him, he could not keep that one vow? I will kill him for this!"

She stared impassively, her eyes betraying no emotion. The marks of Naldrum's wicked rage looked as if they had been cut with a birch switch.

"We have to get you away from here before he sees you!" Kel cried. "We'll ride for the coast tonight. I'll find a ship. We'll go away where he can never find us. Come!" He reached for her cloak. "Come!"

But as he grasped it, the cloak fell open, and Kel saw that she cradled a child tight against her body. The child's face was cold and blue. It did not move.

Kel drew back in horror. What he saw was not possible. He stared at the woman again, aghast. The lips were wrong, but those eyes and that hair, so like Aldís, yet not hers.

Kel felt as if he was falling. *It could not be.* The little girl with those eyes and that hair had died long, long ago.

. . .

Kel realized in that instant he had never learned the name of Aldís' child. He stepped through the doorway and reached for the woman again.

"Please come in. Let me help you," he whispered. As he did, the light of the lamp spread a little further. He saw more faces behind her.

Two more young women, their hair stringy with rain, their faces welted with the same marks. Kel rubbed his eyes in disbelief. They were the two girls of this spring. The soap-maker's daughter and the one whose longhouse he had just left stared at him, bruised, grieving, accusing.

No! He had done what Naldrum ordered! Why did they have marks on their faces? Had Naldrum beaten anyway? Why?

"You must not be seen here!" he urged in a hoarse whisper. "Naldrum will destroy you! And you—" He lunged, tried to grab the first woman. A cry of dread escaped him. "Who are you? *What* are you?"

The women stared back at him without speaking. They edged closer. The dreadful nausea of child-killing swept over Kel.

"I did not want to do it!" he cried. "He left me with no choice!"

Another silent woman appeared. He recognized this one too, a girl from two years ago. Or had it been three years? No, two; and there behind her was another girl, the only one from last year.

And then Kel knew. The *dísir* had sent them. He was to be punished at last.

. . .

Face after face appeared in the mist. They crowded towards the door, forcing Kel back. His feet felt stuck to the cold stones, but his eyes darted wildly as the host of women pushed towards the longhouse entrance, all cloaked, each face showing the marks of brutality.

"What do you need from me?" Kel groaned. "I freely admit my guilt. What must I do? Please let me atone for what I have done."

As if at some signal, the pale women flung their cloaks open. Huddled against each was an infant, tiny blue faces on limp necks, lifeless. Kel trembled, not wanting to see, but his eyes would not close.

So many women. So many children, without the breath I stole from them. Such evil I have wrought for him!

"Aldís!" He threw her name towards the encroaching women as apology, as a reason, as a plea for forgiveness. "Because of Aldís! I never wanted this to happen! You must believe me!"

"You smothered healthy children." The hollow voice of an otherworldly creature. "You killed so that Naldrum did not have to take responsibility for his actions."

"I tried to refuse! Naldrum does not allow it! No matter what I do, or do not do, he will make someone suffer!" Kel cried, his voice breaking. "I hate this duty! But he gives no choice!"

The *dis*-Aldís opened its mouth. A scream exploded from its throat. It reached for his face, its fingers like claws. Kel stumbled backwards, tried to push the door shut against her. A fragment of the woman's cape pressed through, kept the door from closing. Her fingers snaked in, bony bits that curled around the wood, reaching.

Kel put his shoulder to the thick pine boards. He shoved with all his might, but the throng of spirit-women pushed back harder. He lost control and fell against the flagstones. The doorway swelled with women in sodden capes, clawing at him, falling upon him, holding their lifeless forth infants against him. Kel fought for air.

"Aldís!" he cried. "I have to save her! *Let me save her!"* But the women still came, swarming over him. They buried him in a mound of damp flesh. Death-smell choked his lungs. Kel groaned in misery, unable to breathe, and reached for the solace of death.

. . .

"Shhhh," a voice pulled him back from the terror. "Shhhhh. You're dreaming. Shhhh. You're having a bad dream."

A smooth hand stroked his neck, down the top of his back. That soft hand had never known field labor, had never even buckled the harness onto its own horse. A hand fragrant with expensive perfume from Frankish merchants.

No, not Ankya. Kel's heart still pounded with panic from the nightmare. *Go away.* Half-asleep, he felt confusion. 'Go away' was what he told the fathers who knocked. 'Go away' to this woman, to protect himself from whatever danger she posed.

"You traveled all night again, I hear." Ankya's voice, soothing. "Look at you, sleeping on this hard floor. Let me send for my maid to wrap a stone from the longfire for you, to warm you." He felt something touch his thigh, stroke upwards. Her hand?

Kel lay without moving, his face buried in his elbow. He grunted as if sleeping. *I am no different than the men who come here. We all need to escape from Naldrum and his treacherous family.*

"Perhaps later, then" she whispered. "Rest well, brave man."

Once again something stroked against his muscle, this time higher yet on the inner side of his thigh. Slightly too high, slightly too long. The sound of her bare footsteps padded away, and he was alone.

. . .

Chapter Forty-Four

Ankya moved silently towards her father's private room. No servants were nearby. Whoever had knocked so late this night met now with her father in secret.

She leaned against the doorway and pressed her ear against the wood. Almost impossible to hear. It was not worth the risk of being caught.

Ankya dropped onto one of the crowded sleeping benches in the main hall. She would wait as long as she needed, to see who came out of that room.

. . .

The man facing Naldrum trembled. He hoped the headman could not see it. The last time the trader Josson had stood in the *gothi's* presence had been a near-disaster. Today, he hoped to rectify that mistake with news certain to win back Naldrum's favor.

Naldrum, wearing his sleeping-cap, stood glaring at Josson, hands on his hips. "You!" he roared.

"Please, sir. I came with—" But Naldrum cut him off.

"I told you to never come back here again unless you had something of true value for me! How quickly you have forgotten!

And now, the ash-girl has woken me from sleep in the middle of the night because of you! You owe me more than you did before!"

"More, sir?" quavered Josson.

"That infernal slave you sold me has run off!"

At those words, Josson now regretted deeply the fact that he was standing in Naldrum's longhouse. The last time… He forced himself to move away from that horrifying memory.

"I have news for you, *gothi.*"

"This had better be worth it, you slime-ridden rot-gut."

Josson bowed and half-prostrated himself. He was so eager to speak he had to start over several times, which only worsened Naldrum's annoyance.

"Get to the point! One more senseless word and I'll have you dragged outside and beaten!"

Josson took an unsteady breath, his heart thumping. He stammered out what he had heard. "A man is to be tried for murder at the spring *thing* held at Thornes."

"What interest is that to me?"

Another shaky breath. "I heard certain people whisper that you might be interested in the outcome."

Naldrum's eyes narrowed. "Tell me about this accused man. And lower your voice."

"It is a seafarer, whose name many know. One whose ability on the seas cannot be bettered by any other *vikinger* alive. He is a tiller, known for his ability to steer a ship. They call him Tiller Th—"

Naldrum cut off Josson's words with a slashing gesture. "Hush! Do not speak his name! Anyone could hear you." His eyes bored into

Josson's. "This man—this seafarer—is accused of murder? Are you certain?"

"I pledge my life on it, *gothi.*"

Naldrum struggled to keep his face severe, but inwardly, he exulted. What luck! A serious accusation like that could result in outlawry—and best of all, Naldrum had many powerful friends at Thornes.

We badly need someone who can steer the ship I am planning.

"Make haste back to Thornes," he commanded Josson. "I want you to give a message to give some of those who will be on the jury. They must convict Tiller! You must reach them before the trials begin." Naldrum listed the names and made the trader repeat them.

Josson hesitated. Should he ask for a reward? He opened his mouth, but Naldrum grew impatient.

"Go! *Now!*" he shouted. "There is not a breath of time to lose! And then ride back to tell me the result!"

When the longhouse door closed behind Josson, Ankya sat staring at it. She had heard her father's shouted words. What was so important that a common trader had ridden here in the middle of the night, and left just as quickly?

. . .

When the sun rose, Ankya sang snatches of songs, dancing around the longhouse. "One more day to prepare for the spring festival!"

Servants and slaves swarmed in the great hall as Kel gave orders. Baskets of vegetables stood ready to be prepared. Pigs squealed in the slaughter-yard, destined for the roasting-spits. The weaving-women counted blankets, making sure enough were ready and clean for the extra guests expected. Naldrum's wives sorted gifts to be given. Expensive items were reserved for guests of honor, while cheap tokens would be thrown to the crowds: twisted chicken-feet, broken beads, bits of colored thread for embroidery.

Ankya ran up to Kel, brushed against him. "Where is the trader Josson? I heard him come in last night and speak with my father."

Kel scowled. "I have no idea. Your father did not mention it to me. I suggest you go ask him."

"I will, but what if the trader brought a gift my father plans to give me? I don't want to ruin his surprise."

"Ankya, I'm busy. Please."

She stood back and twirled. "Do you like my dress?"

Kel forced himself to look away from her. The garment had the same cut as other women wore, but theirs were linen and wool. The makings of Ankya's dress came from somewhere so far away Kel could not even imagine, a strange white fabric called silk that seemed to be the stuff of clouds. It flowed in a soft fog over her breasts, dropped from her shoulders in a smooth waterfall down her back. It turned the curves of her buttocks into a drift of snow, nestled in the cleft between them.

Snow makes everything beautiful, Kel thought. *Every falling-down fence, every pile of rotted cabbages seems clean under such pristine white stuff. The delicate drifts hide the fetid underneath. That was what Ankya Naldrumsdottir reminded him of, putridness covered in a skin of perfection.*

"Greetings of the festival, Steward Kel," she whispered, pressing her body against him again.

The soft inhale of breath, her little gasp of desire. Those lips that a man had to notice, full and perfect. Ankya watched Kel. Her expression, revealing, taunting, shameless, hid no more than the silk garment she wore.

"Steward?" She inclined her head, still staring intently at him. "Kel!"

"I must be getting to work on—"

"Come over here." Ankya dropped the sing-song child-voice and spoke like a grown woman, rational and determined. She pulled him away from the crowd of workers. "Sometimes I wonder at the wisdom of my father's plans. Do you ever?"

Kel barely kept his mouth from falling open. "You know it would deeply offend your father to hear you doubt him. He expects loyalty from you. From all of us."

"He plans for me to marry some powerful jarl in Norway. I am nothing but a pawn to him. I don't know why that trader was here. My father has said nothing to me. I worry that he carried a marriage offer." She bit at her lip, hoping that Kel knew something, would give her a hint.

What did she take him for? She could not be trusted.

"Ankya, I made a contract to serve your father. Whatever he orders me, I do."

She smiled, her mouth bitter and beautiful. "Which includes ignoring his daughter's desires."

Kel said nothing. Ankya, full of spring lust, needled him. "Perhaps my father's steward still knows himself strong enough for a woman like me." She smiled, the implication in her words clear.

Demon-woman. Impossible to know if she is joking or if she means what she says. Kel looked away. Dangerous to ignore his headman's daughter, distasteful to be in her presence.

"You look dreadful, Kel. What are these journeys that my father sends you on each spring? They clearly exhaust you. Sit with me at the morning meal. I will share the best morsels with you."

. . .

When the time came for eating, Ankya saved a seat beside herself for Kel, but he was nowhere to be found.

He had put a long galloping ride between himself and the longhouse, heading to see his friend Sauthi in the distant fields. Thor-Thunder sensed Kel's mood. He ran hard for the first stretch without needing to be urged. By middle-day, Kel felt as if he could breathe again.

. . .

Chapter Forty-Five

Sauthi offered no greeting. He merely said, "The days are getting longer and snow lingers only in the deepest hollows. Must nearly be the time for spring rites, I'm guessing. Figured I'd see you out this way soon."

"Hey, Sauthi. Good to be here."

"Good to *live* out here. None of the inbred vileness of our chieftain's compound."

Kel paced the grass, bending and picking up tufts of wool. "I see the sheep have begun shedding."

"Aye. I've collected bundles of it. Gives me something to do. I trade them for small items, should a trader happen by."

"Of course." Another long period of silence.

"Bad this year?" Sauthi glanced sideways at Kel.

Kel nodded. He once told Sauthi about the dreaded spring errands, although he had never spoken of reasons for them, or what they entailed.

"How many trips?"

"Two so far."

"You look pretty ragged. Worse than last spring. Something making it worse this year?"

"I had a nightmare last night, about a woman. She looked like someone I once loved—but it was not her, it looked like—" Kel broke off. "It looked like someone else. Someone impossible."

Sauthi waited. Unburdening one's sprit was not a quick matter.

"There were other women in the dream, too. Young girls whose faces I've remembered for years. So many faces." Kel's voice trailed off as he felt once more the crushing weight of the dream.

"How *many* years?" The tone of the question, oddly sharp. "Exactly?"

Kel frowned. How many years had he answered the knocks and ridden on Naldrum's command? Ever since his very first spring in Naldrum's service. He thought back, counted, gave an answer.

Sauthi leaned against his crook. *No.* For once, his eyes left the horizon and closed.

"That many, already?" Sauthi muttered in disbelief. He kept his eyes closed, rubbed his forehead with his knuckle. "Has it been so long I have been out here? And yet still not long enough to make them leave me alone." Old memories, unable to be washed away.

Kel could not make out Sauthi's words. "What did you say?"

Sauthi mumbled again. "I said go away."

"Who? Me? Why?"

"Not you!" Sauthi snapped. "I want the walking disgust that is Naldrum to go away! I want the memories of what I did for him to go away! I want to be free of it, once and for all!"

"I don't understand." Kel had never heard Sauthi speak that way.

"No? Let me make it clear for you." Sauthi's tone became even more hard and rough. "I *know* why you come here, Kel Coesson! I know why you ride away from Naldrum's estate in self-loathing, but always crawl back to serve him again, choking on your anger and shame. I know what it feels like to be caught in a trap, willing to gnaw off part of yourself to escape—but also knowing that escaping will only cause even worse suffering."

Kel, stunned, could not believe what Sauthi was saying. "How can you know these things? I've never told you."

"I know because I *was* you, once, Kel I know what you do for Naldrum—because I did it myself!"

. . .

Kel could not have been more surprised if one of the sheep had started to speak.

"What, you think you're the first one to do his filthy bidding?" Sauthi cried. "Who do you think did Naldrum's dirty work before you came along? Did you never consider the duties of the steward before you? I was that man! Naldrum trapped me just like he has trapped you. And there were others before me." Sauthi turned away, humiliated, but relieved to have finally spoken the truth. "It shames me to admit, even to you, what I did for him."

Two humans, locked in a misery they could share with no one else, stared across the valley. No words existed to ease the terrible burden they each bore.

"How long?" asked Kel. "For you, I mean."

"I lasted for seven years. But I had lost the will to live long before." Sauthi looked with concern at Kel. "You seem close to that yourself."

Kel made no argument. The next question was harder, but he had to know.

"How many?"

The number, unforgettable, deep in Sauthi's marrow. "Eleven." He did not ask the number that he knew Kel carried inside. "I found myself longing for my own death more and more, each time I brought death."

"How did you get away from him? Naldrum has threatened to hurt—to kill—someone I love if I betray him or leave him."

"The same with me."

"And did he—?"

"Naldrum never keeps any of his good promises. The bad ones, he never fails to keep."

"And when you finally left Naldrum, he hurt her."

"Hurt *him.*" No explanation was offered, and Kel did not ask. Brother, father, lover, son; none of the choices mattered to Kel. He saw only the pain etched Sauthi's face, and feared that pain.

"Badly?"

"Deadly."

Sauthi trembled against the crook that held him up.

"Here, friend," Kel said. "You're about to collapse."

A broad rock in the meadow, warmed by the sun, offered comfort. Kel led Sauthi to the stone and helped him to sit. A silence, in which each man looked down long furrows sown with regret and pain, bearing crops of sorrow.

"I won't let the woman I love die," said Kel. "So for me, there's no escape."

Sauthi turned to Kel with merciless honesty. "You can't save her. You already know in your heart that Naldrum will break his word. He cannot bear to be controlled by anything, not even by his own promises! No matter what he says, he *will* torment her one day. He will cheat you because he loves to cheat, even more than he loves to win. He is driven to do it. You have a single choice to make." Now Sauthi was shouting. "How much longer you will cover up Naldrum's misdeeds, Kel? *How much longer?*" Sauthi tried to calm himself and quiet his voice. "Because no matter what you do, eventually, he *will* destroy this woman, whoever she is, and you as well."

"Not really much of a choice, is it?"

"Like the 'choice' we forced on people?"

The reality of Kel's guilt cut through him afresh.

"What's her name?" asked Sauthi gently. "The one you love?"

"Aldís." Saying it, Kel wanted to make the signs of Thor and the white-christ, anything that might protect her from Naldrum.

Aldís? Sauthi choked. The memory of that particular name cut him to his core.

Curse you, Naldrum. All these years, all this distance, and your poison still infects all of us.

Sauthi hardened his voice. "As I said, you cannot protect her. I promise you."

"I'm to just abandon her to his cruelty? I've protected her so long. I cannot just give in."

Sauthi peered intently at Kel. "You've lasted far longer than I did. Far longer than the ones before me. Perhaps you have it in you to do more than just to defy him. Perhaps you will be the one to stop him, once and for all."

Kel swallowed hard. "Don't make me a hero. Do you know why I lasted so long? Because for years, I thought I wanted to be like him. But something started changing. I realized that everything I had idealized in Naldrum was a sham. That all the 'fake rumors' he claimed were spread by jealous people were, in fact, true. I am ashamed that it took me so long."

"The same with me." Years of regret in Sauthi's voice. "But I failed."

"The worst thing? Instead of me growing stronger against him, Naldrum's snare wrapped tighter and tighter—around *me.* He threatened me about Aldís when we first met, long ago. I had hoped that after so much time he had forgotten, but no, he renewed his threats this past Althing. Trapped, I resolved to watch him, to pretend to serve him, waiting for my chance to thwart him. But because of her, Naldrum all but owns me. Yet she hates me because I serve him." A long pause. "You see the truth, Sauthi. I *am* about to break. I too, have failed, and Naldrum will win. I cannot bear the thought."

"You have not failed! You have lived side by side with that beast for all these years! You know him better than anyone in the world. The road may have taken you the long way around, but you are still walking it. I see your strength. What you feel as failure, I see as a blade of iron, hardened by the blacksmith's anvil and hammer, seared by fire, toughened by immersion."

Kel did not answer. After a pause, Sauthi pressed on, excited by a new thought.

"I think that your breaking is not about *your* breaking. I think you sense *Naldrum's* breaking. A way exists to destroy Naldrum. One day his power will dissolve like sand before a wave. Set your intentions, and stay strong, Kel."

Set your intentions. The same thing that Tor had told him. "Someone said almost those exact words to me."

"The dark elves must be trying to work with you. Listen to their truth."

Dark elves. A dark-skinned man Kel counted as a friend. Kel felt the breath of destiny, but scoffed.

The shepherd assessed him. "You have a weighty burden to carry already, and this only makes it heavier. Do not fret yourself with how such a thing may come to pass. Be like the glaciers. Move slowly and deliberately, but always towards the same goal. Let the spring meltwater flow in you as it does in the glaciers, in mysterious ways. You find your path to the sea, where you can drop this huge load and be free of it."

"I don't know. Maybe the knocks are over for this year. Maybe Naldrum will die soon."

"I used to wish for the same thing. Don't count on it. Demons must protect him He has grown so deceitful and so bitter, yet he thrives. Besides, his family is just like him. Even if he is gone, they will spread his evil. They must all be defeated as one."

"But Aldís," Kel began.

Sauthi sighed. He wished he could protect Aldís, and knew he could not. The old deep pain. "I meant what I said. It's a brutal truth, I know, but trying to protect the woman you care about only gives Naldrum time to grow stronger and stronger. You must choose." His eyes dimmed. "Protect that which is already lost—her—or stop evil before evil gets stronger." He repeated his earlier admonition. "You must choose."

"I just don't believe it. I could set my intentions all year, and it would change nothing."

Sauthi fumbled in a ragged pouch. He extracted a small wooden figure. "Take this. Maybe it will help."

"What is it?" Kel asked.

"It belonged to the last child. The one that broke me, that caused me to run away from serving Naldrum even one heartbeat longer."

Kel took the little figure and held it in his hands. A child once held this, a child that Naldrum had wanted dead, and that Sauthi had killed. Disgust at himself filled Kel.

Sauthi was still speaking. "—but I couldn't do it. I couldn't live with myself anymore. She had this little toy clutched in her hand. Instead of killing her, I gave her away, to strangers. She put this little toy in my hand. I think she understood I needed something to hold onto. Night after night, drowning in guilt, I held it, as she must once had. Every breath I took, I prayed that she would live and thrive. Naldrum kept his wicked promise. But this little doll kept me alive through the darkest years. Wretch though I was, at least I saved one child from him."

He broke down. Kel put his cloak around the old shepherd.

"Keep that doll with you, Kel. Remember that one child survived Naldrum's purge. Believe that you can do what needs to be done. Do not ask how. That will come with time. Only know that you can. For all of us, you must try." His voice, pleading.

Kel turned the bit of carved wood in his fingers. A trifle, a nothing, but oddly, the small weight of it in his hand gave a feeling of comfort. A real child had held this, a tiny being who breathed and ate and feared—and still lived, somewhere out there. This little toy, proof that for once, the all-powerful Naldrum had lost, and might again—and to a mere child.

But how? Kel's logical mind tripped him. Again, he yielded to doubt.

"Boy or girl?" he asked, stalling.

Sauthi knew the child's name, knew the mother's name. Could not bring himself to say either. He simply replied, "Girl."

Sauthi longed for the comfort of full confession to Kel, the only living man who truly understood these torments inside, but he could not bring himself utter the last shameful truth.

Perhaps another day.

. . .

Kel touched the top of the piece. "Girl, eh? She was old enough to have some teeth. Look here. She must have chewed on it." Again, the touch of destiny swept over him and chilled him.

"I'll treasure it. Thank you. It's a powerful thing, knowing that this child lives. Once day it may help, as you said. But for now, it feels too big, too impossible. Right now, I need to do something good, something real. I need to work hard and be exhausted and forget the whole mess, if only for today. Any ewes set to lamb?"

"Several every day, pretty steady. A few are coming on. You'll get a chance."

Kel pulled a packet from his saddlebag. "Here, before we get started. I brought you some *dísablót* food from the main house." One of the cooking girls had wrapped a smoked trout.

"Well, that's a treat I don't often get," said the shepherd. He bit into the meat, savored it. "Cook must have felt sorry for you, working so hard." He shifted back into the taunting camaraderie they had shared since Kel, wandering from the compound in distress, had first met and befriended the old man. Sauthi, like Tor, treated him without deference or without the cloying obsequiousness of the compound.

"Maybe the cook knows I'm the steward of the whole damned place, and treats me with the respect you so clearly lack." He smiled. They traded the same jests every year.

"Maybe," said his friend. His sharp eyes flicked to Kel for a moment, then went back to watching the hills as before, the difficult subject set aside for now.

Kel stripped off his shirt. "That's why I come here," he said. "Too much respect back there. You're the only one who treats me like I barely matter at all." The spring air bit cold against his bare skin. "Put me to work."

. . .

Chapter Forty-Six

Tiller's foot jiggled as he waited for his case to be heard by the law council at the spring *thing* in Thornes. The whole prank of getting his high-seat pillars back from Thorgest had billowed into a bitter, rotten mess.

He talked to Styr, repeating things he had said over and over before.

"I told Thorgest exactly what happened. His sons came up and I was half-laughing. I mean, it was ridiculous. We had all worked so hard to get my pillars out and the replacement ones in that I was silly with fatigue. Too tired to even be angry at Thorgest, and I was friends with his sons, so the whole situation was just absurd."

"I didn't expect what happened next. Their blades were out when they rode up. I put up my hands, told them we didn't need to fight. I even offered to give the pillars back."

Styr said nothing. What had happened could not be changed.

"They struck first, Styr."

"I know." Styr believed Tiller.

"I kept trying to settle things down. I understood why they were angry, but they wouldn't listen at all."

Tiller lapsed into silence, then began speaking again, as if to himself. "Einarr. One of my best friends. Odin's eye, Styr. He was always such a scrappy one. Thorgest's son cut him, just a little on the forearm, and Einarr just went berserk."

Tiller leaned over and groaned. Einarr had returned the insult with deadly speed. The four men—Tiller, Einarr, and Thorgest's two sons—had grappled together, rolling on the ground.

Nausea twisted Tiller's guts. "Thorgest arrived not long after. I explained, but why would he listen? With his two sons dead on the ground? No man would."

"But Tiller, he brought some of this on himself," Styr said. "Yes, maybe we all pulled a stupid prank. Maybe his sons overreacted. But Thorgest started it, didn't he, by not returning your pillars to you? If he hadn't been so pigheaded, none of this would have happened."

"He said I was the pigheaded one, because I wouldn't admit I was wrong. We ended up shouting at one another. Gods, Styr, I don't know what all I said to him. The sight of his sons and Einarr, and the smell of blood in the raw air. I was devastated. Angry and heartbroken. And now it's come to this. I should have known he'd file a case against me."

"Everybody around here knew he had your pillars. Maybe they'd have backed him up, told you he had the right to keep them. But plenty of people heard him laugh about them, and say he'd told you not to worry how long he had them. At least they heard him say that before his wife decided she wanted them. And remember, his son attached Einarr first. That matters."

"But this trial—I can't imagine it's more than a formality." Styr's words did not sound as confident as he had hoped they would.

This hearing will be just a formality. Tiller had said those same words, trying to get sailing work for the upcoming season. *Once the law council hears the facts, they will clear the charges against me.* In fact, he had very much believed that to be true. Now, he was not so sure.

"It's Thorgest's word against mine. And there aren't any other witnesses to the fight." Tiller forced himself to still his jiggling foot. It looked anxious, and he did not want people to see that. He needed work. "I should be conducting business at this *thing* to make up for what Naldrum cheated me. But enthusiasm for my work has been tempered by Thorgest's accusation. It'll be a relief when the hearing is finished and the whole damned thing behind me."

The crowd in front of Tiller began to shift and break apart, signaling that the case before Tiller's had ended. The people who had gathered at Thornes had squeezed into a turf-walled sheepfold for the legal hearings, where rough plank seats had been set up. The law council stood and stretched, needing a break from the hard planks, while some who had been watching the proceedings sank gratefully on the same benches to rest.

Portions of small beer were shared into mugs and horns placed on the table in the gathering-yard. The drinks were hastily gulped down before the next hearing began.

Except for their initial conversation, Styr had kept his distance, at Tiller's recommendation. He tried not to stare at Tiller as they waited for the trial. Nervous anticipation grew steadily, as Styr fought feelings of guilt for his own part in the matter.

During the council recess, Tiller looked through the crowd for a distraction. Surely someone likely to talk seafaring was among these farm families. He was glad to see a familiar figure. The old shipbuilder Bjarni Herjolfsson moved slowly across the grass, braced on the shoulder of one of his many grandchildren. Tiller called Bjarni's name.

"Is that my young friend Tiller? Rumor says you got into a scrape with Thorgest and might be at this *thing*. Good to hear your voice. I had hoped to have a talk with you."

The elderly shipbuilder spoke with complete unconcern, as if a charge of murder was a mere inconvenience. Bjarni was a man of deep principles, someone Tiller respected deeply. The shipbuilder's words were a welcome balm. The old sting of having a father who bore the brand of *outlaw* was never far away, and especially now. To Tiller's relief, Bjarni seemed uninclined to discuss the charges against him.

In fact, the old man did not even wait for an answer to his question, but started talking of ships he had built, of how they had been designed for different sorts of voyages and purposes. How one needed a balance between height and girth for a specific kind of load when travelling the rough seas of the North-way, and how the biggest knarr he had ever built was still in service somewhere, a slave galley far to the south.

"I never learned the name of the king or the country. Would've liked to, though." Bjarni chattered on and Tiller half-listened, glad of the distraction.

"…an almost endless voyage…room for a crew, but not too big…extremely stable…survive weather no one could predict…but fast enough to travel quickly…" The old man rambled on about the last ship he would ever build, and how he wanted to craft something entirely new, a vision of seafaring that had never been realized before.

He seemed oddly intent on the concept. His voice changed as he moved from a litany of ideas to specific questions for Tiller.

"What might you be able to add to this grand design?" Bjarni said nothing about who the 'grand design' belonged to. "Eh? What suggestions, young Tiller? You're one to think differently than others. Good ideas, always. I'm counting on getting your thoughts!"

Tiller saw the law council members heading back into the sheepfold. The Thornes headman pointed at him, indicating his hearing was next.

Bjarni was poking Tiller in the ribs now, practically demanding a response. Tiller rattled off a quick answer, but an intuitive one of which he felt oddly certain.

"Bjarni, build her like the women of your youthful memories. Give her a strong body, and the speed and power of a warship so she can fly over the waves like a Valkyrie—but give her, too, the carrying capacity of a mother, because like a merchant's knarr, she'll need to hold the many items her crew will need for such a voyage."

Tiller stood and straightened his kyrtill. He smoothed his hair back one last time, and walked to the door of the trial room. Bjarni, pleased with Tiller's words, stood as well. He started his slow gait in the opposite direction, his granddaughter carefully guiding him towards where horses waited. Already he was turning Tiller's words in his mind. They were exciting ideas he could use.

At the threshold of the hearing, Tiller paused. A thought had come to him, and even though it was a small idea, he felt an overwhelming compulsion to say it to Bjarni as well. Impulsively, he turned where old man was walking.

"Bjarni!" Tiller called. "Make your ship beautiful, too! Whoever crews that vessel will need to feel proud of her. A ship built well will serve them for the voyage you describe, but a *beautiful* ship built well will uplift them. It'll give them strength and courage in the desperate days. They'll need that!"

Why had it felt so critical for him to say those words? Tiller shook off the puzzling feeling. He walked through the sheepfold entrance to face his old friend Thorgest and the accusation of murdering Thorgest's beloved sons.

. . .

For the most part, Tiller had thought little of the law, both in practice and in fact. Law had painful, too-familiar connotations from his childhood. His own father branded an outlaw, and their family torn apart forever. Being around law councils at the *things* brought those feelings of shame bubbling back to the surface, so Tiller usually stayed far away from them. For him, spring quarter-*things* and Althing were only for trading and voyaging opportunities.

This time was different. Tiller had keenly watching the proceedings. They had started with the usual announcement, reminding longtime residents and new ones that every spring of the *things* held at the homestead of the elected regional *gothi.*

"Be the weather fine or foul, icy or calm, we follow the tradition established by the Quarter-mandate spoken into law generations ago. '*Our land shall be divided into four quarters, of Northwest, Southwest, Southeast, and Northeast. People of each Quarter will gather on the waxing half-moon after the equal-day of Spring (and*

Autumn if needed) to hear matters of importance to all, and to decide fairly on disputes of law. Then, on Longest-Day each summer, people from all Quarters will gather together for the All-thing. The Althing will include daily public recitation of the laws of our land, and a daily law council with representation from all Quarters, as well as opportunities for trade and peaceful engagement, all for the benefit of our land and our people."

As the trial began, Styr watched in nervous fear, and Tiller in annoyance. He could not admit that his own rash anger at Thorgest had played a part. Instead, he blamed the entire matter on Thorgest, once a friend but now a bitter foe. Tiller had had to stay in hiding while Thorgest's friends had hunted him. Now they would meet face to face for the trial.

. . .

At Naldrum's compound in Bull Valley, when the time came for the law council to hear local cases, Kel watched in growing horror.

First, the council heard testimony regarding a boundary dispute. Many of the men and women who usually served on the council had not been nominated this year. As seat after seat on the law council filled, Kel realized that the group heavily favored those who trusted Naldrum.

Still, Kel assured himself, what harm did that hold, really? These people were neighbors. They traded regularly and depended on one another for survival. *They'll weigh the issues fairly.*

But at the first vote, Kel's jaw dropped. The law council did not ask for clarification on needed points after the testimony had been heard. Instead, with almost no discussion, they voted. The decision, in Kel's mind, was wrong.

He frowned. What had happened?

"What did you make of that?" he asked a woman next to him. She came often to Naldrum's to trade, and he knew her character. In her face, he saw the same disbelief.

At the next case, Kel watched more carefully. A chill ran along his spine. The jury members had not kept focus on the law-arguers. They watched Naldrum.

With each testimony, he either smiled broadly or frowned. When the time came to ask questions, again, the council voted with only the briefest of deliberations. This time, Kel knew for certain they had sided with Naldrum's view, and another unfair verdict was reached.

As one plaintiff left, Kel witnessed yet another appalling thing. Some in the crowd shoved and kicked at the man as he left the *thing*-court. Never in his life had Kel seen such disrespect for the law or for a neighbor.

. . .

Kel watched, sickened, as case after case followed the same pattern. Now he realized what Naldrum's goodwill tour dispensing butter and his gifts of food to struggling landowners had really accomplished. The headman had corrupted generosity for his own purposes. Kel felt as if he had been hit in the head with a stone.

Naldrum had blinded the jury to true right or wrong. He already controlled much of Bull Valley. Did his headman intent to control this entire Quarter of the land? No man or woman could stand against such a corrupt court! His thoughts whirled, disconnected.

The girl at Althing. Aldís. Stop Naldrum. The knocks. Stop him from ordering me to kill newborns. These decent plaintiffs here deserve justice. Stop this travesty of a thing *trial. It all flowed from Naldrum. Stop him. Stop him. Stop him.* A drumbeat, intense in Kel's head.

As he watched one mockery of a trial after another destroy what used to be the *thing*-court, a hideous new possibility occurred. Sweat ran down the middle of Kel's back, despite the cool air.

Naldrum had applied to be Lawspeaker because of vanity, Kel had thought at the time. Was this sham trial a foretaste of Naldrum practicing for something bigger?

Kel felt sick. Maybe Naldrum could get away with acting the king in his own region, but it could never happen at the country-wide law council. But what if Naldrum somehow managed it? What would happen to Iceland, if a man who cared nothing for law controlled the highest law council in the land?

Three moons until Althing.

Three moons for Naldrum to deepen his corruptions.

Three moons for Kel to find a way to stop him.

Three moons were not enough time. Yet it was all Kel had.

. . .

Naldrum, with the instincts of a fox, watched Kel's face. "Look at him," he complained to his youngest wife, a woman not much older than Ankya. "Our steward doesn't appreciate the work I'm doing to stabilize our community."

"You've been stewing about this for months. Put it to the test," she answered. "Force him to acknowledge you are the authoritative leader here. If he won't obey, get rid of him."

"You have an idea?" He loved the hard light that would glint in his wife's eyes when she sensed weakness.

She turned her head so no one could catch her words. Naldrum snickered and gestured to a house slave. "Go to the stables during the last trial. Bring Kel Coesson's horse here."

He turned back to his wife. "We'll see how Kel reacts to your idea," Naldrum laughed. "Either way, tonight, we're going to have the most magnificent blood-sacrifice of any *thing* ever."

. . .

Spring *things* followed time-honored patterns. First came the courts, so that disagreements were resolved early in the day and amends could be made. Then, for women only, the Ceremony of the Egg, while men mingled and talked. After the Ceremony, games and contests took place. When dusk fell, the host offered a banquet, plentiful with meat and ale—and much later in the night, when all had eaten and drunk their fill, the highlight of the entertainment would take place, a horse-fight amid chants and burning torches. When it ended, the last event of the night would end the celebration: a blood sacrifice to the gods, to give them strength to woo the goddesses of spring.

. . .

As the trials ended, Naldrum stood. "Time for the women to attend their special little event." He smirked, as if the Egg ceremony was something of no consequence. "Women only! Let them through the crowds. Stand aside. Let them pass."

When the women had gathered their parcels and left, Naldrum held up his hands for silence. The remaining crowd, all men, quieted, eager to hear what would come next.

"For those of you who have traveled here today, I have a special treat! Most of you know Kel Coesson, the steward of my properties, and are aware of his skills as a horse trainer. The best in all Iceland!" Naldrum clapped his hands towards Kel. The crowd followed his lead, clapping and nodding in agreement.

Kel stood rooted to the spot. *What was Naldrum up to? Stop him, stop him, stop him.* His throat choked.

"There is no greater honor than going to Valhalla, whether warrior, or a warrior's horse," Naldrum cried. "Now, how many of you have seen Kel's stallion Thor-Thunder? A splendid mount, yes? Better than my own—almost." He allowed time for a laugh to run through the people, then beckoned to the young slave. "Lead in the horse."

Thunder, his halter held tightly, came snorting and fighting. "Look at this fierce warrior!" Naldrum crowed.

Kel whispered furiously. "What are you doing?"

"I have no need to hide my intentions," Naldrum answered. "I'm testing your loyalties. A headman should know if his steward can be trusted to follow orders, even ones he does not like."

He gestured to the crowd. "To give you a truly fine horse fight, perhaps the best you have ever seen, I choose this stallion to represent the house of Naldrum in combat tonight—and Kel himself will be the wrangler in the fight!"

Naldrum basked in the cheering and cries of enthusiasm. Yes, his young wife had offered a brilliant idea. Thunder promised a thrilling fight, but better yet, the victor—and of course it would be Kel's stallion—would become the *blót*-sacrifice after the battle ended.

The people of Bull Valley and beyond hungered for the torch-lit clash of stallions and the taste of horse-meat. But to eat of such greatness? They cheered at the idea of seeing the gods so honored.

Naldrum beamed and waved. "All I need is the approval of the law council—a small matter, of course! The horse rightfully belongs to Kel Coesson. But it can be mine, quickly, and my gift to you for the fights. Therefore, I sue for rights to claim this stallion, as payment for damages my steward caused!"

"You can't do this!" Kel cried. "This is illegal!"

Naldrum's followers on the law council hung back, silent and appalled. Even they could not condone such a brazen snatch of Kel's property. Wary gazes flickered as the men sized one another up, trying to gauge whether it was in their best interests to protest this clear injustice or allow Naldrum such blatant unfairness.

A few brave souls raised their hands to speak.

"What damages do you mean, *gothi?*" Kel recognized a nay-sayer to Naldrum who had made it onto the council despite the headman's efforts. "Kel only acts on your command, so any damages caused would be the result of an order you gave him."

Naldrum had not expected a challenge, and he blustered. "He was sloppy in a matter I assigned him. Sloppy. His sloppiness cost me much gold to right it."

"What sloppiness? What matter?" The challenger stood firm. "We all know Kel well. He's loyal and faithful in his work. Your steward would not ever do less than his very best. Any damages must have been from reasons beyond his control. Be specific, why don't you? What exactly did he do that harmed your name or purse?"

Naldrum had not thought the matter through that far. His mouth hung open as he searched for something to claim against Kel.

His son Drikke stood beside Naldrum. "This questioning of your headman is vile and inappropriate! We do not need to hear such petty bickering! Call the vote!" Drikke shouted. "The council has heard enough! Let them decide now!"

"My neighbors, Naldrum seizing Kel's own horse goes against every protection the law offers!" the protestor cried. "Even a headman must provide full testimony, and there must be time for the defendant—Kel—to respond. The law is clear on this. You cannot call for a vote!"

The crowd pushed against the man, nearly causing him to fall, and shouted down his words. "Vote! Vote! Vote!" they screamed towards the law council.

One by one, the majority of the men and women on the council turned up their palms and shrugged their shoulders with great exaggeration as if to say, *the crowd wants it. What am I to do? I can't stand against them.*

The vote was overwhelmingly in Naldrum's favor.

Drums would beat and torches flare as the night triumphed over day. Kel's beloved Thor-Thunder would rear and strike hooves against another stallion in mortal combat. When the other horse was vanquished, Naldrum would proclaim Kel's horse the winner, and put the ceremonial knife to Thunder's throat and proclaim him as the offering. Bright red would spurt across the chilly night ground, and the magnificent animal would breathe no more.

Even better, Thunder's flesh, hastily butchered, would be gobbled, either cut raw right from the muscle, or spitted on the fire to roast. Bloody and still warm, or delicious and cooked rare, they would tear Thunder to shreds, singing his glory in Valhalla.

The women wanted to stay and talk, but the time had come for the Egg ceremony. They gathered up their parcels and left, shocked

. . .

Kel spoke hurriedly with the council member who had protested against Naldrum.

"This can't be possible! Thunder's too fine to sacrifice for the amusement of a group of drunken revelers! Naldrum's been jealous of Thor-Thunder for years. He's tried to buy him from me, tried to steal him—a headman, stealing from his own steward, can you believe it? He passed it off as a joke, but then he tried to bully me into it. I've never yielded."

"Except that apparently, Naldrum owns the law council."

"You saw it too," Kel affirmed.

"One man controlling so much power. What good can come of that?"

"No good at all. His temperamental whims and cruelty will grow even worse with no controls on him. Cross him, and he'll take whatever he wants, and not enough will stand against him."

"How did this happen? Last spring, we were a law-abiding group of farmers. All that really mattered to any of us was our grain crops and our herds and raising our families in this peaceful valley. A good harvest, enough sun, not too much rain. Now I feel as if we are on the edge of madness—and worse, if we keep going this way."

They stared at one another, aghast.

"But I don't know what to do. What are one or two against the crowd?" The man flinched, feeling as if he should have done more to stand against the crowd.

"This nonsense can't last," Kel said. "Naldrum is powerful here, but soon people will see what's happening and stand against him."

A long silence.

"I hope you're right. At any rate, it'll be time for the horse-fights before you know it. Whatever you're going to do—stand against him and refuse to let Thunder fight, or yield—you don't have much time. I'll leave you so you can think."

The lean farmer nodded to Kel in respect and walked away, worry evident in every line of his hunched shoulders and bent body.

. . .

Kel, however, did not choose to think through a plan. Instead, he charged after Naldrum as the headman strolled from the open meeting area back to the longhouse, where a pit had been set up to roast meats.

The headman walked among a group of admirers. As Kel approached, they lifted their beer horns to him in tribute. Some laughed and reached out their hands to him, gushing *Steward Kel, what an honor for you and your stallion!* Kel gave them only scowls, and the hands dropped.

Kel ignored them. *Bootlickers.*

A lightning fast movement, and Kel grabbed Naldrum's tunic, pulling him close, and pressing his *saxe* against Naldrum's flabby throat.

"What are you thinking?" Kel demanded. "You cannot just take my horse!"

Just as quickly, other knives were drawn. Kel stood surrounded in a circle of deadly blades.

"Back away, or I'll cut him right now," Kel said. His voice was deadly calm.

"Our council approved the action. It's legal," Naldrum choked out to his admirers.

"It's not legal! If you had any understanding of the law, you'd know that."

"Careful, Steward." Naldrum gripped Kel's hand holding the knife. "You do not want to provoke a fight among our guests."

"You mean these people who sold their honor to you? Who once were free, but have now become your virtual slaves? What do I care about them? Nothing! I care about Thunder! I will not let you steal him from me!"

Naldrum tried to edge away, thoroughly rattled. He had expected anger from Kel, but not such open fury. The knife still priced his throat, and around him, the farmers who had pointed their blades towards Kel stood helpless, waiting for Naldrum's command.

This is all my wife's fault. Naldrum's face reddened, a sign Kel knew meant the headman wanted to indulge in a fit of temper. Naldrum strove to maintain the festival atmosphere.

"Put your knife away. I'm glad to compensate you for your animal," he started. "I'm a just man—"

"You are no such thing. You are a crook and a thief." No more pretending. No going back. Kel's full animosity was out in the open now for all to see.

Naldrum's face went from red to white. "You can't do anything about it! You have no power!"

Kel let go of Naldrum's tunic. His fist hardened to iron. "I have the power to beat your lying face to pulp." Kel lifted his fist to Naldrum's nose. The headman's eyes widened in fear, and he whimpered.

Suddenly, calm flowed through Kel. "You're disgusting. I'd only fight an opponent worth the blow." Such an insult would cut Naldrum where it hurt most of all, in his ego.

Naldrum wilted in relief, already beginning to sputter and mock his steward.

"We're not done yet," Kel said. He swung his arm back and slapped the headman with all his strength, hard across the face, and Naldrum went sprawling across the ground. "No one threatens Thunder."

Kel gave the shocked men around him a look of loathing. "Put your weapons away. Naldrum had it coming, and you know it. Let him be a man for once and take his punishment. Besides, you know your odds against me. None of you really wants to go to Valhalla tonight." Kel turned on his heel and walked away.

Naldrum scraped himself up to a seated position. "Say what you want, steward," he said from the floor. "This crowd expects to see your horse fight. You're one man against many. No matter what, I win, and you lose."

. . .

The law had been blatantly ignored, and in his favor. Delighted with his success, Naldrum called out those who had openly supported him. They would have the best seats during the night feast. His slave women would be washed and clean, to reward those headmen with their favors.

He had taken careful note of those who had voiced opposition as well. Those, he announced, would be given poor meat, and little of it, and no beer.

Even his favorites found Naldrum's disrespect for the rules of hospitality appalling. But what could they do? Naldrum cared little for rules, or if dark looks and muttered oaths came his way. His supporters huddled together and pretended all was well and normal.

Those who were undecided quickly realized the advantage of pledging to Naldrum. Soon the festival had changed from an impartial, good-spirited local *thing* to a celebration of all things Naldrum.

. . .

Chapter Forty-Seven

Unaware of what had just happened, all of the free-women walked in small groups across the fields, heading to a sheltered grove where the Egg waited for them. Normally they would chatter together, full of excitement about the upcoming ceremony and the events of the day. Today, their voices were low and worried. Much rested on the success of this year's Ceremony of the Egg.

"You look as if you're carrying again."

"I'm due in three moons. How can we feed another mouth?"

"Did you use vinegar? I do every night, just in case."

"I should have, but I didn't. I've started making our workers use it now, all of the women old enough to bleed. We can't afford any more children at our farm."

"Nor us. Our field hands are too thin. They don't work nearly as hard this year as they did last."

Snatches of conversations back and forth, about shortages of food, of the hardships of the past winter, of hope that the Egg would help this summer be more prosperous.

"Last year was Ankya's first time to serve as Egg. But the weather was bad and too many crops failed. We must pray harder for her, so that she is successful this time."

The wife of the man who had protested at the law circle spoke in a derisive tone. "What if it isn't *we* who failed? What if Ankya wasn't the right choice for the Egg?"

An uncomfortable silence confirmed that others thought the same but dared not say so. Finally, a farm woman who had received a butter-bribe spoke.

"She's rich. She's beautiful. Her father is powerful."

"How does being rich and beautiful and having a wealthy father qualify her? The Egg should be the woman most pleasing to Freya, not to the men of the valley!" the challenger retorted.

Another woman chimed in. "Surely Freya, who loves beauty, wishes Ankya to represent her? Perhaps the goddess is testing you, to see if you have faith enough."

"Testing me? That's ridiculous! When has Freya ever before caused our sheep to get hoof-rot, or our chickens to not lay? Why would she suddenly care about the looks of an honorary Egg? I've never heard such a ridiculous idea!"

"Who are we to question the will of the gods? This is all part of the plan. We humans just can't understand."

No one knew how to argue such an idea. The women fell silent, uneasy that disagreement had tainted their cherished, critical ceremony. The whole point of the Ceremony of the Egg was to be one with the goddess and one with all women, to be in sisterhood and in unity with each another to face the challenges that life presented.

When they reached the circle of trees where the ceremony would take place, they set aside troubling thoughts. A holy hush fell.

. . .

Straw lay scattered on the ground, reflecting the sun and making a blanket of gold. Ankya stood on it, waiting, noble and tall, her feet bare, her eyes painted with charcoal, a crown of flowers on her head. The scandalous gown of the morning was gone. In its place, a cloak of lush velvet covered her from throat to the tips of her toes, hiding the nakedness underneath. The collected women stared at the breathtaking cloak. Like the silk of her earlier dress, most had never seen velvet before.

Ankya did not acknowledge their stares. She had willed herself to become the day-goddess, and a goddess did not engage in chit-chat with human women.

She lifted her face to the sky. "We honor the goddess Freya," Ankya intoned. "We honor her, mother and sister and daughter of the land."

The dozens of voices around her echoed her words. "We honor the goddess Freya."

"We are the mothers and sisters and daughters of the land as well. Only we, who bear children, are bearers of Freya's legacy."

The repeated response, reverent. "We are the bearers."

"We are the keepers of life. That which lives, lives because we conceive, nourish and heal."

The words repeated as before in quiet chant. *The keepers of life...*

"We are the passage to death. When life ends, it is we who bathe the body, who dress it, who gather food and gifts and lead the journey to the underworld."

The passage to death...

Two *systirs* dedicated to Freya moved to Ankya. They unbuttoned the velvet cloak and pulled it from her shoulders. The spring sun made her pale skin glow. Naked and proud, Ankya held herself in regal composure. She wanted to make the lovely, sensuous sign of the bishop's cross on her body, but refrained.

"We are the Bearers of the Egg. We are the Receivers of the Seed," Ankya the day-goddess said. She gestured to the women.

At that, they too removed cloaks, aprons, shifts and underskirts to stand nude in the cool spring air, a little self-conscious but eager to respect the tradition, repeating, "We are the Bearers of the Egg. We are the Receivers of the Seed."

Ankya's assistants unbound her braids and combed their fingers through her hair. The straight blonde locks tumbled down her shoulders over her breasts. The surrounding women unbound their own braids and fingered them loose.

"I give you the Arc of Life, for the gathering and blessing of your gifts." She held forth a semi-circle of wood. The light breeze lifted strands of Ankya's hair towards it. They floated and twisted along the Arc, caressing it as might a lover's touch. At a signal, her assistants slipped the curved arc carefully around Ankya's neck, where it rested on her shoulders.

"We celebrate the flax," she said. "Bring the flax for blessing."

The women reached into their baskets and drew out handfuls of the soft stuff. Stripped of its outer husk and combed through a hatchel, the flax looked exactly like Ankya's hair: pale, gold, and nearly as light on the breeze. Deftly, her assistants accepted the flax and tied it in loops onto the Arc of Life.

"This flax—our linen—covers us and cares for us. We are grateful for the flax. Murmured responses echoed her words.

"We celebrate the wool." This time, each woman carried to Ankya a loosely-bundled length of spun wool yarn. Again, the goddess's assistants tied them to the wooden ring.

Each element of life and sustenance was requested and presented in turn. Women offered items they had carefully preserved since the prior harvest: stalks of grain with the barley or oats or rye grains still in the husk, or lengths of berries strung along a thin thread. Some presented clattering strands, small bones of chickens, cattle, sheep, and goats tied onto strings, or dangling garlands of bird feathers. As each offering was brought forth, one or another *systir* would tie it to the wooden frame. More and more of Ankya's nakedness was covered, little by little.

"Are all the gifts presented?" she asked. Heads nodded *yes*.

Ankya stood, all solemn reverence, and lifted her arms wide. The strands of flax and wool, of berry and bone and barley-sheaf hung down her body from her shoulders to her ankles. The spring air teased the strands, entwining them as they rustled and clicked, moving around her. The women gazed in awe at their creation, symbol of the numerous bonds between women and their world.

"Behold the Cloak of Life!" Ankya cried. They shouted the response happily. Some wiped tears of emotion.

"Now we bind ourselves to Freya with the most important gift of all. Bring forth the eggs!"

The women came forth one last time, each bringing from her basket an egg, nestled in soft wool and carried from home. The assistants held out a small bowl, and each egg was cracked and poured into it. The *systirs* stirred the eggs into a frothy yellow pool.

"We make our offering of eggs to Freya," Ankya intoned. "May the Goddess treat us kindly this coming year!" Her assistants removed the Cloak of Life from Ankya's shoulders and lay it on the ground at her feet, spreading it over the straw.

Ankya lay down and stretched her naked body out across the Cloak, her hands at her sides, her palms up and her eyes closed. The assistants dipped their hands in the bowl of beaten eggs and smoothed the golden fluid over her breasts, arms, between her thighs and over her belly, until they had painted every bit of the Goddess' skin. The egg dried quickly to a smooth finish. She glowed, lustrous and golden, their Goddess In-The-Flesh, their Egg.

Each woman circled the Goddess. They knelt to reverence her, tapping her egg-gold skin and then kissing their fingertips. They spoke aloud personal prayers as they passed by, one by one.

"Behold our offering, Freya. Keep us safe, Freya. May my children thrive... May my son get well... May we have enough to eat this year... May my sister survive her delivery... May my husband regain his strength..." The soft pleas wove the women together in common need, their deepest fears and greatest hopes the warp and weft of struggle to survive that faced them day by day, season by season, year by year. They were bound as one. They did not face their troubles alone.

When the prayers ceased, Ankya lay quietly. Her assistants washed the egg from her skin, soaping and sudsing her with warm lather. Goose-bumps rose on her skin, but a day-goddess did not permit herself to shiver as humans did. When Ankya was clean, she stood for her assistants to dry her and wrap her in the velvet covering again. They cut the ancient wooden Arc from the Cloak of Life, leaving the strands of linen and wool and bone lying on the straw. Ankya touched a torch to it, and the Cloak began to burn.

The women watched, reverent. Part of the Cloak would rise in the air as ash and warmth. Part of it would soak into the fields. The *dísir,* the great invisible world of female spirits, would accept all of their gifts, and watch over them for another year.

The women dressed, turned without speaking and walked in silence back to Naldrum's home.

. . .

Chapter Forty-Eight

If the Ceremony of the Egg was reverent, the games and competitions were anything but. Early betting on the horse-fight had been fast and furious ever since Naldrum had announced that it would feature Kel and Thor-Thunder. Naldrum's admirers, keen on proving their loyalty by wagering for his steward's horse, first congregated around the field bonfires. When they came to the stables to gawk and boast, words quickly disintegrated into brawls.

Kel finally left, closing the heavy stable door against those who wanted to poke and prod Thunder to assess his chance of winning. He stormed towards the blacksmith shed where Tor worked, his mouth set and his mood angry.

"I have a question. Why did you bother to return here, after you took Kandace to the ship with Rota?" Kel blurted. He had wondered about it, annoyed ever since the day when Tor had trudged back into Naldrum's compound and tied on his leather blacksmith apron again. "Why would a man with the great sense you profess to have willingly return to serve this bastard?"

"What would have happened if I didn't come back?" Tor answered in a sour voice.

Kel had not bothered to consider the alternative. "I guess you're valuable enough that Naldrum wouldn't let you just disappear without a proper search."

Tor dared not say *and then how long until Naldrum's men found the widow's longhouse, and took possession of my wife and children?* He had never spoken a word to anyone of his relationship with Kandace. Instead, he simply agreed.

"And who would he have sent looking for me?"

"Me, I guess."

"Damned right. I've heard what people say, that you could track a ghost across the lava fields. Would I have stood a chance against you?"

"Probably not. If not me, then someone would have combed every valley looking for you."

"And if I'm miserable now, Naldrum would have made it much worse. Should I have attempted an ill-conceived escape, or return here where I have food, and decent work, and a place to sleep, with none of my bones broken by a vindictive headman and my skin not whipped into shreds? Not a difficult choice, I think."

Kel glared at the glowing coals in Tor's fire. "Depends."

"On what?"

"Maybe the ghost-tracker would have looked the other way. Maybe I don't need to work so hard for Naldrum any longer."

Tor did not look up, but his hands stilled on the anvil. "Since when?"

"Since he decided that Thunder would be in the horse fight tonight."

At that, Tor did look up. "Oh, no," he grimaced. "You love that horse as if it was your child."

. . .

Perhaps another word would not have cut Kel to the quick.

But *child.*

Tor did not know about all the infants that Kel had sent to their death at Naldrum's order. Of the memories of so many young mothers, screaming *please don't take my child!*

The headman's heartless cruelty had finally come to Kel's own doorstep. Tor was right. Kel did love Thunder that much. Now his own child, as it were, was to be sacrificed to Naldrum's ego.

"Yes," Kel said, a lifetime of sadness in the word.

. . .

Kel felt the final break happen, as just the littlest snap in his chest. Not something audible, not something momentous. Just the quietest splintering, the knowledge that he was done.

Fifteen years of working for Naldrum, over. The growing dislike and distrust, finally too much. Even the thing that had kept him going for so long, his desire to protect Aldís, abandoned as hopeless.

Sauthi's right. If I can't protect my own horse, I can't protect anybody or anything from Naldrum. It's only a matter of time until he needs a new target. Sooner or later, he'll choose Aldís again. By then I may have lost my only chance to fight him.

A deep fissure in Kel broke wide open. Fury and self-disgust poured out, hot as lava.

"Naldrum's taken *everything* from me! He stole the woman I loved—the only one, ever. He knew I loved her, but he claimed her as his, and told me that he'd cut her—not me, *her!* —if I ever tried to get her back. And she went along with him! How could she? It broke my heart, but I wanted her so much I told myself, *if that's the kind of man she desires, then I'll be that man.* Because of that, I did disgusting things for Naldrum, vile things, until I became dead inside, locked in self-loathing. When I saw her at Althing last year, I learned that she *loathes* Naldrum! All this time I thought she had some unhealthy love for him, but she *hates* him. I have *wasted my life* making myself into the very thing she despises! No wonder she hates me. All I have left is Thunder, and now Naldrum wants to kill him, too."

The flood of bitter anger poured out. When it subsided, Kel spoke again, calm but determined.

"Thunder is the last thing keeping me sane. If I lose him, there will be nothing left of me. Can you understand, Tor, what it means, to have *everything* taken from you?"

. . .

The great blacksmith had remained utterly still. As Kel finished, his fists flexed and opened. Abruptly, he turned and grabbed Kel's tunic, half-lifted him.

"You think because I am a slave that I have no one I care about? How could you be so stupid?" The same fury at Naldrum and at himself bubbled up in Tor, hot, demanding release. "I understand far more than you might imagine! I understand *exactly* how it feels to have Naldrum steal something you love, and threaten what you hold most dear. Naldrum threatened to burn Kandace. To *burn* her!"

Kel looked at Tor, confused. "I don't understand. She's beautiful and kind, and it's horrific what he proposed. But you only just met her. How can that matter as much as someone I've loved for years?"

Tor could keep his secret no longer. "It mattered enough that I did not put her to a ship to return her to Haakon."

Kel's face, aghast. "What? Why would you risk so much for someone you barely know? A near-stranger, Tor! Where is she now?"

"She is no stranger. Kandace is my wife. She lives in hiding, in a valley some distance from here, with our two children."

. . .

This pronouncement stunned Kel. "How, by all the gods, have you been able to keep that secret from Naldrum?"

Tor did not answer, nor did Kel expect one. "A wife?" he said. "And children? Ahhh, I see now. They're the real reason you came back here."

"Yes. I couldn't chance someone searching for me and finding them. But ever since Kandace arrived, I have been trying to devise a way to get the four of us away from this land. It's been a useless exercise. I got her away from Naldrum at least. But I miss her terribly. I worry, day and night. So yes, Kel, I do understand what it means to have everything I care about taken from me."

"You've saved them! For now, at least!" Kel's voice raised almost to a shout. "I don't have that option! I have zero chance of keeping Thunder out of the horse fight, not with that crowd groveling around Naldrum. Once it gets darker, during the feast, I'm planning to leave tonight in some way that doesn't attract a crowd with swords chasing after me. The games are starting. Then the feast. After that, I need to be gone. Any ideas?"

Tor frowned. With his tongs, twisted the stirrup he was repairing. "None." He hammered furiously. "I'm just a blacksmith. I only know metal and fire."

And metal and fire flew, as Tor took out his frustration on the broken stirrup. Beyond them, scattered across the hillside, other bits of sparks and fire flew as the wind danced with the roaring bonfires.

And soon, sparks flew between two men who had everything to lose, and little to hope for.

. . .

Naldrum glared at hearing the message that his steward and blacksmith were brawling.

"What now?! Kel knows we're about to start the banquet! He's just angry about his stupid horse! What do you mean, they're trying to kill each other?"

"They were like wild beasts! We pulled them apart. It took many men."

"By Hel, I'll see them both in chains for disrupting my festival. Bring them to me," Naldrum bellowed. *I have to get rid of Kel as soon as possible after this feast.*

. . .

Tor and Kel were dragged into the hall, spitting, glaring hatred and shouting accusations at one another. Naldrum demanded an apology to his guests, who were as appalled by the spectacle as they were entertained by it.

"This is how you treat me? And our guests? How should I reward such poor manners?" he asked.

"No need to punish me," Kel swaggered. "I only have a little time left with my horse. If Thunder is going to Valhalla tonight, I want him to groom him until he gleams. He must be resplendent. I was on my way to the stables. Tor has no business there! He started the fight! Keep this hulk as far away from me as possible."

"A strong man would be at the banquet making toasts in Thunder's honor, eating pig and drinking mead, instead of sulking and hiding in the stables!" Tor shouted. "You are as weak as our *gothi!* You both disgust me!

Naldrum laughed with no humor in his voice. "How dare you both continue to shame me in front of my guests? I think I will amuse myself by forcing you to spend the evening together while we sup and drink!"

"No! *No!* I don't want him anywhere near me!" Kel cried in protest as Tor raged.

Naldrum laughed again as he turned to his guests. "These small nuisances show what a headman such as I must endure." Naldrum summoned a contingent of men. "Take these two down to the stable. Lock them inside, and then hurry back here so that we can officially start the feast. I'll make the first toast to their 'honor'." He clapped his hands. "More ale for my guests!"

. . .

Chapter Forty-Nine

Tor and Kel, hurled into the dark stable, scrambled up from the stone floor upon which they had been thrown. They stood breathing heavily, barely able to see in the darkness. The only light came from where the setting sun filtered through cracks in the stone walls, striping the floor in thin bands.

"Now we wait," said Tor.

The slivers of light lengthened and turned redder, more faint. As they faded into true dark, Kel reckoned that the ale barrels had flowed enough that the banquet guests and house servants would be full of drink. Every year, some of the women who had stripped naked for the Egg ceremony repeated the act in the hall, eager to forget the harshness of daily life in a bit of raucous merriment. The same would be repeated in the groups around the bonfires. No one would pay attention to anything else.

"Now or never, I guess," he said to Tor.

The heavy door had been bolted from the outside. Tor squatted and wedged his fingers in the tiny space under the thick timbers. He strained against the weight and lifted.

It barely moved. Tor repositioned his feet and tried again. A gap opened between the door bottom and the stable floor.

"Now!" Tor gasped.

Kel pushed against the hinge side of the door. The weighty iron post grated against the top of the socket in which in normally rested.

"Just a little higher," he grunted, and Tor heaved again. The post swung clear of the socket.

"Hold!" Kel pushed farther. An opening appeared along the hinge side of the door frame.

"It's clear!" Kel cried in a hoarse whisper. Tor staggered a step forward, still carrying the full weight of the door. Kel squeezed through the opening and guided the hinge-post to a flat rock they had placed for it earlier. Now Tor forced his way through the opening into the dark stable yard. They held their breath, listening. Nothing disturbed the night save the sounds of revelry echoing from the hill fires and the hall above them.

Kel moved the rock and they opened the door wider. Silently, the two men moved.

Only three mounts were ever kept in the paddock behind the stable: Naldrum's horse, Kel's stallion, and Ankya's favorite mare. Tor and Kel felt for their saddles and tack in the dark stable. Soon two horses were saddled and all three outfitted with panniers. Tor and Kel took a brief pause. Their luck had held so far.

"I'll get the things we need from the storehouse. You get the wood."

These would be the most dangerous part of their plan. Kel moved quickly through the night to the door of the new storeroom. His heart hammered as he put his ear to the door. *Good thing Naldrum didn't think to take my keys.* Kel pushed the thick fingers of the iron key through the opening, flinching at the metal screech of the lock as it opened.

No one inside. A quick round of the shelves, and Kel had filled baskets with cheeses and smoked meats. He grabbed wool blankets and an armload of tanned sheep skins, then eased the door open again and looked around the yard. The path to the stable lay empty and dark. Kel pushed his load outside, closed the door and reset the lock, then staggered under the weight of the supplies as he ran back to the stables, hoping not to be seen.

. . .

One figure, hidden in the shadows, did see. Watched but made no sound. Smiled faintly, and moved back inside to the feast.

. . .

Tor pulled bundles of hay from the loft. He mounded them against the turf walls and the pillars that held up the thatch roof, then slipped through the night to the smithy. He loaded a wheelbarrow with kindling, wood staves and charcoal. He dashed back to the stable and spread the wood over the hay, then returned the wheelbarrow to the smithy shed.

One last thing. Tor pulled a glowing ember from the forge-fire, wrapped it a bit of leather, and carried it to the stable. Touched it to the soft dry straw.

As flames leapt up, the wood began to crackle. They waited to see it burn enough that the roof would soon inevitably catch. Once again Tor lifted the door, from the outside this time, while Kel maneuvered the pivot back into the socket. He tossed away the propping stone they had used to get out.

Smoke began to filter out of crevices below the roof. It would be a long while until the revelers in and around the longhouse, eating and drinking and carousing, would notice. By then, the entire stable would be engulfed in flames.

They mounted the horses and spurred them across the meadow in the dark, the hooves silent on grass, and rode away into the night.

. . .

Tor and Kel rode hard until they reached the track that led up towards the wilderness of Hekla. They did not look back until they had gained some height on the mountainside.

At that long distance, they could not see figures running towards the fire, stumbling with drunkenness over the uneven ground in the dark, or the sounds of Naldrum, bellowing in fury that his festival had been ruined.

They would have laughed in mocking satisfaction at those who claimed to hear Kel and Tor screaming while the stable burned hot enough to turn everything inside to powdery ash. They would have smiled in grim satisfaction to hear Naldrum's furious curses the next morning when he realized that not only had someone burned his stable, his slave and his steward, but had also stolen the compound's three finest horses.

For now, all they knew of the chaotic scene in the distance was a fierce red glow lighting the horizon. After one more look, satisfied that their ruse had worked, the two men turned and galloped fast and as far from that glow and all it meant.

. . .

Chapter Fifty

Sometime during that weary night, Tor straightened in his saddle. "This woman you love," he began.

"Don't want to talk about her," Kel answered.

Tor ignored him. "You said she has scars on her wrists?"

"She does."

"Is she called Aldís? The one people call 'the mist?'"

Kel glanced sharply at Tor. "She is. You know her?"

Tor did not answer. "Why do they call her that?"

"Because she has a habit of suddenly appearing and disappearing. Her mother was a Druid—captured as a slave in the Gaelic lands, and brought here. Aldís has some of the inner-sight that her mother had, sometimes. She lives alone, wandering. Comes and goes as she pleases. Like mist."

"Well, my friend, you have done a good deed for me, taking me with you away from our despised headman. This woman Aldís has been a friend to me. Perhaps I can be a friend to both of you, one day."

Kel did not care to hear Tor's thoughts. He only wanted to ride, and be rid of Naldrum, and not think.

The moon rose and crossed the night sky. Thunder knew how to follow the slightest of trails. The beautiful animal had little need of guidance. Kel patted Thunder's neck and breathed gratitude, uncaring of where they rode.

. . .

Tor, however, knew exactly where they were heading. He said nothing to Kel, but once they are off the mountain, he moved his horse forward at each stream-ford and each fork in the trail and chose the route without asking. Tor had covered this ground five times before, and he had pictured it during hundreds of lonely nights and long days of work. He could have walked it blindfolded.

As the eastern sky blushed rose, they looked for a grove off the trail where they could rest, hidden, during the day. Kel pulled the sheepskins from Ankya's mare and threw them on the ground. The two men collapsed, exhausted, and fell fast asleep.

. . .

More long nights in the saddle, and days hidden in thickets. Little by little, the tightness in Kel's shoulders eased. The next dawn, as they ate a hasty meal before sleeping, he sighed. "We'll be dead men if Naldrum ever catches us. But it's so good to feel free." He looked away, embarrassed. "I've grown up around slavery. Never particularly thought to question it. I've been all but a slave to Naldrum. Feeling this freedom, when I've had so much more than you, makes me ashamed of what some of us do to others."

"Same here," said Tor. "It feels as if years have dropped away." He broke a wedge from one of the cheeses and pushed it onto a stick, held it against the glowing coals of their tiny fire. The cheese softened, and Tor ate. Soon he would be home, for that how he now thought of the widow's farm. Afterwards, he lay long without sleeping, for the first time in ages daring to hope.

. . .

More nights of riding. The moon was almost gone, and their progress slowed. The rising sun shone on an overgrown stone with a faint rune carved into it. Tor turned his horse towards it. "Along here."

Kel, weary to his core, did not argue. They entered a narrow valley. He looked about for a place to rest, but unlike other days, Tor made no indication of stopping.

After a while, Kel guessed. "We're heading to the farm where your wife and children are hidden?"

"We are. You can see how isolated it is. No one ever comes here, but it's not just because it's secluded. You need to prepare yourself."

Kel looked puzzled.

"There was a fire. She was burned. Badly." *No need to tell the whole story.* "Eilíf has a beautiful heart, but her face—" Tor paused. "You can thank her, though, for our escape. The way she became a widow gave me the idea of burning Naldrum's stable."

"We're in her debt, then," Kel answered.

"Because of the disfigurement, Aldís told me that those with small minds whisper that the woman has become a troll. No one comes here. She lives as a recluse. If Naldrum believes we died in the fire, we should be as safe here as anywhere in Iceland, for a long while. Where will you go after this?"

"Naldrum is rich in land and silver and butter, and he has allies with swords. I cannot defeat him in battle or wealth. But one girl and her family may have the power to stop Naldrum. I'm going to ride straight to talk to them. If they agree, I'll go to Mani the Lawspeaker—this time, with the witnesses and evidence Mani needs to for a charge against Naldrum."

Tor grunted. "Sounds like a long shot. But long shots land well, sometimes. Against all odds, you and I are here, nearly to my wife and children. One good chance is sometimes all you need."

. . .

Their horses moved silently along the almost-invisible track. Soon Tor dismounted at a small hill. Kel realized he was standing in front of a well-concealed longhouse, its roof overgrown with grasses and a shrub in front of the door.

Tor knocked slightly and opened the door. A woman worked at a loom in the center of the room. She looked up in surprise.

"Kandace," Tor said.

. . .

Chapter Fifty-One

Thornes Thing

Tiller's case had been the last one scheduled. The verdict had come far faster than he expected. Women were anxious to make their way to their Egg ceremony, and men wanted to sort out rules for the games and contest.

Thorgest had had his turn to speak in accusation, and then Tiller in defense. Then Thorgest's law-arguer, and then Tiller again. The *gothi* from the surrounding valleys who served as the law council whispered together. One by one, they had cast their vote. It had not been unanimous—that was not required at quarter-courts, only at Althing—but it had been enough.

No one spoke as the hearing emptied. The testimony had been emotional but clear, and most present whispered that the deaths of Thorgest's sons was regrettable. A terrible accident, but not murder.

There was general shock at the verdict.

Thorgest and his grieving wife Gretta walked off without a word to anyone, relieved to finally have the burden of the trial over. Both of them wiped their eyes, the grief still fresh. *Our dear sons.* They could not speak even to one another. The verdict did not lessen the pain, so raw in their hearts. Thorgest had broken down and cried during his testimony, describing his sons dead on the ground with Tiller kneeling beside the dying Einarr.

Members of the law council stayed tightlipped. The ones who had voted for innocence were dumbfounded by those who said *guilty.* When asked, they remained silent about the reasons for their verdict.

Tiller stood in the mud of the sheep pen with the impossible words still ringing in his ears. Automatic actions took over. He scratched behind an ear, then ran a fumbling hand over his forehead, stunned.

It could not be true.

Some instinct turned him around, pulled him out of the barn, and he stumbled out into the sheep-yard. The setting sun reflected off wet patches on rough tables knocked up for the day, puddles where barley-beer had been spilled. Tiller took in the scene but saw none of it. He passed his hand over his forehead again. What had happened?

He would have a chance to for an appeal, Thorgest's law-arguer had reminded him. The summer All-Thing would be held in thirteen weeks, and because the vote had not been unanimous, the sentence was not final until either revoked or affirmed by the larger, more powerful Althing Council, where *gothi* from all over Iceland would ensure fairness.

But those words—those words—

Tiller had believed the truth to be so obvious that he had not even bothered to have a law-arguer for himself, something common at the quarter courts. He knew many of the *gothi* who sat on the jury. He had done work for many of them. They knew him, knew his values. Admittedly, they knew Thorgest as well, but still! Again, the shocked thought came. *It can't be true.*

Five words. The same ones that Tiller's father once had heard. Those words had splintered his childhood home, had exploded his life, had cast father and son far away from their Nor'way homestead into distant Iceland and a meaner, harder existence. His father's bitterness had dragged them into a downward spiral that ended on a hard, mean tract on steep and thin soil, fields too stony to decently farm, a place of poverty and loneliness that Tiller had escaped only by his wits, and a willingness for the dangerous work of sea travel.

As a child, Tiller had vowed to put those five words in his past, to never speak them again, to never hear them ringing in his memory again. But they had refused to leave him in peace. They rang, cold and heartless, plaguing him in ways no one ever knew, undermining every success he had ever had. Daily, he fought to keep himself distant from them, but now here they were, irrefutable, mocking, relentless. But this time, the words described not of his father, a man of no love and much loathing, but *himself.*

The verdict had been made. The man appointed to pronounce it stood and spoke it aloud.

"Let memory serve that this man, and those who helped him—though we do not know who they were, he certainly had help—this man and any who aided him must bear the punishment, without reprieve or aid, from this moment forward until the sentence time has passed." And then he said the last five words, formal and odious.

They seared into Tiller's brain, deep as the brand that would soon be burned onto his skin, if the Althing did not change it.

Outlawed, for three full years.

. . .

The merchant Josson spurred his horse as soon as Tiller's trial ended. Finally, he would be in Naldrum's good graces again. His old horse lathered, and he cursed it.

"We have to make haste! Didn't you hear him? We have to get there first with this news!"

He walked the horse until it stopped lathering, then used his spurs again. "There's no profit in trade anymore. No one has any money, except the rich. I want a soft job, working for Naldrum. You won't have to drag things along the roadway. Come on, you old bag of fleas. Go faster!"

. . .

Thorgest rode beside Gretta, his first and oldest wife, on the coastline track away from Thornes. Thoughts she had kept inside could not be held any longer. Her voice shook.

"Was she worth it?"

He knew who Gretta meant. "I thought so, once. Now, no. I was stupid."

His new young wife had lasted a month in the longhouse after his sons' death. After that, on the first day that the weather was fit to ride, she announced her divorce from Thorgest, took his horse and the best of the household goods, and disappeared down the valley track.

Gretta had said nothing until now. Thorgest knew what was coming.

"She just *had* to have those pillars. I told you to say no! Her greed has taken everything from us and *you let her*."

Thorgest had truly thought he loved his new young wife. No. It had only been his desire to feel youthful again. She'd have been a better fit for one of his sons.

The anguish in Gretta's voice reminded Thorgest where his true loyalties lay. He reached for her hand. Gretta kept her face turned from him so that he would not see the tears, but he knew.

"It has been weeks now, my wife," he said gently. "Justice has been done. We need to move on."

Thorgest said the words for himself as much as for her. He had known anger in his life, and joy, but he had never felt devastation before. Fear that they would both be overwhelmed and never recover made his next words harsher than he intended. "We can't wallow. It won't change anything."

"We have no one to help on the farm now, Thorgest! The other boys are gone in their own lives. They are never coming back! No one to work with us but a few bondsmen. Everything that we did in hope that we would see grandchildren playing in our home? It is all gone! It is *nothing*, Thorgest! How do I accept that?"

He had no answer for her. The same despair dug a hole in his chest that no-law verdict could begin to fill.

Gretta flung her hands towards the sky. "I feel as if everything I am, everything I have done for my whole *life* has been for nothing! We don't matter to the gods. I *hate* the gods! I used to pray to them to keep our sons safe, but did they care at all? No! And as for the afterlife? To think of our boys in Valhalla, fighting and dying over and over, reborn each day only to fight and die again? I picture them there, and every day, *every single day,* I see the stab wounds in their bodies, the blood on their clothing the day they died—" she wept. "I cannot bear to think of them that way, day after day, for eternity, Thorgest! And I cannot bear to think of them in the cold loneliness of Hel, either, so far from everything they know. And where will you and I go to when we die? Valhalla, or Hel? What if we never see them again? Or even each other?"

She knew that Thorgest would guess where she was going with her words. He had objected to when she had tried to bring it up before, but Gretta had reached the point where it did not matter what he thought.

"Those who follow the white-christ claim that there is life after death. Not like in Valhalla or Hel, but a *joyful* life, where all are reunited and live in peace. I need to believe in something like *that*, Thorgest! I need what the white-christ god offers, Thorgest. I need it desperately! To one day see our sons in that place they call 'Heaven'? To kiss their faces once again, to hold them in my arms and hug them and tell them how much I love them? I need it terribly. I cannot survive without at least hoping for that. I know it is hard for you to leave the old ways in your heart, but Thorgest—" Gretta's voice broke, and she struggled to continue. "Thorgest, you will lose me as well if I don't find a way through this grief. I cannot hold on much longer! Please, for my sake, let us part ways with the old gods. They didn't protect our sons, did they? Let us pledge to this new god. I can then at least hope that they are well, and at peace, and that one day I may see their beloved faces again."

She was silent for a while, her piece said. In a bit, she spoke again.

"Last year, we rode this way home from Thornes with them. "Remember? They raced their horses on this very stretch." Her voice broke again, as she heard in her memory the sound of their laughter when their mounts had careened against one another, and the shouted words of their fierce, joyful competition.

Her precious sons. Brothers who had competed with every fiber of their being, yet who would defend the other to the end, gone. The effort of waiting for the hearing had both exhausted and sustained her, and Gretta felt on the edge of collapse.

Thorgest wiped his eyes. He, too, remembered the boys racing that stretch of roadway. The memory tore at his chest. The only person who could understand that pain rode beside him. All that mattered to him now was to take care of her. He reached for Gretta's reins and pulled both of their horses to a stop.

"I'll do whatever you need," he said. "Whatever helps. You're right in what you say. I've been angry at the gods myself. Such cynicism I felt today, when the cupbearer killed her rooster as the *blót-offering* to start the *thing*! The old gods kept no one safe. Not our sons, not Einar. Not Tiller, even, who we once counted almost as another son. He's as good as dead. But that's all behind us. We cannot bring them back. The only thing that matters to me now is you. I will worship the land-spirits or the white-christ or even a damned troll if it will keep you safe. I love you." His own voice shook. "I need you, Gretta. Whatever it takes."

He kept hold of her reins to give her time. When she finally turned her face to him, wet with tears and grateful, he reached for her and kissed her.

"I love you, Gretta."

"I love you, Thorgest."

She took back her reins and held them in one hand, steadying herself to ride again. With the other hand, she reached for Thorgest.

They gripped each other's fingers tightly as they rode, and the long-ago echo of their sons' laughter drifted in their memories, precious, hallowed, and pure.

. . .

Chapter Fifty-Two

The widow's damaged face only caused alarm upon first seeing it. After that, Kel heard the happiness in her voice as she called Tor's children from the field *come, come right away, your father is here,* and he saw the sweet shy pride with which she introduced her blind husband.

Kel had never thought himself a sensitive man, but then, he had never had a family. The little group in this longhouse—thrown together by fate, disfigured, enslaved, poor, and outcast—encircled one another, blissful, overflowing with wonder and joy.

The widow's hand covered her trembling mouth, and her husband held her as Tor and Kandace enfolded their children. Four people who had suffered so much were together again at last.

No one saw Kel excuse himself from the happy circle. He walked a little way from the longhouse, his back to the door. His heart ached with fervent hope for that small band who had become a family—and ached, as well, in worry for what he would have to face.

. . .

When they ate supper that night, Tor sat next to Kel. He alternated between stirring the *sup* in his bowl and tapping a small rhythm on the edge of the bowl with his spoon. Finally Kel stopped eating in exasperation.

"Just say whatever it is you're thinking about, you great lout."

Tor grinned. "If you're sure." The smile left his face as he leaned towards Kel.

"This woman Aldís—" Kel snorted and started to turn away but Tor gripped his arm, stopping Kel. "You seem pretty angry at her for someone you claim to have loved so much. I don't care what happened between the two of you, but know this: Aldís has been a good friend to me. It's because of her that the woman who cares for my children survived a deadly fire. It's because of Aldís that Josson thinks my children are no longer in this world. It's because of Aldís checking in on them that I trusted they would be safe while I lived at Naldrum's. It's because of Aldís that I know what it means for my children to be Icelanders. She insisted I go to the opening of the last Althing, and helped me to see the greatness that your country has, despite people like Naldrum who try and corrupt it. So be angry at her if you need to, but be fair to her. Who among us is perfect? No one. Neither is Aldís, but she does more than her share of good in the world."

Kel thought of his own debts of gratitude to Aldís. It was because of her that more than one farmer last year had not had their lands stolen in *holmgang* duels, when she had fought at Kel's side as his shield bearer with no thought of her own safety and for no reward. It was because of her that the boy Drikke's horse had injured had healed, like so many others. It was because of Aldís that he, too, had come to understand and appreciate all that Althing and the Law meant to him and Iceland.

What had he, Kel, done to help others in the ways she had? Hardly anything. He had carried out Naldrum's vile orders and felt sorry for himself.

Shamed, he nodded to Tor. He put his bowl on the cup-board and went outside into the springtime dusk.

Kel lifted his face to the skies from which soft spring rain fell, water from *Yngvi,* god of rain, and of peace.

It met wet on his own cheeks. *Let this man and his family find a bit of peace, Yngvi,* he prayed. *Forgive me for my stupid anger. And keep Aldís safe, please.*

. . .

The next day, Kel rose early and rode away from Eilíf's farm. He would say nothing to Mani about two children who lived in hiding with a scarred young widow and a blind poet. He would say nothing to Mani about a kidnapped nun who was no longer a nun, or a slave who had helped him burn the stable of *gothi* Naldrum to the ground.

But he *would* talk to Mani about a crime to be prosecuted at the upcoming Althing, three moons' time from now. Because the night before Naldrum's spring festival started, an embarrassed man had tugged on Kel's sleeve and had asked to talk to the headman in private.

Beside the man had stood the girl who had run from Naldrum's tent at last year's Althing—and she had held a child.

. . .

Chapter Fifty-Three

The cart-trader Josson beat his exhausted horse. Damned lazy beast! Josson had ridden the horse hard for the second time all the way from Thornes *thing* to Naldrum's compound, where, after a quick conversation, the headman had immediately sent him back to Thornes *again*. Josson had obeyed Naldrum's command to ride fast, but soon, irritation and his horse's weariness slowed them down.

On the one hand, Josson enjoyed feeling so important to such a great man. "Naldrum was clearly impressed by my diligence in bringing the news to him. Maybe I can finally get permanent work at his compound." For a while, that puffery filled him, until Josson realized he was hungry.

"Still, the headman might've offered me some hack-silver—just a little! —for what I've done." Josson chewed on this bit of gall, gnawing it thoroughly to extract every scrap of bitterness as he complained to his weary mount.

"First that *gothi* at Thornes sent me riding to Naldrum to tell him about the law case against the *vikinger* Tiller. Then Naldrum sent us back to Thornes to carry his own message. Then to Naldrum's with the verdict, and now another long ride back to Thornes with yet *another* message. And what, for all that trouble? Nothing! Four damned trips between Thornes and Naldrum's. That's worth a silver armband at least!"

Josson mulled how excited Naldrum had been at the news. "That trial seemed awfully important to him. He told me there wasn't a breath of time to lose. Maybe it should've been worth even a gold coin."

His bone-thin horse barely plodded along. Josson's expression fell back into its usual grumpy sourness.

"A gold coin, for sure! But he sent me away without offering even a skinful of *skyr*! No respect at all for the laws of hospitality!"

Josson vacillated between annoyance and pride. *If only someone would come along the roadway and offer him a place to stay with a warm blanket and good food.*

The longer he rode, the more Josson became convinced that he was owed *something* for rushing such important messages back and forth. He reached a fork in the road. One way led back towards Thornes, and the other way led—albeit at some distance—to a certain widow's homestead which he was accustomed to avoiding.

"Could stop there and rest a bit, I suppose," Josson told himself. His horse stood, sullen and drooping, waiting for Josson to decide. "But you know I don't like that place."

He debated the matter with the weary animal. "If you saw her, you'd understand why. Hideous creature! Plus, she never bought anything anymore. Said she felt too guilty, after that fire that killed her husband. Not even one scrap of cloth has she bought in years. I told Tor that's why I never go to her farm anymore."

The mention of Tor reminded Josson that he *had* stopped at the woman's farm last year. "Well, just that once," he said to his horse, as if the beast had corrected him. "That time after I bought Tor from the merchant ship." Now, Josson's empty stomach reminded him how well Eilíf had fed them.

"That ugly wretch owes me," Josson declared to the empty air. "When I stopped at her farm for repairs—how could I help that my harness broke right at her path? —by the time we left, Tor fixed damn near everything on her farm that was broken." Another memory twitched. "Oh! How could I have forgotten? Tor tried to give her one of my oranges!"

Those precious oranges had resulted in Josson being profoundly shamed by Naldrum. At that last bit of evidence, he judged the widow guilty. Now she must pay.

Josson's sour expression turned mean. He kicked his horse towards the widow's home.

"Here we go, then," he said. "Maybe she'll have some of that fine *sup* of hers." He turned between into the two marked stones and kicked his horse with anticipation, his stomach growling.

. . .

The farm, though well-tended, appeared empty. *Trolls hide during daylight.* Josson shivered a little. He tied his horse to a birch branch and walked towards the house, not exactly with stealth, but not in the forthright manner of a welcome guest, either.

His steps slowed more and more as he approached the longhouse door. It stood open, but still no signs of the widow. *One of her sheep must be lambing in a field somewhere,* he reassured himself.

His former unease about seeing the widow had returned. *I'll just slip in there quickly and take whatever food I can find, and leave before she gets back,* he decided, and peeked around the door frame.

. . .

The chunk of smoked ham Josson sliced from a joint in the rafters tasted so good that he decided to take the whole hock with him. The trader dragged a stool under the hanging meats and climbed on it, steadying himself. He stretched, reaching for the rope tied around the hock joint.

A brusque voice interrupted his efforts. "You there! What are you doing? Are you stealing our food?"

Josson lost his balance, and the stool crashed. He fell to the longhouse floor. For a while, his head swam and his eyes could not focus—but when they did, he found himself staring at the last face he expected to see.

Tor, likewise, stared aghast at the trader. *It could not be.*

. . .

"Naldrum said you died in a fire! But you're here?" Josson moaned. His head pounded. He pressed it with a fist. "How can that be? How could you be dead and—" The trader's eyes, confused, his head throbbing. Then his chin shot up and he glared at Tor. "You ran away."

Once again, Tor wanted to kill a man. Not for himself; he could bear anything. But if Josson saw or heard—

And in that instant, Josson *did* see and hear.

"Papa, who is that man?"

Standing behind Tor were two children that Josson recognized, two children that he had wanted to sell, and believed had died—but who now, like their father, also appeared quite alive.

"Run!" Tor cried to his son and daughter. "Tell the widow to stay away from the longhouse!"

He did not say *tell your mother*. The less Josson knew, the better.

. . .

The two men faced each other. Their negotiations would be fast, without pretense.

"What do you want for your silence?" Tor asked.

"Silence? Ha! What is that worth, against telling Naldrum not only that I found his prize slave alive and well, but that I'm gifting him with two fine children also?" Josson could hardly contain himself.

I don't want to kill him. I must not kill a human being, not again. Not ever again. Tor anguished. Yet what other option remained? One only: to give Josson what he *really* wanted.

Tor made himself not think, not feel. "Listen to me. I'm going to tell you what you have to do."

This was how it had to be. There was no other way. After they talked, Tor walked to the field and called his children.

. . .

Tor pulled the knife across his son's hand. The red line showed immediately, the blood promise Josson had demanded. Then Tor cut his daughter's skin, and his own.

Each time, Tor clasped the trader's hand, the children's small fingers under his. Each time, he said the words, *I swear by the blood.* Their young faces watched the trader and their father in innocent worry, not understanding what was happening, only that something of deep importance was taking place.

Tor's admonitions to them, serious, as if he spoke to adults.

We live in this country. We live by its rules. You are young, but you have the spirits of lions. Be brave.

The deal was struck.

. . .

Josson had inadvertently let slip to Tor the fact that Naldrum had told him to immediately ride back to the *thing* at Thornes with a final message that Naldrum planned to make a huge announcement at Althing, and for his allies in Thornes to be ready to support and cheer it.

Tor made the most of that scrap. "Yet here you are, almost a full day's ride from the track, dawdling around and stealing hams. Do you hasten back to Naldrum to tell him you found me? I'll disappear, I promise you—and what will he say, seeing you in his longhouse instead of following his orders to return to Thornes?"

Josson's face fell in confused disarray. He had not thought of that.

"And if you leave here and ride to Thornes? Again, I'll be long gone by the time you get back. You can tell Naldrum you saw me, but I slipped through your fingers. What do you think his response will be?"

The trader hunched over the table, studying a crack in the wood. "Well, he's the one told me to ride to Thornes, after all."

"You think he will care?" Tor scoffed. "Naldrum hates nothing more than excuses that other men make, even if he's the cause of them. You can't win."

For the thousandth time in his miserable life, Josson tasted gall. *Naldrum will never see me as a successful man.*

"But here's the problem for me," Tor continued. "I'm in a bind as well. Eventually, you *will* get word to Naldrum that you've seen me. Once he knows I'm alive, he will scour the countryside until he finds me. Not only will I be his slave again, but he'll take my children—but he'll still be angry at you for making him work so hard to accomplish it."

Josson's glum expression deepened.

"It would seem we're both trapped, trader. Naldrum will again despise you, even if you follow his orders. And eventually, I'll be hunted down."

Josson spread his palms upward in supplication. "What do I do? I'm old. I'm poor. Trading's worse every season. I can't make it much longer." Josson could not admit to himself that much of the fault for failure lay in his own hands. "Naldrum's the only chance I have."

Despite himself, Tor had felt compassion for the scrawny merchant. "There's a way out. We neither of us get all that we hope for—but we get what we need most."

Josson looked up, hopeful. "What do you have in mind?"

"My heart's desire is for my children to be safe. You must leave them here, and never return, and never speak of them to anyone."

Josson's expression, skeptical. "What do I get in return?"

"You get *me.* I give you my word, I'll stay here. Let me spend the spring with my children. Let me help the widow get her crops in the ground and her lambs delivered, so that she will have food for them. Come back here before Althing, and I'll ride as your prisoner to the festival as your prize capture, Naldrum's runaway slave. You can make my return to him the kind of big show he likes. You, a trader who could have made a fortune selling me to someone else but whose loyalty lies with Naldrum, and everyone seeing you make me kneel before him, in front of a crowd at Althing. Much bigger and better than you just reappearing at his compound, all breathless with news but nothing in your hands."

Josson whistled through his teeth. "You're a clever one."

"Not that clever, or I'd have been off this island by now."

"Why should I believe that you'll wait another three months and then turn yourself over to me?"

"You don't have children. If you did, you'd understand. I'll do anything for them." *And my wife,* Tor added in his thoughts.

. . .

Kandace wept, of course. They all wept, hearing the news after Josson had ridden out of sight, but Tor remained adamant.

"If I had struck no deal, Josson would have blabbed his news about us to anybody and everybody. Where could we go, that fast, all four of us? We'd be captured within the week. But this buys Josson's absolute silence for nearly three months. He'll stay completely quiet about this, because *he* wants to be the one to return me to Naldrum. He won't want another soul to know I'm here. We're safe until he returns to get me, at least."

Kandace could not bear the thought of Tor enslaved again. "But then?"

"You and the children must be long gone before Josson returns. As soon as he delivers me to Naldrum, he'll renege on his promise. He'll come right back here and start hunting for the children. Naldrum's men will be at this door in a couple of days."

She groaned. Tor took her fingers in his.

"Something will turn up, Kandace. I could have snapped that man's neck today with my fingers, as I would a chicken-head. But I resisted the desire to do evil. Whoever watches over us has steered us back together and kept us safe so far. I have to trust, and keep following that path."

"Your faith is stronger than mine," she said. "I dread what might come."

Kandace knew that despite his calm manner, the decision had cost Tor greatly. She pointed to the jug of carrot seeds.

"Well, you negotiated the planting season. These need to go in the vegetable garden. Take your son with you to help. Eilíf and I will pluck a couple of chickens and start cooking. From this instant until you leave, I intend to celebrate being together every day."

Tor needed work, she knew, and so did she.

. . .

That night, Kandace offered an idea.

"The bishop, my love," she murmured to Tor. She curled against him on the sleeping bench, the fire low and quiet. A low board separated their section from where Eilíf and Petr's breath rose and fell in slumber. Kandace spoke quietly so as not to wake them.

"What about him?"

"He's a good man, Tor, if a bit of a weak one. As far as he knows, I'm still a nun. He'd help any human being in distress, but I'm certain that the idea of a nun being hounded and harassed would greatly dismay him. We need to find out where he is. I must go there for safety."

They lay together in silence. The reassuring home-smells of the longhouse drifted around them; the smoky fragrance of the hams hanging from the roof and the fresh clean fragrance of spruce branches on the floor.

"He could be anywhere, Kandace. How would we even begin to find him? And how would we get you safely to him?"

"Big obstacles, I admit, but I'm not leaving these shores unless it's with you—so if you must return to Naldrum, I'm staying in this country. Don't argue with me. Bishop Friedrich is my best chance for safety. As far as finding him and getting there, Naldrum wields too much power over many landowners and ship merchants. We need someone with no allegiance to him. Someone he can't control."

They lay in silence, their fingers intertwined. Then both spoke together.

"We need Aldís."

They talked no longer after that. Their bodies curved around each other as if to memorize the feeling. Eventually each drifted into exhausted sleep.

. . .

Chapter Fifty-Four

Once again, Kel sat across a table facing a young woman, an infant, and her family. This truly would be the last time, though.

Like Sauthi, he had crossed a line where he would not protect Naldrum's disgusting secrets any longer. For a painful instant, Kel remembered Sauthi's anguish as he spoke of how Naldrum had killed whoever Sauthi had loved. Kel thought of Aldís, wherever she was, then plunged ahead.

First, he spoke to the young woman's husband.

"Your wife told me you had met at Althing and married two moons later, shortly before she realized she was pregnant. You realized the child was not yours when it was born too soon. You threw a fit, and finally she told you the truth."

The young man, his face red and angry, agreed.

"But then you ignored her pleas to not contact Naldrum. You insisted that she and your father go to Naldrum and demand that he pay the child-rights he owed her. They were at his compound for the spring festival."

Kel had seen the older man and the young woman holding the child at the *dísablót.* He had pulled them aside and warned them as he had the others. But unlike those before him, this man had listened to Kel. He had backed away from trying to talk to Naldrum, and had taken his daughter-in-law and her child home.

“It is fortunate that they did not get to talk to the headman that night. If they you had, Naldrum would have promised everything you wanted. Payment, and to take the child and raise it as his own.”

“What’s so bad about that?” the husband asked.

“Because that’s not what would have actually happened. Naldrum would have sent me to follow you, to kill this child. To beat your wife. To threaten you.”

In a clear, calm voice, Kel told them everything. The number of times he had ridden across the country to a family like theirs. The things he had done, and could not undo.

“You’re exaggerating,” the husband said. “This cannot be true.”

Kel shook his head. “I wish I could say I am exaggerating, but no. And I wish I could say that I disobeyed him, but I followed his orders. For years, I believed him when he claimed that young women made up their stories to extort money from him.”

“If you did that to others like me, why are you being so decent to us?” the young woman asked.

“Because last summer at Althing, I happened to be awake at middle-night, walking. Normally I go to bed early, to prepare for the opening festivities the next morning. I saw a man moving among the lanes between the tents—up one lane, down the next. It seemed odd to me, so I followed him. The way he moved looked familiar. Suddenly, I realized it was my own headman, wearing a cloak that I’d never seen before.”

“And you saw him with me.”

“I did. You came out of your family’s tent—”

“It was my first Althing. I was too excited to sleep.”

"I'm not blaming you. Anyone should be safe at Althing any time of the day or night. But I saw him go over to you and talk. I couldn't stay too close for fear of being seen, but not long after, I saw you walking with him towards his tent, so I followed, and listened."

"He grabbed my arm," the girl said. "Pulled me along, jerking at me. I was a little nervous, but as I said, it was my first festival. He said he was one of the law speakers, and they needed help. Something about the opening ceremony. I never thought to question him. He dragged me to his tent."

"And then—"

"And then he forced me."

Kel had needed to hear her speak those exact words, that last bit of truth, completely on her own. If he had encouraged her to say it, he might still have wondered. But seeing her earnest face, he knew.

"I believe you."

"So now what happens? You say he won't pay the father-fee?"

If only it were that simple. "No. He would have demanded that your child be exposed until it died. He'd have told me to beat you within a breath of your life for naming him as the father, and to threaten to kill your family if you spoke of it again, ever. I wouldn't have beaten you—I never did that—but I would spoken his threats."

"I don't believe all this!" the young husband burst out. "He's a headman with a reputation to protect. He's rich, but he's not above the law! Why would you claim he does such terrible things? How could someone get away with this as long as you claim he has?"

"Because people like me have protected him! You don't have to believe me. What does your wife say?"

"I told you." Her voice was soft, broken. "He threatened me, exactly as this man says. I told you before we went to his compound that it was too dangerous, but you insisted."

The young husband glared, not wanting to believe.

"Something else happened at Althing that I never told you," she continued. "A healer with a yellow scarf comforted me that morning. Told me not to ask Naldrum about child-rights. Trust them, please."

"I understand that you deserve compensation for father-rights," said Kel. "But something much bigger is at stake. At first, I wanted to just stop Naldrum from hurting any more women in this way. But he is planning something big, something dangerous to all of us. Mysterious visitors from the Jarl of Lade come and go. He has been bribing those who are hungry, and spreading lies. Once-respectable farmers, even other chieftains, have allowed him to twist the law to his own purposes—and this is the man who got himself nominated to serve as Lawspeaker when the vote is taken this summer. Whatever Naldrum is planning, it's bigger than Althing even—and it can't be good. I need someone to help me try and stop him before it's too late. Are you willing?"

They were poor folk, and proud. They knew the value of a hard day's work, and they knew how to tighten their belts in a difficult year.

But mostly, they were farmers who knew what happened when rot started and how fast it could spread if ignored.

"We'll help," the girl said, and her family nodded alongside her.

Kel drew a breath of relief. One obstacle done, but more ahead.

. . .

Chapter Fifty-Five

Hunger took a short break from stalking the land. It did not gnaw at bellies as it had over the dark months, because milk animals produced their richest flow in the spring and chickens laid abundant eggs. But the winter just past still haunted the minds of all. Farmers walked behind their plows, eyeing the skies and wondering if again this year the rains would be too heavy. Could they survive, if that happened? Not likely everyone.

Who would die?

Those who were old. The infirm. Newborns, needing to suckle but whose gaunt mothers had too little food to make milk. All were vulnerable, for all needed fat and food to survive.

As bondsmen moved from farm to farm, their iron scissors singing as they cut the heavy winter wools from sheep, they eyed the animals carefully. What if the hoof-rot came again this year?

As women spread flax seeds across finely-tilled plots of soil, they worried about how to stretch lean larders to feel hungry families. Slaves with bellies already thin heaved stones from meadows and pushed themselves beyond fatigue. If one did not work hard, one did not eat.

Fear crept into every nook and cranny of what should have been warm, happy, hopeful days of planting, shearing, sowing. Women of every valley hid a kind of shame, as if they would be responsible for failures. Had they not been the ones to take gifts, each to their own Egg? Had they given enough to the goddess?

They murmured their prayers again and again, and hoped that Freya would be kind.

. . .

Chapter Fifty-Six

Aldís had listened, fascinated, as Kandace told the story of how the *vikinger* called Tiller had rescued her from Trondheim. Aldís had been working her way along one valley after another, following calls and helping with work. To Tor's relief, she had one day appeared at Eilíf's farm.

"The *vikinger* Tiller put me in a large leather sack, to hide me," Kandace said. Her Icelandic had improved, but she still needed Tor's help with some words. "I could not understand what Tiller was saying, of course, but I could see the face of the harbor official through a tiny slit in the bag. There was no mistaking his horror. Later I learned that Tiller was brave as well as creative. He had burned himself to create what looked like oozing sores."

They had all admired Tiller's cleverness. But the next morning, as Aldís and Eilíf darned patches onto grain-sacks, Tiller's 'white pox' trick gave Aldís an idea.

"We can use that same ruse!" she cried. "Kandace needs a way to hide, the way Rota hid her and Tor in a tent-wagon. But you have no wagon! And she and both children for a long voyage in search of the bishop? Day after day, they would need to relieve themselves, if nothing else. Inevitably, someone would see and they'd be discovered."

Eilíf sighed and ran a hand over her worried face.

Aldís leapt to her feet. "But what if we make Kandace and the children very *visible* instead? What if we intentionally draw attention to them? But when people look, they see an illusion? Like a fairing-trick? Something they're meant to see that's not really there." She explained to Eilíf. Without a word, Eilíf rose and ran for Kandace, calling in hope.

The sad, fruitless conversations about escape suddenly took on fresh energy. Worry of '*is there any way*' changed to discussions about small details needed. Every part of the plan was considered, adopted, rejected, changed. New hope gave focus on the solution instead of fearing the danger.

"We'll hide right in plain sight," Kandace said. "We have no other ideas how to get halfway across this country to a man whose whereabouts we don't even know. If it worked for Tiller, it could work for us."

Now, the bigger problem became finding Bishop Friedrich. Asking for his whereabouts might draw unwelcome attention. Aldís had noticed that more and more people, at least in Bull Valley, seemed to have suddenly grown suspicious of white-christ followers.

Worse, what if the bishop had already left their land to go home?

"Kel said that the *gothar* of the western fjords have little liking for Naldrum," Tor recalled. "That's the best place to go for now, since we have no idea where Friedrich might be. I've been to a trading site there a few years ago. It's a rugged place, but beautiful."

They talked of it over and over, scraping the bone thin, trying to plan every possible circumstance. With terrible odds of being discovered and an unknown destination to find, Aldís daily grew more worried that her idea might put Kandace and the children in far worse jeopardy than if they stayed at the widow's house, hidden. As the warm days lengthened and Althing approached, Aldís had taken to walking in the light-night, unable to sleep.

"Aldís, there's no one I trust more than you," Tor reassured her. "Josson saw the children. They simply can't stay here."

"What if I fail?" she asked, glad that they stood outside and no one could hear her doubts.

"Everything that could possibly fail my family, has," Tor said. "And everything that could possibly go right, has. We are on this path, Aldís. There is no other. Just do the best you can."

She shook her head. "I worry I'm more likely to do harm than good."

Tor took her hands. "My friend," he said. "Your fear comes from a place of deep pain."

She took a hand back, wiped a tear. "You're right. I do not trust that good will come from what I do. As if I do not deserve happiness or goodness."

Tor comforted her, his hand on her shoulder. "Many wish you all the happiness in the world, and believe that you deserve it. Some even love you with all their heart."

"How do you know? You're just saying that! Who could you possibly know who would claim such a thing?" Tor did not answer, letting Aldís work it out for herself.

Slowly she put it together. *Naldrum bought Tor. Kel worked for Naldrum. Tor was talking about Kel.*

Aldís stiffened. "You *don't* know! Kel Coesson is not a good man! He most certainly doesn't love me—and if he did, I wouldn't care!"

"I know differently," said Tor. "I know a man who paid a substantial sum out of his own pocket for the freedom of the slave boy that Drikke injured. I know a man whose face changes every time he spoke of you, once I finally put together that it was you he was talking about. I know a man who feels anguish, doubt, frustration, anger, betrayal, hope, despair, and grief over a love he lost years ago. All of them, straight from the heart and plain to see on his face, every single time." Tor's words, quiet but relentless. "I know a man who gave up his freedom to keep you safe, even though you never could have known that."

Aldís broke away from Tor and ran to the edge of the yard. She leaned against the wattle fence of the chicken-yard, her face contorted with pain.

"No! What you say can't be true. I once thought Kel was wonderful. Yes, I once loved him! But he's a brute and a toady to Naldrum. I can't stomach the thought of him now!"

"You don't have to believe me today. But I have never lied to you, and I never would. You may have the sight, Aldís, but in regard to Kel, a wrong understanding shapes your anger. One day, perhaps, you can open your heart to the whole truth."

She did not answer, but kept her back to Tor. He could see her shoulders shaking. He gave Aldís a bit of time, and then changed the subject back to their discussion about the trip to the western fjords.

As they talked, a gyrfalcon wheeled over their heads and perched on a tall dead tree across the meadow.

"Look at that beauty," said Tor, pointing. "She's been hunting here. Showed up not long after we arrived. I'll tell her to go with you. You can listen for her call. She'll show you the way, if you get lost."

“Silly man,” Aldís half-laughed. “A gyrfalcon for a guide?”

Tor’s face tightened into seriousness. “You have the seeing, Aldís. Maybe it flows to and from animals as well. Who knows? But stop being afraid of your gift. Stop worrying that you will misinterpret it. When in doubt, be like our blind friend.”

All that evening, Petr had worked plaiting a basket from birch strips, his mouth relaxed in a gentle smile.

“Look with your being instead of just your eyes,” said Tor. “Trust yourself. I do.”

. . .

Of course, she did not trust herself, Aldís realized. She never had. *How have I not noticed that before?* That was the problem, had *been* the problem ever since Kel. She had trusted her feelings that long-ago Althing, but both Kel and her feelings had betrayed her. She had trusted that he would come find her, but he had gone to Naldrum’s instead, and had stayed with Naldrum. Ever since, Aldís had become skeptical of what the inner-seeing told her, even though time after time it had spoken true.

Aldís frowned. *Why does everything always come back to Kel?*

. . .

Chapter Fifty-Seven

Kel had ridden to the valley where Mani lived, bursting with news that he had witnesses willing to testify against Naldrum at Althing. Kel had made them promise to not breathe a word to anyone. No one must know.

. . .

Mani and Kel talked long after the dinner bowls were empty, after the longfire had dwindled to embers.

The story came hard to Mani. He had never told anyone before, and the memory pained him.

"Dalla and I have never owned slaves. I didn't need or want one, but I saw that girl in the line and, well, I bought her."

The young woman had been a slight thing. Her startling green eyes had caught Mani's from where she stood roped with the other captives.

"She looked so forlorn that before I knew it, I had taken the cattle-marks out of my purse and handed them to the slave-trader."

That one, he had said, pointing.

"Not her," the trader had replied. "She's sick. I'll sell her to someone for a bed-slave, someone who doesn't care that she's not fresh."

Mani started to turn away, disgusted at the man, but the trader blabbed on.

"Can't say who tested her already. I tried to sell her outright to him, but he just wanted the one night. Someone high up, though. I have important clients." The man had settled his cap on his narrow head and leered at Mani. "Paid me the price I asked, and he didn't complain, either. But you're Lawspeaker. I don't want you bringing a case against me for bad trading, so choose one that's healthy. Anyone but her."

"That's the one I'm paying you for. And keep your filthy talk of bed-slaves to yourself. My wife is getting older and needs someone to help her around the house." It wasn't true, but he wanted to end the discussion.

"Your choice, Lawspeaker. Just don't say I didn't warn you."

The slave trader had untied the girl. The others had brightened, seeing a buyer in good clothing who looked well fed. They had called out to Mani in piteous voices.

"Take me too! Buy me! I'll work hard for you!" Cries of their skills rang in his ears as he turned to go. "Turf-cutter! Wool-dyer! Carpenter! Butcher! Weaver! Healer! Stonemason!"

Such a vile business, this stealing of human beings and selling them as if they were cattle. He shook his head *no*. The girl padded after him, her feet bare. She clutched a ragged shawl around her shoulders.

When they were out of earshot of the trader, he stopped. Mani spoke to her in broken Gaelic. "He says you're sick. A fever?"

Already he was having second thoughts. He ought not bring fever or a pox into his homestead. *I'll give her to someone else. Tell them to keep the cattle-mark.*

She shook her head. "No fever."

"Blisters? Pox?"

Another shake.

"Vomiting?"

She looked away. Ashamed, she put her hand flat against her belly.

Oh. *That.*

Mani suddenly realized why the girl's eyes had captivated him. *The daughter he and Dalla had finally had, after so many years of boys.* His wife's joy at their little girl. The child's eyes had been blue, not green, but had had that same innocent shape, that same earnest expression as she pondered how to walk, to eat with a spoon. The same worried look when she struggled to breath, after the coughing started.

"Come on," Mani had said to the slave girl. "It's not far. Let me know if you need to rest as we walk."

. . .

They had several months with the girl before her labor pains started. Dalla, who had been furious when Mani arrived home with the skinny waif in tow, had fallen in love with the girl, had coddled her as she had once coddled her own daughter. She had learned to speak to the girl in Gaelic, comforted her in her own language. Asked her about her home, her mother. Learned that the man who had impregnated her had done things that made the girl turn away and put her hands over her face, made tears come from her tight-squeezed eyes.

She had not survived the delivery, nor did the infant. It had hurt Mani terribly to lose his adopted daughter. The deaths had nearly destroyed his wife.

Mani had made a point of seeing the trader the following year, and not by accident. Mani had asked people to watch for the small caravan with the wheels painted in a certain design, and to call for him when they spotted it.

The man had yielded easily to the glint of silver in Mani's hand. Soon Mani knew who had fathered the pregnancy that had ended the life of his beloved slave-daughter. The name had slithered through Mani's thoughts ever since.

When Mani pulled on the now-ragged gloves she had been so proud to knit for him, or when the sweet taste of blueberries reminded him how she had delighted in collecting then, Mani, who loved the law perhaps more than he loved his wife, found himself infected with the desire to take from that man what had been taken from Mani and his wife, without trial and in careless brutality. A life for a life.

Among the feelings of sadness and loss, the snake-name slid, moving between muscle and bone, hiding and twisting in the shadows of his bowels. *Naldrum.*

"You see, now, why the case is so complex," Mani admitted. "If we bring suit against Naldrum, and anyone gets wind of this, I could be accused of trying to slant the trial, to throw evidence against Naldrum. Even if the council of gothar thought him guilty, they would be forced to declare a mistrial because of my perceived bias.

After that, who would mount a charge against him? Exonerated, he would flaunt his travesties openly. Such a trial would make women *less* safe. Eventually justice might would prevail, but how long might it take? And at what cost?"

Kel had never considered this complexity of legal matters before. "It is so fragile a thing, this thing we call law, isn't it? You cannot hold it in your hand. Yet it is so powerful to those who respect it—and so easily broken by those who do not."

"You have just spoken my deepest nightmare aloud." Mani looked about for any listening night-spirits. He rose and took his bowl to the fire, tossed a scrap of meat to the flames, said the incantation against evil.

"This is how the freedoms of our countryfolk can be destroyed, Kel. Not by hunger. Not by disease. But by selfish greed. All that is needed is a leader willing to blatantly ignore the law in favor of himself and his followers, and forcefully deny that he did. A 'leader' who stoops to using fear and violence to thwart all who stand against him. A man who has no understanding of the importance and value of fairness, who will stack the law councils with those who favor him and his followers. Of course, the same idiots who put him in power will one day regret it when he betrays even them for his own gain, and trades their freedoms to some foreign king, or taxes them to starvation, or uses their sons and daughters to make war, or takes away rights they hold dear."

"If the people put the man in place, then you must start with those people. Surely if you appeal to their good sense?"

"I have studied men and women all my life. What you ask may be more challenging than it first appears. Many who are wealthy act from greed. Gold, sheep, land, butter, horses. Every decision starts with how much they have, not what serves their community. Asking them to not be greedy? Good luck."

Kel shook his head. "But what about those who are not wealthy? They're more likely than anyone to want good leaders."

"They do. But I have noted, with astonishing regularity, that half of our freeholders will ask questions, and learn for themselves. The other half have a different quality. They do not like to question and learn. They prefer someone to tell them what to believe, which makes them vulnerable."

"What do you mean?"

"We have neighbors near and far who feel confused by complex ideas. They look to a leader to tell them what to think. It makes them easily manipulated by a bad leader."

"You're right," Kel admitted. "I've seen it in the faces of good people who like to act, to work, to serve, but who do not particularly like to think things through."

"These same people feel outmatched by law arguers and scholars who embrace complex thinking. They seem to think such thinkers believe themselves to be somehow superior, while of course, they are not; intelligence is a good thing, but a human's value does not rely solely on that. Consider intelligent people who have no ethics! But those who feel intimidated by scholars and thinkers feel more comfortable with men and women who seem equally 'ordinary'."

"Which means what?"

"Which means that they can be manipulated to dislike those who *do* think deeply about law."

. . .

Kel's blood ran cold. Mani had just perfectly summarized the effect Naldrum had had on the trusting folk of Bull Valley.

"But there is more, Kel. Another thing these people share is an innate distrust of anyone different than them."

Kel considered the people he had known across the years. Astonishingly, he realized that Mani was right.

"It's astonishing, how you've describe them! They look to someone in leadership to tell them what to think and believe, they feel outclassed by intellectuals and scholars, and they don't like outsiders! All three things in the same kind of person, over and over. Remarkable."

"That means the fate of our country has depended on the quality of our leaders. If they value the law and fairness, all is well. But if a leader who does not respect the law and fairness manages somehow to gain the ear of those we might call 'simple trusting'."

Kel finished the sentence for Mani. "That 'leader' will sow conflict, for their own gain and to the detriment of our land."

"And they will applaud him even as he strips them of their lawful rights and their prospects."

Both men sat silently as they considered the future.

"There's another quality to such people," Kel realized. "Regardless of their depth of knowledge, they seem to believe—how can I describe this? –that *their* way is the *only* way. About everything! They feel entitled to an opinion about everything, but deny others the right to have different opinions. *Theirs* to decide what is right and what is wrong, as if they somehow have the authority of the gods on their side. Theirs, to say how a person should live his or her life, while others are not allowed to have opinions."

"You're right," Mani mused. "Such a thing flies completely in the face of our laws, which say we are to be impartial in making decisions."

"Look at what is happening in Bull Valley. Some people who devoutly follow the Old Ways welcome the white-christs, but others believe that the Old Ways are the *only* way. It justifies them in hating white-christs and wanting to drive them out of our land, as if they own even the decision of how a man or woman might pray! Naldrum encourages them in such ridiculous prejudice. He uses their fear as a weapon, and revel in what it rewards him."

"The saddest thing is they do not realize that, little by little, they hate more and more. They splinter into smaller and smaller groups of distrust, and grow more and more bitter against those they perceive as different from them. They have grown into a force, Kel. The troubles in our land have frustrated them. All they needed was a bully leader who treats the law as if it answers to his whims, rather than being fair to all. How have they already forgotten that this is *exactly* what our people ran from in the Northway lands? Our forebears loathed the power of tyrants! Those who follow Naldrum do not yet realize that this dangerous pursuit of ultimate control is a fox that will lead them right into the same trap. How can they be so stupid?" He stopped. Thin lines pulled his mouth down in frustration. "The only reason law *works* is because the majority of people respect it. Once that respect is destroyed, such a precious thing may never be repaired."

"You have been watching Naldrum as long as I have."

Mani nodded. “And I have felt powerless as long as you have. He has always been a deceitful, pompous cheat. His ill-gotten wealth makes others perceive him as powerful, someone they want to emulate. One would think decent gothi would spurn him. Yet instead, yearly, he grows more powerful. Look how much stronger he has become this summer than last year. You heard that he wants to become head Lawspeaker? The fool does not know the law at all! How could he possibly teach it and interpret it? He respects none of it, yet he wants to be the person in charge of ‘protecting’ it? Appalling! So yes, Kel, I understand exactly what your concerns are. But because I am who I am, I must uphold the law, even it protects him. Even if I wish otherwise.”

“Mani, I was one of those who once supported Naldrum. I changed my mind. Others will as well.”

“But how long will it take? And will we survive him as a country of free people?

“I cannot speculate about that. All I can focus on is that we finally have a chance to stop him.”

The lawspeaker held onto the edge of the trestle table. “One chance only, so we must work carefully. From what I have learned of people and their patterns, we must assume that at least half of the *gothar* will vote for him, no matter how heinous his crimes. Convicting him may come down to a single vote or two. Because I am Lawspeaker, I cannot help you plan your challenge. I must remain impartial, and merely weigh the evidence as presented. I will listen to your strategy, and if you have enough evidence, I will present the case. But you know as well as I do that failing to destroy Naldrum will only empower him more—so we must not fail. Make sure your witnesses are sound, and their testimony is clear and compelling. I cannot present a trial that cannot be won. Not one this important."

Kel stood, yawning and exhausted. "Fair enough. But you don't have to worry about my dedication to this. I have everything on the line here, Mani. If I accuse him, and I lose, I'm a dead man." He looked about for an open space on the sleeping benches. "Which, by the way, Naldrum thinks I am already, so that's convenient."

Kel fell asleep before he had a chance to roll over. Freedom, even at a fearsome price, brought peace. For the first time in years, Kel's slumber was not troubled by knocks of any kind. He dreamt of the fields of Althing, and a woman who reached for him in love.

. . .

Chapter Fifty-Eight

Spring brought relief from food shortages, for the present at least. But worry still lurked. Rota, visiting again, sensed it.

"I have a messenger sailing to Trondheim this week, *gothi* Naldrum. I need to send Jarl Haakon an update before Althing. It's time for him to decide if he will partner with you. What shall I tell him?"

Naldrum puffed his chest. "Remember that you told me to find something that caused fear? Well, I have. Of course, worry about famine causes fear. But what *causes* famine? Worship of the wrong gods, I have decided."

"The wrong gods?"

"The god of the white-christs."

Rota gazed at Naldrum for a long time. "Harald Bluetooth, the king of the Dane-lands and the Nor'way lands, is Christian, and insists that his subjects must be as well."

Rota probed. "I wonder if you know of the Jarl's feeling about that?"

Naldrum squirmed, uneasy. "No. I never thought to ask."

She laughed without warmth. "I can assure you that the Jarl has no liking for that faith. He follows the old ways."

Naldrum rubbed his hands together. "Excellent. Then you will be pleased to know that for months I have spread rumors that the white-christs have caused the bad weather and crops—and that allowing them to worship freely causes *our* gods to turn against us."

"Admirable. What else?"

"You also told me to create hope. During midwinter, our servants quarreled over our Jul-log. My skald recited a story about those who settled Iceland, and a brilliant idea came to me." He beamed as might a child showing off a prize.

"What?"

"Something that will profit me everything, and cost nothing!" Naldrum told Rota about the old legend of lands that lay in the seas even further west than Iceland. "The idea died years ago, but I intend to beat it to life again."

"How?"

"By sending a ship in search of it! Even if they sink a day's sail away, who will know? I'll be a hero."

"What is your goal from all this fearmongering and carrot-dangling?"

"What you said when we first met. To lead all of Iceland."

Rota smiled. As she had realized early on, Naldrum could be led by ego. He had swallowed the bait and the hook was set. Now, he was hers.

Rota nodded slowly. "A good start. I may have underestimated you."

Naldrum fumed inwardly. *Why must this woman always imply an insult?*

"A *very* admirable idea," Rota continued, and he relaxed a little. "But still too simple. A fight over religion will cause some trouble, but how does it make people see *you* as a *leader?* Likewise, you can dangle your ship as a prize, but how does it make people see you as *the one they want to lead them?* Your plan needs to be much stronger.

Naldrum sat with his mouth open, looking as if she had asked him to do the impossible. "What do you suggest?" he asked.

"Don't make me do the work for you. If you're going to be a leader, maybe you could try a little harder."

. . .

Rota gave Naldrum most of the day to deliver on her request. Instead he alternated between boasting of his prowess in various matters and sulking, demanding that she tell him the answer. Finally, having reached his small limit of patience, Naldrum called for his new steward, a burly man named Randaal.

"The woman visiting us insulted me today. I need you to remedy that."

. . .

Randaal immediately went to where Rota and her guard had pitched her tent. He walked up and without a word, kicked the guard in the groin. The man dropped to the ground and Randaal slung Rota over his shoulder. He carried her back to Naldrum's longhouse, threw her down in front of the headman, and gave her a choice of which thumb he should cut off.

Naldrum beamed. Kel would never have done such things. At last, he had the steward he had always sought, a man untroubled by conscience, willing to do whatever he asked.

Rota laid out her strategy as if placing *tafl* pieces on the game board: king, queen, riders, priestesses, archers, swordsmen.

"It's not enough just to create trouble or dangle a prize! When you get to Althing, talk about the white-christs as enemies—but then *give people a path away from them.* Demand a return to the Old Ways! I'll tell you exactly what to say. And when you talk about the ship, don't just gabble on like a goose about sending it out exploring! First, you must tie it to the return to the Old Ways. Second, there must be a reason that gives—*everyone!* —eagerness for you to succeed, whether they like you or not. When we get to Althing, I'll tell you what to say about that, too. I'll take your simple ideas and make them into a war machine."

"How dare you insult me so! Tell me now!"

Rota, furious and stubborn, refused. "No. And if you try to hurt or humiliate me again, I'll take the next ship back to Trondheim, and the Jarl will send men to skin your family and burn your property to the ground. Do you understand me?"

Naldrum reared back. "He cannot do that! We have laws here!"

She laughed without humor. "Your laws mean nothing to the Jarl. Besides, I've heard that you don't bother to follow your own laws either. Don't play the aggrieved victim to me."

Naldrum looked away. "I'll do what I want."

"You're pathetic. But you're my best chance for the Jarl right now." She called her guard, limping, and he brought her a small chest.

"Here. Wear these at Althing."

Seeing a gleam of gold, he decided to ignore Rota's rudeness.

"I will be the Jarl's willing servant," Naldrum said graciously, intending no such thing. But he reached eagerly for the golden arm bands and slid them onto his wrists.

. . .

Rota changed the subject. "Your slave man, Tor, who translated for Kandace. I want to buy him. A gift for the Jarl, helpful to Haakon the same way he was to you, translating for Kandace."

Why did I just ask that? Rota asked herself. *Absolutely unnecessary.* Still, she was not sorry.

Naldrum glanced around, uneasy. "Tor is not here. I have sent him to do a task for me."

"I'll pay you today. Send him to me when he returns."

Naldrum could not think of a reason to refuse her.

"Excellent," said Rota. She counted out a generous sum of silver cattle-marks into Naldrum's outstretched hand.

This idea of getting something for nothing suddenly seemed a fine strategy to Naldrum. The best strategy, in fact. Others would pay for his ship, yet he would reap all the praise and profits from it. Likewise, Rota would never find out that Tor died in the fire. "I'll just make an excuse the few times I see her each year."

Now, instead of owning a pile of worthless ashes, Naldrum held in his palm enough cattle-marks to buy several *obedient* slaves. *Not a bad way to do business at all,* he complimented himself.

. . .

Chapter Fifty-Nine

"Leprosy, they call it," Kandace said. She described the beggars that had hovered around the walls of towns, pleading for alms. "Some kind of sickness eats their skin—"

Tor flinched, remembering. "You see those poor creatures in southern trading ports. Such a pitiful condition."

Aldís asked to hear the details, gruesome though they were, so that she could explain the "sickness" of her traveling companions to those they met on the road.

Listening to Kandace describe those afflicted with the disease, Aldís realized she had other failures of trust. *If Freya loves us, why do humans suffer so?* She asked that question of the skies on yet another sleepless night walk, but heard no answer. The gyrfalcon, tearing the flesh from some prey, offered nothing of help, either.

. . .

"Put your arms through the sleeves, like so." Kandace had cut holes in grain sacks for her daughter's head and arms.

The little girl did as told, her springy curls pushing through the neck opening, followed by her serious eyes. She stood, arms straight out, while Kandace measured her for pants.

Mask.

Hood.

Gloves.

Boots.

Every single bit of their skin must be covered. People must not see skin the color of seal fur. They must never realize that a valuable child from a far-away land hid inside the shroud.

When the outfit was completed, Nenet put it on and twirled for them. The smallest of slits across the eyes to see and a slit for her to breathe were the only openings in the fabric. Rough cloth took on the form of a small human that looked and moved like a life-size toy.

"Can you ride in it?" Tor asked. In answer, Nenet ran to the field and called her favorite of the horses Kel and Tor had brought.

The mare bent her head, Nenet straddled it, and the horse lifted her. Nenet slid chest-first down the mare's neck and twisted onto her back. She clucked with her tongue and the horse strutted around the meadow.

"Yes, papa! I can ride!" she said. Kandace, watching her, exchanged glances with Aldís. The children had no idea how dangerous a journey they were about to undertake. Better that way.

Kandace bent her head and sewed furiously, each stab of the needle an angry jab at God for putting them in such a heartbreaking situation.

. . .

The completed outfits hung over the trestle table in the widow's longhouse. Eilíf, wracked with grief, spent her days going from the Nenet to Nikea over and over. *One last touch. One last kiss. One last inhale of the smell of their hair. One more gentle holding of their hands.*

Her husband pulled her away. "They need to go soon, Eilíf. We cannot keep them. They must be far away before the day Josson arrives for Tor."

Aldís agreed. "Althing starts in one more moon. The week or two before, roads will become crowded. Right now, though, they are nearly empty, because people are working hard to get everything ready. It's safest right now."

The widow nodded, understanding, but sobbed nonetheless. "Only eighteen moons they have been here. It is not enough."

Aldís, normally so gentle, offered a hard reminder. "Kandace did not see them for years. She could lose them again. Who knows when Tor will see his children again? Save your tears for them. We must all be strong."

Tor, hearing, flinched. *Should I just go with them, too?* he wondered. Over and over again he had weighed the excruciating choice. He cursed the part of him that, once his word was given, would not retract it. Besides that, though, were the practical matters that he had gone over time and again. No silver, no friends, a strange country where travelers depended on the hospitality of strangers, and were noticed, here on an island far from any other land.

I might die a slave, but I can't live without them being safe. This plan, as awful as it was, offered the best chance for those he loved.

. . .

Kandace, Nenet and Nikea pulled on the sickness-suits. Aldís had fastened a type of harness to help the boy and girl ride together on one horse. At first it had seemed a silly idea, but when they stood wrapped together in it, she had gasped in surprise.

"We'll use Naldrum's own words against him!" she cried. "He has been spreading rumors among the valley folk of strange signs, of deformities in animals. Look at them!"

Certainly, hooded and bound together, they made for an odd creature. Four-legged, four-armed, two-headed, clumsily lunging as they tried to move.

"You'll inspire fear. Perfect," Aldís decided. "You two just became one creature."

Eilíf tied the linen thongs around their wrists, to hold on the hand coverings. The deception was ready.

. . .

The shrouds, too, had been treated to be part of the ruse. Bloodied, dirtied, tattered, torn and patched, what had been normal grain sacks now looked unclean and frightening.

Eilíf's blind Petr could not see them, but he smelled the faint stench of dried blood on the weavings. "They must look like some kind of death-walkers," he laughed.

"All the better," Aldís agreed. As they had gotten nearer and nearer to the time to leave, she had been chewing her fingernails to the quick. The more horrific the children and Kandace appeared, the better for them all.

. . .

"The full moon, for good lighting during night travels," Petr voted.

"No, the dark of the moon. Horses don't need light. Darkness is safer." said Eilíf.

Kandace, however, made the final decision.

"I have watched the people of this area during my months here. They are creatures of habit. We can use that." She knelt beside Nenet and Nikea. "Here is a puzzle. On what day of the week do people mostly look inside instead of out?"

Nikea counted on his fingers. "Sol-day, the Sun's day, we reposition the sun-stick, to keep track of the equal-days of spring and autumn and the sun-still days of mid-winter and mid-summer, and start counting the days of the week over. We are looking outside that day, right, Momma?"

Kandace smiled. "Correct, my fine son. Nenet, your turn. Keep going."

"Mani-day, the Moon's day, we check if the moon is full or half, waning or waxing. We start each planting or harvesting on those days, and we use that day to keep count of the months. So not Moon-day. Because if we are always out on Moon day and working in the field, so would other people be." Nenet smiled, her shy grin showing the gap where she had lost her first tooth.

"Excellent, my sweetness. Nikea?"

"Týr's day is next. Petr tells me that the valley folk take turns helping each other with tasks that need extra hands—like raising rafters, or setting foundation stones. So not Týr's day."

"Now Odin's day," said Aldís. "Do you know they call it Wodin's day in the Saxon ports? Such an odd way of saying the same thing. Anyway, that's the day that families try to take a day of rest, and honor their gods, and teach lessons to their children. They play games outside, and they tell stories. Servants have the day off and they walk to other farms to visit. So definitely not Odin's day."

"Thor's day," mused Nikea. "That day we always check the property and make sure that the longhouse and animal pens are safe from bad weather, and that we have firewood cut and ready, and water drawn for days too rainy to go to the stream. So, again, since we're out working, not then." She frowned, perplexed. "We are running out of days, Momma."

Kandace smiled. "Keep going."

"Not Frigg's-day," said Aldís. "Women use the goddess-day to visit each other. To check on women ready to deliver, to help new mothers, to carry food to the elderly ones. They are often on the walking-tracks and roadways."

"And that brings us to lather-day. Might Laugerday—washing day—be the answer?" asked Kandace.

"Oh!" Aldís cried. "Laugerday *is* the puzzle answer!"

"Correct," smiled Kandace. "Now tell me why."

"Because on washing-day, everyone is mostly working *inside* their houses and pens. We wash our clothing and hang it to dry over ropes in the yard, or, if it is rainy, along the longfire inside. We muck out the barnyards and check the feet of the herds. We tidy the wattle pens where the chickens, ducks and geese are kept. We run back and forth all day carrying pails of clean water. When all farm work is finished, we gather in the longhouse, and heat more clean water, and take our weekly bath! Everyone soaps and rinses, we wash each other's hair and comb it. We all go to bed clean, with a good feeling that the home and farm are in order."

"But what does that have to do with our travel day?" asked Nenet.

"Because all the other days, people are looking at the sky, or the roads, or the fields," Kandace answered. "On washing day, they stay on their own property and they are looking at *it*, not the sky or the fields. They don't walk down the paths to the trackways. They almost never, ever travel. The roads are empty, and more importantly, ignored. The longer washing-day goes on, the more they look inside instead of outside. So *that* is the day we should leave."

After a short discussion, the final decision was made. They would set off the evening before washing day, when people had finished work in the fields and went inside for supper. That gave them an evening and a full night to travel. Then washing day, another day and night in which they could travelled almost unnoticed.

That would take them into the weeks before Althing, when most normal tasks were interrupted and families began the work of packing up trade goods and traveling equipment for their trek to the festival valley.

Two days remained until Lauger-day, with nothing to do but wait.

. . .

The small caravan left when Sól crossed the fifth-eighth mark on the evening before washing-day. Aldís had concocted an outlandish garb for herself, cobbled from Tor's stories of fearsome guards in other lands. She rode on one of the horses and Kandace, wearing her sick-suit, rode on the other. Her horse pulled a small cart holding the two children and some basic supplies.

I'll see them again, Tor told himself. *Somehow.*

Aldís wished she could feel something about the future, but nothing flowed from that uncertain tide of awareness. Only the faint strange calling continued, too intermittent to catch. She pushed it away, fearing it meant harm to Kandace. Who kept summoning her, and what did they want?

. . .

They rode at a slow pace, not hurrying in a way that might attract attention, but with purpose, inviting no casual contact. Aldís felt sick with apprehension. She looked around constantly, her heart thundering.

They did not talk. Part of their plan.

Single file. A silent parade, riding long into the still-light night.

. . .

Tor watched as all that was precious to him ride the faint valley track out of sight. When he could see them no longer, he picked up the hoe and returned to the vegetable field, to hack savagely at the weeds that grew there.

. . .

Aldís felt a flicker of *something-not-right.* She glanced back at the children, looking for the small signal—the gyrfalcon feather, held upright in Nenet's hand—that indicated all was well with them. She scanned the road behind, the road ahead. Nothing. Still, the bad feeling persisted.

. . .

Chapter Sixty

Josson found their trail easy enough to follow.

He had not thought of the children after Thornes *thing*. In truth, he had not thought of much of anything until Althing approached.

Then, he had ridden, sick with worry and criticizing himself for being so stupid, straight to the widow's property. He had waited for darkness to slip close to the house.

They were still there. Josson had almost wept with relief.

He had moved back along the roadway and camped, hidden. Watched the road. The tedium of doing nothing bored him to distraction. But finally, his wait had been rewarded.

. . .

Josson saw the strength Aldís had intended to project. And the sick-suits unsettled him. What had happened to them? *That thing of arms and legs. That's Tor's children in that mess, right?* He eyed the group, nervous. *Looks as if they have blood on them.* And who was the other one all covered up in that nasty garb? Not big enough to be Tor, but certainly an adult. Who was it?

Better to follow them and do nothing. He'd have plenty of time to go back and get Tor for Althing.

Josson kept his horse well back so that he was never seen. But that witch Aldís kept turning around looking. How did she know?

. . .

Because it was washing-day, they had ridden since dawn. True to Kandace's observation, the roads had been completely empty. They had paused only briefly to relieve themselves and eat rapidly. The sun had risen early and was in no hurry to set. After a long day on the road, they were all exhausted, but their biggest challenge lay directly ahead.

The road ran straight through a large farmstead where traders and travelers frequently stayed. It was always crowded and busy.

"We'll wait as long as we can and go through when people start to go to sleep." Aldís told them. "It's been grueling, I know, because we are close to Longest-Day. Only a little dark will, and late, but that's our best chance. Can you do it? Can you stay awake and ride the short night, too, so that by tomorrow morning we are well past that farm?"

Her companions nodded, their heads bobbing strangely in the gunny sacks.

"Let's freshen up your clothes," Aldís said. It was a small joke the children had started. Nenet and Nikea sat, sweet and cooperative, as Aldís made a small cut on her forearm. When the blood oozed, she dabbed it around the mouth and eye openings of the sick-suits. A little water, and their 'faces' frightened even her.

"Your turn, Kandace," she said. The two women faced one another, fearful, trusting one another.

"Do it," said Kandace.

Aldís painted Kandace's mask as well, then wrapped a light linen strip over the cut on her arm. She swung up into her saddle again. As the late dusk fell, they headed for the trading-farm, hoping to ride past unobserved.

. . .

When they reached it, no one was out of doors. They stayed to the road, faces forward, steadily moving, making no sound. The sun had set but full dark did not come this close to mid-summer.

Keep going.

Keep going.

Keep going, keep going, keep going.

With every step of the horses' hooves, Kandace fought her fear, her chest almost too tight to breathe. Aldís's horse started to snort and rear, sensing her tension. The two children, in their tied-together state, clung to one another and trembled.

Keep going. Keep going, keep going, almost there, keep go—

A dog barked, shattering the stillness of the night.

. . .

Two merchants stood at a distance from the roadway. Behind them, a number of people had spilled out of everywhere at the shouts. They all held back, nervous about the things in the sick suits.

"You there!" one called to Aldís. "A word!"

She halted her horse, held up her hand for the others to stop. They waited, holding their breath.

. . .

The two merchants came a little closer. With each tentative step, they squinted more, unsure and uncomfortable.

"Stop! Come no closer!" one said. Aldís was glad to comply.

"Those—things with you. Why are they dressed that way?" the man asked.

Aldís knew human nature. People wanted a simple reason. "They have a sickness which is spreading in another valley." Impulsively, she added, "Some say the bad fortunes in our land stem from the white-christ leader who came to our country the last Althing, named Bishop-Friedrich. I am taking these people to him, as his responsibility. Their sickness must leave our valley."

He grimaced. "What kind of sickness?"

Aldís frowned at the merchant. "Do not look at the masks covering their faces! Some who have looked on them have also become sick. They are covered this way to protect us from them." She paused. "To answer your question, I don't know what it is. Blood oozes from the eyes. From nose and tongue. It starts quickly—sometimes as soon as a day. Stop looking at them, I tell you!"

The man stepped back a pace, ready to let them pass, but the other trader frowned. "Why have *you* not fallen sick?"

"Some who look at them get the blood-ooze and others do not. I did not get sick, so I have been forced into taking them to the healer. But that is why I ride in front of them, to protect myself from looking at them." She paused. "Our land has had bad weather. We cannot stand a terrible sickness as well."

The two merchants muttered together.

"Get away from this place, quickly," the first one said. "We wish you a safe journey." As he turned to go, he threw a comment back over his shoulder. "That man you are looking for? The white-christ Friedrich? I heard that he visited Akureyri. Try there."

. . .

They stayed in rigid formation as they passed the compound and the mass of staring people. Kandace felt as if a hundred eyes burned into their backs as they rode through and past the farm. They rode until dawn shone again in the east. In the darkness, they could just make out another small valley lying before them.

"We made it," Aldís breathed. 'It worked once, and it will work again. We should be safe."

. . .

As the staring people returned to the longhouse, another man slipped in among them. A slight trader, an inconsequential man. He sought out one of the merchants who had spoken to Aldís.

"We've met before. You're a man of trade. Silver interests you?"

"What kind of stupid question is that?"

Josson ignored him. Following Aldís and Kandace all day had left him drained and exhausted. "That woman and her charges are not what they appear."

“What are they, then?”

“Those who do not want to be approached or questioned. My advice? Follow them. Watch them in secret. If I’m right, I know someone who will pay more than you could earn in a year for whoever is under those coverings. But you have to make sure they’re not what they seem.” Josson’s small eyes glared. “If I’m right, take them to Althing, and ask for me, Josson. I’ll be there, and I’ll tell you who he is. Whatever silver he pays you, I want a share.”

. . .

Chapter Sixty-One

"Probably a week's ride," the fisherman said. He eyed the creatures in bloody garb and kept his distance. "No, I'll not take any payment. Sorry to say, but it might be unclean from whatever curse follows your group. Take it, with my good wishes. You're hungry, I can tell. But keep your cattle-marks."

Aldís had circled her small group well north of Althing, but she had made a wrong turn on the unfamiliar passages.

The fisherman pointed to the track that led to the Westfjords. "Follow this until you reach the river crossing. Then the right fork. Keep following the setting sun. It's in the far north this time of year, you know. It'll lead you northwest. Once you get to a place called Birth-valley, it's straight on to the western fjords." He gave Aldís a keen look. "But it's a long, lonely road, even for those in good health. A weary journey for just you with these sick ones."

"I have no choice," Aldís said. Getting lost had cost valuable time. They needed to get far from Althing before the roads became crowded with travelers haunted her. The man could hear the weary concern in her voice.

"I hope where you're going that they have the right spells," he said. "You're braver than I am to ride with such cursed folk." He made the sign of Thor to protect himself and help them. "Here. Take these. Not many folks will want to trade with you." He handed her two more large fresh cod and a basket of salt-fish. "It'll help get you a bit farther along the way."

. . .

The merchant who Josson had pointed towards Aldís had followed Josson's advice, trailing the riding party as they struggled along the roadway. Twice he had nearly turned around, fearing that he, too, would contract the bleeding disease if he kept staring at the riders, but the amount of silver Josson promised bested his worries. That evening, he lost the trail, but found it again.

. . .

"Bless that fisherman. I'm so sick of dried meat and smoked eggs." Kandace sharpened her small knife, preparing to gut the fish. "Nikea and Nenet, stay close. This ravine is far below the road, but we cannot take any chances."

"How much charcoal do we have left?" Aldís asked. "Enough for a week?"

Charred wood did not smoke. When it was gone, they would have to eat their food cold, or not at all.

"We should only cook one time a day. It may last then."

The smell of salmon made their mouths water. Getting lost had cost precious time. Hungry for food and tired to the bone, they did not hear the man standing on the trail, well above where the ravine dropped off at a dizzying height.

He looked around once more, saw no one and nothing, and cursed. “Where did they go? What a waste of time this has been! That stupid trader! I should never had listened to him.” The long curve of the mountainside ahead lay empty and desolate. No sign of any riders met his eyes, and no tracks indicated that anyone but he had passed there.

He put his foot in the stirrup and mounted. Swung his horse around, kicked it, and smelled salmon roasting over an open fire.

. . .

Warm on her fingers, delicious on her tongue, Aldís sighed with pleasure at the taste of good fresh food. She closed her eyes for an instant, full of bliss to simply rest and eat. When she opened them, a pair of boots interrupted her peace.

The group looked up, at first merely surprised, and then in dread.

“Finish your supper,” he said to them. “That salmon smells delicious. I’ll have some of it.”

“Please,” Aldís said. “Please, we—”

“No sense begging, miss,” the man answered. “Nothing you might say will change my mind. You’re worth a lot, apparently, so I’m going to take you to Althing. But it’s not personal. No need for me to be unkind or starve you along the way.”

He drew his sword and laid it on the rock right at hand, then squatted down and reached to pull a piece of cooked fish from where it lay on a clean stone.

Kandace leaned over and whispered to Aldís, but the tracker interrupted them. “No talking. I don’t intend for you to plan to tie me up while I'm asleep and run off. In fact, I'll make certain that doesn't happen. Give me your rope."

. . .

Chapter Sixty-Two

Tell no one, Kel had implored the girl's family.

Good intentions, possible to keep while the small family was secluded on their farm making preparations to travel. But once on the road, the camaraderie of travel proved too tempting an outlet.

A long night of sharing food and conversation seemed innocent enough.

"Naldrum. Such a liar. Attacks young women. I know personally." The young husband looked over to where his wife sat across the fire. "He does the worst things. Things you can't imagine."

"Naldrum's been nominated to be Lawspeaker. Did you know that?"

"It's disgusting. But it won't happen. My wife is going to testify against him at Althing. Going to put a stop to his cruelty."

"Sounds exciting. Tell me more!"

. . .

In the morning, the fellow traveler was nowhere to be seen.

. . .

Chapter Sixty-Three

Tor was as good as his word. Josson rode up to the widow's and saw three figures raking hay in the small meadow. He whistled a sardonic hello.

Eilíf and Petr dropped their rakes, but Tor finished the row before he looked in Josson's direction. He carried his rake to the shed and put it carefully away. Washed his face in the bowl beside the door.

"Well, you're here," Josson said. "Had a bet with myself that you wouldn't be."

Tor made no reply. He felt for the bag that held his children's soul-stones. He had meant to give it to Kandace before she left, but with all the details to remember, Tor had overlooked that tiny important one. Shook out his traveling cloak and folded it up. Took a water-bladder from the ones that hung near the door. Put his short *saxe* blade on the table as a gift for Petr and Eilíf. Breathed, silent, and prepared himself.

Eilíf and Petr stood nearby, each with hand on his arm. The house was heavy with sadness.

"Where are your brats hiding?" Josson made a rough attempt at humor. "Send 'em out. Nothing for them to fear. Uncle Josson maybe brought 'em a treat."

"You once planned to sell them into slavery," Tor answered. "Did you think I had forgotten? Do you think I trust you to keep your promise? My children are where you will never find them."

Josson's gaze shifted. *Damn tricksters. I could have made a pretty bit of coin from those two. Maybe I still will, if that tracker does his job.* Josson's pretense of friendliness ended. He jerked his head towards the door. "Might as well get going. Long way to Althing, and I intend to enjoy every bit of it, thinking how pleased *gothi* Naldrum is going to be at seeing you."

. . .

Chapter Sixty-Four

"Tiller! Tiller, Tiller, *Tiller!* I am thoroughly sick of hearing about Tiller!" Fatimah cried. "You have the silvers he gave you. You say you love me. It is almost summer now! Why did you not make an offer of marriage to my father during the spring *thing* at Thornes?"

They stood behind the longhouse, where no one would hear. Styr pulled his beloved close.

"I do love you, Fatimah. I am intent on marrying you. But you saw what happened at Thornes! Tiller's in great danger. Men ride still, searching for Tiller. They carry swords. They intend to kill him. They don't want to take any chances that Tiller will be absolved on appeal at the summer Althing."

"What is that to you and me? This whole mess was his idea!"

"But I went willingly, Fatimah. I can't marry you until Tiller is cleared. If he loses his appeal and is outlawed, blame might come to me somehow. Don't shake your head no. It could happen! I won't have you marry a man who carries a charge of thieving."

Fatimah's downfallen expression broke his heart, but Styr could see she understood. "There is more, Fatimah. He told me to leave him with the pillars before Thorgest arrived, to protect my job here at your father's farm. Every day I think about how if I'd stayed, Thorgest's sons would have seen three of us and only two of them. The fight might never have happened. Maybe Tiller and Thorgest would have argued and worked it out over mead and money. But Tiller thought only of me and you, and not himself. I need to be ready to do whatever I can to help him—even if it means putting our plans on hold. What kind of friend would I be to desert him now, when he needs allies the most?"

She turned her face away and buried it against his shoulder. "You're a good man, Styr. This is why I love you!" She punched him lightly with her fist. In reply, he looked around quickly and gave Fatimah a quick kiss.

"But Styr, I'm serious. If you want to marry me, we can't wait too much longer. Of course, no one but you wants me, but I barely managed to avoid the bride-fair at Thornes. My mother will be *determined* to get me in the one at Althing. And if someone proposes, just to take me as an extra wife, a sort of free slave, and my mother accepts—and she *will*, Styr, no matter how poor the offer—my father won't go back on her word. He's the same kind of man you are." Fatimah did not mention that her mother would undoubtedly be pleased to receive a low offer, affirming the worthlessness of her limping daughter. "Please, Styr."

"I'll speak to him," Styr said. "But in private, before Althing.

"Promise me," Fatimah said.

"I promise. But for the crops are in and nothing we can do now except wait on the weather. From now on, any day your father doesn't need me for work, I'll be with Tiller. They're less likely to get him if he's not alone."

. . .

Chapter Sixty-Five
Midsummer at Althing

Kel kept his head down and hood pulled forward so that no one could see his face as he moved among the early crowds at Althing. Naldrum would soon enough learn he was here. No sense alerting the headman any earlier than necessary.

What would Naldrum think, Kel wondered, at seeing him? Already Kel had overhead bits of conversation about how he had perished in the terrible fire at Naldrum's stable. Kel pictured the headman, jaw slack and eyes bolting out in astonishment at the sight of his not-so-dead steward. Then the most dangerous days of his life would begin.

For now, Kel wanted to visit the sooth-sayer again. He had come early to Althing, hoping to ensure everything was in place for Mani and the accusation against Naldrum.

So much at risk. Such a slim chance for success at stopping Naldrum. With nothing to do now but wait and worry, whatever relief the *saith* might give, Kel would welcome.

. . .

Horses and herd animals had churned the pathways to mud. The area cordoned for the slave market offered the only way across the roadway on foot.

. . .

Kel had always avoided the slave market at *things* he attended. The sight of fenced-in humans for sale sickened him, even though he had worked among and overseen slaves his entire life. He walked around the area, averting his eyes from the misery inside the ropes.

Was that someone calling his name? Kel ignored the sound. Probably just someone who thought he still worked for Naldrum and who hoped for a favor. Best to have as little to do as possible anyone here.

He walked faster as he left the slave market behind. Soon he stood at the tent of the soothsayer. Kel rang the bell at her tent opening and cracked his knuckles, wondering if she would remember him, almost afraid of what her visions might show this year, with so much more on the line.

. . .

The *saith* listened with her ears and eyes and senses. The latter told her more than Kel's words.

"You have decided to make something of your life," she breathed. "Even if you lose it. Good. The clean-fire burns high in you, even though you cannot feel it because you have so much worry." She waved her hands in the air. "Spirits of summer, keep him strong."

"Will we win?" Kel asked. "Will we stop Naldrum from becoming Lawspeaker? From corrupting the Law Council the same way he has corrupted so many of the *gothar* of Bull Valley?"

"No," she said.

The abrupt word shocked Kel, and he protested.

"How can you be so sure? We *must* stop him!"

The *saith* laughed. "I'm not sure at all. I said that just to test your resolve. Despite it, you still intend to try. That is the way it must be. Now that I have proclaimed that you will fail, it frees you to try harder than you might have if I had told you victory was certain."

A rueful smile, acknowledging her truth.

"Valhalla is peopled with warriors who wield swords," she said. "But those who fight with will and wit win the seats of honor, next to Odin, who prizes wisdom. Go out to your battle. Fight to the bitter end. Fight with everything you have, with all you are."

She stood and held the tent door open. "You came seeking certainty. If life is anything, it is uncertain. When you learn to embrace the uncertainty instead of fearing it, you truly live."

Kel left a silver bead in her dish as payment. As he bent to leave the tent, the sooth-sayer reached for his tunic.

"Wait—" she said. He froze.

The *saith* spoke to the spirits, inwardly, so that Kel could not hear, and then aloud. Her voice sounded hollow and far away.

"Two forces that twist in your life come close together," she said. "Take care that you do not destroy one in slaying the other."

Sunken eyes returned to normal. "Go," she said, closing the door.

. . .

Two forces that twist in my life. Kel remembered sensing that Naldrum twisted around Aldís, suffocating her, and the feeling that to set her—and himself—free, he had to follow his destiny, no matter where it led.

He thought of the knife hidden in his boot, and another in Thunder's saddle. Naldrum always kept his steward and guards armed, despite the ban on weapons at Althing. Kel needed to be prepared for anything.

. . .

Aldís gripped the pointed stakes of the slave-market fence. *I am certain that was Kel! Why did he ignore me?*

She huddled with Kandace, miserable. "I failed you, my friend."

"We knew the risk. There was no alternative." Kandace held her daughter Nenet on her lap, with her other arm around Nikea. Stripped to the waist, she shivered with cold. "I do not fault you. Don't punish yourself. We will find a way out of this."

The words brought no consolation. They stood roped in a line of those to be sold. The red stripes across Aldís' back showed the foolishness of trying to escape.

Aldís groaned. *Like mother, like daughter.* For the first time, Aldís knew more of how her mother had once felt, roped to others, her past stolen, her future stretching only to bleakness. *I thought I understood, Mamai,* she whispered. *I didn't. I'm so sorry.*

. . .

Chapter Sixty-Six

Kel knew Naldrum would arrive at Althing any time now. All night and all day, he had watched for that familiar entourage to fill the track. When Kel saw Naldrum's banner, he waited long enough only to ensure that the headman rode among the entourage, and then left unseen. The chieftain had no idea Kel was alive. Best to alert Naldrum to that fact in the most public way possible.

. . .

"We'll open the welcoming barrel as soon as this short meeting is over," Naldrum spoke his annual words to the loose gathering of farmers and families who stood around him. "And I know many of you have had a ghastly winter. The word *famine* now lurks around every farmhouse. Never fear. I have something amazing to announce this Althing that will jolt us out of bad fortune into plenty again! But first, I see we have some newcomers this year." He beckoned to his new steward. "Let's have this fellow say a few words."

Naldrum gestured to the man to begin, as he has always directed Kel. "Steward, tell them what to expect from Althing."

. . .

Randaal, coached by Naldrum, had rehearsed his words carefully. Still, the man was making a mess of it. Kel listened, his frustration increasing with every garbled sentence.

It's Althing. It matters. Get it right! he fumed. Naldrum's new steward clearly had no appreciation or understanding of these important traditions.

Kel had planned to wait until the speech was over, and interrupt as Naldrum opened the keg of beer, to shock and shame him during his little pompous ceremony, but found himself unable to bear the travesty of the new steward's speech. Kel strode forward and pointed at Randaal.

"Get off your horse," he said.

"Kel!" Ankya jumped from her new mare and ran to him. "What am I seeing? Are you truly alive?" She began to weep with joy.

Naldrum turned pale. *Kel Coesson is dead. I saw the ashes after the fire myself.* Had Kel Coesson somehow regrown his body and come back to life as a death-walker? "Make the speech!" he roared to his steward.

Naldrum's new steward Randaal, good at intimidating others but nervous and feeling stupid at public speaking, tried again but faltered. "At Althing, you can buy new clothing and eat food."

Kel reached for him. "Get…off…your…horse!" He pulled Randaal down and swung up into the saddle.

Naldrum felt for the small knife hidden in his sleeve, more nervous than he had ever been, uncertain of how one fought off a thing that looked alive but was not.

. . .

The words came easily to Kel from years of memory. *The days ahead will be different, for this thing is like no other. Here, you stand on hallowed ground, for this is Althing. This festival, this All-thing, is the Assembly for All Iceland!*

He could see Naldrum backing away little by little, putting others in the crowd between himself and Kel.

"Naldrum of Bull Valley!" Kel cried, and the headman froze in place. "I, Kel Coesson, your former steward, with firsthand knowledge and witnesses, accuse you of the crime of rape! Worse, the act occurred on this hallowed ground of Althing!"

Naldrum tightened in fear. Death-walker or not, he could not allow such a claim. "That is a preposterous lie!" he cried.

"That is for the Law Council to judge," Kel replied in a voice pitched to carry to the edge of the group of people. "And you farmers who have allied with this man, think carefully about your loyalties. You cannot follow a tyrant and still claim to honor the laws of Althing. One will fall, so choose! Do not decide only for yourselves. Decide which fate you will give your children. Will your children have their freedoms cobbled like slaves to one man's ambition? Or will they grow up as true Icelanders, with the rights and freedoms promised by our laws?"

Kel swung down from the saddle and gave the reins back to Naldrum's new steward Randaal. "For the gods' sake, man," Kel said. "If you're going to make a speech, learn what you're talking about." He walked away quickly, leaving Naldrum at the center of an uneasy group.

Kel did not fool himself. People were sheep, and sheep followed. They did not think for themselves.

But a few would question. That was all that mattered, to have a crack in the wall. To have some, enough, stop blindly believing Naldrum, and start asking themselves where the real truth lay.

. . .

Aldís could not sit. The slave-ropes made it impossible, forcing her to stand so that potential buyers might see her.

Explaining to her captor that she, Kandace and the children were free-beings had not helped. All he would say was that he was leaving them with the slave-seller, who would hold them until Josson arrived.

. . .

"Bath-boy!" Aldís shouted. "Bath-boy! Over here!"

Aldís saw a young man moving along the line of roped slaves. He offered his hand to each, along with a few kind words.

"Do I know you?" he asked her.

"We met last Althing. You were working at the bathing-tubs. We spoke." She studied his face. Still thin. Still sad, but tempered with kindness. She had not seen that in him last year, only loneliness.

"I remember you," he said. "You're the one who told me to find something of my *ygdrassil*—my tree of life—to keep me sane."

"And you did?"

"I did." He seemed much older than the boy she had comforted last summer. "Everything has changed since then. My master died.

The woman who bought his tub-business does not starve us. I'm still a slave, but she at least treats us as if we are human, not nuisances. I still long with all my heart for my family. But they are not in Eire any longer. There is no going back to find them. My father is dead. Perhaps one day I can find my little brother, but the truth is that likely I will never see him or my mother and sister again. Nothing could ever take the pain away. But I have learned to fill some of that hole in my heart by helping others, as you suggested. But you are free. Why are you in the slave market? How can I help?"

. . .

Kel felt something grab his shoulder. The knife almost came to his hand before he caught himself. "What do you want?" he growled.

A young man stood near him, a thrall-collar loose on his neck. "There's something you need see."

"What is it?"

"Just come with me."

. . .

Ankya had trailed Kel ever since he had taken over Randaal's speech, taking care to keep Kel from seeing her.

Ankya pressed her fingers against her mouth, overwhelmed. When the bath-boy led Kel away, she followed.

. . .

Chapter Sixty-Seven

Aldís, exhausted and chilly in the evening air, knew Kel by his walk long before he saw her in the cluster of slaves. Her heart leaped. The bath-boy had found the man she had described.

"Kel! Kel Coesson!" She screamed his name over and over, determined that he would respond this time.

Kel stopped walking, his head cocked, listening.

"Kel! Over here!"

That voice. Kel ran forward, searching. Among the slaves slumping in their ropes, he saw the face he could never forget, and his heart began to hammer.

"Aldís!" he called. Kel leaped over the fence and ran to her.

. . .

The slave-seller shook his head. "No. I need hard silver, not promises of payment." He jerked on the rope that held Aldís, Kandace, and the children. "Bring me something of enough value, and I might let you have one of them."

"She's a free woman! They all are free!" Kel raged.

"Can you prove it?"

"Of course, I can't prove it! But you can't prove they are slaves, either!"

"I already have a promised buyer for this group. Are you buying today or not?"

"I'm telling you, I have enough to buy all four, and I *want* all four—but I did not come to Althing expecting to purchase slaves, and did not bring silver! Ask anyone! I worked for *gothi* Naldrum for years. I led his clan into the Law Circle!"

"Are you his steward now?" the slave-seller asked.

"No."

"Then you have no backer for your promises. Hard silver, or trade goods. Nothing less."

Kel thought wildly. Naldrum had just arrived. Kel knew well the headman's schedule at Althing. First, the barrel of beer to draw his followers in, and then, when the praise and adulations began to bore him, Naldrum would walk among the wealthier trade tents. Then he would head to the slave market.

Every year, the same schedule.

Kel had, at most, a day-eighth before Naldrum saw Aldís, Kandace, and two children in the slave market. The slave-seller had positioned them in the front, a prime sale sure to win high bids.

Kel could not let that happen. But he had only one thing of value here at Althing.

Thor-Thunder.

. . .

"I'll give you my horse for the woman Aldís," Kel cried. "Everyone knows the stallion Thor-Thunder." He felt gutted at the thought of putting up his beloved companion, but it was the only way.

"I'll borrow another horse, and ride to where I have silver stored. I'll return before Althing is over to redeem Thunder and buy the other three."

The man did indeed know of Kel's stallion.

"Done," he said. "I'll hold them until the night before the closing ceremony. If you don't show with the silver, your horse is mine and I'll sell them to whoever I please."

"No," Aldís said. "I can't leave Kandace and the children here by themselves!"

"You have to, Aldís. Naldrum won't hurt Kandace—too valuable—but if he sees you, there's no telling what he might do."

Aldís knew Kel spoke the truth. She stretched her neck for the slave collar and rope to be removed. She embraced Kandace, Nenet and Nikea until the slave master tore them apart.

Kel clasped the shoulder of the bath-boy who had fetched him. "That horse is my best friend. He's in the farthest meadow. Please take good care of him until I get back." He held out payment, but the boy refused.

. . .

As Kel led Aldís away, half-fainting with hunger and exhaustion, he put his arm around her.

"What happened? Why are you here with them?" Kel asked, but all she could do was weep, half in relief and half in grief.

. . .

Kel left Aldís at his tent in the common-grounds. He searched out people at Althing who knew him, borrowed what he could, then sprinted back towards the slave-seller, hoping he could at least put some silver as a down payment on Tor's wife and children.

Kel stopped short at the sight of Naldrum's gold-embroidered cloak at the slave-lot.

Unlike Kel, Naldrum *had* come to Althing expecting to purchase slaves, but he had never anticipated such a windfall. The headman opened his purse which he had filled from the silver-chest in his tent and counted into the slave-seller's hand the amount requested, without, for once, quibbling. Kel watched helplessly as Naldrum accepted the rope that held Kandace and her children. The headman laughed as he led them towards his tent.

Behind Kel, a cloaked figure watched the exchange.

"You promised me!" Kel raged at the slave seller.

"Promises can be bought, with enough silver," the man smirked. "I was supposed to hold them for a trader named Josson, so I said an impossible price, one I never imagined he'd give. But Naldrum paid every bit of it. I told him the sale isn't final until Althing is over, but if he wants to keep them in his tent, I have three fewer mouths to feed until then. Plus, he said if anyone made a better offer, he'd double it. I'd be a fool to pass on that."

Defeated, Kel went back to the crowded common-grounds where he had left Aldís to rest. The cloaked figure trailed him. Clad in nondescript clothing and muttering a spell to keep Kel from noticing, it drifted silently in his wake.

. . .

Aldís wrapped her hands around the bowl, grateful for the warmth of the barley pottage and the small fire before them. She slurped greedily at the *sup*.

"Once a day, the slave-seller put a vat of cooked oats in the yard. We had to dig our hands into the mess and eat with our fingers, as if we were animals at a trough. It was awful. The dirt from our hands got into the oatmeal. I could feel the grit of it in my teeth."

"You're safe now. At least as safe as I can make you. I'm not exactly safe myself these days."

"I know. When I arrived at Eilíf's longhouse, she told me about how you and Tor escaped. Naldrum really does think you both died in the fire. I heard a rumor that he made a big show of mourning for both of you and his horses, the day after the fire. He actually asked for donations to be put in a burial mound for you."

"He's vile in every way. I'll wager he used every bit of it just now to buy Kandace and her children."

"How on earth did you and they end up in the slave market? Wait. Where's Tor?"

"He'll be here soon enough," Aldís muttered. "He's turning himself back in to Naldrum."

To Kel's horror, Aldís explained Josson's inadvertent discovery of Tor and his family at the widow's house, and the abysmal bargain Tor had made to save them.

"Kandace and I left with the children. We disguised them as best we could, to make our way to the western fjords. Naldrum isn't liked there, and we hoped to find that man called Friedrich in those parts."

Kel did not know whether to feel fury at the cruelty of life, or anger at Tor for such a stupid idea. Why must Naldrum *always* win?

"Tor should have killed that damned trader!"

"Tor lives by a different code than most."

"Why does being decent always allow evil to win, though?" As that thought tormented Kel, he realized that the superstitious headman, already frightened at the apparition of his former steward as a death-walker, would see another one when Josson arrived with Tor. Kel started to laugh.

"What's so funny?" asked Aldís, but Kel could not answer. The tension of the last year poured out of him in one great torrent of laughter, until he lay back on the ground, weak and relieved.

"Actually, nothing is funny at all," Kel said, wiping his eyes. He sat up and grew serious. Reached for the hand that held her now-empty bowl.

"Listen, Aldís. I came here to Althing for one reason, and one only. I don't know where I'll go after that. Maybe leave Iceland forever. But for now, the very dangerous reason I'm here is that I came to try and stop Naldrum from a corruption he's sowing among the Law Council. Today, I formally accused him today of raping a woman—that girl you helped last Althing. She's agreed to testify against him. But just in case something goes wrong—because things do—since you are here, I want to ask if you might speak against him as well. I know it would be hard for you. But people who know you hold you in high regard as a healer. They'd vouch for you. It might make the difference between Naldrum getting off or being declared guilty. Would you be willing?"

Aldís's eyes widened. "You burned down his barn, and now you've accused him of a crime. This is the Kel Coesson I once knew! How did this all happen?" A warm feeling filled her.

Kel weighed what he should say to Aldís. Could he tell her everything? She'd been through so much. Better to skip the awful parts, the shame that he could not face, and just stick to the facts at hand, Kel decided.

"I took a long, wrong road, Aldís. But it still got me here. The girl's father-in-law—he too, will testify that Naldrum raped her—brought her to Naldrum's spring *dísablót.* They had finally pried from her the truth about who had sired her pregnancy. Like all the others, he had brushed aside her protests and had come to Naldrum's to demand child-rights."

Aldís, silent for a long time. The warm feeling disappeared.

"Others?" she muttered.

"Yes. Every spring." Kel mumbled, ashamed. Reluctant to tell her, he still would not lie. "I did what I had to do."

"You cut them, Kel? Like this? For Naldrum? How could you!" She held out her scarred forearms, her voice bitter again.

"No, Aldís! Never that! He told me to beat the women, but I never did. I only took the children they claimed were his. Their deaths, but nothing else, is on my conscience."

Her face, stone. "Only that? How decent of you."

"I knew what would happen to those women otherwise. I did it as gently as I could."

"Again, how very decent of you. I'm such a fool. I honestly thought it was just me, until that girl last year. Then I hoped it was just the two of us, her and me. Now I learn that Naldrum has done this over and over? I thought I hated him before."

"It's why I must stop him. He can't keep getting away with this."

Aldís wiped her eyes. She fought for breath. The question that had tormented her for years demanded asking.

"What is it, Aldís?"

"His men came a few days after you visited me and—" her words stumbled slightly— "my, um, daughter. I'd always wondered why you told Naldrum about her."

"I never said a word about her, or about seeing you! How Naldrum learned of her, I promise it wasn't through me."

Kel wanted to ask Aldís what had happened to the little girl. He'd made discreet inquiries years ago. Something about a sickness in winter. No need to press Aldís now on what must be a painful memory. The details did not matter now.

Aldís mulled the enormity of Kel's words and actions. He had done terrible things for Naldrum. He was risking everything to confront the man. He had given Thunder to get her from the slaver. But now he was asking her to testify against the man who had had her tortured.

"I have avoided Naldrum so long." Her face went ghostly white. "Because of what his men did to me. I stay only with people who I know will not betray my whereabouts to him. To confront Naldrum openly, in a court of law? What he does to me after that will be so much worse."

Kel saw the trembling. "I hate to ask you, Aldís. But everything rides on this. We may never get another chance."

She looked away and shook her head. Kel tried again.

"Aldís, this isn't about you and me. It's not even about Naldrum and that girl last year. It's about something I've always looked up to, something I've always been proud of. Something you love as much as I do, I know it. It's our *land*, Aldís! Our *law*. We are an imperfect people, but what Icelanders have accomplished—to be a country of law, law that serves all people, instead of people serving a king—we are part of something noble, Aldís. An ideal. Something true. This beautiful valley symbolizes it. You can't put into words how important it is. It spans time and personal matters. It's imperfect, but it must be incorruptible. I know you believe the same way. It's the first thing I loved about you. I have everything on the line here. Please, Aldís. This is hard. I need you."

Love of the same ideal throbbed in Aldís' chest, but the memory of torture cried out as well.

Kel saw the battle in her. "I'll never forgive myself for what I did. But I give you my word, Aldís. I'll burn every last breath in my body to stop him from hurting anyone else that way."

"Alright, Kel," Aldís said. "I'll testify against him in court. I'll be your witness. If he kills me afterwards, so be it. Surely the Valkyries will welcome me to Valhalla, knowing that I stood against such evil."

He gripped her hands in thanks.

"But you did evil, too, Kel. To this day, I cannot fathom why you served a man like that, or why it took you so long to stand against him. I've lost too much. I'll be your ally now, but I'll never forgive you."

Kel wished he had told her the other reason for his actions. *I also did it to protect you.* Too late now, and far too weak an excuse.

"Thank you. It's all I can ask." He reached out to Aldís and took her face in his hands, pulled it close. Forehead rested against forehead as the enormity of what was at stake rose and swelled against the chilly night air.

. . .

Aldís and Kel had spoken to one another in low voices, their campfire at a distance from others on the common-grounds. Neither had noticed the cloaked figure that, little by little, edged closer among the tall grasses until their words came clearly.

As Aldís and Kel closed their eyes in the sad embrace, the lurking figure edged away again, carefully, quietly, and imperceptibly.

. . .

That night in her family's festival tent, Naldrum's daughter Ankya lay with her eyes half-closed, thinking. Finally, Naldrum noticed and asked her if she felt well.

"I feel wonderfully well," she replied.

"Then what causes you to lie so long, looking exhausted?"

"I am thinking about something. A great idea. A gift for you."

Intrigued, he prompted her to say more, but Ankya refused. "Soon," was all she would say.

. . .

Chapter Sixty-Eight

As he had for many years, Mani the Lawspeaker stood in the center of the stone circle of hallowed ground, the court of the council of *gothar*. All of the land's thirty-nine regional leaders sat in proud attention, strung along seats in a large circle. In another circle in front of them, and one behind them, each *gothi* had two law advisers, to whisper advice to the gothi as the trials proceeded. In a wider, ragged circle stood those who had come to hear the trials, whether for entertainment or because they would serve as witnesses.

The crowd filled the entire space. Word had gotten out that the first case was a rape accusation against the headman Naldrum. Admired by many, abhorred by as many more, all had come to see the spectacle.

Mani waited impatiently for Kel to arrive. *So much hanging on this. Where is he?*

Finally, he saw Kel hurrying forward towards the Law Circle. Kel's face was set in anger. Aldís raced along beside him. Mani fought to keep his composure.

"What is this? Where is the witness?" he demanded.

"I've just come from the girl and her family. The girl has retracted her statement. She won't testify against Naldrum."

"No." Mani felt sick at hearing the words he had dreaded all morning.

"She's been beaten, badly. Her face is a mess and her arm's in a sling. Her mother and father roughed up, too. They had brought the infant to Althing as proof of what happened, but it's disappeared. They won't say anything about who did it. I found them packing to leave Althing. They flat-out refused to come to the Law Council. I told them that if Naldrum isn't stopped now, he'll become an even bigger threat, but they wouldn't budge. Whoever the headman used to threaten them—and I suspect it's his new steward, the man's a brute—he accomplished exactly what Naldrum wanted."

Mani tried to hide his despair. "You have no case, then," he said.

"Maybe not. We have one last witness," Kel said. "It happened long ago, but Aldís the healer is here. Will you accept her testimony?"

Mani thought quickly. "I'll have to. It's all you have. We don't have the option of backing down now. Naldrum will have us both killed before we leave Althing. You for making the charge, and me for agreeing to hear the case. We'll have to do the best we can with what we have. Aldís, do you know how important this is? Your testimony has to be impeccable."

"I know." Her voice, unsteady, gave no reassurance to Mani. She had been with Kel, and had seen the family that Naldrum had had beaten.

But she had also seen the fury in Kel's face at their treatment. *Maybe he had spoken truth, when he said he tried to find a line between one cruelty and a far worse one.*

What if I everything I have thought about him is wrong? What if he is the exact opposite *of what I have believed all these years?* The thought shook Aldís to her core. *The old Kel, the one I fell in love with...maybe he has been here all along.*

But here stood Naldrum, glaring at her. Panic, anger, and the desire for justice warred. She reached for Kel's hand and closed her eyes.

"I'll do my best," Aldís said. "What he did to those people was terrible. They're too afraid to stand up to him. He has to be stopped. I have no family. Nothing to lose. I'll testify."

Mani drew a deep breath. "May good prevail." He turned to the restless crowd to begin. "I call the council of *gothar* to order! As many of you have heard, we have a special trial that must take place first, because one of the members of the Law Council is the accused. We must determine his fate immediately, so that he can either remain on the Council or be replaced."

A murmur of excitement ran through the council.

Mani continued. "Naldrum, headman of Bull Valley, a *gothi* known to all of you, has been accused of—"

A sound from the parade route echoed along the speaking stones. Mani hesitated, then began again. "Accused of—"

He saw the faces of the *gothar* twist away from him, craning towards the sound as it grew louder. By now most of the circle of onlookers had stood, stretching to see what caused the commotion.

. . .

Naldrum's daughter Ankya moved through the circle of *gothar* like a dream. She held a pair of good-luck sticks over her head and struck them together in solemn rhythm in the same pace as the drumbeats that opened the Court.

Ankya wore her transparent white dress of the *dísablót,* with nothing underneath. The lustrous silk folds of the scandalous gown lifted and flowed, weightless. It drifted around her body, now concealing, now revealing every entrancing detail. She had painted her face and darkened her eyes in the way of the Egg Ceremony to give herself the face of the Goddess. Men and women could not take their eyes away from her appearance.

Ankya did not return their gazes. She focused on her father, almost floating towards him. She moved through the crowd and between the council members, striking her good-luck sticks and never taking her eyes from Naldrum's.

"My daughter, why are you here?" Despite his embarrassment at the spectacle she had created, Naldrum could not help but admire how lovely she was.

"I have come to save you, father," Ankya replied. Her forehead furrowed slightly, as if speaking took great effort.

"Daughter, this has nothing to do with you. Go back to our tent. I will see you afterwards."

She smiled. "Father, for once, I must disobey." Ankya turned to Mani. "I must speak to the witness Aldís" she said in a low voice. "Privately. Before the trial begins."

"It is against the Law to pressure or threaten a witness," Mani replied.

"I'm not threatening her," Ankya smiled, enigmatic. "I simply need to make sure she has all her facts."

. . .

Mani nodded. “Come to me, just the two of you. Whatever you say to her, I must hear as well. You stand within the Circle of Law, and your testimony, whatever it is, must be true. Everyone else—you, Naldrum, and you, Kel, move away from us, out of hearing.”

Naldrum began to protest, but Mani lifted his hand. “I have spoken.”

Even Naldrum did not dare to openly disobey the Lawspeaker. He and Kel moved away. Kel ignored Naldrum, but the headman could not stop himself from making cutting comments about his former steward to the amusement of his supporters.

“Further away,” Mani directed, wagging his finger at Naldrum. “And keep silent. Have some respect for the court.”

The headman scowled and complied. When Mani was satisfied that only he and Aldís could hear, he directed Ankya to speak.

. . .

“I heard Kel talking to you last night,” Ankya began. “He wants you to speak against my father. Why do you want to hurt him? He has done nothing to you!”

Aldís pushed up the sleeves of her linen shift and showed the marks to Ankya. “He did this to me. Do you call that nothing?”

“Accidents happen. Punishments occur. I have no idea under what circumstances you necessitated that injury. Poor woman. It looks to have been painful, I must say.”

“Get to it, young woman,” Mani directed. “The entire council sits waiting while you talk.”

"This woman has experienced pain, she says, from my father. I would like to offer her something of significant value—to compensate her for her suffering."

Ahhhh. Mani understood now. If Ankya had approached Aldís privately, she would have been accused of tampering with a witness. To do so publicly—albeit only with him listening—changed everything. And to offer Aldís compensation for a wrong was technically within the law.

"Nothing you could offer would be as sweet as seeing your hideous father reap the cruel harvest he has sown for so many years." Aldís voice, bitter winter.

"Perhaps not. Perhaps yes." Ankya leaned towards Aldís, her eyes sparkling. "Nothing you know about. But something you don't know about? Perhaps—" Her voice trailed off.

Mani huffed in frustration. "Get to it, girl!" He had not meant his voice to carry as far as it did.

Ankya touched Aldís's shoulder with her fingertip. She traced down Aldís' arm to her elbow, then, slow and seductive, ran her finger up the front of Aldís' dress to where it covered her nipple.

"Once a child suckled here?"

Aldís lifted her hand to slap Ankya, but the girl moved, quick as a cat.

Tears of hatred and pain came to Aldís' eyes, but did not fall. "Stop tormenting me," she said. "Whatever you want to say, have it done."

"I just thought you might be interested to know—I would certainly be interested, in your place—about a girl with hair exactly like yours." She considered Aldís' locks, fingered them. "Yes. So unusual. Not like mine, or others in our land. Blonde, like we are, but curling like the little wavelets right at the edge of the sea. The same exact hair."

Aldís struggled to breathe. What was Ankya saying?

"And with those wavelets, her eyes, the same unusual color as yours. Her face, the same features as yours. So strange, isn't it?"

Aldís reached for Ankya, grabbed folds of the silken dress with both hands, wrenched her close. "What do you mean?"

Again, that luminous smile. "So strange, that you lost a child, and that a girl lives who looks so much like you she could be your twin, only much younger."

What Ankya was inferring could not be possible. Sanity warred with absurd hope. "What do you know? *Tell me!*" Her voice faltered.

"Shhh," Ankya said. "This is a secret. Between me and you. And this man. Even my father does not yet know about it." She giggled, waggling her fingers at Mani.

Aldís ignored the remark. She grabbed Ankya's hair and air-thin gown again and shook her, words staccato between the shakes. *"What…do…you…know…about…that…child?"*

Naldrum ran over, slammed into Aldís. "Stop attacking my daughter!"

"Your daughter? Your daughter!" Aldís choked. "What about *my* daughter?"

Naldrum's mouth dropped open. His face turned to Ankya. "What has she told you?" The thought of Ankya knowing about the infants he had had his stewards dispatch sickened Naldrum.

Ankya did not answer his panicky question. Instead, again, the odd giggle. "Everything about them, exactly the same."

Aldís swayed. Mani realized she was on the verge of collapse. He gripped her elbow and ordered Naldrum away, then turned to Ankya.

"You are offering information about someone, somewhere, who you say looks like Aldís, and you are, I assume, inferring that this young woman is somehow related to her? And you want something in exchange for information about the person is? And I assume you will only give this information if Aldís refuses to testify against your father?"

Ankya clapped her hands as if she had been handed a gift. "Yes! Refuse to testify!"

"What you have just done may be quite illegal, Miss." But what could Mani do, save put Ankya in the shun-yard for a day or two?

Aldís could not speak. She looked at Ankya, hating herself for the plea that she knew was in her eyes.

Naldrum, watching from several paces away, fretted. *Ankya doesn't know anything.* Still, whatever his daughter had said just unsettled Aldís to the point that she could not speak.

Aldís' face went gray. She swayed again, and Mani gripped her more firmly.

"You must decide, Aldís. The council is waiting."

She could not speak. Her eyes, going from Naldrum to Ankya. *Can it be possible my daughter still lives? Or is this bizarre young woman just lying?* Aldís, sensing desperately, knew that what Ankya said was the truth. *A truth that could not be.*

Sounds came to Aldís as if from a great distance. She saw Mani's lips moving, realized he was speaking to her.

"Aldís. This trial hangs on your testimony. If you speak, Naldrum will be almost certainly be outlawed. There should be enough votes to convict him. Whatever Ankya is talking about may be of no consequence whatsoever. The girl is not right in her head, Aldís. People have exposed themselves to great danger in an attempt to see justice done. Choose carefully, *please*, Aldís."

Naldrum's shouted towards Mani. "Remind her that if she accepts whatever information my daughter offers, the charges will be dropped, and I will not be outlawed. Be very clear!"

"The headman is correct," Mani confirmed. "If you do not testify, Naldrum will be cleared of charges for lack of a credible witness. The entire matter rests on your decision."

Kel shouldered his way past Naldrum into the terse small group. "I demand to know what is happening!" he cried. "What is taking so long?"

"Get away!" Mani roared. No matter how badly he wanted to see Naldrum pay, the law came first.

"No," Aldís mumbled, her voice weak. "It doesn't matter. Let him stay. Forgive me, Kel. I… I… I have to know." She reached for Ankya's hand and grabbed it, pulling the girl with her away from the Law Circle.

Mani wished that he could show the anger and defeat that burned in him. Instead, he sucked in a deep breath and turned to face the circle of *gothar* and their advisors.

"The witness withdraws her testimony," he said, again using his formal Lawspeaker voice. "Due to lack of evidence, the charges must be declared void." Mani could barely say the words. "The accusation against *gothi* Naldrum is dismissed."

Naldrum crowed in triumph. He strutted to Kel, shoved his chest against Kel's. "You can't beat me," he gloated. "No one can beat me! You were a fool to think you could. I have many friends here. You won't survive the week."

"You know the rules at Althing. No weapons, no fights, save in the holmgang duels. You can't touch me here."

"You believe that, Kel?" Naldrum's voice sarcastic. "Watch your back anyway. You've crossed me for the last time."

. . .

Chapter Sixty-Nine

Kel ran after Aldís, furious. He caught up with her as she clung to one of the tall stones under the Law Rock. She sat crumpled, her face pressed against the rock, sobbing.

"Why, Aldís?" he shouted. "Why, every Althing, must you dismiss everything that matters to me, the way you always do? Were your whisperings with Ankya some attempt for her to convince you, woman to woman, to punish me for the wrongs I've done? I freely admitted my guilt, but it wasn't enough for you, was it?"

"No," Aldís, her face still pressed against the rock, agonized.

"I have everything on the line! I traded Thunder for you!"

"She said—" Aldís sobbed. "She said—"

"I don't care what she said! You just ruined this trial! I'm a dead man walking, now, Aldís. My life is worth nothing, but I don't even care about that! I care that our one chance, *our one chance*, of stopping Naldrum is gone. We will never get another opportunity. Because of you!"

"Please," she whimpered. "Let me explain."

"Nothing you can say will change anything." Kel felt uncontrollable fury growing in him. For the first time in his life, he felt the urge to strike a woman. *Get away from her,* something inside him cried.

"Please—"

"No. Tell somebody else. For years I've wondered why you pushed me away when I've done everything in my power to protect you. I don't care now. You've deserted me for the last time. I'll never trust you again. I never want to see you or speak to you, not ever again. You always said, back before, how much you loved the law of our land. How much you loved what Althing meant, the same as I did. Now was your chance to prove it, but it turns out to have meant nothing to you. I never want to hear your voice again! How stupid of me to love you all these years, when it meant nothing to you. You played me the same way Naldrum has, but this is the last time. Congratulations, Aldís...and goodbye."

. . .

Naldrum watched Ankya, perplexed. Yes, people had whispered—in his hearing, and intending for him to hear—that something was not right about his daughter. Yes, she behaved differently than other people sometimes.

He was still determined that Ankya would one day marry a prince or a king. *Woe be to anyone who mocks her then,* he often consoled himself.

But today, she had saved him. Yet even as she had, he knew Ankya's behavior was aberrant. He had followed Ankya out of the Law Circle, had pulled her away from Aldís, had practically dragged her back to their family booth. The whole way, Ankya had giggled to herself, repeating one phrase over and over.

"...just like her...a girl who looks just like her...a girl who looks just like her..."

When they reached Naldrum's quarters, he ushered her into the tent and closed the flap tightly behind them. "What are you going on and on about, Ankya?" Neither he nor Kel had not been able to hear any of the interchange between his daughter and Aldís.

She looked at her father, her eyes unfocussed, wandering. "I once saw a girl who looks like that woman Aldís."

"So?" Naldrum did not particularly care, but perhaps talking would help Ankya to move out of this strange mood. "When did you see such a girl? And where?"

Her eyes drifted, as if they looked different directions at the same time. "You once took me to the trading post at Gásir. I saw her there. A little girl, younger than me. A perfect copy of Aldís."

Naldrum came suddenly to alert focus. "Say that again, daughter?"

Ankya's gaze returned to sharp clarity. "Yes, Father. She was with one of the traders. A woman who was selling pots. The girl was there with the pot-seller, but she looked different, as if they didn't fit together. When I saw the woman Aldís—last year, at Althing—it took me months to remember where I had seen that face and hair before. When I remembered, I could not believe how much Aldís looks like that little girl I had seen."

"How long ago was this, Ankya? And how old the girl?"

Ankya thought back, and reminded Naldrum of a trading voyage on which he had taken her. "The girl was about three years younger than me, I think."

Naldrum counted in his head. *Inconceivable—but possible.*

Long ago, he had heard a rumor that Aldís had born a child the summer he had met her and had hired Kel. Naldrum could not remember for certain if he had lain with Aldís that Althing. Still, he had charged Sauthi with dispatching the child. Better to be safe than sorry.

Any offspring who looked like 'exactly like Aldís' should have rotted in a field by now. Naldrum had not thought of Sauthi in years. As his thoughts pawed through the past, Naldrum realized that Sauthi had left soon after the order to expose Aldís' child.

Had Sauthi betrayed him? Naldrum froze, shocked, as the possibility solidified in his mind. He motioned for his messenger.

"I need you to start a search. Two of them, in fact," he said. "First, seek a merchant who trades in earthenware pots, possibly in Gásir in the western fjords. A child once lived with her. I want to find that girl." Naldrum described the features Ankya had noticed. "And a man once worked for as my steward fifteen years ago, a man named Sauthi. I want him found as well. Bring him to me unharmed. We have some old business to settle." He turned back to Ankya.

"Very good, Ankya," he said slowly. "Very well spoken, daughter. You shall have a new headdress tomorrow for this."

"I don't want a new cloak. I want a new knife. A fighting knife!"

"You want a *saxe*, daughter? Then I will buy you one. Just don't use it on me."

"Stop treating me like a childish girl, and I won't." Ankya glanced at her father with disdain. Then, imagining the knife she would choose and the ways she could use it, she giggled. "That reminds me! Now I can tell you what I was thinking about last night in our tent!"

Naldrum asked with no small amount of nervousness. He had heard the seriousness behind Ankya's threat.

"First, I was thinking of this missing child," she said, almost gleeful. "Next, I was thinking of what you have told me, about your plans for a mystery-ship to sail to the western seas. I thought of your desire for people to return to the Old Ways, instead of these white-christs—but then I started thinking about how the white-christs claim to eat the flesh and drink the blood of a human man, not a *blót* animal sacrifice, which seems much more powerful. And do you know that I thought of next?"

He could not begin to fathom.

"Father, we should find a blood-sacrifice to bless your ship. Not just any sacrifice, for not even the finest horse would do for such an important voyage!"

"Then what, Ankya?" He felt annoyed at her erratic rambling and her odd fascinations.

"The missing child, Father, of course! The one who looks like Aldís. Take her to the shoreline when your ship sails. Cut her! Just like a little lamb to the slaughter. I could even do it, with my new saxe! Just like a proper white-christ sacrifice, but instead, a human child—and a child of a woman you hate!—for this great voyage, as a sign to the gods that we are sincere in our intent to return our land to the Old Ways."

Naldrum's eyes widened and his mouth sagged open. Inadvertently, he stepped back from his daughter and made the sign of Thor.

But as instinctive as the horror that rose in him also came certainty. Ankya spoke true. Goosebumps raised on his arms at the idea. So profane; how many lifetimes had it been since the Old Ways actually condoned human sacrifice? So illegal, outlawed for time out of mind, yet such a seductive, illicit idea that it thrilled Naldrum to his marrow.

He knew he was a powerful man, but Ankya—! *My daughter has it in her to be a true Gothi of All Iceland,* he realized.

Appalled at her cold and ruthless idea, yet fascinated by her logic, Naldrum suddenly feared his favorite child as much as he loved her. He looked at her with newfound respect. In his eyes, Ankya saw capitulation.

She triumphed at her success. She would get a new saxe. She would be the one to cut the girl.

As she twirled about their tent, Ankya pictured Kel's strength against her father's cowardly weakness and mundane thinking. She knew how to get something done far better than her father did.

Kel loved that woman Aldís. That woman Aldís had once had a child. The child likely lives. We will find it and cut it—and that cutting would hurt Kel and Aldís as nothing else could. And then Kel would see how much smarter Ankya was than Aldís, and at last, he would be hers.

. . .

Chapter Seventy

Rota, arriving at Althing, heard about the accusation against Naldrum with little surprise but great frustration. While she hastened to dismiss the issue among Naldrum's faithful—*no, it's nothing, I'm sure*—inwardly, she fumed. *Had she wasted all that time with him?*

But the instant that Mani dismissed the case, Rota went to work. From booth to booth she moved, making generous payments to the merchants for all sorts of wares while she chatted with them. To the wealthier headmen and women, Rota gave expensive gifts, and among the poorer people, she distributed cheap trinkets that she had bought from the festival booths. *Naldrum,* she said to each.

. . .

"Such lovely ivory carvings. I'd like two, please."

"I must have some of your fur trimming!"

"How can I refuse such beautiful embroidery?"

"The red of that wool dazzles me. I'll buy your entire supply."

Each time, as her purchases were wrapped in rough linen, Rota asked questions. "What do you hope for in the coming year? Or, "What challenges trouble you? Who do you think bears the blame for them? Does the law punish them adequately? "What do *you* think should be done to them?"

Little by little, she built on the foundation Naldrum had started. Within a few days, Rota knew who was steadfast in their opinions and who was pliable, who was forthright in principles, and who could be swayed for a promise of payment, power, or prestige.

Rota added other simple questions, designed to keep them nodding *yes, yes,* and then made suggestions. Listening, suggesting, listening, suggesting. By the end of each conversation, she had convinced these men and women of what they had always suspected was true: *that they knew better.*

That their opinions mattered more than others.

That those who disagreed should not be allowed to have a say.

And little by little, they finally felt emboldened in taking the law into their own hands.

. . .

Also, Rota suggested, perhaps the law should not be so fair to all. Wouldn't it be better if it favored her new friends? Wouldn't it be better if it allowed more punishment and retribution against those who disagreed with them?

Yes, yes, Rota agreed, as if these people had suggested the idea and not she. *Yes, yes.* As each day of Althing passed, more and more she fed one singular message: that Naldrum believed as they did, and would force others to fall into line.

So easy to lead them. "When Iceland began, so much good, before all these troubles started." She hesitated, leaned in, lowered her voice. "When the Old Ways prevailed."

The replies fell into line just as she had primed them.

"So many outsiders cause conflict. They weaken us. The Old Ways, and those who follow them, offer our only hope. If we go forward, we will lose what we are, what we hold most dear! We must go back, not forward!"

To the most powerful of the pliant, Rota opened the small wooden trunk her servant carried.

"Please, allow me to offer you a small token, a greeting from my master Haakon Sigurdsson, the Jarl of Lade, who lives in Trondheim in the Nor'way lands. You have heard of him, yes? No? Then perhaps you have heard of the *gothi* who trades most with him, the headman Naldrum? Oh, good. Yes, you will see that Naldrum wears these simple bands, as a sign of his loyalty to the Jarl."

As the unwitting recruits to Rota's campaign slipped on the gold bands and stretched out their arms to admire the sight, she added, "Others agree with you. Talk to them. Look for others wearing these same arm bands. Oh, I nearly forgot. *Gothi* Naldrum will be making an important announcement very soon. Please make sure you hear it when he does!"

No one failed to note that the 'small tokens' were anything but. They clearly represented a man of immense wealth. At Naldrum's name, their heads nodded eagerly. Rota smiled, watched them put the bands onto their wrists, and slipped away to find another conquest. By the time Althing ended, she would have put all the votes Naldrum needed to be Lawspeaker right in the palm of his hand.

. . .

The trader Josson, with Tor in tow, arrived nearly at the end of Althing. Josson knew this was the best time to make a dramatic entrance. The first days of Althing were crowded with exciting events, and his entry with Tor would be of less note. Something striking towards the end of Althing fetched far more attention from bored fairgoers.

Josson wanted nothing to detract from Tor's grand reappearance. He had no way of knowing how close Naldrum had come to wearing outlaw marks on his *own* hands, in which case Josson's gambit would have failed.

As they approached the Thing-valley, Josson dismounted. "I want to make a proper entrance."

"What does that mean?" Tor asked

Josson squinted. "Not just you riding alongside me, free as a bird."

"You want to truss me like a hog for slaughter." *Such a pathetic man, this trader. So eager to curry the favor of another weak man.* "I agreed to this bargain. Why would I care how you dress it up?"

They made their way through the festival grounds. Those who remembered Tor from the year before goggled at seeing the once-proud blacksmith stumbling behind Josson's horse, his hands roped behind him and his ankles fettered.

. . .

Day after day during the ride to the Althing valley, Josson had pictured Naldrum practically falling to his knees in gratitude. Instead, at seeing Tor in the flesh again, the headman first stared in astonishment, and then fear. He threw the joint of roast goose he had been eating into the dirt as he backed away from Josson, cursing.

"First Kel comes back to life, and now Tor? That's not a human, you stupid trader! That's a *revenant!* Tor's death-walker has tricked you!"

Naldrum made the sign of Thor across his chest. *What dark magic had they used?* He wondered how to protect himself. Maybe this was part of the curse from that white-christ woman Kandace. He gathered up his cloak to run away.

Rota had been seated beside Naldrum, whispering to him about their newest allies. She looked up and saw Josson and Tor, and smiled widely.

"Ah! Here comes the slave Tor that I bought from you, *gothi.* Excellent. Give me his rope." She reached her hand to Josson.

Naldrum froze, unsure of what to do.

Josson bowed and smirked, awaiting Naldrum's gratitude. "I captured this slave on behalf of the *gothi,* madam. I am returning him to headman Naldrum, not you."

"Captured him?" Rota swung to Naldrum and immediately saw his discomfiture. "You told me Tor was on a mission for you, but this trader is dragging him here in ropes and chains. You sold me a runaway, didn't you?" Rota hissed. "You didn't even know where Tor was when you took my silver, did you?"

Naldrum hesitated. He could not very well tell Rota that he had sold her a dead man, that Tor was not alive, that what she saw was a death-walker masquerading in human form. He could think of nothing to say to escape the dreadful situation.

"Give my slave to me!" he cried to Josson. "What were you thinking, dragging him in here like that in front of everyone? Did you *intend* to humiliate me? Because you have!"

Rota stepped between Naldrum and Tor. "*My* slave, you mean," she said. She drew her dirk. "What everyone says is true. You can't be trusted. Not at all. I demand retribution!"

"Spare me your high and mighty attitude," Naldrum snarled. "You have played games with the truth yourself. Perhaps we are not so different." He called to Randaal, the burly man who had taken Kel's place as steward. "Go get my captives!" he cried.

. . .

Naldrum's steward Randaal returned leading three figures. Seeing them, Tor groaned.

"You told me you were putting this woman on a ship to go back to Haakon," Naldrum gloated. "Perhaps you can explain why she was captured recently, riding towards the western fjords?"

. . .

Kandace and Tor faced each other, their sadness palpable.

"What did we do to deserve such misery?" she asked him in their own language, full of grief.

"It seems we are not meant to be happy, my love," he said to her.

"*Why not?* Who decides which humans get happiness, and which do not? Cruel, hateful people sleep safe in their beds, yet we, who have never hurt anyone, suffer again and again!" Kandace wiped her cheeks. "For years, I was faithful to Christ, both in my childhood land and after the nuns found me. For years, you have trusted in Allah's justice. You have kept his Word, no matter what it cost, even respecting the bonds of slavery! Here, the people of this land, many of them kind and good, sacrifice and pray to their pagan gods, yet they receive nothing but hunger and troubles. All of us great fools hope and pray to some great Force that we foolishly believe cares about us, and loves us, and will help us, but for what? Yet Naldrum, who believes in no god, in nothing but his money and power, thrives, while all we others struggle? Why?!"

"I don't know, Kandace. I have no answer for you."

They stood trapped in misery. Faith, so long their foundation and ally, drifted away, useless and empty.

. . .

Josson still held the rope that held Tor's bindings. His hopes had been crushed at Naldrum's angry words. Once again, his dream of impressing the headman had blown away, ashes before the wind. He would receive no reward for Tor now, it was clear. But the children were still valuable. Perhaps Naldrum would want them.

"*Gothi* Naldrum," Josson leaned forward. "The children?"

"What?" Naldrum snapped.

"Tor's children—"

"Tor has no children!"

Josson looked confused. "No, *gothi.* These belong to him."

"Why must you *always* be the stupidest man alive? You think I would believe such a ridiculous lie?"

"*Gothi!* They came with Tor, when I bought him! I intended to sell them, but he told me that they had fallen into a waterfall and died."

From the corner of his eye, Naldrum saw Tor sag at Josson's words. The motion told Naldrum that Josson spoke truth. He stretched his hand to the trader. Josson took it, delighted and astonished.

"Tor must have hidden them and told Kandace where they were. She was trying to help him by escaping with them!" Naldrum beckoned to his new steward Randaal again. "Fetch a fine cape for this fellow and give him a gold piece! He will have a place in my household. This bumbling imbecile has served me better than any man ever."

. . .

Kandace saw Tor nearly fall to his knees. "I couldn't hear! What did they say?" she cried.

"The children," he gasped. "They are negotiating for them. I have failed you all."

Fire filled Kandace. "No!" she cried, and leaped towards Naldrum.

She bit at his face and tore at his eyes with her fingernails. Naldrum screamed in terror. His steward seized Kandace, trying to pull her off the headman, but she fought as a berserker, a she-bear in mortal combat for her young. Naldrum fell to the ground under her attack, writhing and twisting in the dirt beneath Kandace.

As Naldrum squealed and bawled, Randaal grabbed at Kandace and flung her aside, then pulled the headman to his feet again.

Naldrum stood panting, his hands on his balding head, bleeding from claw marks.

"She will die!" he shrieked to the onlookers. "This witch must die!"

. . .

A messenger ran to Mani the Lawspeaker. "There's a mob around one of the headmen!" the messenger cried. "They are about to fight, Lawspeaker! You must come right away!"

Mani sprinted towards where the messenger pointed. *I am too old to move this quickly.* Still, he ran. The taboo that forbade fighting at Althing had never been broken—and it would *not* break, not while he had breath in his body to prevent it. Mani panted, held the stitch in his side, and ran faster, and Kel ran beside him.

. . .

In the beer tents, Konradsson heard a woman screaming. He listened carefully. It seemed as if he recognized the voice. As she cried out again, he realized.

"It's the nun Kandace who was at Naldrum's!"

Konradsson shouted to no one in particular, as he too dashed towards the melee.

. . .

Mani saw the ugly crowd gathered Naldrum. He took stock of the situation, trying to learn quickly what had happened.

A slave woman, defiant and desperate, knelt with her arms around two children. The slave Tor shouted at the men who held her. The headman Naldrum, bleeding and shrieking at the woman, backed fearfully away from Tor. The woman Rota, Haakon's secretive agent, glared at Naldrum.

Mani felt panicked. No matter what, he must preserve order in Althing. But the mob shouted louder, making ugly threats of violence.

. . .

"What is this mess?" Mani shoved between people to the center where Naldrum stood. He had no reason to pretend politeness to the headman any longer. "How dare you defile the Althing with a fight!"

"She started it!" Naldrum bawled. "I am innocent!"

The throng surrounding them quieted a little at the appearance of the Lawspeaker. Mani took in the circle of faces. Disgust, worry, compassion, resentment, fear—but most of all, anger. One spark and they would be at one another's throats. Mani needed to sort things out quickly.

"I don't care who started what, or why. You're a headman. You're supposed to help keep the peace. Whatever happened, you have to help calm this down."

. . .

Glances shot at Naldrum, sharp as arrows, and shouts. "You told us this white-christ woman in her strange clothing was not welcome in our land! You claimed you would burn her at the spring festival, yet here she is! Odin's justice, are you afraid of her? Here's your chance to keep your word. Do it!"

Others pleaded differently. "She says she's not your slave! You can't go around just capturing freeholders! For the love of the gods, let them go!"

Naldrum hung torn, inept and incapable. He tried to think of what to do. The glances of the crowd grew sharper and darker as people pressed closer, each side demanding what they saw as justice. They began to shove at one another.

Naldrum could see no way out. The only thing that mattered was convincing people of his supremacy. If people lost faith in him, his whole plan would be ruined.

"I paid well for her and her children. You're not going to just get to steal them from me," Naldrum ignored Mani and bleated at Rota.

Rota was surprised to hear her own voice. "Look at them!" she cried. "So pitiful! That woman belongs to my master Haakon. Give her to me!"

Naldrum seized on the unexpected escape Rota's words offered. He would likely have to choose between Kandace and Tor. The slave man offered enormous benefit that Naldrum could use immediately—and if Tor *was* a death-walker, would get him away, forever.

"Yes! Let us pity them!" he started, making it up as he went along. "This woman has attacked me, but the real issue is this slave man. He was disobedient. He ran away and has been brought back. You should not have to own such a disobedient man, Rota. I will return your silver and take him back into my household." Naldrum made a show of stripping off the hacksilver armbands he wore, holding them out.

Caught off guard, Rota began to protest. She had not wanted Naldrum to take Tor back. She whispered, furious. "What are you—"

Naldrum's hissed reply burned her ears. "You never returned Kandace to the Jarl. Don't give me a reason to send that news to him."

. . .

Konradsson pushed through the melee. He faced the small group in the middle of the fracas, trembling inside.

"I wonder if I might offer some help here," he began.

"Get out of here, you sniveling coward!" Randaal said. "Your kind is at the root of this problem!"

Naldrum took up the attack. "Yes! You… this woman…your white-christ ways defile our land!"

. . .

Friedrich had told Konradsson about his dislike of this particular headman.

"Over and over, I told myself, *mine is not to judge."* Friedrich had said. Remembering that effort, Konradsson tried to act as the bishop might have. He offered no disagreement as his words slid across the muddy ground to Naldrum. He had no purpose in fighting this man. What mattered was getting Kandace and her children away from him.

"You are right that they belong to the same faith that I do. Give her to me. Let me remove her and her children from this sacred valley, where their ways are not welcome."

"Take his offer," Tor muttered to Rota.

"Why?" she whispered back. "Come with me back to Trondheim, Tor. You'll be safe there."

"Safety does not matter to me. All I have lived for these last years was to find my wife." Tor's throat choked with emotion. "Sell me back to Naldrum in exchange for them. I don't care what happens to me. Let Kandace and our children go with Konradsson. Just get them away from Naldrum. Please!"

. . .

Rota handed Tor's rope to Naldrum. *They came so close to having a chance,* she consoled herself. *I could do no more, especially with what Naldrum is about to announce.* But she knew better. Deep within, Rota felt shame.

. . .

Naldrum shouted to the crowd. "The time has come! I have an important announcement to make!"

Anger that had reached a boiling point suddenly diverted. They watched to hear what the headman might say. It would have to be as significant as Naldrum was promising.

Mani breathed a sigh of relief as he saw the danger subside. One more day. One more disaster averted. *I am most definitely getting* far *too old for this.*

But he also realized that he felt more alive than he had for years. *Maybe I am not as old as I think.*

He also wanted to hear what Naldrum had in mind. Might as well find out now rather than from rumors later.

"To the Law Circle!" Naldrum cried. "I want every headman and woman to hear this!"

. . .

Naldrum, anxious to make a show of his prowess, made the most of the occasion. He dragged Tor, yanking at the rope to make Tor stumble.

Council members who had been disbanding after the day's hearings rushed to take their seats again. Mani held up his hands to have an orderly process—after all, they were in the Circle—but Naldrum's supporters, wearing their gold arm bands, shouted to let Naldrum speak.

"This slave threatened me!" Naldrum lied. "I could whip him, to show all slaves that such behavior will not be tolerated, but is that enough?"

"No!" cried his supporters. "He deserves to be outlawed!"

"Yes! And he *will* be, at a trial later today, I promise you! Before that, let me share exciting news. I was going to announce it at the close of Althing, but now is as good a time as any."

A murmur of excitement ran around the Law Circle.

Naldrum held up his hands for silence. "Some of your leaders—those of us who actually *care* about your wellbeing—understand how difficult the last few years have been for our people. Too little land! Too little food! Bad weather! Sickness! Too many strangers, and their strange ways!" He glared at one of the headmen who wore a cross on his tunic, and made a mocking gesture, crossing himself as he had seen the man do. "Have you ever thought that our gods are angry at us for being so welcoming to strangers, and for abandoning the Old Ways? For allowing those who disrespect our gods to spread their filth and lies in our land?"

Many on the council roared approval. Ever since last Althing, they had whispered in secret of such things. Rota had done her work well—and now hearing Naldrum speak these words aloud gave life to their angry suspicions.

Those wearing the gold arm bands shouted loudest.

"The time has come to set things right again!" Naldrum continued, encouraged. "At this fifty-first year of Althing, we must rededicate our country to the Old Ways. I proclaim a new era for our next fifty years: *The New Days of the Old Ways!*"

The words rang like poetry, full of power and hope, catching imagination.

No one clapped or cheered. They stood like children, awed and docile, until a tremendous roar broke out.

. . .

Naldrum had not expected such an awed reaction. He foundered briefly and regained his momentum.

"As we embark on this new era for our land, it seems fitting to make a mighty sacrifice to our gods!" He flapped his arms. "A great gesture, to show how much we still honor them and respect them! To show them that we are a worthy people, so that they will shower us with fortune!"

Excited chatter broke out. What could Naldrum possibly mean in addition to his remarkable announcement?

"What could be a grand enough gesture? It will have to be a great, great effort on our parts. And so that you do not have to trouble yourselves at sorting out such a complex problem, I am proud to tell you that I have found the perfect solution!"

Now people leaned forward to hear every word, some in anticipation and excitement, and others in dread.

"A ship is being built—a magnificent ship, the finest ever made, to sail in the spring. But to where? We all know the old rumors that land may lie in the oceans west of us. Maybe so, maybe not. But has anyone bothered to look for a long, long time? No! But I, your beloved chieftain Naldrum, have decided to sponsor a new search—and if we find land, those who support me and the Old Ways will be given the first pick of land there, *for free!*"

A great roar went up. Even those who disliked Naldrum found themselves intrigued by the idea.

He laughed to himself. *Like Hel they will get anything for free. I'll give them the land after I charge them a fortune for passage on my ships. Look at their stupid faces, eating this up.*

"And who will go on this ship to look for such land? On a very dangerous mission?" He let the question hang in the air, let them desire the answer.

"Outlawed men, that is who! Men who are strong, but who do not deserve to live among decent folk! And since this man Tor is my slave, he will be my gift to you. Tor will be the first chosen to sail on this ship!"

Cries erupted from the crowd. "Let me sail for you, *gothi!* Let me be one of your chosen!"

"No, my people. This mission has far too much danger to risk the lives of the good people of this land. We will fill the ship with outlaws—and rid our land of their menace at the same time." Applause and cheers broke out, but Naldrum held up his hand for silence.

"This man is valuable property of mine. Look how big and strong he is! What a wonderful addition he will be to the crew of this vessel!"

The crowd could be held back no longer. They surged to their feet and cheered. Feet stamping, hands clapping, good-luck sticks pounding together. The roar was as deafening and wonderful as anything Naldrum could have wished. He basked in the glory of it, waving to his fans—until he realized they were not shouting *Naldrum, Naldrum, Naldrum!*

Their chant echoed against the stones of Thing valley. "Tor! Tor! Tor!"

Naldrum seethed, his teeth on edge. Why were those clods cheering Tor instead of him? *It doesn't matter,* he consoled himself. *They'll see me as their hero soon enough. That* vikinger *Tiller will lose his appeal tomorrow. He will be outlawed for murder, and I'll put him on the beastly vessel to steer it. Tor will go on it, and die—really die! —out on the western seas somewhere, and never return. Those outlawed this year will be more than enough men to sail the ship. This Althing has been nothing but gloom and doom so far, but now I have wrought a miracle, as that misled bishop would say.*

A small final inspiration occurred to Naldrum. He held up his hands one more time, and the crowd waited, breathless.

"And when they find land—when, not if! —when they return to us, what then? We will reward them like the heroes they are for undertaking this perilous voyage!"

The cheers, impossibly, came even louder. Naldrum bowed deeply to the crowd and swept out of the Law Circle, waving like a king as he departed.

"I'll be the next Lawspeaker whether Mani wants it or not," he said to Rota.

She gave her enigmatic smile. "I'll see to it that you are. In the meantime, don't do anything to destroy all the work I have done on your behalf."

Don't try to get Kandace back, she meant, and Naldrum knew it.

"As if I care about a couple of Haakon's slaves," he snorted. "You insult me, as always, Rota. I have far bigger interests to attend to."

Not without my help, thought Rota. *Cross me, and I'll dump you like a rotten rat.*

Ankya watched Rota's expression. It intrigued her. This strange woman, who Ankya had mostly ignored, apparently held quite a bit of power over her father.

I need to study Rota, Ankya decided. *And I need to make my own plans.* She thought briefly, and went in search of her father's new steward Randaal.

. . .

Randaal hated women, Ankya could tell. She brought her maid and a piece of gold to him, holding it in her palm where he could see it.

"I need your help with something," she said.

He spat on the ground, barely missing her dress. "Why should I care?"

"Take off your tunic," Ankya told her maid.

The girl's eyes widened. "No!"

Ankya slapped her. "Ignore me again and he'll be the one slapping you. Take off your tunic."

The girl, her furious eyes downcast, pulled the tunic over her head. She stood in her undershift, the lines of her body clearly visible.

"Stop covering your chest with your arms. Stand up straight and let him see you," Ankya commanded. The girl dropped her arms, lifted her chin, glared at the horizon. The breeze made her nipples stand out under the thin fabric.

"See?" Ankya pointed to her maid, then twirled the bit of gold in her hand. "I have pretty things you want."

Randaal did not bother to argue. "What do you want in return?"

"That voyage my father announced. I want you to volunteer to go on it."

"On a ship of outlaws, sent off for three years to nowhere, who are all likely to die? By Hel, no! I'm your father's steward now. I'm an important man. Why would I leave such a good position to do that?" He practically sneered at Ankya.

She stayed calm. "First of all, because that ship offers you freedom. It might go anywhere. Here, there is only one Naldrum.

Look at the woman Rota, who works for Haakon. Have you seem the luxury of her possessions? Her necklaces? Her horses and her tents? Haakon pays her *far* more than you for doing much easier work." Ankya let that thought sink in. "In other lands, there are men whose fortunes dwarf my fathers, lots of them. That outlaw ship might be your ticket to a much better position."

His small eyes diminished into a squint. "Why would you betray your father by tempting me to leave him?"

"Because I want things my father doesn't understand. You want things he can't—or won't—give you. We can have an arrangement."

"A bit of *fukke* and gold aren't enough. You have something else in mind. What is it?"

Ankya smiled. "Oh yes. I most certainly do have something else in mind. Something I think you would like very, very much."

. . .

Ankya pulled Randaal farther aside where her maid could not hear. She explained everything she had suggested to her father about finding the missing child and using it as a sacrifice—but added the new exciting part that she had only just now realized.

"A sacrifice on shore before the ship leaves? What a massive acknowledgement of our devotion to the old ways! But is it enough? Only a few fishermen will see it, and then forget it. What I envision could be so much bigger. So much more powerful. That is where you come in."

She explained. *A new land. A girl-child, a virgin, her blood consecrated to the gods, to the Old Ways, spilled on the beach of whatever land you find.*

Randaal did not take his eyes from Ankya's face as she spoke. Something in him grew deeply aroused at what she was saying. Ankya could see the desire for what she described take him, and knew he was hers.

"You would be the one to do the sacrificial cutting, of course. You're the only one I could trust. You understand these things the same way that I do."

Ankya tuned her words to the deep cruelty she knew lay in Randaal's heart.

"Think of it. The dagger, in your hand. Her little chin in your other hand. Lifting it, so that her pale throat is exposed, just like a she-goat at a spring or autumn blót." Ankya could see the effect her seduction was having on Randaal. "But not a goat. A living, breathing girl. Yours, to take as long as you want. And who could stop you? No fear of retribution. No consequences. All nice and legal. Approved, even."

Randaal pursed and opened his lips over and over. *Too much to think about.* The craving he felt for the image Ankya had created made him almost mad with desire.

She finished. "Those who witness this girl sailing off to eternity will repeat it to others, and they to others. The story will become much larger in their minds than if they had seen it done on our own shores—and you will be the hero of the story."

Randaal tried to follow all that Ankya was saying, but the slave girl was standing there in her shift, her nipples hard now in the cooling air. He pictured cutting her instead of the sacrifice-child. Would Ankya just stop flicking that bit of gold about, catching the light? Randaal had never held a piece of gold in his life, and his fingers twitched, wanting it, wanting *all* of what she dangled in front of him.

Finally he burst out, “Fine! I’ll go on the ship. I’ll do what you want! Give them to me!” He snatched towards the gold in her hand, but just as fast, Ankya closed her fingers.

“I’ll hold this for you. You’ll just spend it on whores at Althing. No need for that when my slave girl will serve just as nicely, and for free.”

She gave the girl a little push towards Randaal. “No marks on her face or arms during the festival. She has to serve me all through Althing, and I don’t want people whispering and wondering who’s hurting her. After Althing, when we get back to our compound, you can do what you want. Now here’s what you have to remember.”

Randaal repeated the words Ankya told him. “I’ll volunteer to go on the ship. I’ll talk your father into doing the sacrifice at the new land, not when we depart. I get to cut the girl as soon as we reach land, any land, new or not.”

They shook hands. “We are agreed, then,” Ankya said, and gave him her bright innocent smile. She bowed, a mocking gesture. “Here’s her dress. I’ll need her back by when the Kalendar calls the time for sleeping.”

Randaal grunted in response as he stared at the maid’s body. Ankya laughed softly to herself, and went to plant the next seed of her plan. Her maid stood staring at Randaal, horrified that she was being given to him.

Randaal grabbed her by the arm and marched her to his tent and tied the flaps closed. He pointed to his sleeping blanket. When she protested, Randaal threw her to the ground, and kept his hand over her mouth the entire time so no one could hear her screams.

. . .

Rumors of the outlaw ship immediately swirled from the Law Circle throughout Althing. Styr stood in front of Tiller, insisting that he fight the punishment.

"Even if this is true, you don't have to go! No matter what Naldrum says, he can't just *force* you onto his ship, if it exists! Any outlaw has the right to pay for passage to another land, stay there until the three years are up—"

Tiller cut off Styr's impassioned plea. "It doesn't matter. Nothing matters."

"What do you mean?"

"I'm just done, Styr. There's no fight left in me. I've always been looking for one scrap or another, or one adventure. Some kind of way to prove to myself and to others who I am, what I'm capable of. To earn their respect. Maybe to earn my own respect. But after what happened to Thorgest's sons, I just don't care."

"But it was his fault from the beginning—or his wife's, at least."

"Thorgest warned me, last Althing. I laughed at him and didn't listen, so it was my fault too, Styr. He was within the law. And if there's one thing I loathe, it's people who don't take responsibility for their own actions. I won't be like that." Tiller was thinking of how Naldrum had refused to pay him for kidnapping Kandace from Lade

Garde in Trondheim. "Naldrum has all but ruined me, financially and personally, because he wouldn't admit he made a mistake, and wouldn't take responsibility for his commands. I refuse to be like that bloated troll."

Styr was losing ground, and he knew it. He made one last attempt. "You know the trial at Thornes was unfair."

"It was. I have no doubt that Naldrum bribed the law circle there. But what really matters, in the end? Thorgest was the closest thing to a decent father I had. But because of my anger and pride, three of my friends are dead, and the man I counted as a foster-father is heartbroken over losing his two sons. Is that fair? No. Can either of us undo what happened? No. I'll stand for my trial, and I'll tell the truth., I don't have nearly as good a lawspeaker as Thorgest will. Naldrum has paid for him to have the best there is. But I'll do what I can, and if I'm convicted, the last thing honor I can give Thorgest and his dead sons—my friends, once—is to take the punishment like a man."

"But your own father—"

"I don't speak of my father. You know that."

Tiller clapped his loyal friend on the shoulder. "Cheer up, Styr. I'm still a free man, at least until my trial tomorrow. Let's go get something to eat. I highly doubt this nonsense will come to pass. It's probably just another trick Naldrum is playing on people. But if there is some great dangerous adventure at sea to be had, I'll be one they'll want to send. No one has a better reputation than I do for sailing. If I can accept that, you might as well also. Plus, maybe it's better that way. At least I won't have to face Thorgest's friends everywhere I turn."

They walked to the food tents. Styr trudged in defeat, but Tiller moved as a man relieved of his burdens, cynical, unsurprised by human pettiness, but prepared to endure whatever might come.

"My friend, there is one other benefit to this trial finishing," Tiller added, jovial. "You can give up fretting about me and make a proper proposal to Fatimah. She's a wonderful woman and you deserve one another. Just because my life is at an impasse doesn't mean yours has to be."

. . .

When the Kalendar called the sleeping-time, the sun still glowed bright in the north-western sky. Ankya fussed about the tent, annoyed that Randaal had not yet returned her maid.

At last she heard his knock on the entry-board. "Come in!" she cried, smug that Randaal *had* obeyed her, after all.

But the knock was not Randaal. A *gothi* she did not recognize stood in the doorway of the tent. In his arms he carried the unconscious body of her maid. Several men and women stood behind him, angry.

"What happened to her?" Ankya cried. She could barely make out her maid's features.

"You father's steward Randaal did this," the man answered, his voice grim. "A group of us pulled him off this woman."

"Put her down—no, not on my pallet, she's bleeding! Put her here, on the ground."

Ankya bent over her maid. Randaal had gone too far. Damn him! The vote for the next Lawspeaker took place tomorrow. This was going to spread through Althing like wildfire, and her father was going to be furious.

The girl moaned through swollen lips.

"Thank the gods, she is speaking! She is alive!" Ankya said. "Leave us so that I may tend to her!"

The headman made no move to leave. "Randaal will be charged for this. Even the youngest children know the rule of no violence at Althing except at the holmgang duels. Your father may be powerful, but he can't protect this beast of a steward. We've already sent someone to bring a charge before the Law Council."

"Get out!" Ankya cried. "Do you not see how you are distressing her?" She thrust the group back from the tent door and tied it closed.

"Take him to the jail pens," she heard the gothi command. "He can't be allowed to run loose."

. . .

Ankya bent to her maid. "What did you do?" she hissed. "All you had to do was go along with him and everything would have been fine!"

"What he wanted," the girl mumbled. "Unnatural," Her shaking fingers moved to her lips. She pulled a bit of broken tooth from her mouth, spat out another one. Her other hand fluttered against Ankya's belt, pulling at it.

"Oh, stop grabbing at me and stop being such a ninny! I had a bargain with him! As soon as you're better, I'm giving you back to him. Your little show of defiance has proven nothing!"

The maid struggled to breathe, forced the words out. “My blood is on your hands,” she said.

With that, the fingers prying around on Ankya’s belt found its target. The fancy golden knife that Naldrum had given to his daughter knew its first blood as the maid plunged it into her own chest.

“No more of your people,” she laughed, blood bubbling from her lips. “No more.”

. . .

Ankya’s face settled into a vicious frown. To Hel with this horrid vixen! She stood up, took her *saxe* from her maid’s hand and wiped it onto the girl’s shift. What to do now?

By the time Naldrum had returned to change his tunic for the evening festivities, Ankya had covered the dead maid’s face with a scrap of rag. Sadly, she relayed to her father how she had cautioned the girl against flirting with Randaal, how volatile he could be, and how her maid had not listened.

“And now look at this,” Ankya mourned. “Dead, here in our tent. She’s killed herself from grief.”

Naldrum had moved as far away from the body as possible. “Get that bloody thing out of here!” he screamed at his daughter. “I want no parts of this! The vote on who will replace Mani as Lawspeaker is tomorrow—*tomorrow*, Ankya! I can’t have this kind of scandal associated with me! This foolish maid of yours might cost me everything!”

“What will you do, Father?” asked Ankya.

"Randaal must be outlawed, as soon as possible! I'll cast the first vote. It's imperative that I disassociate myself from him before the Lawspeaker vote."

"Of course, Father," Ankya soothed. "I'll testify against him if you like. But on the bright side? He's sturdy as an ox. One more outlaw for your ship, and a man who's loyal to you. That's a good thing, yes?"

. . .

Ankya went to find Randaal in the jail pens. She professed dismay that her maid had provoked him. Wept, telling him that her father had already turned against his own poor victimized steward. Assured Randaal that if he pleaded guilty to the crime and did not argue it, she would still see to it that he got the prize he wanted most, the one that would make all this nonsense worth it, a girl-sacrifice…the first, but perhaps not the last, Ankya hinted.

Once again, with very little time to plan, things had not worked out as Ankya had envisioned.

No, she realized. *Better.*

. . .

Mani conducted the emergency trial in record time. Word of Randaal's violence had spread even faster than that of Naldrum's outlaw ship. No one came forward to speak in Randaal's defense. The brute pled guilty, smirking all the while at Ankya. Naldrum decreed Randaal would be part of the crew for the outlaw ship, and Mani made a short speech, reminding all that protecting the safety of Althing was just one example of how law must be respected and obeyed, lest such abhorrent practices flourish.

The second trial of the day was Tor's. Mani felt only grief at having to preside it. The travesty that was happening to Tor sickened the aged Speaker. Still, he was bound to observe the Law.

"Guilty," was all Mani said. "Outlawed."

Nothing about the pronouncement changed Tor's fate. He had suffered another humiliation at Naldrum's hands. Still, the enslaved man stood tall and proud, undefeated, while Naldrum crowed victory.

"Bring Randaal and Tor for the outlaw marks to be cut!" Naldrum cried. "I'll oversee the man doing it myself. For Randaal, to show everyone how much I disapprove of his actions—and for Tor, so that all will know again what happens when a man dares defy me."

Ankya's cheeks flushed with anger. Naldrum adjusted his words.

"Ankya, my darling daughter, you have been such a support in these matters. Certainly you deserve to have revenge for your maid! Get out your blade. The honor of cutting shall be yours, my love."

. . .

The year earlier, when Kel had sliced the first set of outlaw marks on Tor's hands under order from Naldrum, Tor had focused his thoughts on his children, safe at the widow's farm, to block the pain.

Today, just before his own trial, Randaal had whipped Tor, inflicting physical agony on top of his emotional pain. Now the enslaved man hunched at the branding-table in a daze of agony, preparing to endure the next torment.

As Ankya drew her small golden blade from its hilt, Tor stared straight at the corrupt headman. With the loss of Tor's faith, pure hatred shone from his eyes.

"At least Rota took my wife away from you," he sneered.

Naldrum paused. "Your wife? Who is that?"

Even through the pain, Tor realized his mistake immediately. He slumped against the cutting table.

"Your *wife*," Naldrum drew out the word in delight. "So Kandace *was* the one I sent Tiller for! What an amazing performance you have been doing, pretending she wasn't." He reached for Ankya's golden saxe, touched it to his lips. "What a lovely gift your words have given me. Now that you have blurted out the truth, I promise you that no expense or trouble will keep me from getting her back. I am good friends with the Jarl, who bought her from the slavers in the first place, did you know that? Just because she's going to that simple-minded bishop doesn't mean she's safe. The Jarl will release his claim to her, and I'll take her for my own."

Tor tried to protest. "You bought me from Rota for their safety. Rota will not be manipulated like your other cowardly grovelers."

"Perhaps she is not as powerful as you think. I will do anything the Jarl wants—anything! —and pay anything he wants, to get your wife back. And then I promise you, your woman will become my bed-slave, while you drown somewhere in the endless seas to the west. Everyone knows there is no land out there. You will never return to save her. I want your dying thought to be of me rutting between your beloved wife's thighs."

. . .

Ankya poised her knife, thrilled that she was being allowed this important task. The blade was not razor-sharp as Kel's had once been, and she did not know how to press properly, to make one straight smooth slice that cut skin but spared tendon and muscle.

She hacked at Tor's hands, gleeful. When the '*X*' marks gushed blood from the back of both Tor's hands, Ankya laughed, stood up, and waved the knife in the air. She felt giddy from the experience. How her father loathed Tor! And how exciting it had been to grip Tor's wrist with one hand while she sawed away with the other. The feeling of the man's bone and skin gritty under her blade, the sound of him crying out in pain as he tried to pull away, so intoxicating. It gave her a rush of pleasure better than any mead she had ever tasted.

As Ankya wiped her blade clean and put it back in its embroidered scabbard, Tor sagged, past pain, his head on the table between his bleeding hands. A thought circled in his mind, a feather drifting and catching in the wind. *My own voice betrayed Kandace.*

"I will never speak again," he promised himself. The words, broken, came through lips bleeding and bitten, the barest whisper. "I never want to hear the sound of myself speaking again. Never."

One last thing still needed to be said—and after that, silence.

. . .

Chapter Seventy-One

The Blue Beads

Kel waited for Naldrum to swagger off, surrounded by sycophants and admirers who chattered excitedly about the 'New Days of Old Ways'. Soon the law circle had emptied of the council of *gothar* and onlookers. Only Mani and Kel remained beside Tor.

The bleeding man struggled to sit up. "I need you to do something for me," he croaked.

"Anything."

"Kandace and my children were heading to the northern fjords in search of Bishop Friedrich. Aldís was with them."

"Yes," Kel answered.

"Rota has Kandace and the children now. Do you know where Aldís is?"

"She left Althing. I don't know where she went, nor do I care."

"I need you to find her, Kel. That priest Konradsson means well, but he can't protect them. Aldís knows people, and so do you. Konradsson will need your help, and hers, to get my family to safety."

Anything but riding with Aldís for days, Kel wanted to say, but he could not refuse Tor.

"I'll stomach the sight of her one last time for you, my friend."

"Konradsson told me that the bishop *is* in the western fjords. Please find Aldís, and then get Konradsson and my family out of here. As far away from Naldrum as possible."

"I will," Kel replied. "You have my word. Naldrum has many enemies in the western fjords. He won't dare to go there. They'll be safe."

"And Kel, if I come back from this impossible voyage, find me. Tell me where they are, so I can go to them."

Kel nodded.

"But because I probably won't come back—"

"You will. Don't say that."

"Don't be stupid. We both know the odds."

Kel grimaced. "Honest enough. If you don't come back, what then?"

"In my pouch." Tor nodded his head at the small bag on his belt.

Kel untied the leathers, opened the bag and turned it upside down. The two soul-stones for his children were in it, plus one other bead, a blue so bright it glowed.

"I gave that to Kandace as a gift the day we were engaged to be married. It's not particularly valuable, but she loved it. She always wore it. I found it lying in the dust of the roadway the day she was stolen by slavers. I always thought she may have torn it off and flung it down as a sign to me. It was the one thing I couldn't bring myself to sell, before I traded my freedom to try and find her," Tor said. "I've kept it all these years. Please give it to her to wear in memory of me."

Kel put the shining blue bead and the two soul-stones into his own pouch. "I won't fail you."

The sun glowed red on the horizon as Kel walked towards the horse meadows. Damned if he cared about the slave trader's claim to his horse. He'd saddle Thunder and ride. Aldís had left on foot along the road out of Althing. He'd catch up with her quickly enough.

Find her, return to Althing, collect Tor's wife and children from Rota, get Konradsson, and take them to the western fjords.

Then I never, ever, ever have to see Aldís again.

. . .

Tiller had known that his chances were slim. At his trial, Thorgest spoke as if his great heart had broken. His words moved all who heard them—but so did Tiller's words about his beloved carved pillars.

The law-arguer that Naldrum paid for Thorgest did not depend on emotion, or right, or promises made and broken. He knew his business of law, and he knew it well.

Once again, Mani grimaced at the verdict.

"Guilty," he said. As with Tor, there would be no speech.

Only four other words. "Outlawed, for three years."

. . .

The final session of the Law Council loomed over the gathering. Unsettling violence of the last few days—Randaal's attack on the maid, the wrenching drama of Tiller's and Tor's trials, and the significant number of men branded as outlaws—had cast a pall over the festival.

Now, talk of Mani's retirement and the vote for the next Lawspeaker dominated Althing, as the time came for the votes by the Law Council.

Across the past weeks Naldrum and Rota had worked tirelessly, spreading promises to headmen and women willing to listen. On the afternoon of the last day of the festival, they sat taut with anticipation.

The drums for the Law Council sounded the opening of the Law Council the way they had every morning of every Althing for fifty-one years. *Boom... boom... boom... boom...* Thirty-nine beats, one for each leader present.

Gothi from the East, West, and North and South quarters paraded silently into the Law Circle flanked by their law-advisors. Mani, walking in beside his sons Mothur and Bright, felt as if he was holding his breath.

Likely others were as well. Mani had spoken to many who would vote—not to influence them towards Bright, as that would be wrong, but to gauge the mood of the valley leaders. His certainty of last year that Bright would easily beat Naldrum had ebbed to mere hope.

A heartbeat of silence as the leaders all stood in their places.

The pound of Mani's ash staff on the ground.

The thunder of the drums.

Mani raised his hands and opened his mouth to say the words he could put off no longer.

. . .

"I call this Council of Gothar into order for our final duty this year!" Mani cried. He requested the roll call of names. His assistant sat with a leather rune-skin at the outside of the Circle, making marks to count those present. This vote had to be correct, with no errors.

When the roll call was completed, Mani raised his ash staff again. The *gothi* and their law-arguers hushed so as to hear every word.

"As you know, I serve two functions here at Althing. As direct descendent of our country's first Lawspeaker Úlfljót, the one they called 'Ugly Wolf', I am *All-sher-jar-gothi*, the All-Chieftain who must open and close each Althing. This year, I will give that honor to my youngest son Mothur. When I close this Althing, when I had the ash staff to Mothur, he will be All-Chieftain. For as many years as he is able, Mothur will carry the ash staff. He will stand on the Law Rock and formally open Althing, and he will dictate the day that Althing concludes each year. Please give him your respect and support in the years to come."

No one else had been directly descended from the first Lawspeaker, so of all present only Mothur or Bright could serve in this capacity. The gothi clapped dutifully, and shouts of "Mothur! Mothur" came from most of those assembled.

"Now, for a weightier matter. I have served as your Lawspeaker for four terms now. Twelve years. It is time that I turn that duty over to another, so that our people have the benefit of other voices in interpreting and strengthening our laws. As you know, last year, two men were nominate for this honor. One is my son Bright—a renowned legal scholar, and the other is Naldrum, headman of Bull Valley. You have had a year to make your acquaintance with them, and to form your decision. We will now proceed with the vote."

Mani could see that many of the leaders around the circle had pushed up their sleeves. Slender golden bracelets flashed on their wrists. What did those signify?

"The vote will be a roll call vote by name, to ensure that all have voted, that none have voted twice, and that none have failed to vote."

The votes, name by name. Mani noticed that most of those who wore the gold bracelets voted for Naldrum—but not all of them. *Why?*

Two vote-counters stood next to Mani, putting stones in a dish as each gothi spoke their choice.

Mani's heart pounded. *Naldrum. Bright. Bright. Bright. Naldrum. Bright. Naldrum. Naldrum. Bright. Naldrum. Naldrum. Bright.* Neck and neck, the pile of stones in each bowl mounted as the votes were cast.

The group waited, breathless, as the stones were counted. The first counter and then the second whispered their total to Mani. His weary eyes closed for a brief moment, and then he held up the ash staff.

"The vote-counters agree. Those who wish Naldrum to serve as Lawspeaker equal nineteen votes. Those who wish Bright to serve as Lawspeaker, twenty votes. Bright has been elected Lawspeaker for the next three years. The vote is final."

Mani felt dazed. Bright had won by such a slim margin. A single vote! *How had Naldrum nearly won over the educated, well-liked Bright? How had that crude headman captured the loyalty of almost half of the valley leaders?*

Mani did not have long to wonder. A tumult broke out. For the first time in memory, and to Mani's horror, the gothi of the Law

Council stood shouting at one another, waving fists and shoving at one another.

Now it was Bright's turn to feel dazed. Certainty grew in his gut that there was no way for either him or Naldrum to successfully lead with such division among the voters. With that certainty came a decisive, bold idea, and equally bold action.

Bright strode to the drummers, gave quick instructions—and the drums thundered again, silencing the ugly turmoil.

Bright gestured to his father to raise the ash staff. When Mani pounded it down, the drums stopped. Bright stepped forward.

"I have studied the law since I was a mere boy. What I am going to say may sound unbelievable to many of you—but those who have listened to my father recite the law each year will recognize that what I am about to do is perfectly legal. And it is, in my opinion, wise."

Mani felt dread start inside. Bright could not mean—

But Bright *did* mean. "I accept your vote as Lawspeaker, and I thank you. But I accept it in the realization that we are a people weakened by bad crops and poor trade, and now we are weakened further by political differences. Some of you think Naldrum is better suited to lead us out of this quagmire, and some of you think I am. But *all* of you trust in the man who stands beside me. We cannot go through famine and worry with divided minds. I intend to invoke a never-before used clause of our law that allows a Lawspeaker to appoint another to serve in his stead, should there be need."

No one spoke.

"And there *is* need for continuity, for strength, for trust. Because of that, I, your duly voted Lawspeaker, appoint my father Mani to serve for another three years—and I request that you acknowledge acceptance of this action by your voice vote and applause."

The crowd stood shocked at what Bright had done, but the wisdom of his words impressed them. Those who had thrown their lot in with Naldrum knew that even though the vote had been close, Naldrum had lost. Better to try again at the next election, they reasoned, than let Bright take the mantle—for once that happened, Bright would serve for decades, as his father had done.

The others, appalled at the prospect of Naldrum leading them, knew Bright's skill with the law. They, too, saw the strategic wisdom in his move. Another three years under Mani's guidance, and the corrupt pestilence of Naldrum might be vanquished without bloodshed or anger.

In twos and threes, both sides began to chant Mani's name and clap. With equal parts dismay and pride, Mani realized that Bright's gambit to save the integrity of the Lawspeaker position had worked. He bent his head in acceptance, nearly weeping.

"I will be an old, old man by the time this term is over," he said to Bright. "But after that, I hope to see you installed as Lawspeaker. A finer, man cannot be found in all our land. I am proud of your wisdom today, my son, as much as I dread the three years to come. Naldrum will not take this defeat easily. I fear that he will be like a wild dog, yipping at the heels of a horse and rider, and threatening anything that defies his desires."

. . .

After the vote, one of the *gothi* wearing a gold bracelet pulled Mani aside. He had a good and honest face, and he looked troubled.

"I need to unburden my conscience," he started. "But I want to make sure my words won't be repeated."

"You have my pledge," Mani said, and he meant it.

"I told Naldrum I'd vote for him, but I didn't. I'm a little concerned about how Naldrum might take it. He's the type to hold a grudge for a long, long time—and to be vicious in exacting revenge."

"I won't discuss details, but I know that to be true," Mani said.

The man's worried expression did not relax at all. "I just hope Naldrum leaves my family alone. But no matter what, when it came down to the vote for Lawspeaker, I couldn't vote for him. I just couldn't!"

"You want to tell me why," said Mani.

The man's eyes darted around, worried who might notice him talking to Mani. "It was that business with Randaal," he said. "I mean, I liked everything Naldrum had to say about returning to the Old Ways, and how he promised good fortune to those who stuck by him. Who doesn't want more profit? But that beast Randaal? Who chooses a man like that as his steward? Kel, his former steward, was a good man. Everyone respected Kel. But this new fellow is all mean eyes and a shifty demeanor. Naldrum and his daughter said the woman killed herself from grief, but I talked to some of those who caught Randaal beating her."

Mani simply listened, needing to understand every iota that had to do with Naldrum.

"So as the vote came, I asked myself what kind of headman chooses such a brute to be his right-hand man? Maybe I'd make a bit more profit if he was become Lawspeaker, but would such a man even honor our laws?"

"I have my own doubts about that," Mani admitted.

"And who's to say what the gods actually want? Maybe they'd be offended we chose such a wicked man to lead us. Odin prized wisdom. Naldrum doesn't. Thor is straightforward and strong. Naldrum—well, you know his reputation. He cheats everyone he does business with. He's made a fortune by refusing to pay others. Would the gods want us to partner with such a man? I had doubts, but this whole filthy mess with Randaal? A man has to choose between what's right and what's wrong. And everything about Naldrum smells wrong to me. He might promise things we want—but at what cost to our countryfolk?"

Mani felt enormous relief at these words. He did not fool himself that in three years Naldrum would try again, and he expected the stakes to be higher when that day came.

But something about the man's assessment gave Mani hope. People did have a sense of right and wrong. They might set it aside for a little while, and they might be dazzled by a gold bracelet or the promise of more pigs—but in the end, more would choose a leader who seemed to possess true character over a false prophet promising profit.

It was enough, Mani told himself, to keep him going. He would do all he could for the next three years to keep Iceland a place of law and fairness—and then, by the gods, it was going to be Bright's job, whether his son was ready for it or not.

. . .

Chapter Seventy-Two

The party riding north to the bishop spent the first few days barely speaking. Kandace hushed her children, hoping that time and shared work mend some of the wounds between Aldís and Kel.

. . .

Konradsson, on the other hand, chattered happily about every detail he noted in their long ride north: the soft nests of eider ducks, the already-shorter days, the quiet of the northwestern fjords. His efforts at standing up to Randaal last year and Naldrum this Althing had given him yet another boost of courage.

"I once feared coming home to this land so much!" he told Nenet and Nikea, trying to cheer them up. "But look how lovely it is! So strong, so open. The air, so fresh. The mountains, so majestic." He gazed around in awe. "Your father was wise to bring you here. Yes, some of the people can be a bit rough, but one finds that everywhere. This land demands strength. It will serve you well, growing up here."

"I thought you hated it," Aldís remarked.

"I did hate growing up here. I hated my memories of my youth. But one can become a different person than in one's youth. One can grow and change. I am trying to do that."

She rode in silence. *Can one?*

“How do you do that?”

“By letting go. By not caring what others think of me. I used to be so worried about everything. I was a thin boy, not healthy. My parents did not show me kindness. A burden of shame clung to our entire family, and as the youngest and weakest, much of the weight of that shame fell to me. My father beat me unmercifully. My mother refused to take my side, even when she should have. When we had to interact with other families, boys bigger than I was would kick me and punch me.” *Even grown men.* Konradsson’s eyes grew shadowed as he remembered the brutalities, especially from Randaal. *No need to go into the terrible details. The children riding nearby should not hear that.*

“Yet you seem unafraid now. Because of the white-christ?”

“I suppose I should say yes, but the truth is, it has been less a matter of falling on my faith than of praying for the strength to stand on my own two feet. I was afraid then, and people took advantage of that fear. When I stopped fearing others, stopped trembling and bending, they stopped raising their fist.”

“If only you had known it was that simple when you were a child.”

Konradsson smiled. “I dearly wish that. But to spend my days looking back in wistfulness seems a waste. Better to spend them looking forward to doing good for others. Even if they are not ready for it, I can plant the seed.”

“You are a wise young man,” Aldís smiled. “But a truly inept rider. For Odin’s sake, get off your horse and tighten the belly strap before your saddle falls off.”

. . .

Kel listened to such traveling conversations without partaking. He hobbled the horses each night, and directed the children in tasks to set up camp each evening when they became too weary to ride any longer. Despite his gruff demeanor, in a few days they felt trust for the silent, dependable man.

"Papa likes Kel. He told me so. I do too."

"I think he is safe."

A little silence.

"Do you think Kel would let me sit on his lap? Like I did with Papa?

Another pause.

"I think he might."

"Good."

In their small way, Nenet and Nikea included Kel in the small clan of those who mattered to them. He did not know how preciously small that group was, or how terribly important, or how difficult to gain entry. He only knew the surprise of a little girl climbing onto his lap, unasked, as the flames dwindled to embers in their campfire that night.

"Well, then," Kel said. "What is this?" He had never before held a child. *Except the infants, ever so briefly.* The ever-ready shame swept over him, made him want to shove Nenet away. *I'm unworthy of your trust. Choose anyone but me.*

But as he struggled inwardly, Nenet's small hand slipped into Kel's and her little head rested against chest. A small sigh *safe here* escaped her.

Kel's lips trembled. "Well then," he said again. But his arm tightened around the little girl, to give her welcome. Gratitude filled him. He blinked rapidly, swallowed hard.

Aldís, across the fire, saw Kel holding the little girl and patiently explaining the road they would follow up the western fjords. Tenderness welled up in her heart, but just as quickly, rage burned that feeling to nothingness. She got up and walked to the stream to wash their supper things, wiping her eyes where Kel could not see.

. . .

Bishop Friedrich got up where he knelt in the warm soil, digging carrots from his little garden. A movement caught his eye. Far along the roadway, almost too distant to see, someone rode. Perhaps more than one person? Friedrich shrugged, turned to the next row, wrapped his fingers around another carrot-top and pulled.

As he reached the end of the row, Friedrich looked again. What had been a blurry dot in the distance, he now realized was a small cavalcade riding along the roadway. In this distant fjord? Friedrich peered, intrigued, then shrugged again and started on a row of turnips. It would take whoever it was quite a bit of time to reach him. He grasped the vigorous bunch of turnip leaves and pulled, pleased to see a fat globe lift from the soil.

. . .

Friedrich carried the bulging basket of turnips and carrots into the modest longhouse where he lived. A good day's harvest. The moon indicated that Sunday came in two days. He'd have time to clean these, take a bath, wash his dirty trousers, and welcome the neighboring farm families to a meal at his tiny church, as had become his custom the last few months.

Nothing harsh would be present, either on his menu or his mind. Nothing that judged these people for the ways they had followed their entire lives. Only a gentle welcome, an introduction to a different way of seeing the world and what came after. No battles were needed to get into Heaven. No Valkyries. No cold, lonely gates of Hel and no frost-giants for those who, not living a warrior's life, had simply died plowing their fields or from old age. No, Heaven was warm and golden and welcomed all who wanted to come.

The message had been well received. Friedrich felt hopeful that the several conversions of local people to Christ would inspire more across the rest of the summer.

. As the riders drew nearer, Friedrich recognized one of them as his protégé and fellow traveler from the monastery in Germania. The young priest sat taller and straighter in the saddle than ever before.

"Brother Konradsson!" Friedrich forgot the decorum required of a bishop. That life seemed long ago and far away. He pulled off his hat and ran towards them. "Brother Konradsson!"

. . .

Friedrich had prayed long and hard, nearly every day, about the wisdom of forcing the man he always thought of as 'young Konradsson' to return to Iceland. Now, as Friedrich gripped the younger monk's shoulders and gazed with joy at his face, his prayers were answered. The face that smiled back seemed different, somehow, calmer, and more settled. The hunching-forward of his shoulders was gone, and the anxious expression had left Konradsson's eyes.

"My brother in spirit!" Friedrich cried, and embraced the younger man. "I cannot tell you what joy it gives me to see you!"

Konradsson searched his mentor's face just as carefully. The self-doubt he had seen growing in Friedrich was gone, and so were the frown lines. The older priest seemed healthier, and younger.

"You have found peace here," Konradsson said.

"I am doing God's work in a very real way. I work in a manner that our Father might find surprising, but it is respectful. I'll tell you all about it later. Now, is this our Sister Kandace I see riding with you? My happy greetings, Sister! And *gothi* Naldrum's steward Kel as well!" Friedrich beamed.

Kel shook his head. "Steward no longer, sir." He left it at that.

"Ah, I see. I'm sure you had good reasons for parting ways. Now, please let tell me the names of these friends with you." He gave his warm smile to Aldís, then twinkled up at the two children. "Starting with these fine creatures!"

. . .

Friedrich had not wanted to ask directly, but when Kandace introduced Nenet and Nikea as her children, he had an opening.

"You have children? And you do not wear your nun's attire?" The bishop's earnest face seemed confused.

Kandace lifted her eyes to his. "Ah, Your Grace," she began, but he interrupted her.

"Please, not my formal title, here, child. We are far from all those things. Brother Friedrich suits me better now. I prefer it, if you don't mind."

"Well, Brother, this will be a long story—and it's one you should know from the beginning."

. . .

By the midday meal, Friedrich had heard the full tale, from Kandace's abduction in Morocco to Tiller's rescue of her from Haakon Sigurdsson's stronghold, about the snowstorm on Hekla, and her daring visit with Tor to Rota—and how Rota had let Tor take Kandace to Eilíf's. She told of how Tor and Kel had escaped from Naldrum, and how Josson had found Tor and his family at Eilíf's. How they had worn the sick-suits and set off in search of the bishop, and had nearly reached the beginning of the western fjords when they were caught and taken to Althing. How they had stood together as a family one last time before Tor was led off in chains—and how they had made their way, thanks to Rota again, up to this distant valley.

Friedrich knelt down to Nenet and Nikea. "Blessed are those who hunger and thirst," he said. He stood and took Kandace's hand in his. "Blessed are the peacemakers."

"Thank you, Father," Kandace murmured. She had existed in a fog of sadness ever since her parting from Tor at Althing. For the first time, her heart felt the smallest measure of comfort. "Tor wanted us to be with you, because Naldrum is powerful, and he will stop at nothing to get us three back. Do you think we really will be safe here?"

"I do. My longhouse is small, but you will stay as my guests for now. It will be easy enough for Konradsson and me to build on a room for you and the children, if you want? In fact, I have been thinking of starting a school! Perhaps God has answered my prayers about that by sending you. Might be willing to help me?"

Kandace could not believe her good fortune. Konradsson had led her to the bishop in this remote valley. They would have a home even more isolated than Eilíf's farm had been. Kel, Aldís and Konradsson would know where she was, so that if—she corrected herself, *when*—Tor returned, he could find her again.

Overcome, she nodded at Friedrich and gulped. "It would be the least that I could do for you."

His smile grew even wider at that. "But you have travelled so far to get here! Let us talk of tomorrows tomorrow. For now, you must rest, and eat, and enjoy some of my not-quite-so delicious but still, if I may claim so, excellent ale."

. . .

As they ate, the bishop drummed his fingers on the table.

"Is there any way we can get your husband back from Naldrum?" he asked. "I have no interest in buying a slave, but certainly, in this case…"

"No," she said. "That man intends to destroy Tor. No pile of gold in the world would be big enough to get him to sell my husband to you. All it would do is make Naldrum connect you and us—and that's the last thing Tor would want." She bowed her head and wiped her eyes. "I wish to God there was a way, but there is not."

Friedrich's tiny longhouse could not fit seven people for conversation. As soon as they had eaten, they moved to the small church next door to finish talking.

Kel chafed, wanting to leave as soon as he could. He had kept his promise to Tor. Now every breath felt constrained. He wanted to ride Thunder hard and fast, not the walking pace they had kept the last many days.

Kel stood and reached his hand out to Friedrich and Konradsson in turn. "Thank you, sirs. I need to be getting on my way. I may not agree with you on the gods we worship, but I know decent people when I see them. It's been an honor." He knelt and hugged the children. "Take care of your mother." Held Kandace in a long embrace. "You're a strong woman. Count me as a friend."

"Where will you go?" she asked. "You're not safe where Naldrum's influence reaches."

"I don't know. Maybe to one of the Saxon seaports. There's a trading center not far from here. It's usually pretty busy around midsummer days. I can come by each year to check in on you. Maybe I'll go visit the land you and Tor came from. See the place that made such fine human beings. I could take you back there to wait for Tor, if you like."

She shook her head. "My husband's ship will leave from Iceland. I'll wait for him here. Godspeed, my friend."

Kel stood to go. He supposed he should say goodbye to Aldís but no words seemed right, and his tongue felt stuck. So much troubling history lay between them. So much pain and betrayal. She had been weak, betraying his lawsuit against Naldrum. Kel would never forgive her for that—but that same woman had tried to take Kandace and the children north by herself. So brave. So decent.

At least he could part on good terms. "Goodbye, Aldís. Fare well." It was all he could manage.

"Fare well, Kel." No smile, but genuine gratitude for his help.

. . .

Chapter Seventy-Three

As Kel turned to go, he remembered the soul-stones. He pulled his pouch from his belt and spilled the contents on a small table.

"Here," he said to Kandace, picking out the beads. "Kel knew you would want these."

As Kandace closed her fingers around the precious gift, Nenet's small hand went across the table. The little doll that Sauthi had given to Kel lay in the pile of items. Nenet reached for it. Her luminous eyes went to Kel's, asking.

"You can have it," he said. "It served its purpose. It helped me break ties with Naldrum. I no longer need it."

A kind of gurgle came from Aldís, a choking gasp. She sat staring at the doll, her eyes wide.

"Where did you get that?" Aldís managed to ask. At her voice, Nenet dropped the toy and backed away.

"An old friend gave it to me, as a kind of good luck charm."

"An old friend. A good luck charm." Her words came from far away, lost.

"What's it to you?" Kel wanted nothing more than to be done with this mess and away from the surging confusion that Aldís always created in his chest.

“The friend… Was he…” Aldís could barely speak. *What was the man’s name? So long ago. Such painful memories.* She struggled to remember. “Did they call him Sauthi?”

Kel, surprised, half-hostile, expecting criticism. “Yes. You know him?”

Aldís wondered if she might be dying. She hoped so. “Sauthi’s the man who took my daughter and killed her. She had this doll in her hand when he rode away with her.”

. . .

Time stilled to nothing as Aldís and Kel stared at one another. The enormity of her words broke through Kel’s anger.

“Oh, gods. I’m so sorry, Aldís.”

He watched the woman across the table from him. Shards of terrible memory cut her into a heart-wrenching reflection of a destroyed life. All she had was tragedy and sorrow. The shadow that was Aldís wanted it to all go away.

Kel saw her distress but had no idea how to help. “I thought—I heard she had gotten sick,” he tried. “I heard she—a lung sickness—”

“No. Sauthi took her. Out of my arms. The little cap I made her had slipped over her eyes. I could see her reaching for me, not able to see me. Crying. The hat in her eyes. Trying to see where I was. She had the doll in her hands. I remember it exactly. Every detail. She couldn’t move her cap. She couldn’t see me. Couldn’t see me trying to get to her.” Aldís’s eyes saw only the past, her voice dull. “She was crying as Sauthi rode away with her. The other man held me and laughed."

"Sauthi said it came from his last one," Kel said. "The last child Naldrum sent him to—" Aldís had said it, the word 'kill', but Kel could not. Not about her beloved daughter.

Still Aldís did not weep. She just stared at the little figure on the table, her eyes too wide, her face and body too still.

Clumsy, Kel tried, but fractured her again. "Sauthi gave it to me, to encourage me. He knew I wanted desperately to break away from Naldrum. That's why I said it was a good luck charm. I'm so sorry."

Aldís throat strangled. "That toy you call a *good luck charm?* I made it for my daughter. Sauthi took my baby girl from me, and he killed her, and he kept her toy for himself. What kind of monster would do such a thing?"

Without thinking, Kel reached for Aldís, took her hand in his. He had a strange feeling of being trapped in a frozen truth, thawing one tiny drip at a time.

"I don't think it was the action of a monster. He said the child—I'm sorry, I mean your daughter—*gave* him her toy. As if she understood the pain he was in and wanted to ease it."

"*His* pain? How dare you."

"Naldrum traps people, Aldís! He gives them no choice. I know that trap too well myself. I never told you that the reason I stayed with Naldrum so long." The words tumbled out from him, faster and faster. "Naldrum trapped me by threatening you. He constantly reminded me that if I ever left him, he would harm you. I could not bear the idea of you being hurt! Sauthi had been trapped in the same way. Somehow, with a child's innocent heart, your daughter understood that Sauthi suffered dreadful pain, even as he inflicted it on others. He told me he had seen profound kindness in her eyes, much more than one could ever imagine coming from one so young."

Part of Aldís had always wanted to believe that Kel was a good man. She heard what he said about Naldrum's threats, and believed him. But it was too late for her to worry about Kel's pain, and too little. An avalanche of pain filled Aldís and swept her away.

She pictured her little girl. So small, so generous, handing the doll to Sauthi. Yes, it was probably true. Her chubby fingers would willingly give anything, to anyone who asked.

"She was so sweet. She would do that," Aldís choked. "But he still killed her. My baby. How could he?"

No, Kel thought. What had Sauthi said? *'But I couldn't do it—I took her away...'*

He braced himself to say something to Aldís that might only wrench her into even deeper anguish.

"Aldís, Sauthi *didn't!* He tried, but as he was about to, she handed him her doll, and he just couldn't do what Naldrum ordered. I give you my word, your child did not die by his hand that day."

Suddenly, truth rushed forward in a torrent of understanding. "Oh gods, Aldís. The girl Ankya was going on about. You thought it might be your daughter!" Understanding swept over Kel. No wonder Aldís had run to Ankya, had grasped for hope. What mother wouldn't?

Aldís moaned. "I did. But when I dragged Ankya from the law circle, she just mouthed strange vague words, going on and on about a girl who looked like me. She could not—or did not—say where she had seen the child, or how long ago." Brief promise had flickered, but despair had quickly blotted it out again. "I realized she didn't know anything useful. Only just enough to torment me into not testifying. I'm so sorry."

Kel remembered his hateful words to Aldís at the Law Circle. Shame released long-held bitterness.

"I've never understood one thing, Aldís. You said Naldrum forced himself on you. Even if his child had all of your goodness, how could it possibly matter so much to you? You *loathed* Naldrum!" He grabbed for the little wooden toy as if to demand an answer from it as well, but accidentally knocked it across the table. Aldís leaped to catch it before it fell to the floor.

At that, finally, the wall inside her began to crumble. The secret she had kept for so long could not remain untold any longer.

"I never said she was his," Aldís sobbed. "I said he owed me child-rights—and he did, in a way, because he took her real father away from me."

Aldís lifted her tear-streaked face to Kel. Years of sorrow and loss carved valleys of pain.

"Kel, she was yours. Yours and mine. She was ours."

. . .

For a long while there were no words, only two people holding one another. Acute pain and overwhelming relief, astonished joy and intense grief.

"I have a daughter," Kel said, wondering. He held Aldís' face in his hands, his heart full of anguish and tenderness. "With you."

"You cannot possibly forgive me for never telling you. I am so sorry." Aldís pulled away, bent over, clutched her arms in misery.

Kel pulled Aldís back to him. "It's not a matter of me forgiving you. It's not even a matter of whether I can forgive myself, or you yourself. There's been so much pain between us, Aldís. So much anger. But for now, all that matters is that you are safe, and that we have to find her."

Aldís leaned against his chest and sobbed in pain and relief. Kel held her tightly, wanting to crush the hurt from her heart.

"She has grown up her whole life without us! *That* will be impossible to forgive. If I had told you sooner—"

"Aldís, stop. We know the truth now. The future is all that matters."

"And how will we ever find her? She could be anywhere," Aldís asked, distraught. "Naldrum will know by now what Ankya meant. He is searching for my—our—daughter already, I am sure."

"Of course, he will search for her. But we have things he does not have! We have your remarkable ability to hear thoughts that fly on the wind. Now that you know that our daughter lives, you will be listening for her! Does he have anyone with intuition like yours? No! And he does not have his best tracker any longer. I don't mean to sound cocky, but Aldís, I'm the best tracker in all of Iceland. He does not have either of us helping him. He has us working *against* him! We'll find her, Aldís! Before he does, I promise you, we'll find her. Believe it, my love."

Aldís lifted her head. "Kel," she said, but that was as far as she got.

A kiss, tentative, hopeful, trembling, remembering; each wondering if the feeling had been real, so long ago, when their time together had been so short.

The kiss steadied Aldís. She stood taller, a warrior's stance.

"You're right. We *will* find her. We must!" Now her voice came clear and strong. Their daughter might be alive. Fierce hope filled Aldís. "It won't be easy. But we won't stop until we have her safe."

"Now, we won't! You have my word. We'll ride today. We'll go to every single farm in Iceland, if need be. We will find her, somehow, and get her so far away from Naldrum we'll have to learn to speak a new language."

Two people, wanting to believe, stared at each other. Embers of long-denied desire flashed into fire, refusing to wait any longer. Aldís' knuckles went white. She pulled Kel close and lifted her lips to his again.

. . .

Friedrich touched Kandace on her sleeve. He nodded towards the door with his head. "Let us give them a little time," he whispered.

Konradsson had not moved the entire time. He stared at the two people who had barely spoken to each other during the long ride, dumbfounded.

"But your honor," he appealed to Friedrich. "In the chapel? It is not seemly!"

Friedrich put a finger to his lips and shook his head. He gestured to Kandace and the children to follow him as he led the way out of the small church door. When Konradsson did not come, he sent Tor's son back in to fetch the gawking young priest, and closed the door silently as they left.

. . .

Inside, the lovers had eyes only for each other. Their fingers traced each other's faces in tender remembrance, hungry to have back what had once brought them together.

For now, they let go of the lost years. The only thing that mattered was the future. As they clung to each other, their bodies remembered what they had felt so long ago, had so long wanted to feel again: *hope.*

Hope in the promise of Althing had once joined two young people who had yearned to believe in the magnificence of humans might achieve, no matter the flaws of mortal beings. Belief that they might truly find their cherished daughter, recover their love, and become a family filled them now. Streams of feelings long dry began to flow again, washing away pain, nourishing that hope.

Above them, the face of a carved wooden angel gazed down. Its smooth blind eyes could not see their embrace, and its carved ears could not hear the whispered cries. But still, its lips curved in a smile of joy, and a blush flushed soft across its cheeks.

. . .

THE END

A preview of Book III

VIKING: The Green Land

Cast Off

west coast of Iceland, spring equinox, circa 980 A.D.

"Leave! Leave now!" The headman's voice rang over a pounding surf as the sun sank into the waves and the sky grew dark.

They were wise to chain us, Tiller muttered to himself. He stood on the shoreline, shackled like the other men, and stared at the ship waiting for them. It had silenced their rough boasts of coming home heroes to all the silver and women they could want. Seeing the ship, they felt fear as they faced the far likelier prospect of dying at sea.

Even Tiller, always at one with the waves, felt the same dread. *Too late to escape our fate now,* he thought bitterly. As he looked over the smooth curves of the ship, Tiller realized with a sudden shock that he knew this ship, even though he had never seen it before.

'Build that ship like the last love of your life,' he had said to an aged shipbuilder in what seemed a lifetime ago. *'Give her the body of a strong young woman, and the speed and power of a warship so she can fly over the waves like a Valkyrie—but give her, too, the carrying capacity of a mother, because she'll have to store much for the monumental voyage you describe.'* He had added, as an afterthought, *'and make her beautiful. Whoever crews that ship of yours will need to feel proud her.'*

The headman called again. At his words, a crowd of people herded the crew towards the ship and shoved them up the boarding plank. One by one, the men of the crew lifted their wrists for the manacles to be unlocked and the watching crowd cheered, but as the irons rattled off, the crew began to argue loudly, shoving at one other.

A woman was pushed aboard last, her wrists chained as well. She would serve as Fishgirl – cook, healer, and crew's helper - for the voyage. As the torches flickered on her face, Tiller could clearly see wet tracks of tears.

"Stop fighting!" the headman shouted at the crew. "The moon has almost cleared the hills. Get to your oars! The ship is heavy and the surf is high. You will have to row hard! Be ready!"

He turned to the man who counted the moons and seasons. "*Kalendar*, be ready as well, to call out the release-ropes."

The Kalendar nodded. The man who kept track of the seasons had prepared for months, watching carefully the winter daylight lengthened, growing equal to the night.

"Only one or two more days," he had reported yesterday to the headman. "Spring is almost upon us, *Gothi*."

"And the moon?" the gothi had asked.

"Full tomorrow night. It will rise just after Sól sets in the sea." The Kalendar had hesitated. "A rare thing, and to nearly coincide with *even-day-and-night*? Inconceivable! It foretells a remarkable voyage."

"Ready the ship and the men!" the headman had cried. "They will sail at moonrise tomorrow!"

Last to be unlocked, Tiller watched the sixteen men who would be his shipmates for the next three years. All were seasoned in the ways of the sea, and like him, all were outlaws. Beyond that, they were as different from one another as any lot of men might be. Some were tall, some short, some disfigured by scars and others handsome. Some seemed talkative and others stayed morosely silent. Tiller saw all of humanity in their faces: strength, weakness, greed, fairness, brutality, and humor. What did they see in his own face? Did they see the uncertainty in him? The willingness to risk their lives to prove himself right?

The woman who would be their Fishgirl desperately looked from face to face of the people on the shore, but no one met her gaze. She did not watch the headman as he unlocked her wrist irons, but only saw the god-face of the moon rising over the shoreline hills, and her face filled with dread.

How old? Tiller wondered. She looked to be about twenty-five. Still no finger-ring for marriage? For certain, not because of her looks. The entire crew was eyeing her. Any fool could see trouble coming. *Why the oath they'd been made to swear? To 'protect her, at all cost, until we find land'?*

More importantly, why a Fishgirl at all for this voyage? Women usually served on short journeys, a couple of weeks or a month at most. Had anyone told this one how long they'd be gone, and how terribly small were their chances of returning? What would compel her to agree to come with them? Unlike the men, she did not carry the mark of an outlaw.

"Rowers, ready oars!"

Strong hands gripped the long oak poles, and the crew prepared to pull the ship through the surf.

Tiller held the steering oar. Through it, he could feel the waves frothing against the strong hull. The ship bucked against the ropes holding it, and exhilaration knifed through Tiller, reckless and hard.

Those sweeping timbers longed to be free of land, and he in turn longed to feel the strength of her surging through the open sea.

"Almost ready!" the headman shouted. "Release the ropes on my command!" He cleared his throat.

Oh, gods, he was going to give a speech.

"You on this voyage are headed straight into the heart of danger. We will pray to the gods every day that your courage will set us all free…"

"Every day alive is dangerous for outlaws!" shouted one of the crewmen. "We're not brave! We're dead men! What difference at sea or on land?"

The headman frowned and continued his speech, with words of hope in stark contrast with the grim faces on board.

Tiller's thoughts drifted. He had not murdered anyone, but no one else from the fight had survived to say so. Men he counted as friends had tumbled to the ground and bled out, their open eyes as colorless as the sky. With them went testimony that might have saved him.

Guilty, the Council had said at the trials at the springs trials at Thornes Thing. *Three years outside the law.*

Being outlawed might as well be a death sentence. Outlaws enjoyed no protections that the law had once offered to them. Take an outlaw's tools, and he could complain to no headman about the theft. Take his fox-traps and the furs he had prepared to sell. Take his last rind of cheese, his last crust of bread, and give them to your own sons and daughters, and no one would stop you from letting him starve. Take his cloak for your own, and let the rain drench him, and there was no one to whom he could turn for recourse.

Helping an outlaw was forbidden. Giving him shelter and food meant risking the same fate. Convicted men who could afford passage left for other lands. Those less fortunate gnawed hard barley grains and hid in hillside crevices in freezing cold, not daring to risk a fire.

At the midsummer country-wide Althing, Tiller's law-speaker had pled his case again, but the council had affirmed the guilty verdict.

After the hearing, one of the *gothi*-councilman appeared at the jail-pens. Gold threads embroidered through his rich cloak glittered in the light of the sun, and he lifted it carefully above the muddy ground.

"Come over here." He had beckoned with his free hand. "I have a proposition for you."

Tiller's heart had beat hard, but he kept his eyes steady.

"The stories that have spread throughout this Althing. I assume you've heard them?"

Tiller had hardly dared to believe they might be true. He nodded.

The gothi continued. "Everyone knows the situation here in Iceland. In the time of the Great Settlement, people came here relentlessly. Almost immediately, all of the land was claimed. All the forests were cleared, and all of the soil tilled. For four or five generations, there has been no new land left. No more farms to feed the grandchildren and great-grandchildren of the families who settled here. Yet more mouths are born every day, more slaves are bought and brought here. They, too, have children who must be fed. The terrible truth is that too much food is needed from too few fields." He rubbed his hand across a forehead lined with worry. "With the crop failures these past years, even the people with good land are struggling. You know what is happening to those whose farms are on thin soil."

The dreaded word *famine* had at first been whispered. Now, every meeting along the roadway brought news of places where people were starving.

The councilman cleared his throat awkwardly. "It's been almost ten years since anyone went *viking* to look for Gunnbjörn's skerries."

At those words, Tiller knew that the rumors were true.

. . .

Gunnbjörn's skerries. Maybe land, maybe not; a something in the sea far to the west, barely glimpsed by Gunnbjorn Ulfsson's crew nearly a hundred years ago after a disastrous storm.

"You want us to make another attempt to find them," Tiller said flatly. "Because outlaws are desperate, and expendable."

"Not want, Thorvaldsson. Need." The councilman's voice was almost pleading. "Every headman here at the Althing brings the same problem. Their people are dying for want of fields and food. If there's even a *chance* that an empty land is somewhere out there, can you imagine what that would mean to our people? We must try! That means an opportunity for you. A ship is being built, a specially-designed one. We need a crew who will go to search for whatever Gunnbjörn's men glimpsed."

Tiller had remembered then, too, the elderly shipbuilder who had asked *How would you design a vessel for an incomprehensibly long voyage?* The old man had been vague about the reasons, but had listened carefully to Tiller's ideas, and had disappeared into the crowd again.

How long had the council been planning this? How long had they been watching him?

The councilman eyed Tiller to gauge the condemned man's reaction. Fury built in Tiller, but he held it in check.

"I know what you are thinking," the *gothi* continued. "You have the means to buy your way to another country and try to ride out your three years. You know as well as I do that anyone who goes on this voyage will likely die on the sea. There will be storms, bitter cold, fights on board. You may starve, or perish of thirst. And to go so far out onto the waves…" The councilman shuddered. "Freakish things live out there, they say. Monsters in the waves who swallow ships that sail too far from land." He forced a laugh. "But your odds may be just as bad on land. Too many traders know your name, if not your face. Show up in Dublin or Danmörk and someone will turn you over to us for the reward-silver that will be offered. Where could you not be found and hunted down? Do you want to live as a fugitive running and hiding for three years, or go searching for glory? Find a land where we can send people to live, and you'll have everything you could want. Gold, silver, slaves, silks, furs, fame, and freedom."

Tiller had heard the stories of Gunnbjörn's skerries since childhood. After a disastrous voyage, Gunnbjörn Ulfsson had finally steered his battered ship back home, all but sinking and with most of the crew gone. The few *vikingers* who had survived told frightening tales. "*We were steering for the North Way, but we were blown west by a terrible storm. Hideous, a man-killer. A ship-sinker. We took down the sail. Not one of us believed we'd survive it. Waves…*" Their faces would still go ashen remembering the horror of that night. *"The sea tore at us like an enormous animal, berserk, clawing and screaming from every direction. Maybe the sea-goddess Rán wanted to punish us for being so far west. She pulled most of our crew overboard. Swallowed men whole in her great mouth."*

The ship had wandered, lost. Fog had swirled around them. *"That fog was as thick as cream, unnaturally warm, a feeling of something unhealthy. Were we even still alive? Maybe we were already dead, and Loki's daughter Hel was pulling us to Niflheim."* Niflheim, the *nothing-home* that lay at the very edge of the world, was a place hidden by clouds and mist. Those not chosen at death for Valhalla went there, where giants of ice guarded Hel's gates.

The storyteller would hesitate, his haunted eyes remembering. The fog had suddenly lifted. They had seen something hulking in the water, gray and white, something enormous of stone and ice. Should they sail closer? They had barely survived so far. Why tempt Hel's ogres, or perhaps some huge sleeping sea-beast? If those were the actual gates to Niflheim, would there be sharp terrible rocks, tearing what was left of their hull? Would they become slaves for the dead?

Fearing for their lives, Gunnbjörn's crew had turned the ship in the opposite direction. They prayed with every passing wave to see the shores of home again, and vowed to carry a warning to others. *"The sea-goddess Rán spared us for a reason! We tell others, so that they do not go where the seas end. That place belongs to Hel. All must stay away."*

The warnings of Gunnbjörn's crew had fallen on deaf ears. Many ships went in search of those shapes in the sea. Most never returned, and the voyages had diminished over luckless years. The last attempt several years ago had ended in horror.

Going to find Gunnbjörn's skerries was like being outlawed. Both usually meant death.

. . .

"What's your decision?" The Althing councilman had interrupted Tiller's thoughts. "Everyone knows your reputation as a steersman. Will you go?"

Bitterness ate into Tiller's gut. "When my neighbor Thorgest accused me of stealing from him and murdering his sons, everyone knew the truth. I only took what was mine. Those high-seat pillars belonged to me. I never wanted the fight, never intended for anyone to be hurt. I trusted in the law, certain I'd be found innocent. Now I know why all of you on the Althing Council ignored my law-arguer. You convicted me because you needed me."

"What difference does it make? However you got here, you're an outlaw now. Be practical."

"Do I really have a choice? You'll find one way or another to get me on your ship. I'll save you the trouble. Sea dangers don't cut a man as deep as deception from those he trusts."

But as he spoke, premonition had swept over Tiller. Gunnbjorn's skerries were he had always longed to go. He was meant to find them.

. . .

Now, as he waited for the local headman to finish his speech, Tiller wondered about that feeling of fate. A future-knowing? He winced. Maybe he was becoming too like his father, desperate for recognition, imagining his own importance. But by the gods, *Gunnbjorn's skerries!*

By the time he had grown enough to listen, the tales were old and tired, the patina of promise worn away. Some still clung to the possibility of rich land waiting in the west. Tiller's father Thorvald had been one of them, spinning stories about wealth to be found. As a youth, Tiller had pretended to be Gunnbjörn Ulfsson, finding the longed-for land. Later, loading crates as ship's boy, in his imagination he was carefully outfitting a merchant knarr with supplies for a new settlement.

Well, you're on that knarr now, he thought as the headman's speech droned on. *And you're not Ulfsson, you're Thorvaldsson, with all the stigma that name carries. Not exactly the dreams of your boyhood.*

Tiller shook off the feeling of destiny. He was an outlaw, and the son of an outlaw. Who was he to think he had any chance of succeeding where so many others had failed before? He was going to die out there. But the old longing skirled deep in him, like the smoke rising from the shoreline torches, and he knew he still longed to try.

Tiller kept his eyes on the stars as they came out, thinking of the course he would steer. The rowers waited for the command to pull. Firelight flickered on the long wet oars. Thin edges of moonlight tipped the waves. Beyond, all was now blackness.

The headman rushed his carefully-prepared words to match the moonrise. "You set off tonight, watched only by the moon-god, so that nothing in the sea will notice as you leave land in the darkness. The ship has been charmed with powerful spells. It is stocked with provisions for a long voyage. We have done all that we can to protect you, and we ask of you this: if there is land to find, find it. Find good land for us, green land, a place where people can live and thrive. Know that your journey offers hope for our people. A new birth! But make no mistake: there will be no warm arms to welcome you. This ship is your midwife, and your mother is the sea. Our future and yours lies in her cold embrace. We may never know what happens to you, but we will sing of your courage in sagas."

At that, the gleaming white circle lifted above the hills. Their moon of destiny—or disaster—floated, full in the night sky.

"It is fully risen! They must get underway immediately!" The Kalendar's anxious voice rang out as the bottom curve of the moon-god Máni came clearly into view.

"Pull away the boarding plank!" the headman roared.

Fish-gutters, who had arrived for the spring spawning and were camped in hovels along the shoreline, jeered. "Plenty of land at the bottom of the sea! For certain, you'll find some there!" Their mocking words concealed hope they dared not admit, a longing that was buried in the lines of their too-thin faces.

The headman silenced them. He gestured to the rope-holders. "Release the ropes! Push off the ship! Row now, men! Pull hard! Row! Row!"

At the gothi's command a score of people waded forward to press their hands against the sleek lapped timbers of the ship. Cynical sarcasm shot through Tiller. How many who had jeered today would one day say, *'I pushed them off,'* telling grandchildren of a part in the great discovery?

The rowers leaned forward, pulled back hard, and the voyage was born. Long years of experience told Tiller's limbs to shift from land-legs to sea legs.

The woman who would be their Fishgirl lurched at the motion. Hair blew wildly and tangled in the wind. She cried out once in agony as the ropes were released. Her eyes locked on Tiller's.

"We die, either way, you and I," she croaked towards him, looking furtively back over her shoulder at the crew. "There is no coming back for us."

What was she talking about? Tiller needed to focus all of his attention on the rudder as he steered them away from the breakers. He gripped it hard and ignored her stare.

No one called good fortune as the knarr left. There was only silence, except for crash of waves and the wind blowing across the beach. It had been forbidden to make the good-luck striking of sticks, or to ring bells to bring safe journeys to the ship. No sense alerting whatever lurked in the deeps.

The pale faces of the crowd on the shore watched, stony and still. So much hung on this ship and the small band on board. Dozens of hands lifted in a wordless fare-thee-well. Their silence pulsed with a mute plea for land, for food, and the dark width between the knarr and the shoreline slowly widened.

Salt spray cut across the bow as strong arms pulled the ship steadily through the waves. The rowers watched the fires of the torches on shore grow fainter and dim to nothing. Tiller could see the men's eyes in the moonlight, fierce and focused as they rowed in unison, the reality of what lay ahead locked away inside for now.

We'll all be sick of one another and the sea soon enough, Tiller thought. How long until one of the crew panicked under the crushing uncertainty? It was only a matter of time until knives were drawn and blood spilled. *We're as dangerous to each other as the sea is to us.*

Screaming birds wheeled overhead, ghost-pale. In defiance of the headman's orders, two small vessels darted from a nearby cove and came alongside, calling encouragement.

"Get away, damn you! You were told not to come!" roared the man who had shouted at the headman. "Too much splashing waves! You want a sea-troll to come before we barely get started?"

Tiller knew full well who was on the boats following them. He called to the men who had risked their lives to shelter him for the last months, "Go back. I know you wish us well. I'm in your debt. When we return, I'll do whatever I can to repay you."

As the men in the small crafts turned away, the knarr slipped past the headlands and they were utterly alone on the nighttime sea.

Tiller felt strong and unafraid. Was it out there, somewhere? That lustful, longing promise of land? Wild exhilaration surged in him again. He and the crew would work all this night without rest or food. They would push themselves to go further and further away from land. For now, their only hunger was the yearning to return as heroes, or not at all.

. . .

When she could no longer see the shoreline, the woman dropped to her haunches and huddled between two crates. She buried her face in her arms and kept it there until the first rowing change. At the gong, she kept her chin down, but her eyes slid to the men.

The full moon gave them dead faces, gray and grim, their eyes black pits. They moved in unison, eerily quiet. The only sound was the creak of oars and the slosh of water.

Gods, how had this happened? Her mind reeled in terror. Clawing for something to hold onto, her eyes landed on Tiller's face. It held hard lines that had not been there before. She noted that his hair had been cropped since the trial, and his beard was clipped close against his jaw.

Why did I say that to him? That man can't help me, the woman thought, angry at herself. *No one can. I am an utter fool. I should be at home, looking for a husband. Starting the spring planting.* She squeezed her eyes closed and looked for courage inside but found none.

Like it or not, a game that would hold her life in its balance had just begun.

If you enjoy digging a little deeper, some book club discussion topics and a few author's notes follow for you to explore.

Reviews welcome and appreciated at Amazon.com

Contact Katie via:

Facebook

Instagram

Goodreads

Amazon Author Page

Find a typo?
I greatly appreciate corrections!
Please email me via KatieARitter@gmail.com and I'll fix that rascal right up. Thank you!

BOOK CLUB DISCUSSION TOPICS

Was Aldís right to forgive Kel? He did terrible things for Naldrum.

Do you think their relationship has a real chance of strength and healing again, or not?

What does Kel's dream tell you about his character?

What is your opinion of Kel's staying with Naldrum so long? Should he have made his break earlier, or was staying the only real option?

As Ankya grows in power, should Naldrum trust his own daughter?

What benefits did an imperfect democracy offer versus being a vassal state under a ruler such as Haakon Sigurdsson?

Elements of this story were inspired by Iceland's famous 'Njál's Saga', the story of a family feud that lasted several decades. Do you see evidence of such feuds in modern times? Why might this be so?

Friedrich is clearly going through a process of self-examination and change. How is this good or bad for his calling as a priest?

Without Styr, Fatimah's future seems limited to being a second-wife, perhaps poorly treated. In her day, would she have any other options?

In the feud between Thorgest and Tiller, which man was justified: Tiller, in taking back his pillars because of a verbal agreement between friends? Or Thorgest, in sticking to the letter of the law?

Like Konradsson, have you ever experienced unexpected courage?

Eilíf has endured terrible circumstances and is quite poor, yet she has happiness. What does she have that makes this possible?

Dalla, Mani, Aldís, and Kel each have a great love of Iceland's democracy and rule of law. How aware were you that a great deal of western democracy and modern law were influenced by Icelandic traditions on one small island over a thousand years ago?

Why does Tora stay with Haakon? Would you, in her situation?

Tor stuck to his principles to the last. Was that wise or foolish? Did he have other options? What should he have done, or not done?

What should Kandace's perspective be now? Does it seem at all likely that Tor will return safely to her?

AUTHOR'S NOTES

Ordinary lives have extraordinary importance

Many readers enjoy tales of the rich and famous, especially in historic fiction. Some books make every hero stalwart and handsome, super-masculine, and of course rich. Every heroine is beautiful. Most are royalty, or at least entitled.

I'm a carpenter's daughter. Far from rich and not entitled. Growing up, I was quite the ugly duckling. Because of that, I find myself taking the road less travelled, trying to show the quiet heroism implicit in the daily struggles of everyday people.

Life is quite difficult for the vast majority of humanity. Despite their challenges, people do amazing things. They create. They produce. They find joy and hope in the worst of circumstances. I'm in awe of that, so I wanted to give life and breath to characters like them, who have no magic powers, no time travel abilities, no wealth, no resources. People who struggled and who had tremendous flaws.

People like you and me, maybe.

I wanted the odds to be stacked against them. I wanted them to know their weaknesses, how very unlikely their chances of success. To feel frustrated, small and powerless, with nowhere to turn. I wanted them to feel like massive failures and colossal f**k-ups—and to keep trying to do good *anyway*, because then, we can learn from them. Working with the characters in my books, I tried to imagine how I could live, enslaved, and mistreated. How I might handle a life with no choices, like Kel's. How I might run away from myself like Aldís, but in running just keep finding myself again. How I might struggle as Mani did between what was legal versus what was ethical.

Book characters are not real, but remarkable examples such as Atticus Finch demonstrate their ability to shape our perspectives and our lives. I'm far from being that skilled a writer, but I hope you find something in the characters of these books that resonates in your life.

Trees in Iceland and how deforestation may have happened

Iceland's earliest documents speak of the land being forested from mountain to sea (except for in lava fields, of course.) Now, barely any trees can be found. What happened?

Experts have different theories. I have mine.

It's estimated that between 70,000-100,000 people lived in Iceland in the 12th century, and people had been living on the island for two hundred years. They needed wood to build homes and ships. They needed wood to heat their homes via longfires, and to cook their food. They needed wood to smelt iron from bogs in parts of the country. They needed wood for charcoal to support the small blacksmith operations common to many farms. Even at modest population estimates…that's a lot of wood.

They also cleared forests, whether birch or spruce (we don't know) for grazing land for sheep, goats, cattle and horses, as well as for crop fields—wheat, barley, rye and oats were all grown during the warmer Settlement years—and for root vegetable plots.

I believe that wooded hillsides eventually reached a tipping point of no return and erosion became an issue; that deforestation on steep hillsides resulted in the 'land-slip' (their word for landslides) for which Erik the Red's neighbor killed two of his farm workers, and he killed two of his neighbors in revenge. The more forests were cut or cleared, the harder it became for them to regenerate, especially on steep hillsides with thin volcanic soil.

While the people in this story still had mostly-plentiful supplies of trees, we can only begin to imagine the hardships endured by Icelanders for the centuries after the demise of their forests, with little left for fuel, for building or blacksmith work, and with little ability to grow grains due to a colder climate, and limited trade or economy.

Fortunately, they persisted, and their heritage endured. Iceland today boasts a thriving economy—and happily, reforestation has gained much national attention and support.

Research, and why this all still matters today

Viking-era Iceland abounded with amazing stories. They were developed and repeated by *skalds* (poets) for more than three hundred years until they were written down.

No one knows how much of the sagas were based on real people and events or what parts were pure fiction. No one knows how the verbal sagas evolved over those early hundreds of years, as social values changed. Christianity arrived, pagan ways were outlawed, the country became a vassal state to Norway, and Althing was disbanded (and later reinstated). Along the way, the climate cooled, volcanoes erupted on the Reykjanes peninsula for three hundred years (10th century to 14th) and trade interactions with other cultures ebbed.

What we *do* know is that the sagas carry such strong elements of human nature—love, lust, honor, betrayal, faith, foolishness, riches, fairness and greed—that they still fascinate.

Beyond storytelling, Viking-era people were remarkable in many other ways. They were master shipbuilders of the strongest, most flexible ships ever imagined. They were utterly fearless seafarers, both trading and raiding. It’s no exaggeration to compare them to today’s Elon Musk, engaged in all sorts of innovation.

And in Iceland, they created the world’s first democracy. Let that sink in: *THE WORLD’S FIRST DEMOCRACY.* Their astonishing model for self-government was based on law lasted for years. It directly influenced the modern democracies of today

They lived in a harsh climate, yet thrived. They played games, chess among them. They loved debating law. They were devoted to art, not only the literary traditions of their powerful *sagas*, but Viking-era Nordic artisans created remarkable works of gold, silver, iron, beadwork, leather, wood carvings, and the written language of runes. These items are instantly recognizable as “Viking” a thousand years later.

Even the words we use today to communicate with one another have deep, wide Viking influence. An *astounding* percentage of English-language words come straight from Old Norse. Though spelled differently, if you pronounce them phonetically, the direct connection quickly becomes apparent.

One of my writing goals is to create interest in learning more about Viking-era Iceland, Greenland and the North-way lands. We owe it to ourselves and them to learn as much as we can about this complicated, innovative culture and the people who built it

ACKNOWLEDGEMENTS

I'd like to give a shout-out to the amazing community of writers. They're willing to help and encourage one another, non-competitive, and welcoming. My local writer group includes the immensely talented Travis Madden, Cheryl Dishon, Connie Matsumoto, Ruut DeMeo, Steven Trumble, Jackie Brooks, Gracie Hosford, Scott Beard, Michael Barron. I'm indebted to them. My larger writer community is a mix of hist-fict and indie writers of all genres. They provide invaluable experience and advice—and they share it willingly, starting off with Louisa Locke, successful author of Victorian cozy mysteries, for her unflagging support and education of indie writers.

Thanks again to Bibi Bendixon and Gordon Giffen, faithful beta readers, for wading through the breakup of one prequel manuscript into two full-length novels. Gratitude, gratitude.

Gaelic artist Zaff Bobolin in Hawaii created the (dazzling!) Nordic horse gracing the cover. You can find her work on ZaffWorks.com.

Thanks again to Emily Sweet @SweetBookObsession of Instagram. Emily, who several times has recommended my work to her followers. Emily is such a great resource to the Instagram reader community.

I'm grateful to folks all over the world who manage hundreds of websites from which I've drawn one tiny detail or another. You represent the pooled knowledge of our species. Thank you.

Amelia Buttercup, I couldn't do it without you…and to my beloved husband Mark and our three sons, infinite love.

Gratitude again to Soffia Arnadottir and Gérard Chinotti, kind friends in Iceland, especially for that wild-harvested blueberry jam!

As in VIKING: The Plains of Althing, I'd like to feature a special group of friends here, where they will be most easily seen.

There's only so much one can do via book, website, google-drive research. I needed a boots-on-the-ground trip to Iceland to see sites about which I was writing. To breath the air there. To *feel* the land.

Wonderful friends stepped up to help fund the needed trip via Indiegogo. They travelled with me in spirit, from a freezing-cold September pre-dawn landing across the approximately 1600 miles my husband Mark and I covered in four days. This book could not have happened without them. I am honored to share their names with you:

Cynthia Ballard
Bibi Bendixen
Susan Stiles Dowell
Winnie Drier
Ricardo Druillet
Rick and Robin Duszynski
Leslie Fortune
Ari Gabinet
Savitri Gauthier
Mairi Giffen
Bill Guerin
Lisa Jan
James Johnson
Lynne Jones
Donna Katunick
Michael Katunick
Gary Levine
Mary Lou Locke
Don Lyman
Sarah Mackie
Joe Newcomb, posthumously
Nancy Palmer
Dave Richter
Meg Pohe Rose
Janet Schiller
Peggy Taliaferro
Steve Van Holde
Tobyanne Ventura
Mary Frances Wagley
Cathy West

Finally, thank you for choosing to read this book. With gratitude,

Katie

Made in USA - North Chelmsford, MA
1111740_9780997876598
05.21.2020 0315